The
Little
Brooklyn
Bakery

Julie Caplin is addicted to travel and good food. She's on a constant hunt for the perfect gin and is obsessively picky about glasses, tonic and garnishes. Between regular gin tastings, she's been writing her debut novel which is set in just one of the many cities she's explored over the years.

Formerly a PR director, for many years she swanned around Europe taking top food and drink writers on press trips (junkets) sampling the gastronomic delights of various cities in Italy, France, Belgium, Spain, Copenhagen and Switzerland. It was a tough job but someone had to do it. These trips have provided the inspiration and settings for the trilogy, *The Little Café in Copenhagen*, *The Little Brooklyn Bakery* and *The Little Paris Patisserie*.

🐦@JulieCaplin
fwww.facebook.com/JulieCaplinAuthor

Julie Caplin

The Little Brooklyn Bakery

A division of HarperCollins Publishers

www.harpercollins.co.uk

Harper*Impulse* an imprint of
HarperCollins*Publishers*
The News Building
1 London Bridge Street
London SE1 9GF

www.harpercollins.co.uk

This paperback edition 2018

First published in Great Britain in ebook format by HarperCollins*Publishers* 2018

A catalogue record for this book
is available from the British Library

ISBN: 9780008259761

Set in Bi~~...~~ by ~~...~~ ~~...~~ingshire

Prin~~...~~ YY

For Justine, who shared the very first New York adventure

Chapter 1

'It's a great offer,' said Sophie, with only the slightest sense of regret that she had to turn it down. One day she would visit New York. 'But I don't see how I could go at the moment.'

Angela screwed up her face. 'I understand, it's really short notice, I could bloody kill Mel for breaking her leg.'

'I don't think she did it on purpose,' Sophie said gently.

'Well it's bloody inconvenient, and while I've got plenty of people queuing up to take her place in New York for six months, you're my best food writer. You would be *brilliant*.'

'That's kind of you, Angela—'

'Kind?' Angela raised one of her scarily plucked, almost-to-the-death, eyebrows. 'I don't do kind. This is honesty. You're a brilliant writer and I wish ...' she shook her head, 'and don't you dare repeat this, I wish you would spread your wings.'

'And you're desperate,' teased Sophie.

'Well, there is that.' Angela laid down her pen with a self-deprecating laugh. 'But at least think about it. It's a fabulous opportunity. Job swaps don't come up that often and if I didn't have the twins, I'd be off like a shot.'

'What about Ella? She'd love to go,' suggested Sophie.

Angela tipped her head to one side. 'That girl is twenty-nine going on twelve, she'd be an absolute disaster.'

'She might not be that bad.'

Angela raised the other eyebrow, 'And I know how much you help her. I don't think she'd survive without you.'

Sophie gave her a cheeky grin, 'So you can't send me to New York, then.'

With a bark of laughter, Angela flipped her notebook closed, 'We'd manage.' Her face sobered as Sophie rose to leave. 'Seriously, Sophie, say you'll think about it.'

Sophie returned to the main office where everyone was still talking about the horrible crack of bone when Mel leapt off a table in the pub at the end of her *I'm-swanning-off-to-New-York-for-six-months* leaving do. Across the way, the limp helium balloon, bearing the words *We'll miss you*, still bobbed above a chair. Someone really ought to take it down before the incoming, very American-sounding Brandi Baumgarten rocked up to take possession of Mel's desk.

The poor girl deserved more than the current palimpsest of sticky rings of prosecco and crumbs of Monster Munch (Mel's favourite) littering its surface. Grabbing a pair of scissors, Sophie advanced on the balloon and, with a satisfying snip, cut it down. She'd done the right thing turning Angela's offer down. The thought of taking over Brandi's desk on the other side of the Atlantic was far too much of a terrifying prospect. And poor Brandi, coming here. To a strange city. All on her own. Sophie almost shuddered. Maybe she should make her some cookies, big fat squidgy ones with lots of chunky chocolate to welcome her and make her feel at home. And coffee. Americans did coffee big time. Perhaps a little welcome-to-England pack. An A–Z of London. An umbrella. A …

'Earth to Soph. How do you spell *clafoutis*?'

'Sorry. What did you say?' She tugged the balloon down and punctured it with her scissors.

'Well done,' said Ella, the other cookery writer on *CityZen*. 'I meant to do that. Well, I thought about it. And how do you spell *clafoutis*? I can never remember.'

Sophie reeled off the spelling and sat down at her desk opposite Ella.

'What did Angela want? You in trouble?'

Sophie shook her head, still slightly bemused at the suggestion that she should go to work on their sister publication in Manhattan, the American *CityZen*. If she told Ella she'd never hear the end of it.

'How was your weekend?' Ella screwed up her face. 'Oh for feck's sake, spellcheck's changed it to *clawfoot*. Can you spell it again for me? I went to that new French place in Stoke Newington. A bit of a trek but … oh, how was *Le Gavroche* on Saturday? Oh … no, he didn't!'

Sophie winced and summoned up a blithe smile. 'Unfortunately, we didn't get there. His mum was ill.'

'Oh, for crying out loud, the woman's always ill.'

'She can't help it,' Sophie protested, ignoring the inner bitch that agreed wholeheartedly. Was it wrong to wish Mrs Soames could time being unwell just a tad more conveniently? 'And it was an emergency this time. Blue-lighted to hospital. Poor James spent all night in A and E waiting for news.'

With a scowl Ella said, 'You are too bloody nice. And far too damn forgiving. He doesn't deserve you.'

'I wouldn't love him if he wasn't so nice. How many men do you know that put their family first?'

Ella pursed her pale-pink sparkly lips. It looked as if she'd been pillaging the beauty editor's cupboard again. 'True. Greg forgot Mother's Day, my birthday and our anniversary.'

Sophie wanted to roll her eyes but refrained. Greg barely remembered anything but his next five-a-side football fixture.

'You're such a brilliant cook,' said James, putting down his knife and fork. Sophie nodded, rather pleased with the way her Massaman curry had turned out, sweet and spicy with the right amount of heat, and the potatoes not too soft and not too firm.

They were sitting in her spacious kitchen, with a candle burning between them. Mondays were her favourite night of the week when she would cook a special meal because she knew James had been running around after his mother all weekend. He lived with her three days of the week and stayed at Sophie's flat the other four. Sophie suspected Mrs Soames wasn't really that unwell but liked having her son at home. And who could blame her?

'I should marry you one day.' He winked and picked up his wineglass, swirling the ruby-red liquid and sniffing with appreciation. As well he might, it was a very nice Australian Merlot that she'd tracked down on the recommendation of the wine writer at work and had cost a small fortune.

'You should,' she replied, her heart bumping uncomfortably.

It wasn't the first time he'd said something like that. And she'd thought on Saturday, at *Le Gavroche*, the second anniversary of their first date ... well, she'd hoped ...

'So how was work today?' That was the lovely thing about James, he was always interested.

'Remember I told you Mel left on Friday? She broke her leg. Can't go to New York now.' Sophie hesitated, and laughed. 'Angela offered me her place.'

'What ... to go to New York?' James looked alarmed.

'Don't worry, I turned it down. I wouldn't leave you.'

James smiled and patted her hand, 'If you really wanted to go, I wouldn't have minded.' He paused and then pulled her hand to his lips. 'But I would have missed you dreadfully, darling. I'd hate it if you went away.'

Sophie got up and stood behind him, wrapping her arms around his chest, glad that she'd not given too much credence to Angela's flattery. She would love to go there one day. Maybe she and James could go together. A honeymoon, perhaps.

James turned and nuzzled her neck. 'Early night? I'm knackered. Driving back from Cornwall is such a killer.'

'I need to tidy up.' Sophie gave the utensil-strewn kitchen a quick look, wishing she hadn't made quite so much mess and that James wasn't always so tired, but she could hardly ask him to help when he'd just driven over two hundred miles.

And she really couldn't complain. How many people her age had a kitchen like this? Or lived in a palatial flat in Kensington? Dad had insisted. It would have been mean to say no. She loved him to bits but that didn't mean she was going to let him help her find a job (have a word with someone on the board), or send her to an expensive private school (she was already settled in the local comprehensive) and it didn't feel right using the title.

By the time she'd tidied everything away and went into the double bedroom, James was sound asleep and the room was in darkness. He never remembered to leave a bedside light on for her. Quietly, she undressed and slipped into bed beside him, snuggling in, but there was no response. Poor thing was exhausted. Dead to the world. She smiled and pushed his floppy fringe from his forehead. He was a good man. Looking after his mother, without a complaint. Sophie closed her eyes. She was so lucky. Who needed New York?

Running late, see you there. And it's my day off but love that you're so loyal Kx

Sophie smiled at the text. Kate was even worse than she was, always trying to cram too much in and she could bet her last pound that Kate had stayed overnight at her boyfriend Ben's last night, which was the real reason she was running late. They were still in that loved-up, passion-boiling-over, can't-bear-not-to-touch-each-other-all-the-time phase. Not that Sophie could quite recall anything like that with her and James. Theirs had been a much gentler, soft landing into love rather than a plunge off the cliff-edge. Sophie wasn't sure she'd know how to deal with that sort of fiery sexual chemistry. It wasn't her style at all and part of her wondered if it wasn't a tiny bit selfish. Shouldn't love be gentle, embracing and warm? Something that grew with nourishment and care. Although she couldn't deny that Kate's happiness and *joie de vivre* were heart-warming, and when Ben suddenly narrowed his eyes while looking at Kate, the intensity of his look gave Sophie goose-bumps.

As she waited for her cappuccino, listening to the industrial hiss of the espresso machine operated by one of the Saturday girls, she gave the Danish pastries a second look. She shouldn't but they looked so delicious. Nope, it was no good, she couldn't possibly resist the cinnamon rolls.

Balancing a plate in one hand, the cup in the other and trying to keep her shoulder straight so her bag didn't slip off and bash any of the tables, she managed to weave her way through vacant chairs to her favourite spot in the corner, looking out onto the busy street.

Unfortunately, her usual table was taken by a tired-looking woman with a young baby who was squeaking with indignation, her big blue eyes flashing outrage as she waved a plastic spoon at the pot of yoghurt her mother held just out of reach in one hand. Sophie could see why the pot was out of the danger zone. The little girl had already managed to smear most of it into her hair and her mother was trying to clean her up. From where Sophie stood it looked more like octopus wrestling.

She sat down at the adjacent table, watching their antics with a gentle smile, and was about to turn away when the young woman looked up and shot her a vicious glare, her mouth pinched tight in sneering disgust.

Taking a far-too-hasty gulp of hot coffee, which burnt its way down into her stomach, Sophie looked away, shocked by the fierce, direct hatred which made her feel almost as if she'd been physically assaulted. She took a couple of deep steadying breaths. The poor woman was probably very stressed, it wasn't personal. Plastering a smile on her face, she took a more measured sip of coffee and looked over at her, hoping that a reassuring, friendly face might make the woman feel a bit better.

Whoa, she got that wrong. If anything, the spite on the woman's face intensified, wrinkles fanning out around her lips like an ancient walnut, and she was dabbing angrily at the child's face, the wipes in her hand flying like sheets in the wind.

It was impossible not to feel the woman's distress. Sophie hesitated for a second. She couldn't ignore the poor woman, who was clearly very unhappy.

'Are you alright?' asked Sophie with a tentative smile, feeling as if she were attempting to reason with a lioness.

'Am I alright?' spat the woman, as the little girl began to wail, and then the mother's face crumpled, falling in on itself, the anger and spite replaced by pure misery. 'Oh Emma, baby.' She scooped the little girl up, sticky fingers and all, and hugged her to her body, rubbing her back. 'There, there. Mummy's sorry.'

Sophie felt the slight pang of envy and the very merest tightening in her womb. One day ...

The little girl held on tight to her mother and stopped crying, lunging with sudden glee towards the yoghurt pot. Her mother smiled, resigned, and shook her head. 'You pickle.' She pressed a soft kiss on the top of the child's candyfloss-soft curls and put her on her lap, moving the yoghurt pot in front of them, giving her the spoon.

With a calm measured look, although her eyes were still full of anger, the woman stared back at Sophie. 'You asked if I was alright?' Her eyes sparkled with unshed tears, her head tilted defiantly.

'Yes, did you want a hand? It looks like hard work.' Sophie smiled at the little girl, who seemed a lot happier now. 'She's gorgeous. Although I don't envy you the mess. Do you want me to get you some more napkins or anything?'

'Gorgeous and *mine*,' said the woman, looking alarmed, wrapping a protective arm across the little girl's chest.

'Yes,' said Sophie warily. Surely this woman didn't think she was a child-snatcher or something?

'Although that doesn't bother you, does it, Sophie? Sharing things?' The woman's tone turned weary and her shoulders slumped, an expression of pain darting across her face.

Sophie's smile froze into place. Something about the woman's tone suggested she should have some inkling of what was going on here. How did she know her name?

'I was just trying to help.' She regretted even making eye contact now.

'*You? Help?*' The woman let out a bitter laugh. 'I think you've helped enough. Helped yourself to my husband.'

'Sorry?' Sophie's hand stilled as she paused to take another sip of coffee.

'Are you proud of yourself? Miss Rich Bitch with your flat in Kensington and Daddy's country estate in Sussex. I looked you up. Lady Sophie Bennings-Beauchamp.'

Sophie's mouth dropped open. This woman had done her homework. None of her colleagues at work had any idea. She kept her passport well out of sight from prying eyes. In fact, Kate was the only one who had seen it and at the time, she'd been professional enough not to say a word.

'I don't use—' she protested automatically because she always did, but the woman interrupted.

'Nice cushy life. No wonder James would rather spend half his life with you. No washing hanging everywhere. No babies crying in the night.'

'James?' Sophie stiffened. Even as she opened her mouth, she knew her words sounded like every last cliché in the book. 'What's he got to do with this?'

'James Soames. My husband. Lives in London four nights, Monday, Tuesday, Wednesday, Thursday. Comes home to his wife and daughter in Newbury Friday to Monday.'

'But he goes to Cornwall.' Sophie's legs felt leaden as if she were weighted into her seat. 'He's in Cornwall now.'

'No, he's not, you stupid cow. He's mowing the lawn at 47 Fantail Lane in Newbury and then he's going to build a swing for Emma.'

Chapter 2

Her heart bumped uncomfortably as the *Fasten Seatbelts* sign blinked on. Too late now to change her mind. To wonder whether her snap decision had been too hasty.

All around her people were gathering the belongings they'd spread around their seats on the seven-hour journey, packing up laptops and iPads, turning down corners of books, folding up blankets. Across the aisle through the window she could see lights twinkling, coming into sharper focus as the plane descended. Her ears popped, feeling full and heavy.

With a thud and bounce, the wheels touched down, the roar of the engines going into reverse thrust as the plane decelerated. She was really here, with a purseful of dollars, an address in Brooklyn and a suitcase packed with a desperately slim wardrobe to tide her through the next six months. Had she even packed a warm jumper? Gloves? Didn't New York get really cold in the winter?

Still pondering the ineptitude of her packing, she forced out a tight goodbye to the smiling cabin crew, refusing to give in to the overwhelming temptation to grab one of them and beg to fly back to London with them on their return leg.

It was tiredness, she told herself, as she tramped up the echoey tunnel, the floor bouncing slightly beneath her feet as the rumble of cases rebounded from the metal walls. Ahead there was so much to navigate, customs, a taxi, meeting strangers and a new home. For the last few hours she'd existed in an almost pleasant no-man's-land limbo, not needing to think about anything beyond choosing which film to watch, whether to have the beef or chicken and how to break into the plastic packaging of the bread roll.

Grasping the handle of her cabin bag as if it might give her some kind of magical courage, she followed the trail of people ahead, most of whom were head down with intent, clearly sure of where they were going. She rounded a corner and came into the huge passport area, instantly looking up at the American flag hanging from the ceiling. Nerves shimmered in her stomach. She knew all her paperwork was in order, but she'd heard horror stories about American customs. It wasn't looking too good. Only a few of the booths were manned and the queue was enormous. As it snaked its way forward she gripped her passport tighter and tried to look innocent, an automatic response to the gun-carrying officials wearing stern, shoot-you-in-a-second-and-not-bat-an-eyelid expressions on their faces.

By the time it was finally her turn, she felt exhausted but also irritated. The plane had landed nearly an hour and a half ago, her body clock was working on UK time and she was used to European indifference and laconic inspection. This lengthy eye-scanning, finger-printing process at silly o'clock, when her legs ached and she felt positively light-headed, was testing even her considerable reserves of Pollyanna-like amiability. Long minutes passed as the middle-aged customs officer scrutinised her passport with a stone-like expression, his greying eyebrows drawn together but separated by a trough of wrinkles. He looked at her, down at the pass-port and then back at her. Her stomach tightened. The spaced-out feeling in her head made her sway slightly. He looked back at the passport again.

'Is this for real?' he asked, his eyes widening as he once again looked at the passport and back at her. 'Lady Sophie Amelia Bennings-Beauchamp.' It took her a minute to attune to the heavy nasal American accent and then she nodded with a well-what-can-you-do smile and a tiny shrug.

'D'ya have a tiara in your baggage?' The direct question held a confusing combination of aggression and curiosity.

Some imp of mischief made her say, very seriously, 'Not this time. I tend not to travel with the family jewels.'

'That so, ma'am. Or should I call you your ladyship?'

'Sophie's fine.'

He looked appalled.

'Or Miss Bennings,' she added with a smile, pleased that she'd broken his scary official person's expression.

'Not Miss Bennings-Beauchamp.' He pronounced it *Bow-champ*, leaving her wondering if she should explain that it was really Beecham, but she decided against it. Not at this time of night.

She leaned forward and whispered, 'I try and travel incognito. So, I stick to Miss Bennings. It's easier that way.'

He nodded and put his fingers up to his lips, his eyes

sweeping over her shoulder and around the room. 'Mum's the word.'

'Thank you.'

'My pleasure, Lady Bennings-Bowchamp.' He winked at her and then frowned. 'You're working?' His eyebrows sank deeper over his eyes. 'L1 Visa.'

'Daddy gambled away my inheritance,' said Sophie out of the corner of her mouth, starting to enjoy herself.

'That so.' He shook his head in sorrow. 'That's bad, your ladyship.'

'And I couldn't sell the family heirlooms. So, I had to get a job.'

'Well, that don't seem right,' he stopped, his whole face screwed up in sympathetic distaste, then with a respectful nod, he added, 'but good for you, your ladyship.' There was a brief pause before, as if jolted back in line, he remembered he had a script. 'So where will you be staying for the duration of your trip?'

She reeled off the address she'd memorised.

'Brooklyn?'

'Yes,' said Sophie, smiling at his palpable disappointment. 'Isn't that very nice?'

He straightened and lifted his chin. 'Born and bred, ma'am, I mean your ladyship. Brooklyn ...' he winced, 'has changed a lot over the years. It's very hip now. Not like in my day. I hope you like it.'

'I'm sure I will.'

'Can I ask you a question?'

'Of course.'

'Do you know the Queen?' Expectant hope glittered in his eyes.

Sophie straightened and carefully looked over her shoulder before turning back to him, widening her eyes as if warning him that what she was about to divulge was top secret. She lowered her voice, 'Yes, the family spends Easter at Buckingham Palace every year. Prince Philip's an absolute sweetie and William and Kate's children are such cuties. But don't tell anyone I told you. We're not supposed to talk about it.'

With a quick salute, a forefinger to his eyebrow, he nodded. 'Mom's the word. But you tell her hi from me. The name's Don. Don McCready.' He beamed. 'Wait till I tell my wife, Betty-Ann, I met you. She just *loves* the royals. She's gonna get such a kick out of this.'

Neon lights blurred as the cab sped past, the road still busy even at this time of night. Sophie wrinkled her nose at the unpleasant post-take-away smell hovering in the back of the shabby cab, the ugly metal grill separating the passenger seats from the front and the cab driver's surly indifference to her. A stream of Spanish came from the mobile phone mounted on the dashboard, punctuated occasionally by the driver's monosyllabic responses. She settled back into the battered seats, watching the street scenes through the scarred windows, as the car veered from lane to lane. It looked like the America she'd seen on television as a child in old episodes of *NYPD Blue*. People of all races loping along the pavements. Nail bars rubbed shoulders with *tire-replacement centers*, the alien spelling striking home, and unfamiliar fast-food franchises – Golden Krust, Wendy's, Texas Chicken & Burgers – as well as the ubiquitous McDonalds, Dunkin Donuts and Seven Eleven, which looked the same, but also different somehow.

For a minute, it was oh-so-tempting to tap the taxi driver on the shoulder and ask him to turn around, go back. She took in a deep shuddery breath. *Man up, Sophie, you chose to do this. Your choice.*

She pulled out her phone and re-read the email about the arrangements. The company had fixed up an apartment for her. A one-bedroomed place in Brooklyn, within reach of the subway and an easy journey to work. For a moment, she let the image of Mel's limp balloon dance in her head. Brandi Baumgarten's desk would be ready and waiting for her on Monday, just thirty-one hours from now. Scrolling across the touch screen, she brought up the subway map she'd downloaded. It looked horribly complicated compared to the tube map she was so used to. Taking a deep breath, she closed the app. Tomorrow there'd be plenty of time to get her bearings and work out the journey to work.

The taxi had slowed, turning off the main highway, and here the streets were suddenly interesting, lots of bars, vibrant with crowds of people, pavement seating full, a world of nationalities in the bars and restaurants they passed. With a sudden screech of brakes, the taxi stopped and almost before he'd halted, the driver turned around.

'Forty dollars,' he spat.

'Is this it?' she asked, peering out of the window at several shop fronts.

'Number 425 – right there, lady.' He indicated with a contemptuous thumb. 'Just like you asked for.'

'Oh, right,' said Sophie, uncertain as to how he could see any numbers. Maybe it was a locals' thing and she was looking in the wrong place.

The taxi driver had already got out and was heaving her cases onto the pavement.

'Thank you,' said Sophie politely, as she rummaged through her purse with the unfamiliar currency and located a fifty-dollar bill. She knew tipping was big in America and had a sudden moment of panic. 'Keep the change.' She had no idea if it was too much or too little but at nearly three in the morning, she just wanted to find the promised key safe, get into her room and collapse into bed.

He snatched up the money and jumped back in the cab before she could say another word and the red back lights of the car disappeared down the street, two eyes glowing in the dark like a fading demon.

With two suitcases and her cabin bag she stood on the pavement, sudden fear clamping her heart as she surveyed the shop fronts. Not one of them had a helpful number on the door. She looked down the street which stretched away into the distance. It was a very long street. A few people were about, and from the nearby corner loud voices shouted.

She turned back and jumped as a man appeared from nowhere. At well over six foot five, he was the tallest man she'd ever seen, with long, lanky, slightly bowed legs that seemed to bounce as he walked towards her. Her momentary fear at being surprised and alone in the middle of the night in a strange neighbourhood receded when white teeth from ebony skin grinned at her.

'Hey lady, you OK? You look a little lost.'

'I'm ... erm ... looking for number 425.'

He loomed over her, smelling rather bizarrely of rosemary. With a surreptitious sniff, she also identified basil.

'That'd be right here above Bella's Place.' He pointed to a bakery and then she spotted the narrow doorway squeezed between two shops. 'You must be the English girl.'

'I must be, yes.' The scent of basil was stronger now and she blurted out, with drunken jet-lagged stream of consciousness, 'You smell of herbs.'

''Erbs,' he corrected. 'Herbs and Spice and All Things Nice.'

'That's what little boys smell of,' said Sophie, now feeling a bit like Alice.

His grin widened as he pointed to a shop front a few doors down. Sophie nodded, feeling a little stupid when she realised *Herbs and Spice and All Things Nice* was the name of his shop.

'You just arrived?' He laughed. 'Course you have, otherwise why would you be out on the sidewalk in the middle of the night with a bunch of baggage? I'm Wes, let me give you a hand with your things.'

Too weary to argue, she nodded, relieved to find the key safe by the door which gave up its contents as soon as she punched in the code. Wes led the way up the narrow staircase, carrying her cabin bag and suitcase with ease while she struggled up behind him, following the scent of herbs which spilled from a couple of pots wedged into his canvas satchel slung across his body.

On the top floor he stopped outside a bright-red door. 'Here you go – 425A, Bella's just upstairs. She rents this whole building.' He took the keys from her and did the honours, dumping the case in the tiny hall and flipping the light switch. 'Welcome to the neighbourhood.' He fished out a rosemary plant and handed it to her, before saluting, ducking under the doorway and loping away down the stairs with a cheerful whistle.

Tired as she was, the brief, friendly encounter with a man who'd given her a herb pot made her feel that maybe life in Brooklyn might just be bearable after all.

The hallway opened into a lounge with several doors leading from it. She had an impression of polished wooden floors, two long tall windows through which the ambient light of the street spilled and a shadowy collection of furniture. She put the pot down on a table and opened the nearest door. Bingo first strike, the bedroom. A double bed, quilt, pillow, all bare of sheets. Bugger. It hadn't occurred to her to pack those. Sod it, still fully clothed, she pitched forward onto the naked duvet, wrapping it around her. Her last thought, her teeth could have an extra minute's brushing in the morning.

Chapter 3

Despite the god-awful time of 5 a.m., she was wide awake, her body clock, even after only five hours' sleep, hell-bent on London time and, according to her biorhythms, enjoying a leisurely nine o'clock lie-in.

With a groan Sophie rolled over, feeling grimy, travel stained and full-on icky, her body still crimped from the plane journey. She stared up at an unfamiliar ceiling as half-hearted daylight clawed its way through the flimsy curtains. As usual, the thoughts began to crowd in. Memories of the last two years, fighting like gremlins coming up through the crevices. Nope, not going there. Refuse to go there. Shower. Unpack. Find tea. They were the priorities.

She swung her legs over the side of the bed and planted them firmly on the wide-planked wooden floor and looked around the room. Just about enough space to swing a very small kitten, but clean and obviously newly painted. The tasteful shade of sage green was complemented by the cream-painted woodwork of the headboard and a matching chest of drawers and an oval mirror hanging above it. Space was tight, so the bed was pushed up against the opposite wall and there was no sign of a wardrobe.

She found the reason when she pushed open the second door leading from the bedroom. It opened into a tiny hallway with a built-in wardrobe and, at the end, another doorway which led into a long and very narrow bathroom. However, the shiny, glossy brick tiles and immaculate, gleaming chrome fittings more than made up for its corridor-like dimensions.

At the sight of the state-of-the-art shower, chrome-filled with numerous taps, heads and levers and big enough to take a rugby team, she peeled off her clothes and stepped into the blissful streams of hot water. It was only as the water streamed through her long blonde hair, from two different directions, that she realised that there was no shampoo, no soap and no towel. She blinked hard at her stupidity. Why hadn't she thought to pack towels and sheets?

As she shook herself like a dog to try and dry off, using her jeans as a bathmat, she glared at the idiotic image in the mirror, her hair wrapped in her T-shirt to soak up the drips.

For God's sake, she was normally the person who could be relied on for having packed spares for everyone else.

She went through her case pulling things out, appalled at the random contents and glaring omissions. Hair straighteners. No hairdryer. Fourteen pairs of knickers. One bra. Three tubes of toothpaste. No toothbrush. Tweezers. No nail scissors. Her second-favourite cookery book. And decaffeinated tea-bags? Just when she could have mainlined caffeine with bells on. Who drank decaffeinated anything? There should be a law against it.

Sitting back on her heels, she looked back at the last week with sudden clarity. Lord, hindsight was a wonderful thing.

Now, when it was far too bloody late, she could see that her packing had been done in a blur of denial and downright indecision. Convinced she wouldn't ever really leave. Right up to the last minute when the taxi driver rang the bell, she'd not really been sure she'd go through with it.

Biting her lip, kneeling among discarded shirts, jeans and Converse hi-tops, she picked through her final days in London. Once she'd said yes to Angela, it was as if she'd stepped on a treadmill and had neither the will, the energy nor the reasoning capacity to do anything but keep putting one foot in front of the other. Misery, it had turned out, was a useful shield, blurring away reality until it was too late to get off the treadmill. The taxi was there, her passport was in her hand and she had two cases and a cabin bag at her side.

And here she was. In America.

'Right.' She stood up, tugged the T-shirt from her wet hair and looked firmly at herself in the mirror. 'You are here now.' She glared into her own eyes. 'You, yes you, Sophie Bennings ... Beauchamp, Bow-champ to the nice customs man, need to knuckle down. Sort yourself out. Sheets. Towel. Toiletries.'

Those stupid omissions at least gave her a mission for the day. She had to go out and buy those as an absolute minimum.

'And shopping.' For Pete's sake, she was so wet, she hadn't even explored her new home. And she was talking to herself. 'And what's wrong with that? Come on. This is an opportunity.' Saying things out loud made her feel less stupid. Perhaps she ought to buy one of those self-help manuals, come up with a few more convincing mantras. 'It is an opportunity. Some people would kill to be me.' OK, kill was perhaps going a little too far, but all her friends had been frankly envious. Not one of them had said, 'Oh, God just think how big and scary New York is and how lonely you're going to be.'

Her exploration didn't take long. The apartment was small, but perfectly formed. Modern, urban and very sophisticated. Not what she was used to at all, but as she stood in the open-plan lounge-kitchen, she nodded to herself. OK, she could live here. The polished, wide-planked, wooden floors were lovely and the huge sash windows let in loads of light and provided a great view out over the street. There was a television and a black box thing, with several remote controls, which she glanced at briefly with a wince. That had been James's department. The bright-red sofa, with grey cushions positioned opposite a fireplace, looked inviting and welcoming.

On the other side of the room, along the back wall, was a long galley kitchen, with white brick tiles on the walls separating units of glossy, dark red. A wooden-topped island with a breakfast bar created a division between the living room and the kitchen. It contained the sink, drainer and more counter space, and she was pleased to see that the hob, oven, fridge and sink were arranged in the perfect cook's triangle of practicality.

When she opened a couple of cupboards to find ubiquitous Ikea china mugs and plates, she was unable to decide whether they were disappointing or reassuring. One half of her hoped that there'd be some exoticism – chic American branded crockery, proof that she'd flown 3,000 miles to be here. But the other half – the more dominant half, to be perfectly honest

– was relieved by the sight of the familiar tall-bodied mugs and the chunky primary-colour plates. They said, *See, not so far from home after all.*

With a nod of approval, she was about to turn when her eye caught sight of an unexpected door, tucked out of sight at the end of the run of units.

'Oh, hello.' She stepped through the door out onto the deck, immediately tipping her face up to let the warm sunshine dance on her skin. The sun burnt bright in a cloud-free sky. For a minute she stood there, letting the heat wash over her. The golden glow held her in a timeless embrace, giving her battered spirits an immediate boost.

'I want to see the sunshine after the rain, I want to see bluebirds flying over …' she hummed as she surveyed the bistro table and two chairs and the empty planter, which begged to be filled with herbs. She would speak to Wes, the mysterious herb man from last night. Musing whether to add a chilli plant in there as well, she turned to survey the backdrop landscape of rooftops and secret insights of backyards. You could see down into the neighbouring plots. Some held climbing frames and swings squeezed onto tiny lawns, while others held compact decks handsomely furnished with expensive-looking garden furniture. She came back to the refrain, 'Sunshine after the rain,' and swallowed back the lump, fighting against tears. OK, so it was going to take a while, a long time before she saw anything flying over mountains or otherwise, but one day she'd feel better. She cast a bitter look at the second bistro chair.

With a sigh she went back into the kitchen. She needed to keep herself busy. There were lists to be made. If only she'd packed a bloody pen. She knew she was putting off the moment when she had to leave the apartment.

And there, taped to the back of the door, was a large piece of greaseproof paper, a jagged tear down one side as if someone had grabbed the first thing at hand, with a note scribbled on it in what looked like bright-blue Sharpie pen.

Welcome. Pop down to the café and say hi. First coffee is on me and I'll throw in breakfast, because I didn't get to the store for you. Your landlady Bella

Coffee. Now the thought was in her head, her stomach growled. When was the last time she'd eaten a proper meal? She couldn't stay here all day ... actually, she probably could ... but she needed stuff, towels and sheets. This gave her the perfect excuse to get going and stop being such a wuss.

Grabbing her guide book and purse, she hastily packed everything she thought she might need and headed out.

For a moment, she stood utterly entranced by the window display, which she'd completely missed the night before. A picture of Audrey Hepburn in *My Fair Lady* in her iconic black-and-white Ascot costume was suspended mid-air above what Sophie could only describe as the most magnificent display. Matching black-and-white decorated cupcakes arranged on two candelabra-style cake stands stood like ladies in waiting behind a five-tiered wedding cake, its elaborate icing and shape cleverly referencing the design of the hat. Underneath the picture was a quote:

Nothing is impossible, the word itself says I'm Possible! Audrey Hepburn

Reading it, Sophie gave a nod. She needed to start being more positive. Her can-do spirit seemed to have evaporated. With a professional eye, she studied the cakes, marvelling at the precision and creativity, until the door opened beside her and someone came out of the café, followed by a waft of coffee.

Her stomach complained again and she grabbed the door as it started to close. The minute she stepped inside, she paused and closed her eyes, inhaling. What the sunshine upstairs had started, the familiar magic alchemic smell of butter and sugar, eggs and flour finished. She felt lighter, as if some invisible weight had dislodged itself from her shoulders, as she registered the soothing hint of vanilla, the richness of chocolate, the sharp citrus of lemon. The scents swirled around her, grounding her. She almost laughed out loud. Grounding her, really? But it was true, for the first time in two weeks, she felt a bit more like herself again. And then she spotted the notice above the counter. *You've got 86,400 seconds today. Have you used one to smile?*

Taking the message to heart, she let her mouth relax into a broad grin, taking another discreet sniff. This almost felt like home and suddenly she wanted to be in the kitchen, mixing, stirring, tasting and baking.

She opened her eyes and headed for the counter. Her eagerness felt rusty and unused. Now she was dying to see what was available, where all those delicious smells were coming from and what she could learn. She'd never been to America before, there was a whole new world of food to explore. Her eyes lit up. Oh yes, there surely was.

'Good morning. How are you today? What can I get you?' asked a petite redhead with a mass of curls bundled up in a bright-green scarf, wiping down the coffee machine.

'Hi, I'm ... very well, thank you. I'm Sophie. From upstairs.'

'Sophie!' The girl squealed, dropping her cloth and racing around the counter, and putting her hands on Sophie's arms, surveying her with bright-eyed enthusiasm, rather like a great aunt who hadn't seen her for years. 'Hey! It's so great to see you. I'm Bella. Your landlady. I've never been a landlady before. Is the apartment OK?' She let go of Sophie and gesticulated eagerly, letting her hands take a share in the conversation. 'Do you need anything? I'm sorry I didn't get any groceries in. I think maybe I should have, I didn't know but then we had a rush order and I just ... well it's always mad on a weekend. Welcome to Brooklyn.'

Sophie laughed and held up her hands to fend off the rush of words and the semaphore fingers, and to reassure the other woman. 'It's all fine. The apartment's lovely. And a nice man called Wes helped me carry my cases in. Even left me a pot of herbs.'

'Ah yes, the luscious Wes,' Bella's mouth dipped slightly before she continued, 'he's a sweetie. And always pushing those herbs.' She nodded towards the aluminium pots of lavender on the tables. 'Phew, it was a rush to get it finished in time, but when Todd, he's my cousin, said the magazine needed a short-term rental, I couldn't turn it down. Now what can I get you? Are you horribly jet-lagged? Is it the middle of the night for you?'

'No, it's early afternoon but I'm trying not to think about

it. Coffee would be lovely, thank you.' Normally she was a die-hard tea drinker but she knew New Yorkers were fond of their coffee and she suspected getting a decent cup of tea would be a challenge.

'Gee, I love your English accent, it's so cute.'

'Thank you.' Sophie had to beam back. It was impossible not to. Bella bounced around like an animated pixie caught in a whirlwind, her hazel eyes sharp with interest and intelligence.

'How about something to eat? I made these lavender-and-vanilla cupcakes this morning, or there are carrot-and-cinnamon or orange-and-lemon.'

'St Clements,' said Sophie automatically.

'St what?'

'It's cockney rhyming slang, orange-and-lemon flavours are sometimes called St Clements. It's one of my favourites.' For some reason she softly sang, 'Oranges and lemons say the bells of St Clements.'

'Aw, that is so cute. I've never heard that before.' Her face took on a dreamy expression. 'Cockneys. They're in *Mary Poppins*. I could do a whole theme. Supacallafragilistic cakes.'

'I love the window. Did you design that cake?'

Bella beamed and Sophie swore the dusting of freckles on her nose danced too. 'Sure did. You like?'

'Love! It's amazing. Those black-and-white frills and the sugar-paste feathers are so clever.'

'Awesome. Thanks. Now you must be hungry, so what would you like? First one's on the house.'

'Mmm, they look delicious.' Sophie's stomach grumbled

obligingly as she examined the contents of the glass cabinet. One side was stacked with interesting-looking loaves, walnut-and-raisin, rye, five-grain, along with cheese-and-herb plaits and pumpkin-seed rolls, while the other had rows of beautifully decorated cupcakes, topped with pale cream frosting and sugar-paste flowers like Easter baskets, as well as several fruit-topped cheesecakes, a line of giant cookies, chunks of melted chocolate glistening, and a couple of full-sized cakes.

'Do you make all of this?'

'No, I don't have time. The celebration and cupcakes are mine. And I live in hope that the wedding-cake side will take off. The cheesecakes come from the fabulous Maisie, who lives around the corner and bakes them while her kids are at school. She uses organic cream cheese from the family dairy upstate in Maine. They are to die for. And the breads and bagels are delivered in daily by a two-man team. Ed and Edie. Well, a man-and-woman team,' she laughed, 'their company is called Two Eds. And their slogan is *When it comes to breads, two Eds are better*.'

Sophie groaned, 'Oh my word. I just got even hungrier. And if the cakes in the window are anything to go by ... you should have plenty of customers.'

Bella pulled a face. 'It gets a bit crazy in here at the weekends. And this week has been crazier than normal. I had two birthday parties, two hundred and fifty cupcakes to make and then ice and decorate with baseball players. I tell you, those little striped shirts are darn fiddly. But then, who doesn't love a cupcake?' She caught Sophie's eye and winked.

Sophie grinned back, 'I love the sugar-paste flowers you've

done,' she pointed to the cupcakes on display. 'They look such fun. I'd love to learn how to do those.' She gave them a considering look. 'I'm a cookery writer, so I do a lot of baking. Testing recipes.'

'Really? Todd didn't say what you do. That's so cool. Maybe we can swap some ideas some time.'

'That would be wonderful. There's something about baking that ...' Sophie sniffed the air again, feeling a tiny bit better about being here.

'Oh, I think I'm going to love you. Yes, there's something about baking ... it's almost magical. I love seeing the customers. Coming up with new ideas. Watching their eyes light up. Cakes make people smile.'

'These look gorgeous.' Sophie peered down at the tray of cakes in front of her. 'They must take hours.'

'They do ... but they're worth it and every single one is hand-crafted with love,' Bella beamed. 'Although it's hard work, but it's my business. Well mine, the bank's and my granddad's. He owns the lease on the building.

'Now, is there anything you need? It's the first time I've let the apartment. The renovations were only finished ten days ago.'

'Seriously, Bella, it's all gorgeous. Everything.' Sophie bit her lip, she didn't want to mention the lack of bedding, as it really wasn't Bella's responsibility, but she had a feeling she'd make it hers.

'Well, let me know if there's anything you need.'

'No, it's great and I love the deck.'

'Just watch out for the mossies. They're nasty.'

'Mossies? As in mosquitoes?'

'Oh yeah. If you're planning on sitting out there, get some citronella candles or a fan. Now, coffee? A latte, drip coffee, iced coffee, cappuccino, macchiato, flat white, Americano, espresso?'

'Cappuccino, please. The last drink I had was on the plane. I'm gasping.'

'Garsping,' teased Bella, elongating the vowel. 'Gee, your accent is so cute.'

Sophie winced, glad she hadn't asked for tea, and watched as the other girl set to work with quick efficiency, tapping out the old grounds, tamping down new, quickly twisting the silver filter into place while pouring milk into a jug with her other hand.

'Take a seat and I'll bring it over.'

Sophie sat down at the only free table, a bistro set in the window, and took a good look around at the bakery. She loved the eclectic decoration and how it had been divided into specific areas, each one with its own distinct style where the sofa, chairs, cushions and throws took their inspiration from the wallpaper design in the wall panel nearest them.

Towards the back there was a large archway and beyond it you could see the kitchen, the table still covered in flour and utensils as if the latest batch of goodies had just been finished.

With a happy sigh, Sophie sat back in her chair. She already loved this place and Bella had given her such a warm, friendly welcome, suddenly she didn't feel quite so far from home. She pulled out a notebook and her guide book, there was so much she needed to do but her head felt a bit too buzzy and cotton-woolly to get a proper grasp on what she should think about first. Jet-lag was a bummer.

The underground map looked horribly confusing and she couldn't figure out the names of any of the lines, there seemed to be so many different options. She glanced over at Bella, busy behind the counter, she'd ask her for some help. She could do this.

Nerves shimmered as she looked through the window at the busy street. She was really here. London was several hours ahead and in the safety of the café she felt that perhaps if she took one day at a time, she could get through the next six months.

It would be late afternoon in England. What would James be doing? Was he still with his wife, Anna?

'Hey, I hear you're Sophie.'

With a jolt, she looked up to find a man looming over her, the sun streaming in through the window, outlining his shape but making it difficult to see his features. From the way he nodded over at Bella, who was gesticulating with those wild arms again, it was obvious the American girl had indicated who she was.

Twisting a chair so that the back faced him, he swung his leg over the seat and sat down grinning at her.

Immediately she was irked by his confidence, the casual attitude, so utterly sure of his welcome. She gave him a tight smile.

'I'm Todd.' He held out a steady hand which she had no option but to shake. His grip was firm and dry.

She stiffened, wanting to move backwards. He exuded self-assurance which made her feel doubly inadequate, out of place and alien.

'Bella's my cousin. I found this place for you.'

What did he want? A bloody medal?

Politeness forced her to nod and say tightly, 'Thank you.'

'No problem.' He lifted his head as Bella approached with Sophie's drink and cake. 'Hey, Bella babes. Can I get an iced coffee?'

'Hi Todd, what brings you this way so early?' She put the coffee and cake in front of Sophie. 'I thought you'd still be sleeping off last night's party.'

'Who said I'd been home yet?'

'Stupid me, of course you haven't.'

She turned to Sophie. 'This is my cousin, Todd McLennan. Party animal extraordinaire.' She leaned down and gave him a hug. 'So where was it happening last night? Or rather, should I ask who was it last night?'

'You wound me.' He put his hand over his heart, grinning at Sophie. 'Don't believe a word she says.'

'Do believe everything I say. He's bad news where women are concerned.'

'Bella, Bella, Bella ... you do me wrong.' He sighed. 'I never lie to them.'

'True, but they always think they'll be the one to reform you.'

He shrugged and leaned over to dip his finger in the frosting of Sophie's cake, winking at her as he did. 'I can't help it if they don't listen.'

Sophie narrowed her eyes as Bella slapped at his hand.

'Keep your mitts off, that's Sophie's. She's probably not had any breakfast yet.'

'Sorry,' he said, his mouth stretching into a wide smile, 'neither have I.'

'Have you even been home?' asked Bella, shaking her head.

'Yes, slept snug and tight in my own bed, if you have to ask. Now are you going to bring me a coffee or do I have to beg?'

Sophie refrained from snorting, as if he'd ever had to beg for anything in his life. Just looking at him, in his casual linen Ralph Lauren shirt and smart navy shorts, with expensive, if scuffed, loafers on his feet, you could tell this one led a charmed life. Almost as if he could read her disparaging thoughts, he gave her a charm-fuelled, dazzling, film-star smile.

'So English, how are you finding Brooklyn?' He leaned forward on the back of the chair, focusing all his attention on her as if he really wanted to know. She had the feeling it was a practised move, that came as easily to him as breathing.

'It's Sophie, and I've only just arrived, so I've not had a chance to find anything yet.' Her words sounded stiff and starchy.

He leaned forward and pulled her notes and map towards him. 'Bergen Street. The F line 47th/50th.'

'Sorry?' Hell, she sounded even more prim and prissy.

He simply grinned. 'The route to work. That's what you were looking up, weren't you?'

Was he some sort of mind reader? She frowned.

'You're doing the job swap with Brandi. I suggested Bella's

place when they let the other girl's place go. Man, bad luck her breaking her leg, but lucky for you, I guess. Never thought they'd get someone to fill the post, that quickly. Were you second pick or something?'

'Something,' snapped Sophie with uncharacteristic sharpness, stung that everyone would think she was second choice, when she didn't want to come in the first place.

'Hey!' He held up his hands in quick surrender. 'I'm not suggesting you're not as good.' Unexpected sympathy brimmed in his eyes, as if he knew it was more complicated than that. 'The subway can be a bit confusing for a first-timer. Bergen Street is a couple of blocks away. I could show you after coffee.' He lifted his shoulders. 'We're going to be co-workers.'

'What? You work at *CityZen*?'

'Sure do.' His eyes twinkled wickedly and he raised his eyebrows in suggestive challenge, 'I write the *Man About Town* column.'

Clearly she was supposed to know about that. She should have checked out the magazine in advance, which is what a normal enthusiastic person, who'd been offered an amazing opportunity to come and work in the most exciting city in the world, would have done.

Suddenly she was sick of herself, sick of her seesawing emotions, sick of feeling sorry for herself and sick that James had done this to her. She'd spent her childhood rising above things, being sunny and positive despite everything her Dad's ex-wife had thrown at their family. James was not going to take that away from her.

With a deliberately bright smile, she responded, 'That

sounds fun.' As soon as she left here she would find the first newsagents (didn't they call them newsstands here?) and pick up a copy of *CityZen*.

'Oh it is.' Those film-star teeth flashed again, although did she imagine it, or did the smile not quite reach his eyes? She got the impression he'd said it many times. 'When you love your work, it doesn't feel like work.'

'I'll second that,' said Bella, sliding a tall glass of iced coffee in front of him. 'That'll be four dollars.'

He dug in his pocket and pulled out a handful of crumpled bills, like tissues, handing one to her before swiping another taste of frosting from the cake.

'Oy, get your own.' Sophie tapped his hand smartly and moved the plate closer to her side of the table.

'You're no fun, English,' he moaned, taking his time, licking the big dollop of frosting from his finger. 'Man, this is good.' He shot Sophie a sudden, horrified, disapproving look, 'Please tell me you're not a crazy person who considers her body a temple and thinks sugar is sin.' With a surreptitious glance out the window, he added, 'There are way too many of them in Brooklyn already. The soya-and-sushi sisterhood. All quinoa and chia seeds.'

Sophie burst out laughing, finally succumbing. It wasn't his fault that she currently hated the world in general. 'I'm definitely not a crazy person.'

'Damn, and here was I hoping to guilt you into handing over the cake.'

'No way.' She put her arms protectively around the plate. 'I love my food.' With a rueful smile, she added, 'A bit too much.'

Shamelessly he gave her body a once up and down, his eyes dancing with appreciation and merriment. 'Not from here, you don't.'

With a ladylike snort, she ignored the faint blush that stole along her cheeks, knowing better than to take him seriously. She'd got his measure. This was one man you should never take seriously and you'd be a fool if you did. And she was not going to be a fool again. Ever.

'I have to run a lot to balance it all out.' At least she'd packed her trainers, if not a sports bra. 'Bella was right, you are bad news, aren't you? But I appreciate the thought.' She was never going to be stick thin, but who wanted to be like that if you were miserable and starving? Regular running kept her between a size twelve and fourteen.

He grinned, unrepentant, and for a second their eyes met. She grinned back at him and picked up the cake, taking a large deliberate bite.

'Ouch, I felt that.'

'You were supposed to. Mmm, it's delicious.'

'Sure you can eat all of that? It's a mighty big cake. Lots of calories.'

With a deliberate lick of her lips, ignoring the hopeful expression on his face, she savoured the tangy citrus sweetness of the frosting around her mouth, sighed heavily and gave him a smug look. 'Oh yes, I'm going to enjoy every last one of them.'

'You're heartless, English. Heartless.' He shook his head in mock sorrow, his lips curving in shared amusement.

'You'd better believe it,' she said, taking another thoughtful bite of the soft sponge, enjoying the exchange and ignoring the little butterfly-like flutters dancing in the pit of her stomach. Nothing to see here, she told herself firmly. Good looking, charming and totally shallow, light-hearted fun and nothing more. It was a while since she'd flirted with anyone and it felt rather liberating, especially when it didn't mean a thing.

'So, Mr Man About Town, can you fill me in on the local neighbourhood? I need to find somewhere to buy bed linen and towels.' She paused. 'Although maybe you're not the best person to ask.'

'Excuse me.' He pointed to himself with his thumbs. 'Man About Town. In touch with my feminine side.'

'Really?' She gave him a direct look.

'And no, I'm not gay.'

'I never said a word.'

'It's an inevitable side-effect of working on a women's magazine. You absorb shopping stuff by osmosis. If you want serious thread count – see, I know this stuff – Nordstrom Rack for quality and discount, or T.J.Maxx for discount and a free for all. Just a couple of blocks away on Fulton Street. Here, let me mark on the map for you.'

'I need to find a supermarket too, to buy ...' she couldn't quite bring herself to say 'groceries'.

'A supermarket.' He pursed his lips around the word, lifting the smooth column of his throat. 'Jeez, I love how you say that, it's so prim and proper.' He grinned recklessly again. 'Kinda sexy.'

Sophie rolled her eyes at him, ignoring the thought that

someone must have invented the word for him. 'You need to get out more.'

He laughed and scooted his chair closer to hers, pulling open the map. 'Here, got a pen? I'll mark a couple of *grocery stores* for you.'

'I don't have a pen.'

'Here you go.' He rooted in the canvas-and-leather man bag slung over his shoulder. Of course he had a man bag, he was so a man bag sort of man.

'Associated Supermarkets on Fifth and Union Street is good. Not the nearest, but definitely one of the nicer ones. Turn right out of here, go down Union Street and then it's a good six blocks but worth it. I'm guessing you can cook if you're the new food columnist. I'll have to get you to cook dinner some time, as we're practically neighbours.'

She raised a single eyebrow at his casual assumption, a trick she was inordinately proud of. 'Sounds like a plan,' she said, before adding just as he took a sip of coffee, 'and you can do my washing.'

With a choked laugh, he nearly spluttered his drink all over the table. 'I like you, English. Funny girl. We're going to get on just fine.'

Sophie gave him a considering look.

'Come on.' He rose to his feet and held out a hand to help her up. 'I'll show you the way to the subway station and then from there you can walk on down to Fulton Street, to get your home wares. We'll take a rain check on dinner as I'm sure you want to get settled. And I doubt you've got any laundry yet ...' He waggled his eyebrows suggestively. 'And you do know washing in the States is something completely different?'

As she put her hand in his, there was no little frisson of electricity, no gentle sizzle between them, no ... a bloody great thunderbolt of lust that almost floored her. Todd McLennan was more than bad news, he was the sort of news that she needed to stay well, well away from.

Chapter 4

For most of the subway journey, Sophie had been fascinated by the fantastically chic woman opposite her wearing a perfectly tailored black suit and her hair swept up in a perfect chignon. Despite her sleek elegance, Sophie couldn't help staring at the clumpy white trainers on her feet. It made her smile. The epitome of New York chic and practicality.

She pulled her cardigan around her. The carriage was a bit too cool, although she shouldn't complain, as the fearsome air conditioning made a welcome contrast to the rich, warm fug of the London underground. The train streaked along, the station names unfamiliar and yet familiar, *East Broadway*, *2 Avenue*, *42 Street Bryant Park*, *47–50 Street – Rockefeller Center*, and then suddenly *57 Street*, her stop. With a quickening heart she grasped the pole as the train jerked to a halt, her pulse racing as she stepped out with the crowd swarming towards the exit.

New York proper.

She'd still woken at stupid o'clock this morning but had enjoyed a leisurely coffee out on the deck. Yesterday, after

Todd had shown her the subway and helped her buy her a monthly metro card, he'd directed her down Bergen Street and then down Hoyt Street which led straight to Nordstrom on Fulton Street, with T.J.Maxx right next door. Even without looking at the map, it had been pretty easy to navigate. Despite her love of London, she had to admit she was rather taken with the straightforward grid system. It made finding her way back via a rather fab grocery store, so easy. She still thought, despite Todd's protestation that it was impossible to get lost, that it was perfectly possible if you didn't know your East from your West or your North from your South. Some of those streets went on for miles.

Laden down with new bedding and a bale of towels, after spending far too long browsing among designer goodies, she'd only bought the basics in the supermarket and had treated herself to the rare convenience of a ready-roasted chicken. There was even a choice. Rosemary and lemon, garlic and herb or Caribbean. She'd also bought a copy of *CityZen*, leafing through it as she ate her solitary supper.

When a seat came free on the subway, she sat down, taking the time to have another look at the magazine. No one ever need know that her first port of call was the *Man About Town* column. Todd's picture leapt out from the glossy pages, his blue eyes enhanced perfectly by the open-necked shirt he wore. It was a great photo. The slight curve of his lips lazily (and yes, sexily) smiling up at her, as if he knew exactly what she and every other woman on the planet were thinking. She pursed her lips with a tolerant smile and shook her head. Todd oozed charisma and charm ... and he knew it. He was the sort of person you should treat like an adorable puppy, knowing that his winsome friendliness was totally indiscriminate.

As the train pulled into the station, she tucked the magazine back into her bag and let herself be carried along by the swell of people. She found herself deposited outside on the pavement, almost projected into the blare of the New York traffic. She stopped dead, exactly the way she hated tourists in London doing, but really! When you looked up, you kept looking up and up and up. Ignoring the tuts around her, she cricked her neck as she followed the line of the skyscrapers. She was *really* here. Manhattan. For a moment she stood and stared upwards, taking in the sight of the towering giants dwarfing everything around them, feeling slightly dizzy. The frisson of anxious nerves that had danced and sung in her veins since she'd woken to the alarm in her apartment vanished with a sudden unexpected bolt of excitement. New York. Seen in countless films, it felt both familiar and strange at once. This was going to be her life for the next six months. All the fear and roiling uneasiness that had been stored up for the last ten days, tightening the tendons in her neck, lining her stomach with nauseous intent and pinching at the muscles in her shoulders, suddenly gave up its grip. With an almost involuntary little skip, she turned and checked her bearings. 57th Street.

She walked quickly, matching her pace to blend with everyone else, her nose alert to the smell of hot dogs and pretzels as she passed a couple of fast-food stands and her ears picking up on the American accents around her. Ahead, a tower block with a jagged silhouette of diamond-shaped glass panes beckoned. Recognising the magazine headquarters, she picked up her step. Up close it was even more imposing. What looked like hundreds of floors of steel and glass rose upwards from the original 1920s stone building which now made up the base.

Following the tide of people, trying to look nonchalant – after all, she was one of them now – she entered through the double doors and almost gasped. It was much cooler inside but the space was huge. Two escalators rose several stories up, alongside a wall of glass and water, the sound of the rushing liquid amplified by the space. She gulped. The country mouse had come to town.

Turnstiles guarded the entrance which people gaily slipped through. She turned right to the reception desk and waited while the girl behind it finished tidying the paper on it, before fixing a bored gaze upon her.

'Can I help you?'

'Yes, hi, I'm ...' Words deserted her. 'I'm ... here ...' The name of the woman she was supposed to ask for had vanished. Completely wiped from her memory. 'I'm starting work here today.'

'Department?'

'*CityZen* Magazine.'

'Name?'

'Sophie. Sophie Bennings.'

The girl scanned her computer screen, her mouth tightening as if it really was too much trouble. Her frown deepened. She looked at Sophie again.

'Can'tseeyoudownhere. Needa name.'

'Pardon?' Sophie could barely interpret the girl's accent and quick-fire delivery.

'I need a name.'

'Erm ...' Sophie's mind went blank. 'Trudy ... Trudy ...' No, it had gone. 'Hold on a minute.' Rummaging in her bag, she searched for her mobile. Why hadn't she been more organised and written everything down?

Security was clearly tight. And she had no clue where she was supposed to be going.

The girl looked over her shoulder. 'Morning, Sir. Can I help you?'

Dismissed summarily, Sophie paled and cursed her own stupidity. Emails. There were emails with everything in them. Where was her phone? She pulled out her purse. Make-up bag. Keys. No phone.

With horrible realisation, she remembered. Faffing about with the unfamiliar American adapter, plugging her phone in to charge.

'Hey, English.'

'Todd! Hi,' her voice squeaked unbecomingly in utter relief.

'Morning. You found your way here OK, then.'

'Yes, but I've left my phone behind and all the paperwork. I can't remember who I was supposed to ask for.'

'No problem. I'll take you up.' He leaned over the desk. 'Hey, Terri. She's with me.'

An instant smile lifted the girl's perfectly made-up mannequin face. 'Hey Todd, how you doing?'

'Good, you?'

'Better if you'd take me out for lunch.' Her chin dipped in coy invitation.

'Now Terri, you know I don't mix business with pleasure.'

'A girl can try,' her eyes lowered with seductive promise. 'You don't know what you're missing.'

'I know,' said Todd mournfully. 'It's a burden I have to bear.'

With a quick rueful pout, she pushed a pass over the desk. 'Here you go.'

'Thanks for rescuing me,' said Sophie as he guided her through the barriers towards the huge escalators, unable to stop herself adding, 'even though you put yourself in the face of danger there.'

He gave her a cheerful grin. 'One likes to do one's duty. They're pretty tight on security here. You could have had a long wait while they checked you out.'

Sophie stared around her. 'This place is impressive.'

'You get used to it.' He shrugged. 'We're up on the thirty-third floor.'

She followed him through a seating area filled with bright sunshine to the bank of lifts, and they sailed upwards with a stomach-dropping whoosh, and in seconds the doors opened with a ping. Her nerves settled with instant relief at the sight of the familiar logo of the magazine on a large glass panel. This looked more like it. Beyond the glass, she could see desks ranked just like back in London. Suddenly everything didn't feel quite so alien and intimidating.

With a wave at the girl on the reception desk, Todd pushed her forward.

'This is Sophie. She's the job swap with Brandi.'

The young woman looked up, a quick expression of appalled horror crossing her face, which she masked almost instantly.

'I'll let Trudy know you're here.'

After a ten-minute wait, which seemed agonisingly long, Sophie was led down the hall to a glass-walled office in the corner.

'Trudy, this is Sophie. The job swap.'

'Sophie, nice to meet you. Erm ...' said the tall, dark-haired woman, rising and smoothing her hand down a slim-fitting pencil skirt before holding it out.

She looked at the receptionist, her eyes flashing some hidden message. 'Right, erm ... take a seat. I'll be right back.'

Sophie sank into the chair and stared out at the view beyond. New York spread out before her, the green of what had to be Central Park, the trees – so small from up here – reminding her of heads of broccoli, the intricate layout of rooftops a long way below which looked like Airfix models, detailed with water towers and air-conditioning units, and in the distance edging the park, more skyscrapers, blinding white in the brilliant sunshine like sentries on the border. Did you ever get tired of this view, she wondered. It was incredible.

She waited, the minutes ticking by. The tension was back, poking at her shoulders, the muscles bunching. Something was wrong. Surely they were expecting her. It had all been confirmed by email. Admittedly in a rush, but now she could remember Trudy Winkler, Editorial Director. They'd exchanged several emails, copied into the HR Manager. Sophie told herself not to panic. They probably hadn't got her desk cleared. Maybe it still had balloons and crumbs covering it.

Trudy came back, a smile plastered on her face. 'Right. Well ... actually, there's been a slight hitch. Nothing to worry about.' She smoothed her skirt again. 'We, erm ... well. When ... erm, Mel, wasn't it, had her accident, we didn't think anyone could fill her place ... Oh, this is embarrassing. One of the board offered his friend's daughter an internship ... to cover Brandi's job.'

Sophie's fingers curled over the edge of her seat, holding on tightly.

'Don't worry ... it's fine. You can job share with Madison ... it's just we need to find you another desk, it won't be with the other cookery writers, I'm afraid, but we'll find—'

The phone rang on her desk and she grabbed it like a lifebelt.

'Ah, thanks. That's great. Perfect. I'll bring her over.'

A real smile lit up her face. 'Problem solved. Come on.'

She led Sophie through the office, where heads were bent over their laptops with studious intent as if they didn't dare look up and acknowledge there'd been a booboo. Only one girl caught Sophie's eye, her bright-red lips stretching in a slightly smug and triumphant smirk. Immediately Sophie knew. This was Madison, the intern. But as Trudy led her across the room past a few more desks into an area by the window, the girl's expression changed to one of dismay.

'Sophie, let me introduce you. Todd writes our *Man About Town* column.'

'Hi, we meet again.' Todd flashed her his usual lighthouse-beam grin. Seriously, that smile should come a health warning, it belonged in a Hollywood blockbuster.

'You two have met?'

'Remember I fixed up the rental on my cousin's place?'

'Yeah, of course. You're our regular Mr Fixit. Need a new screen for your phone, know where to buy fresh Oregano or find a holiday let in the Hamptons? Todd is our man.' Despite her brusque words, she shot him a wry, fond look. 'And somehow, Todd has managed to appropriate a second desk.' She wrinkled her forehead. 'And I have no idea how he did that or how it gets to be in this state.' Trudy gave the messy surface a plaintive frown.

'Hey English, we're going to be roomies.' He swept a pile of paper from the surface of the desk and dumped it into a box which he then put under his own desk, with a cheerful shrug. 'No idea what any of that is but I haven't looked at it in a month.'

'I'll pretend I didn't hear that, Todd McLennan.'

'Work, boss. Work,' supplied Todd.

Trudy sighed, but smiled back at him. 'That's what you're calling it?' She turned back to Sophie. 'I'm still not sure why we employ him, other than he's cute to look at.'

Cute was the understatement of the century but she said it without irony. Maybe familiarity bred immunity.

'And the readers love me.' He tilted back in his chair, his hands behind his head.

'Unfortunately, he has a point there.' She lowered her voice. 'Voted most popular column last month, and he's won a couple of awards, but we try not to let it go to his head.'

At that point Todd, with a silly cartoon gesture, as if he didn't take them terribly seriously, pointed to a couple of crystal-glass trophies on the shelf behind his desk which were doing sterling work as paperweights to teetering piles of paper.

'However, he has volunteered to clean this desk up for you.' Her pointed look had him jumping to his feet.

Ignoring him, she focused on Sophie, 'I'm really sorry about the mix-up. But if you can get yourself set up here ... without the aid of a hazmat suit, hopefully ... then you can join us for the editorial meeting at ten-fifty. Todd'll show you where everything is.'

Sophie nodded, noticing Madison gliding up behind Trudy.

'Hey Todd.' The younger girl flashed him the sort of predatory smile a prowling jaguar would have been proud of. 'Look Trudy, maybe I should swap desks. Let ...' she nodded towards Sophie, 'have Brandi's desk. It's with the other food writers. It probably makes sense. I can sit here with Todd.'

Sophie just bet she could.

'And how would I get any work done, Maddie? I'd be constantly distracted by your gorgeousness.'

Oh please. Sophie schooled her face into polite indifference. He had to be kidding.

'Oh Todd, you're such a charmer,' said Madison, dipping her head coyly.

Really? That sort of cheese was digestible?

'I know,' he said cheerfully. 'But English here is going to help me with a new feature, so it probably makes sense for her to be in the vicinity.'

News to her. Sophie stuck her tongue firmly in her cheek,

which only Todd could see. He gave her a twisted grin. 'Yeah ... er ... An – um – Englishwoman Abroad, checking out what's new in New York.'

Madison frowned, or at least tried to. Her forehead didn't seem to want to wrinkle like normal people's did.

'Oh, OK. Well, if you change your mind or finish your feature, I can always help on another one. I know all the most exclusive bars and I can get you into the member-only clubs.'

'I'll bear it in mind. Thanks, you're a doll.'

Trudi smiled pleasantly, the epitome of diplomacy. 'Right, well, we'll leave you to it. See you at the editorial meeting.' She turned on her heel, making a pointed pause when Madison didn't immediately follow.

'I'll see you around, Todd. Maybe we can have that drink sometime.'

Todd waved a casual finger at her. 'You bet.'

Sophie stood helplessly, while Todd unearthed a phone extension from underneath a stack of magazines. 'I knew there was one here somewhere.' He stepped forward and then with a wicked grin said, 'Let me clear these sex toys away.' He paused, sorting through a pile of boxes before offering her an open one with a large pink plastic shape nestled in purple tissue paper. 'Unless you'd like to try a couple out and review them for me. For the column.'

Sophie gave him a level look which he cheerfully ignored.

'Maybe not.' He dropped the box on the floor and nudged it under his desk with his foot. 'Here, grab these a second.' He shoved a handful of flimsy silk underwear into her hands. 'Help yourself to anything you fancy. They're not my size.'

'Fan mail?' asked Sophie dryly, beginning to wonder quite what the scope of his column was. The one she'd read entitled 'West Bank' had been a recommendation of the best restaurants and bars, with multiple escape routes for those dates that went *West*, as well as a guide to decoding what men meant when they said certain things on a first date. It had been funny, witty and irreverent, poking fun at men's hapless approaches to dating.

Todd let out a bark of laughter. 'Funny, English. Funny. No, they're samples. Sometimes I recommend gift-buying ideas. I get sent all sorts of stuff.'

'So I gathered.'

'Comes with the territory of being New York's *Man About Town*, aka expert on everything.'

Todd's idea of tidying up was simply transferring most of the mess to a pile behind his desk, but she could hardly complain as it meant she now had a clear space to work in. A bit too clear. She gave the bleak desk a baleful look, regretting not even bringing her own notebook to lay claim to her new territory. Digging in her handbag, she pulled out a solitary biro – it was the one Todd had lent her yesterday morning – and put it out in front of her. It looked a little sad. Lost and alone. Her mouth twisted.

When she looked up Todd was studying her.

'You OK? You need anything?'

'Fine,' she said with a wan smile. 'I don't suppose you've got some paper I can borrow to go into the meeting. I packed in a hurry ... I didn't bring ...' On her desk at home, she had a pretty pot with pens, a magnetic bird that held paperclips and ... a photo of James in a silver frame. Pain pinched at her heart.

'Sure.' He tossed towards her a lined foolscap pad emblazoned with a company logo. The phone on his desk shrilled. 'Todd McLennan. Hey Charlene,' his voice dropped an octave and he leaned back in his chair and put his feet up on the desk. 'Course I haven't forgotten. Charlene, how could I forget you?' He winked at Sophie.

She rolled her eyes and his grin widened.

Utterly shameless. Sophie stared at the soles of his trendy lace-up boots.

'Seven o'clock is just great, Charlene. Can't wait.' He put the phone down.

'Was that Charlene by any chance?' asked Sophie, amused. 'Worried you were going to forget her name?'

'It has happened,' replied Todd. 'But it's a good psychological trick, builds rapport.'

Sophie could see exactly why Bella had said he was bad news.

'And now on to the November edition. The fashion section is all sewn up. We've got the "Hundred Best Boots for the Fall" feature. Health, we're focusing on supplements and vitamins that beat lethargy and tiredness. We're testing cookers for best buys.'

As Trudy spoke, Sophie glanced around the meeting room, receiving tentative nods from the people assembled around the large oval glass table. She'd been introduced at the start of the meeting with little fanfare or fuss, which suited her fine.

This was more like it. Familiar and routine. Apart from the American accents around her, it was just like an editorial meeting at home. Already their ideas were sparking a few of her own, plus she'd come armed with a few feature suggestions up her sleeve and had been scribbling a few notes on the foolscap pad.

'Sophie, this'll be your first rodeo. Any ideas?'

'Well, Brandi emailed the outlines for Thanksgiving—'

'She left notes,' piped up Madison, her voice strident and a steely look of determination in her eye. 'I've got it all taken care of. It's not like it could wait.'

'Oh,' said Sophie because she had no idea what else to say.

'Well, with due respect,' drawled Madison in that deceptively casual tone which you knew really meant business, and was not respectful at all, 'you were over a week late.' With an insincere smile, she shifted in her seat, deliberately drawing attention to her long elegant limbs, and slight hint of tasteful cleavage. 'So, I've got the recipes for a cheese grits-and-corn pudding, hints for perfect roast turkey and a darling recipe for pumpkin pie with walnut crust.'

All of which had been in Brandi's outline.

'That's great,' Sophie paused and gave a light-hearted smile, 'and just as well, as being English, I know nothing about Thanksgiving ... yet.' Everyone laughed. 'And I have only the vaguest idea what cheese grits are, but I'm hoping while I'm here to pick your brains and find out more ... but I was thinking of perhaps an English afternoon tea feature.'

Madison smirked. 'Isn't that a bit too precious? This is *CityZen* magazine, not *Good Housekeeping*. Not grannies and their knitting.'

Sophie turned to her, with an even bigger smile, pumping up the enthusiasm. She'd been up against far bigger and bitchier foes and could out-smile anything Madison could throw at her. 'Yes, but we would put a *hygge* spin on it, look after yourself and family and friends in preparation for those miserable dark nights when Daylight Saving comes in and the clocks go back. Scones and jam, I mean jelly, toasted teacakes, warming spicy parkin and delicate fairy cakes. In front of a roaring fire.'

'Oooh yum,' said Trudy with an approving smile. 'Love it, love it, love it, especially the *hygge* angle, even though I have no idea what parkin is, but I'm sure it will be delicious. I'll make sure I'm around the day that recipe gets tested.'

'And who doesn't love a fairy cake?' piped up a very camp voice on Sophie's left, making everyone laugh again.

'Interiors, can you do anything in conjunction?' asked Trudy.

'Oh yeah,' came an enthusiastic voice from the end of the table, where three women sat in a cluster, all nodding in unison. 'We're loving a bit of *hygge*,' said one.

'Cosying up the house in the fall,' added the second.

'Fireplace décor,' chipped in the third.

'Mantelpiece mania.'

'Toasting forks.'

'Burnt oranges, autumn tones.'

'Velvet piles, sumptuous fabrics.'

'Great, ladies,' said Trudy, holding up her hand, clearly used to handling the trio. 'And Paul. Does that sound like something the sales team can get a handle on?' She turned to the tall blond man sitting next to Madison, who bore a distinct resemblance to a less-bulked-up Chris Hemsworth. He immediately gave an enthusiastic thumbs up, ignoring his neighbour's less-than-discreet eye-roll.

'Certainly can. I can see a year-on-year increase in ad sales for this issue compared to last year's, which is great because revenue for this quarter is already up.'

Trudy held up her hand. 'You do good work Paul, but spare me the sales figures until the senior management meeting.'

He beamed at her. 'Sure thing.'

'You're off to a good start, Sophie,' said Trudy.

As everyone's attention turned back to Trudy, Sophie looked up. Paul gave her an encouraging smile, his eyes holding hers for that brief too-long second which no one else would have noticed, but it made her feel a touch warm. She focused on Trudy's voice.

'Sophie, after this meeting, I'll get the team to show you the test kitchens and the studio. We've got a great roster of freelance food photographers. And the interiors team can help you dress the set for a photo shoot.'

Madison's mouth settled into a sulky slash and she shot Sophie a look of dislike, but Sophie responded with a cheery smile. 'Great. And I'm looking forward to Madison's cheese grits and corn pudding recipe.'

Years of snuffing out pettiness with good cheer had stood her in good stead. Madison was a rank amateur in comparison with Sophie's dad's ex-wife.

The meeting drew to a close and as everyone drifted out, Paul stopped at Sophie's chair.

'Hi, I'm Paul Ferguson. Sales Director.' He held out his hand.

Sophie took it and received a warm, dry and firm handshake. 'Sophie.' She winced. 'Obviously, because Trudy introduced me ...' There was a definite twinkle in his eyes as she drew to a flustered halt.

'Good to have you on board, Sophie. If there's anything I can give you help with, I'm up on the next floor.' With a quick lift of his eyebrows he looked upwards and added with a self-deprecating wink, 'The executive suite. We have superior coffee up there,' he paused, shooting her another twinkle-filled smile, 'but we're good at sharing. Come on up any time.'

Sophie nodded, trying to act naturally. She was so out of practice at this stuff. Maybe he was being super-US-style open and friendly, but her gut was telling her that there was definite admiration here.

'Thanks, that's great. I'll remember that, next time I er ... need superior coffee.'

'Make sure you do,' his smile was warmer this time and he held her gaze. 'I'll look forward to working with you, Sophie. And if you need anything, like I said. Just call. In fact,' he pulled out a silver card holder, 'here you go. My direct line. Welcome aboard.'

As soon as she walked into the test kitchens, the familiar sense of rightness settled upon her. This was home. She would always be OK here, even if the size and the state-of-the-art equipment along with the view of Central Park were pertinent reminders that she wasn't in London any more. Everything was that much bigger and better. Her head buzzed with names and details as she was introduced to food technicians and the rest of the food-writing team. They all seemed friendly and envious, in terms of food, of her previous proximity to Europe, especially when she talked about her recent trip to Copenhagen.

By the time she came back to her desk, she'd decided that she was going to be alright here. Things were vaguely familiar, although she was going to have to get her head around cup measurements, which in her book related directly to bra sizes and not flour, butter and sugar. The big question was how many hours could she spend at work each day?

There was no sign of Todd but in the centre of her desk was a hard-backed notebook, with the words *My Little Black Book* etched in gold on the front, and on closer inspection, she saw that the first few pages had been ripped out. There was also a battered stapler; a box of pink paperclips; a selection of pens with various company slogans on them, in a white tin with a red circle bearing the words *Japanese Condom Tin*; and a green Perspex ruler printed with an advert for multivitamins. On top of the notebook was a yellow sticky: *Desk-warming gifts. Todd —*

With a reluctant smile, she touched the embossed letters of the notebook and then with a shake of her head, she opened it for a second time and, picking up a pen, wrote the date and started writing out a to-do list. Todd McLennan was too charming for his own good.

Chapter 5

'Hey there Sophie, how is it?'

Kate's voice spilled from Sophie's phone, propped on its side on the breakfast bar of the kitchen, her slightly blurry image dancing across the screen.

'Hi Kate. How are you?'

'Little bit tipsy. Me and Ben have been out for dinner with Avril and Christopher. She sends her love, by the way. She's not drinking, so I drank her share of prosecco. And Ben was being sensible because he's playing football tomorrow. He's going to bed.' Kate raised her eyebrows in mock disgust and in the background Ben's figure appeared and waved.

'Night, Sophie. Hope it's going well.'

There was the sound of a door closing and Kate leaned closer to the screen.

'So how are you? Are you cooking loads of brilliant food? New York delis are supposed to be amazing.'

'Mmm,' replied Sophie with a guileless expression and a noncommittal nod, thinking of the succession of ready-roast chickens she'd eaten since she'd arrived. Chicken and salad nearly every night for two weeks. So much for being an award-winning food writer with an explorer's quest for new and native tastes.

'And how are you?' repeated Kate, leaning even closer to the screen, as if that would help her get a closer look at Sophie's guarded face.

'I'm fine,' said Sophie with a gentle smile.

'Sure?'

'Yes.'

'Well, I'm not going to talk about James, unless you want to.'

'Definitely not. This is a James-free zone.'

'So what's it like? Have you been up the Empire State Building? Have you been to Central Park? Have you done any shopping? Or are you too busy? I get the impression that New York is so busy and people work really hard there. Is it crazy?'

'Yes, it is a bit. The subway's crazy. Manhattan is busier than London. But I've got into a good routine.' She made her eyes deliberately bright as she talked. Why couldn't she match Kate's enthusiasm?

Perhaps because the routine was quite dull.

Up at seven-thirty. On the subway at eight-thirty, coffee at Starbucks at nine-fifteen. At her desk at nine-thirty. It was all very Abba's 'The Day Before You Came'. Except there would be no one coming for her this time. During the day she was fine. The job was absorbing, busy and familiar, and she was getting plenty of sleep. Most nights she was in bed by nine.

'The apartment is lovely. Look.'

Using her phone, Sophie gave Kate a quick tour of the apartment, showing her the deck first before the kitchen, bedroom and bathroom.

'That shower is to die for,' said Kate when Sophie finally returned to her breakfast-bar perch.

'Yup, it is rather nice.'

'Now all you need is a nice man to share it with you.'

'Kate!'

'Well, I've been thinking.'

Sophie winced.

'I saw that. Meeting Ben after Josh was the best thing that happened to me. You need a rebound man.'

'A rebound man?'

'Yes. Someone to have some fun with to help you get over James. A fling.'

'I'm fine,' said Sophie severely.

'What time is it there?' asked Kate, surprising Sophie with the sudden change in subject.

'It's six-thirty.'

'Six-thirty?' Kate's voice sounded accusing.

'Yes.'

'Six-thirty on a Friday night and you're home alone. You've been there two weeks. You haven't been to the Empire State Building. You haven't been to Central Park. Have you?'

Unable to lie, Sophie shook her head.

'You haven't done *anything*, have you?' Concern shimmered in the other girl's face, evident even through Facetime blurriness.

Sophie pulled a face at Kate.

'I'm worried about you.'

'Don't. I'm fine. Honest. It takes a while to get your bearings. Everyone's so busy and it feels like life goes at such a speed here. I've met lots of people.' Sophie crossed her fingers out of sight. 'My landlady Bella runs the bakery downstairs. She's very friendly. Lives upstairs.' Sophie wasn't about to confess to Kate that she hadn't seen Bella since she arrived two weeks ago. 'And her cousin, Todd, he works at the magazine. Writes the *Man About Town* column. He's really nice. He's been really helpful at work. Showed me the subway station on my first day. Helped me crack security at the magazine.' She told Kate the full story and then told her about Madison, and Todd volunteering his desk.

'He sounds rather nice,' said Kate.

Sophie laughed. 'Nice doesn't come close. Todd is drop-dead gorgeous. Look him up on the magazine website. He's also a grade-A womaniser. Not my type at all. Everyone at work is very nice and I've got so much to do to get up to speed. Taking over someone else's job is—'

'Oooh! Talk about blue eyes.' Kate's head was turned to the laptop to her left. 'He is *gorgeous*.'

'Good photography,' said Sophie instantly, remembering her first reaction to Todd's by-line picture on the website.

'Methinks you doth protest too much,' said Kate.

'He's well out of my league and very popular with the ladies. There's a nice guy in advertising.'

'Ah-ha,' said Kate.

'You're like a bloody terrier, woman. I've only been here five minutes. It's going to take time to get my bearings and get to know people.'

Kate's mouth firmed. 'No Soph, not normally.' There was a long pause. 'Not with you. You make friends with everyone, instantly. I think you're hiding away. That's not like you, Soph. Be honest. I'm worried about you. I thought getting away from London would be good for you and that New York would be a new start. It feels like you're hibernating.'

Sophie stiffened. This was why she'd avoided calling or Facetiming anyone back home. Thankfully her parents were away on a six-month cruise and she could get away with brief texts and WhatsApp messages. In the throes of packing and closing up the house they'd been distracted enough not to ask too many questions about her hasty decision to move to New York, and she might have just omitted to tell them about James.

Kate's face stared solemnly at her from the phone screen and in the corner her own scared face stared back at her. The words 'cornered rabbit' had never been truer.

For a minute she tried to think of a dozen other things to say, but she couldn't lie, not to Kate, and the horrible truth she'd been trying to avoid came spilling out.

'I miss him. I know he's a shit. I know he lied his arse off. I hate him.' Her heart clenched and she sucked in a breath. 'But I … I miss him.' She was not going to cry. 'So much. It's like there's this huge hole. Everything I knew and thought … it's like it's been scrubbed out and there's nothing left. I feel empty and it feels impossible to look forward. I'm too busy looking back. Everything I thought … it wasn't anything. It was based on one huge lie. Part of me still can't believe it. And I still … I still love him. And I hate that I do.' Her mouth crumpled and she blinked hard. 'I really hate that I … s-still …'

'Oh Soph, sweetie. I wish I was there. I'm sorry.' Kate held her hand over her mouth, her eyes semaphoring worry and concern. 'You're so far away. I wish I hadn't encouraged you to go now.'

Sophie sucked in another breath, feeling it catch in her chest. She couldn't do this to Kate. It wasn't fair. With real effort, she forced a smile onto her face. 'Kate Sinclair, don't you dare start feeling guilty. I chose to come here. And I wanted to. I'm just feeling a bit sorry for myself tonight. You're right. I haven't been trying enough. I haven't been trying at all. Must try harder. I promise this weekend I will go out and start exploring. And I'll make a bit more effort at work to get to know a few people.'

Kate gave her a watery smile. 'Atta girl. Sorry, I didn't mean to nag. I miss you.'

'I miss you too, but I promise I'm ... or I will be OK. But you're right. I've been hibernating. From now on, I'll get out there.'

Sophie closed her eyes as she switched off her phone. Without Kate's voice, the apartment felt alien and empty. It was far too soon to go to bed, which was what she did most nights when the loneliness got too much to bear. Although most nights she was still awake at eleven. Staring up at the ceiling. Wishing she could turn the clock back. But that was cowardly, and it couldn't change what James had done. Being ignorant didn't make it any better. Or remove all the lies.

There was a particular crack on the ceiling. It curved from the window to the corner of the room, widening at the two-thirds mark before narrowing and disappearing again. It had become a visual reminder of her battle to keep thoughts of James at bay, as if they were crowding behind that crack, trying to work their way through, and that's when she had to work extra hard not to think of him. Not to think of all those evenings pottering happily in the kitchen, cooking special meals for him. Not to remember waking up in the mornings with his tousled dark head next to hers. Not to long for those evenings simply snuggled up on the sofa, slobbing out after work, watching some TV detective series they both enjoyed.

With a sigh, she stood up and tucked the phone in her pocket as she looked around the kitchen. Had Kate picked up on how spotless the place was? How unnaturally she'd overdone things the previous weekend when she'd binge-watched nineteen episodes of *Friends*.

Through the open window she could hear laughter floating up from the street, the pounding bass from a passing car, and smell the warm city air, a smoky mix of onions and diesel. Brooklynites had come out to play on Friday night. She stood by the window for a while, people watching. A group of young men in jeans, baggy T-shirts and back-to-front baseball caps walked together, nudging and teasing each other as they loped along the pavement, moving aside for single late returners from work, determinedly walking the last leg of their commute, bearing shopping bags like champions bringing home the bread. The cheerful noise and bustle below heightened her sense of aloneness and the paralysis that seemed to have set in, stopping her from leaving the apartment.

What she hadn't told Kate was that she doubted her own

judgement. It had proved so false, some days she found it impossible to make a decision. It wasn't as if she'd even decided consciously to come to New York. There was no weighing up the pros and cons, examining what it would really entail. No, she'd grabbed at the offer, grasping it with desperate, greedy hands as if it were a life-raft amidst the storm of fear, rage and utter despair.

Just as she was about to shut the window, she heard a loud rattle from inside the building, followed by a bang, a crash and then a loud curse. 'You're fucking kidding me.'

Hurrying to her door, she opened it and ventured to the top of the stairs. In an ungainly tangle of limbs, Bella sprawled on the landing at the top of the next flight of stairs below. Sophie hurried down.

'What happened?' she asked as she helped Bella up.

Wide-eyed, Bella clutched her hand to her chest. She'd clearly given herself quite a fright. Sucking in a quick breath, she said, 'Tripped on the last step. For a horrible darn minute, I thought I was going to take a header straight down.' Bella's lip quivered and she hauled herself to a seated position, rubbing at her knee. With a sniff she nodded, her eyes bright with unshed tears.

'Are you OK?' asked Sophie, feeling useless, standing over Bella.

'I will b-be in a mo.' She closed her eyes tight and carried on rubbing at her knee, her teeth gnawing at her lip. 'I daren't look. I'm trying to think really positive here, but right now I can't think of a single angle. Are they all completely ruined?'

Sophie peered down at the frosting-spattered stairs. A rainbow of bright blobs of red, yellow, blue and green was liberally dotted everywhere. Paintball splats on virtually every tread.

'Difficult to tell. Some of them ... might ... be salvageable.' The doubt was clear in her voice. From here they looked pretty battered.

'Aw, shit!' Bella angrily dashed at the lone tear that escaped. 'Shit. Shit. Shit. I just spent the last three hours icing six dozen of the little fuckers for an engagement party tomorrow, and now I've dropped half of them.' She rested her head on her knees, hugging them, saying in a muffled voice, 'I'm supposed to be delivering them before I open up tomorrow morning.' She lifted her head, sniffing as more tears ran down her face. 'I'm going to have to s-start over,' her breath hitched, 'and I'm ... so tired.' She burst into noisy sobs.

'Hey, it's alright.' Even though she didn't know Bella that well, Sophie sank down beside her on the top step and put her arm around her shoulder.

After several ragged breaths and discreet sniffs, Bella calmed down. 'Shit, I'm sorry. I'm not a crier but ... it's been a tough one.' She started to rise. 'Aw, sheesh, look at the mess. What the hell am I going to do? It's going to take forever to clean this up and then I'm going to have bake a new batch and let them cool before I can decorate them.'

Sophie put a firm hand on her shoulder. 'Just take a minute.'

Together they surveyed the wreckage. 'Rainbow cakes?' asked Sophie.

'Yeah, I'm starting to regret that now. I store commissions upstairs because there's not enough room in the kitchen downstairs.'

'Well, it makes for a good show,' said Sophie, trying not to smile. There really was colour just about everywhere.

Bella let out a tiny giggle as together they surveyed the vibrant mess. 'I never do anything by halves.'

'Perhaps you've missed your calling. You could always take up interior decorating. It looks very colourful.' Together they burst out laughing.

'OK,' said Sophie, suddenly feeling like her old self. 'First things first. We identify all those that are salvageable. You can probably scrape off the icing and redecorate some of them.'

'I dunno.' Bella winced, her face already looking a bit brighter. 'Some look pretty darned battered. It was one of those spectacular toss-'em-all-up-in-the-air babies.' She shook her head, a couple of red curls escaping her scarf. 'I guess I'm lucky I didn't take a header after them.'

'Why don't you sit down, have a coffee and a rest? You look quite shaken up and you probably want some ice on that knee. And then I can start cleaning up down here and we can make a plan. I can help. Be your assistant. And with two of us, it'll be a lot easier.'

Bella stopped and looked back up the stairs. 'It's Friday night? Aren't you on your way out somewhere?'

'No. Thought I'd have a night in.' Sophie's smile was so brittle, she wondered if her face might crack.

'Normally I'd say no, it's fine, but I'm so pooped, I could really use the help. But I ... I can't let you clean up.'

'Yes, you can,' said Sophie with a determined glint in her eye. 'Leave it to me. Give me that tray, and have you got a bin bag?'

Sophie helped Bella hobble up to her flat and settled her in a seat, with a bag of frozen corn on her knee. Bella's flat was similar in layout to the one below, except it had a ladder reaching up to the ceiling in the kitchen and a lot of empty shelves, with plastic cupcake holders.

'I normally transport the cakes in those, but they only hold a dozen and I was being lazy and trying to do one trip down the stairs, so I put them on a tray. Serves me right.'

Bella pointed her in the direction of cleaning cloths, and Sophie carried a washing-up bowl down the stairs to deal with the mess. As she scooped up the random dollops of buttercream, she smiled to herself. This was not the most glamorous way of spending Friday night, but it beat not having anything to do.

Half an hour later, Sophie had just about finished when Bella came hobbling down the stairs clutching a bottle of wine and two glasses.

'What's the damage?' asked Bella wearily as she stood on the last step. 'I brought vital supplies.' She held up the bottle.

With a frown, Sophie indicated the tray to her left on the hall console table. 'Ten can be re-done. But the rest are goners, I'm afraid.'

'Sheesh, that bad. It's gonna be a late one. Although dinner's sorted. As much as you can eat mashed-up cake.' She grabbed one of the cakes. 'If you scrape the dust off.'

Sophie grinned. 'I already ate, but for wine, I'm happy to stay, help and be your sous chef.'

'Are you sure? It's Friday evening and the night's still young. I'm plain sad, there's no need for you to be too.'

Sophie responded with a shrug and a half-laugh. 'It's not like I'm doing anything else tonight.'

Bella gave her a narrow-eyed stare. 'Sorry I've been mega-busy. I should have been more neighbourly and been in to say hi. You've been here two weeks. I can't believe that. But it's gone so darned fast. Come on.' She waved the bottle and glasses and led the way through a side door. 'This takes us straight into the kitchen. I keep thinking that maybe I should have gone into catering. Someone said to me last week that' – she bookmarked with her fingers – '"Cupcakes are so last year and wedding cakes are too specialised." There's more money in general catering – you know, finger food and buffets. But seriously, what would you rather have? A great big sugar-kiss delivered in a little work of art in a cupcake case, or a chicken drumstick in sesame and soy? No one ever said, *Let them eat chicken*, did they?'

Sophie laughed. 'True.'

'And there's something about a cake. It says love. It says sugary yumminess. It's like a tiny hand-held hug. Cakes are for Christmas, celebrations, holidays and birthdays. Weddings. For happy, happy days. That's why I love making them. The world needs more happiness.'

Sophie smiled, thinking of Kate and their friend, Eva, back home. 'Someone once told me that things taste better when they're made with love.'

Bella clapped her hands together. 'I love that. It's so true. Especially when you're making a wedding cake. Cutting the cake is the first thing a married couple do jointly. It symbol-ises their partnership.'

'I'd never thought of it like that. That's lovely ...' Sophie paused, trying not to let the familiar sense of bitterness take hold. It was a constant presence lurking on the edge of her consciousness, just waiting for a chance to dig in and take over. 'If it works out.'

'Oh dear. Are you divorced?'

'No, single. Very single. And staying that way for the foreseeable future.'

'Bad break-up?' asked Bella, wincing sympathetically.

'Something like that,' sighed Sophie.

'I'm not sure what's worse. Having someone to break up with or not quite getting there.'

Sophie raised a quizzical eyebrow.

Bella looked stubborn for a minute. 'There's someone I'm interested in but he's too stupid to live.'

Sophie flinched and took a sudden interest in the kitchen work surfaces. She wasn't sure she could cope with anyone else's emotional distress at the moment. Thankfully Bella didn't say any more and turned her attention to the wine bottle, pouring two hefty glasses of white wine.

'Gosh, this is lovely.' Sophie turned around.

Opposite her there was an oak dresser which was filled, no not filled, rammed with a massive variety of different china plates. There was no discernible theme to the display of plates on the narrow upper shelves, which featured umpteen different shapes and a dazzling array of styles: retro fifties block patterns, vintage florals, stark contemporary designs – all bundled together in a rainbow of colours where emerald green rubbed shoulders with peacock blue, vivid pinks, pristine white and scarlet. There were more plates in teetering stacks on the open shelves below.

Following Sophie's gaze, Bella shrugged. 'I collect plates. You never know what you'll need for a display.'

Next to the dresser was a floral sofa that looked as if, once you sat in it, it might be hard to escape from, a wooden coffee table piled with papers and magazines, and a couple of plain pink velvet armchairs.

All this should have looked incongruous against the stainless-steel benches and modern glass-fronted fridges on the opposite side, but those were also filled with colour and shape, so the two sides worked together. Bella clearly liked a bit of colour. The benches were dotted with bright utensil pots filled with china cake slices, wooden spoons and whisks.

Sophie felt herself relax. Kitchens were good places to be. You knew where you were in them. There was something safe and reassuring about knowing that when you were baking, if you added the right quantities and the right ingredients, and did the right things, you'd know what you'd get. A well-stocked and well-resourced kitchen like this was like coming home.

'Cheers,' said Bella, holding up her glass.

'Cheers.'

They chinked glasses.

'Thanks, Sophie. I really appreciate this.'

'I haven't done anything yet.'

'Aside from cleaning up. And offering moral support.'

Sophie looked around the kitchen. 'So, what would you like me to do?'

'First, I need to get cracking on making a new batch of cakes. So, if you can be my go-to girl on weights and measures and weigh out all the fixings, that would be awesome. My basic recipe is here.' She pointed to a laminated sheet pinned to a pin-board. 'Scales over there. Sticks of butter in the fridge. Dry goods in the pantry. Eggs on the shelf. Thank goodness I stocked up this week.'

Thanks to her crash course in conversion over the last two weeks, Sophie had got a handle on things and knew that a stick of butter equated to half a cup of butter or four ounces in English measurement, so she set to following Bella's swift instructions to assemble all the ingredients beside a professional Kitchen Aid.

'I've got one of these at home,' said Sophie, stroking the smart red enamel like a pet.

'Silly me, I completely forgot you're a foodie. You can cook then.'

'Just a bit,' said Sophie, laughing.

'You can make the batter, while I mix up a new batch of frosting and re-ice these ones.'

'I was going to ask you if I could watch you one day. I'm working on a feature on afternoon tea, English style, and I wanted to make some cupcakes and come up with some autumn, I mean fall, themed toppings.'

'Ooh, I'd love to help. Fall leaf colours would be good. I could do a seasonal display. I'd have to think flavours.'

'Ginger. You could make parkin cakes.'

'Parkin?'

Sophie explained what it was. Soon the two of them were

bouncing cake recipe and ideas back and forth, and by the time the first batch of cakes came out of the oven they'd drunk most of the bottle of wine.

When the second batch of cakes went in, they sank to the floor, clutching their glasses with the very last dregs of the wine. In tired silence, they watched the cakes in the oven slowly rise and turn golden.

Sophie sighed and took a last sip of wine. 'There's nothing quite like that moment when the cake goes *pouf* over the top of its case. It makes me feel like there's some sense in the world. All's well when it does what it's supposed to.'

'I'd never thought of it like that, but you're right. There's nothing quite like that moment. *Pouf.*' Bella waved her wineglass at Sophie. '*Pouf* is the perfect word. Although why we are sitting here when I have a perfectly good sofa over there, is bonkers.' She awkwardly raised herself to her feet and hobbled over to one of the pink armchairs, lowering herself gingerly and putting her bad leg on the messy table. Sophie followed and sank into the sofa opposite.

'Sophie, you're a godsend. I think if it hadn't been for you I would have wept hysterically on the stairs for the whole night.'

'Your knee not so good?' Even from the sofa Sophie could see that Bella's injured knee was almost double the size of the other.

'No. It's sore. And very stiff. Shit, I hope I can drive tomorrow.' Bella leaned over and prodded it. 'It's very swollen. I can hardly bend it.'

'Is there anyone else who could help deliver them? Could you put them in a taxi?'

'Not really. To be honest, it's a two-man job. I need someone to hang onto the boxes. I usually ask my friend Wes, but ...' she tightened her lips, 'I was going to ask you if you could help out.'

'Course, I don't mind. I'd offer to drive but ...' she pulled a face. She couldn't remember the last time she'd been behind the wheel of a car. Living in central London, she used public transport all the time.

Bella winced and looked at her watch. 'I can try calling the cavalry ... see if Todd's available. What's the chance of him being around on a Friday night?'

'Slim,' suggested Sophie. 'In fact, I'd say given that I've been fielding his calls all week from a stream of lovely girls, he's bound to be out on a hot date.'

She'd already decided he was like Macavity, the Mystery Cat – i.e. never there. Certainly not at his desk when she was in the office, although there were definite signs of habitation. Usually empty coffee cups and cookie crumbs. The switchboard kept putting his calls through to her extension and she'd been the recipient of several very perky, friendly repeat calls from women trying to track him down. To be fair – and that was one of Sophie's strengths, she was exceedingly good at being fair – the women were always absolutely charming and, rather bafflingly, completely understanding about his failure to return their calls.

'Aw, poor Todd. He's so busy. If you could tell him that Lacey called again, I'd be grateful.' Poor Todd. *Poor Lacey,* more like. She'd called four times this week. While Cherie with the lisp had called three times and high-pitched, giggly Amy twice.

'Well, I'll have to call him,' said Bella, wiping at her forehead with her arm, leaving a streak of flour across her face. 'I can't think of anyone else with a car.'

She tapped her fingers on her phone screen. To Sophie's surprise, the phone only rang twice and then she heard Todd answer.

'Hey Todd.'

'Hey Bellabella. What you up to?'

'Having a disaster. I need your help.'

'Shoot.'

'Would you be able to help with a delivery tomorrow morning? I need to get six dozen cupcakes over to the other side of Greenpoint.'

Sophie waited, expecting a slew of questions and excuses.

'Sure. What time?'

'Early, I'm afraid. I said I'd get them there for eight because I thought I'd need to get back to open the shop. My Saturday girls don't start until ten. It's a bit late to phone the client and change the arrangements now.' Bella winced.

'No problem. I'll be there at seven. You'd better have a coffee ready.'

'Todd, you're an angel.'

'Does that mean I qualify for a lifetime supply of heavenly cupcakes?'

'You bet. See you tomorrow.'

'Laters.'

Bella turned to Sophie. 'He's a star. So will you go with him? Sorry, you've probably got plans.'

'Of course I can help.'

'And you should be finished by nine.'

Great. That just left the rest of the day to fill.

Chapter 6

'Hey English,' said Todd, immediately stepping forward and relieving her of the first box of cupcakes. He had that healthy, wholesome glow of a character from a TV ad, bright-eyed and bushy tailed, in a crisp white cotton button-down-collar shirt and denim shorts which showed off perfectly even-tanned legs.

She wasn't sure why she had, but thank goodness she'd washed her hair, blow dried it into soft curls for a change and put on some make-up. She didn't feel like a bag lady next to him. Even better that she'd put on her favourite cobalt-blue linen shirt that did wonders for her eyes and cut-off shorts that showed off her legs, which apart from her hair (on the days like today, when it behaved itself) were definitely her best attribute.

Not that, scrubbed up, she came anywhere close to matching his golden beauty. No wonder he had a harem of women panting down the phone to speak to him.

'Morning Todd.' She was deliberately brisk. The stupid sudden fluttering in her chest could just back off. Hormones had a lot to answer for. That must be it. Normal healthy response. She was not the sort of girl who had crushes. She was far too sensible, and after James, a relationship-free bastion of singledom.

'How many boxes have we got?' He grinned, eyes twinkly and direct. The flutter intensified and she had to suck in an extra breath.

'J-just another two.' She shot him a perfunctory, polite, see-your-thousand-watt-charisma-has-no-effect smile in response.

'Cool.' His grin didn't so much as dim. 'My car's in a no-waiting area around the corner. You can't miss it.' He was already heading off down the street, calling over his shoulder. 'I'll take these if you can bring the others.'

She took a steadying breath, watching him as he strode off. God, he had a nice backside. Broad shoulders, tapering down to a trim waist and that ... yeah, that backside. What the hell was wrong with her? Objectifying the poor man. She gave herself a stern mental shake.

She marched back into the kitchen to grab the last two boxes.

'Here's the receipt. You need to give it to the customer. They've already paid. Good luck and don't take any risks. Make sure Todd drives like an old lady. I feel this batch is jinxed.'

'Bella, don't worry. I'll guard them with my life.' They exchanged knowing smiles. They'd finally finished very late the night before.

Carrying the two boxes, she rounded the corner and nearly stopped dead. Todd was right, you couldn't miss his car. So much for the assumption he'd be a BMW or Mercedes type of man. She had to slow her steps down, while she schooled her face. She didn't want to hurt his feelings but it took a second or two to mask her surprise. This car was a mess, without doubt the scruffiest, tattiest thing she'd ever seen. And so not Todd, who usually rocked the preppy look with his crisp chino shorts and perfectly pressed linen shirts. The ancient Golf had a huge dent in the driver's door, the bumper at the back was missing and the panel of the rear door was bright blue, in ugly contrast to the dark racing-green paintwork of the rest of the car. As she neared she could see that the paintwork on the bonnet had bubbled with pale craters, looking like skin peeling after a nasty case of sunburn.

'Interesting car,' she said straight faced, handing the boxes over to him. Despite the distraction of the car, she was still unable to stop herself ogling his pert bottom as he leant into the rear seat to stow them next to the others.

When he turned back to her his face danced with mischievous wickedness. 'Pisses the hell out of my dad when I go home and park it on the drive. Lowers the tone of the neighbourhood.'

She laughed. 'I bet it does. I don't want to be rude, but this would lower the tone of a rubbish tip.' She shot the wheels a dubious look. 'Does it actually work or is it like Fred Flintstone's car and we have to run?'

'I'll have you know, Gertie …' he paused and patted the car door, 'is a loyal if occasionally temperamental old girl. She doesn't like winter mornings, but then who does?'

'As long as she starts today and gets these cakes to …

wherever we're going, I don't mind. Bella is counting on us.'

Suddenly serious, Todd straightened up and pulled his keys out of his pocket. 'I wouldn't let Bella down.' Then his face lightened and with his usual engaging grin, he said, holding out his hand, 'Come on, strap yourself in and prepare yourself for the ride of your life.'

'That's what I'm worried about,' she said primly, her eyes twinkling as she pressed her lips together, trying not to smile back at him. He was totally incorrigible. 'I'm grateful no one round here knows me.'

He slapped a hand to his chest. 'Shsh! You'll upset her.'

Sophie climbed into the back seat next to the boxes.

From the driver's seat, he handed his phone back to her. 'Here, you'll need to navigate. The sound doesn't work when it's charging and it's low on battery at the moment. I know my way until we cross Fulton Street and then I'll need directions.'

The car coughed to life with a roar and a bit of splutter but Todd looked unconcerned as they pulled out onto the one-way street, his fingers tapping on the steering wheel in time to the music blaring out from the radio. Interestingly, Sophie noticed as she looked at the floor and the back seat, the inside of the car was absolutely pristine.

'Take the next right here,' said Sophie, holding Todd's iPhone in one hand, while the other kept a gentle guard on the boxes of cupcakes to keep them from sliding around the back of the car. 'We must be nearly there ... Yes,' she checked the screen, 'up this street and then second on the right.'

'Two blocks, English,' corrected Todd, catching her eye in the mirror with his usual sunny smile. 'We'll make an American of you yet.'

'You can try but I come from a long line of very English English-folk.' As evidenced in the heavy leather-bound Bible in the library which traced the family tree right back to the court of Charles II.

'Challenge accepted,' said Todd.

'What? That wasn't a challenge, just an observation.' Sophie rolled her eyes at him in the mirror but of course received his usual grin.

Todd's battered car turned the final corner, into a street of brownstones.

'It's nice round here.'

'Up and coming. They film *The Unbreakable Kimmy Schmidt* here. And a couple of other things.'

'I've heard of it, but not seen it.'

'Big hit. Funny.'

Sophie resolved to check it out on Netflix. That would give her something to watch this week.

With the cakes safely delivered, she hopped into the front seat of the car for the return trip.

'Have you had breakfast?' asked Todd.

'No, it was too early and now it's too late.'

'Welcome to New York, it's never too late for brunch, unless you've got plans.'

Sophie hesitated for a second, remembering her conversation with Kate the previous evening. A few weeks ago she wouldn't have thought twice, in fact she'd probably have already suggested a coffee or breakfast.

'No, no plans. Brunch would be … great. If you've got time.' It would be a fabulous way of killing a few hours and would make her feel that she was at least starting to make an effort to get out and about.

With a rueful grimace, she realised that actually not much had changed. In London, she'd spent a lot of hours at the weekends killing time. Large chunks of her life had been held in abeyance while she waited for James to be around. It made her cross to realise how much time she'd wasted. On weekday evenings she'd been desperate to savour every precious moment of his company, so they'd stayed in the flat. Of course, now it made complete sense. It had lessened the chance of discovery, bumping into someone who might know him. Missed trips to the theatre, to exhibitions, to new restaurants. Not going to Kew Gardens at Christmas, not going to Notting Hill Carnival, not going to Proms in the Park.

And now she was in danger of repeating the same mistake here. Of staying indoors. Not venturing out on her own.

'For you, I've got all the time in the world.'

Sophie rolled her eyes again. 'Yeah, I bet you say that to all the girls.'

'Of course I do.' He flashed her an irrepressible grin. 'There's a great place near Bella's. *Café Luluc*. It will be ridiculously busy, but worth it. A Mexican family runs it. They do fantastic brunch. I can go get rid of the car, if you don't mind waiting in line.'

'You mean queuing,' Sophie's repressive tone was tempered with a wry smile.

'You queue, I'll wait in line.' He winked at her.

'Go on, then.' She couldn't help smile back at him, his easy-going cheerful attitude was infectious.

Standing in the sunshine, watching everyone on Smith Street, was no hardship. Todd had told her he'd be a while, as despite his resident's permit, it could be tricky finding a parking space. She didn't mind the wait; it was fun people watching, especially in a different city. Why hadn't she done this before?

Experience told her that a queue this long meant that the food would be worth every minute. It also gave her plenty of time to give the menu a thorough examination. Her passion for food and English collided in happy accident, after she spectacularly failed her A levels. Deciding to take a year out, she got a part-time job in admin at the local paper and a waitressing job in a newly opened gastro-pub in the village. The food at *The White Hare in Haresfoot* was some of the best she'd ever tasted and when she wrote a review and showed it to George, the editor of the paper, he promptly published it and gave her a job writing a food column.

'What's with the frown?' asked Todd when he finally joined her in the queue.

'It's so hard, I can't decide whether to have the eggs Florentine or the brioche French toast with apple compote. Or maybe I should try the omelette with wild mushrooms and Asiago cheese. I've no idea what Asiago cheese is.'

'So why would you try it?'

Sophie took off her sunglasses and gave him her best schoolteacher reproving stare. 'It's important for your food education.'

'Right.' Todd nodded, for once trying to keep the smile from his face.

'I'm serious. You should never stop trying new things. You might miss out on something amazing.'

'I'll take your word for it. So how did you get into the whole food-writing thing?'

By the time Sophie had told him the full story, they were ushered to a booth at the back of the restaurant and sat down on red vinyl seats at a white-clothed table. When the couple sitting next to them had their food served, Sophie couldn't help leaning over and asking what they'd ordered.

They responded with instant open friendliness and enthusiasm that made her doubly ashamed that this was her first proper weekend outing since she'd been here.

'Now I'm even more undecided,' she confided to Todd, sneaking another look at their neighbours' eggs Benedict. 'They look yummy.' She strained her neck, watching a waiter taking out three plates to a table near the front of the restaurant. 'Everything looks divine.'

'Close your eyes and stick a finger on the menu,' suggested Todd, leaning back against the seat, his arm lazily topping the booth.

Sophie drew herself up and, widening her eyes, gave a mock outraged gasp, 'I couldn't possibly do that.'

He laughed. 'I knew that. Crunch time. The waiter is heading this way and I am starving, so you're going to have to make your choice.' He leaned forward with mock threat. 'And I will order without you.'

'Oh.'

She huffed and puffed as the waiter patiently stood with his notepad exchanging looks with Todd.

'I'll have the brioche French ... oh, actually, can you tell me what Asiago cheese is?'

'It's a nutty, firm cheese, not as strong or dry as parmesan or pecorino but very similar.'

'Right ...' she pulled a face and turned to Todd. 'That makes it even harder.'

Todd rolled his eyes and turned to the waiter. 'She'll have the brioche French toast with apple compote and I'll have the wild mushroom and Asiago cheese omelette.' He turned back to her with a quick aside, 'You can share mine,' before also ordering coffee and orange juice.

'Tea for me, please.'

Scribbling on his pad as he went, the waiter scooted off.

'You didn't have to do that. Now I feel guilty.'

'Well don't. I've eaten here plenty of times. I like omelette and for my food education, I thought I'd try the cheese. And you can try both.'

'That's very kind of you.'

'Kind is my middle name,' said Todd airily.

Sophie studied him from under her lashes. With some people kindness could be quite self-serving, almost calculated. Todd's came naturally.

'So how are you finding New York?'

She shrugged. Evasive, her eyes studying the ornate plasterwork on the ceiling. 'I've only been here two weeks. And most of the time I've been at work.'

Scepticism flared in his eyes, when she brought her gaze back to eye level.

Defensive now, she fingered some stray salt grains on the table. 'There's plenty of time. I'm here for six months.'

The raised eyebrow had her digging in deeper. 'There's no hurry. Everything will still be there tomorrow and every day after that.'

'Yeah, but it's New York. The city that never sleeps, remember? You must have been downtown at lunchtimes.'

'Erm ... not really.'

'What?' He gave a suspicious look.

'I tend to grab a coffee and ...' she shrugged. She'd got into a routine of popping down to the coffee shop in the atrium to grab a drink, sitting people watching, pretending she was engrossed in Facebook or something on her phone.

'You should try to get out. Central Park is less than a block away.'

'I ... guess. It's just ... quite.' She hated sounding so defensive. 'Gosh, sorry, I'm not normally this pathetic. I didn't want to ... I mean, I wasn't expecting to come and I had to turn everything around quite quickly, and it's all been ...'

'Overwhelming?' he asked softly.

She shot him a grateful look. 'Yes. I feel like I've been pitched in at the deep end where everyone else is travelling at warp speed and I'm in the slow lane.'

'You'll get the hang of it. There's nowhere quite like it. But it's easy to be lonely here. Become anonymous.'

'It is in any big city.'

'True. So why didn't you want to come here? The Big Apple. Everyone wants to come to New York.' He lifted both arms up with a quick, mocking jazz hands.

She shot him a sharp look, surprised by his unexpected insight.

'How did you know?'

'I'm not just a pretty face, you know. I listen. You were going to say you didn't want to come.'

She winced. She was too ashamed to tell him the whole story.

'I was quite happy. Then I split up with my boyfriend and I thought, why the hell not?'

Todd raised a sceptical eyebrow. 'How long had you been with him?'

'Two years.'

'Two years! Get out of here. That's longer than some marriages last.' He paused before asking quietly, 'And is it permanent? No chance of getting back together? Or is this a way of showing him what he's missing? Is he likely to come chasing after you, with a ring box?'

She shot him a withering look, disappointed by his cynicism.

'Oh this is permanent, alright.' The circling bitterness, which she normally kept in check, burst out. 'As permanent as possible.'

'Funny how love turns to hate so easily.' Todd didn't sound

the least bit amused, his voice was tinged with weary disillusion. 'Or rather it's not funny at all. It seems to happen with remarkable ease.'

Sophie swallowed hard. 'And sometimes it doesn't.'

She wanted to wake up and find out it had all been a huge mistake and that the James married to Anna was in fact a different James Soames. Unfortunately, Anna had brought two photos with her that day. The sight of James in a morning suit next to his glowing bride and the look of tenderness on his face as he gazed at a new-born Emma had physically hurt. The intense pain in her chest had robbed her of breath.

'I find it interesting that there is such a fine line. How does a couple go from being not able to live without each other, to arguing over who gets the toaster?'

'We weren't arguing about toasters.' Sophie swallowed hard. 'We never argued. Which just goes to show. Love is blind.' In hindsight, she'd been blind, deaf and dumb. There'd been clues aplenty.

'I never got that phrase. Love is blind. Is it? When you're "in love"' – those horrid quote marks with his fingers told her exactly what he thought – 'don't you examine every little thing they do? Analyse everything they say. Dissect the meaning of every last word and phrase. I suspect you can be blinded by love, although it's probably lust. Dazzled by sexual attraction.'

'So, you don't believe in love?'

Todd snorted. 'It's an idea, a social concept, if you will.' She heard the New Yorker in his voice, and it was almost as if a different person were speaking. 'Songs, books, they all talk about being love. I get that you can care about someone. You can be in a mutually respectful relationship. You can promise to be faithful ... but at the end of the day, humans are intrinsically selfish and self-seeking. We look out for number one. That ideal of love being all-encompassing, hearts and flowers, self-sacrificing, that's fiction. Your books and songs.'

'Wow.' Sophie paused as she sieved the words one by one through her filter of despair and betrayal, and found to her relief that despite what she'd been through she was still able to say, 'That's quite depressing.' She smiled, as a little bit of the iceberg of pain lodged firmly in her heart, melted. 'Despite everything with J—' she refused to say his name out loud, give him any more room in her life, 'I still believe that one day, I'll find love with someone else.'

'So in the meantime, you're in ... what, in an emotional holding bay, that just happens to be New York?'

Sophie wriggled uncomfortably in her seat, stung by his rather accurate summation. 'Something like that.'

'That's a terrible waste of living.'

'What?'

'This is one of the greatest cities on earth. Brooklyn is one of the best neighbourhoods to live in. Six months. You can only scratch the surface. You should be making the most of every last damn second.

'You should check some places out. Prospect Park. DeKalb Market Hall, north of Fulton Street. About three blocks over. I've heard it's a real foodie haven. There's a great flea market up at Kent Avenue. What are you doing next weekend?'

'I ...' she lifted her shoulders.

'Aside from chores?' pressed Todd.

'I've got to do my washing sometime.'

'Babe, we've had the washing talk already. Your laundry isn't going to take all day. You need to get out there. Although you can still cook me dinner.' He cocked his head with a hopeful look that had Sophie laughing.

'Great. It won't stop you doing my wash— laundry, although I'm not sure I want you handling my underwear.' She was surprised that there was no washing machine in the apartment. She'd rinsed a few things through by hand.

'I'm pretty good at handling underwear.'

'Why doesn't that surprise me? I'll pass though.'

'English, a tip. There's a service laundromat on Hoyt Street. Five bucks for a load. Washed, dried and folded.'

'That's good to know. I'd never have thought of that.' She sat up straighter, brightened at the prospect. 'I am *so* going to do that this afternoon.'

'Welcome to America.'

Chapter 7

The laundromat smelled soft and clean, the soothing hum of tumble dryers cushioning the noise of the street outside. It was like fabric softener for the soul. Sophie handed over a large sack of washing and paid her five dollars.

'When will it be ready?' she asked.

'Five cock. You come,' said the ancient Vietnamese lady tapping her finger on the Formica counter top. 'Five cock.' Even though it was childish, Sophie bit back a snigger.

'Today?'

The lady looked affronted. 'Yes.'

'Great. Thank you.' That was good service. Thank goodness for Todd's advice yesterday afternoon.

The woman had already stomped off like a bandy-legged Rumpelstiltskin to one of the dryers, where she started pulling out sheets bigger than she was.

'Oh, I forgot to say. Todd sent me.'

The woman dropped the sheet. 'Todd. He good boy.' She beamed. Was there any female he wasn't capable of charming?

Sophie left the shop with the promise of clean underwear later that afternoon, feeling she had achieved something. OK, so it was only washing, but it made her feel normal. As if she were starting to get back to normal. A big tick on her weekend list. Now all she had to do was fill the rest of today.

She could keep walking, except that Hoyt Street, or at least this part, seemed a lot less fancy than Smith Street a block away. There were a couple of grocery and deli shops, the windows plastered with flyers and adverts for cheap offers; corner shops with grimy windows and hand-written signs promising cola at fifty cents; a scruffy pharmacy, a chicken and pizza fast-food place and a bike shop. The metal grills and the basic shop fronts were a far cry from the smart wooden trim finishes and fancy sign-written shop names a street away.

Two teenagers in oversize hoodies and enormous trainers eyed her as they leaned on bikes against a lamp-post. Conscious of two pairs of eyes burning into her back and feeling slightly vulnerable, Sophie picked up her pace and scurried down the street towards home. All her good intentions to explore the area evaporated.

As she drew level with the bakery, she spotted Bella beckoning her enthusiastically through the window.

'Hey Sophie! Good morning, come and meet the Eds.' Bella bounded up to her and dragged her past the busy tables into the warm kitchen, filled with the slightly steamy air of hot ovens and freshly baked batches of cakes.

'This is Edie and this is Ed. Guys, meet my new neighbour, Sophie. And I think you met Wes when you arrived.' Wes, leaning against the dresser, nodded and gave her a wide smile and saluted her.

'Hey Sophie,' the two people sitting on the sofa chorused

in perfect unison, both lifting their hands in identical economic waves, rather like a pair of spookily in-tandem twins, even down to their clothes' similar muted shades of green and brown. Both were very thin, with sharp angular features and short cropped hair in an identical shade of mousey brown, although Ed had considerably more hair on his chin than on the top of his head. It was the sort of magnificent beard that you saw in adverts for trendy beer or featuring lumberjacks.

'They make and supply all the bread for the bakery,' explained Bella.

'And the bagels,' piped up the more feminine-looking one of the pair.

'And the bread rolls,' added the other.

'Coffee?' asked Bella. 'Grab a seat. We were having a tasting. You can give me a second opinion.' The coffee table had been cleared of its papers and in the centre was a large bread-board with several different loaves which had been sliced open.

'That would be lovely, thanks.' She sank into one of the armchairs.

'Here.' Ed immediately thrust a chunk of bread at her. 'Try this. Honey and walnut.'

Edie huffed. 'Not fair.'

'She can try yours next,' said Bella. 'Honestly, they're so competitive.' She handed Sophie a rich, dark coffee.

Both Ed and Edie grinned. 'But of course.'

'By the way, Sophie is my new tenant upstairs. The one I was talking about. From London.'

'Cool,' said Ed, pointing his finger at the bread and urging Sophie to get a move on.

She took a bite of the still-warm bread. 'Mmm, that is delicious.'

Ed gave his opposite number a smug nod. Sophie was still trying to work out the relationship between the pair when Edie leaned forward and kissed him on the nose. 'She hasn't tried mine yet, buster,' she said as she cut a wedge from the nearest, very pale loaf. 'Here, this one has a bit of subtlety about it.' She shot Ed a superior look, tilting her nose in the air.

Sophie hurriedly bit into the crust, aware of the four pairs of eyes on her. This was clearly serious business.

'Seeds,' she looked at the bubbled, waxy interior of the bread, 'chia seeds.'

Edie straightened and beamed. Sophie chewed, trying to get a handle on the familiar taste. 'Yoghurt?'

'I like her,' said Edie to no one in particular. 'It's my cholesterol-busting bread. Chia seeds and yoghurt. See, these English people have got taste.'

'They're both lovely,' said Sophie. The honey-and-walnut was much nicer but the shadowed, anxious looks from Bella and Wes suggested that the wrong words might start World War Three right there in the kitchen.

'OK, sold,' said Bella. 'I'll take a dozen of each next week.'

'Great,' said Edie, beaming. 'Now break out the cupcakes, babe. I'm fed up with the healthy crap. Those chia seeds have played havoc with my system this week. And thanks for the vote, Sophie. So what brings you Stateside? Apart from proving that my bread tastes better.'

'I told you, she's hiding out after a bad break-up,' announced Bella. 'And she needs to get out more.'

Sophie opened her mouth to protest and narrowed her eyes. 'You've been talking to Todd.'

'Yeah, I spoke to him last night. He gave me a lecture about not keeping an eye out for you.'

'Sorry. He shouldn't have.'

'Yes, he should. You've been here two weeks and not met anyone.'

'That's terrible. We can help,' said Edie, bouncing slightly on the sofa. 'We can introduce you to a few people in the neighbourhood.'

'Yes!' said Bella. 'There's Frank and Jim, they run the boutique across the street. They're always good for a drink and they give great discount in the store.'

'Oh yes, they have that really cute little guy who works on Saturdays,' added Edie.

'Little guy because he's about sixteen,' said Ed, poking her affectionately in the ribs as he turned to Sophie.

Edie ignored him. 'Wes, you know the guys down the road that run the cycle store. We could introduce Sophie to them. They have the most delicious legs. Lovely calves. Steel thighs.'

'Who's talking about steel thighs?' asked a dry voice, appearing in the doorway hidden behind a pile of cardboard pizza boxes.

'Maisie! Just the person.' Bella ran over and removed the pile of boxes from the plump arms of a very smiley, short woman. 'You know loads of people.'

'That's because everyone is a sucker for her cheesecakes,' rumbled Wes, taking the boxes from Bella and sniffing appreciatively. 'Mmm, they smell good.'

'Cinnamon and caramel, a new recipe. And a couple of strawberry and chocolate cheesecakes.'

'Mmm, I love your chocolate cheesecake. Remind me, Ed, to grab a couple of slices when we leave. I need to keep my strength up. I've got a dozen loaves to knead this afternoon.'

'Am I too late for a coffee?' asked Maisie. 'I've got a twenty-minute window before Carl divorces me for abandoning the twins with him.' Somehow she'd crossed the room and had wedged her ample bottom into the armchair, her eyes dancing as if she were bursting with happy secrets. 'And why do you need loads of people?'

'Maisie, this is Sophie.' Bella grabbed a mug from the dresser and filled it from the half-full cafetière on the side. 'She's taken the apartment upstairs and doesn't know a soul in New York – well, apart from us. Oh and Todd, but he doesn't count.'

Maisie laughed, taking the coffee. 'Well Sophie, you've landed in the right place. Bella's Bakery is the place to meet at this end of Smith Street. We can introduce you to plenty of people.'

'And she's a foodie,' said Bella. 'She writes for *CityZen*.'

'And she likes my chia-and-yoghurt bread.' Edie held a piece out towards Maisie, who pulled a face.

'I guess someone has to,' teased Maisie, pushing it away as Edie laughed good-naturedly. 'Although if you're interested in food ... has anyone tried the new Mezze place? Hummus to die for. Although the twins made it interesting. You ever tried removing a pomegranate seed from a five-year-old's ear? A family adventure, I can tell you.'

'Didn't you just hold her upside down and shake?' asked

Ed, tipping his head on one side as if giving it careful consideration.

'Sheesh, Mr Practical. And that right there, is why we're not having kids any time soon.' Slapping her hands on her hips, Edie's bony arms protruded like a pair of twigs.

Maisie hooked an arm through one of them and pulled her into a hug as everyone burst out laughing.

'I'm assuming you don't have any rugrats, Sophie?' asked Edie.

'No.' She swallowed hard, an image of James's little girl covered in yoghurt coming back to haunt her. 'No kids. No boyfriend. No husband. Free. Single.' *And adrift.* She'd been one of two for so long. Suddenly she realised everyone was staring at her and that her words had shot out like staccato bullets. 'Sorry.' Her face flushed and she looked down at the floor.

'Don't you worry, honey,' said Maisie, patting her on the arm. 'We've all been there. We'll look after you. You'll find your feet in no time. Pretty gal like you will have the boys falling on their butts for you.'

'Yeah,' said Edie. 'And only half of them will be complete idiots.'

Right on cue, Ed shot to his feet and collapsed dramatically, writhing on the floor.

'See,' said Edie, laughing affectionately and bending to tickle Ed in the ribs.

On Monday, as she snagged the last seat on the subway, Sophie still felt warm all over after the previous day in the bakery.

Bella's friends' unconditional welcome had been like an enveloping hug and this morning she was ready to take on the world, or Manhattan, at the very least.

When the phone on Todd's desk rang, Charlene's now-familiar voice definitely made her feel as if she'd been there forever.

'Hi Charlene.'

'Hey Sophie. Don't tell me, he's not in yet? I guess it's still early.'

Sophie gave her watch a sceptical glance. It was well after eleven.

'Can you tell him I called? Honestly ... he is so hard to pin down.'

'Yes,' said Sophie, trying to sound helpful, when all she wanted to do was to tell the girl to cut her losses. 'I'll leave him a message.'

'Thanks, you're a doll.'

And you're a poor misguided fool, she thought as she put the phone down.

'Hey English.'

'Do you have some sixth sense that tells you when I've hung up on one of your harem?'

He shrugged. 'What can I say? It's karma.'

'Karma is supposed to happen to good people.'

'Aw Sophie, who told you I was a bad person? For that, I won't share the cappuccino with chocolate sprinkles I brought up for you.' He held up two cardboard cups with lids on.

Disarmed, Sophie shook her head at him. 'Thank you. Your sixth sense for coffee is equally good.'

'What can I say? It's a skill. Although you are very predict-able, English. You like your routine.'

'I'm ...' Sophie laughed. 'Yes, I am. I like my mid-morning coffee.'

'You going to share those cookies hiding in your drawer?'

'Nothing gets by you, does it?' She opened the desk drawer and pulled out the small tin of shortbread left over from the biscuit testing the previous week. She still couldn't bring herself to refer to them as cookies, especially not when they were short-bread. As she took a bite of the melt-in-the-mouth buttery biscuits, she wondered how they'd go down with Bella's customers.

'Mmmm,' said Todd, snagging a second one before she could close the tin. 'So how was the rest of your weekend?' he asked.

'Good, thanks,' Sophie smiled as she thought of the laughter and teasing in Bella's kitchen. It had been a while since she'd laughed so much. 'I met a few of Bella's friends and your laundry lady. A woman of few words. But I think I might be in love.' Picking up a bundle of fresh-smelling, still warm, folded clothes was something of a revelation.

'Ah the lovely Wendy. And did you do any exp—'

'Morning, guys.'

'Hey Paul. Haven't seen you down here for a while. Slumming it?' Todd gave him a friendly slap on the back.

Paul nodded at Todd and then turned to Sophie, giving her a warm, very direct smile which made her feel a little flustered.

'Or are you after tickets for the Yankees game?

'No, thanks man. I'm playing in the squash tournament. But if you've got any for the Mets versus Yankee game coming up, I might clear a window. I came to see Sophie.' He turned to her and gave her another smile, the sort that felt like you'd been caught in a lighthouse beam. 'I've been thinking about your afternoon tea feature and the *hygge* thing and I wondered if you fancied a coffee so that I can pick your brains?'

'Yes, of course. Erm ... when?' She lifted her half-drunk coffee. 'I'm kind of ...'

Paul pulled out his phone and scrolled through the screen. 'How about over drinks after work? I'm free this evening.'

'OK. Sure.'

'I'll swing by about six. There's a nice place across the street.'

Sophie heard Todd tut under his breath.

'There are no nice places across the street,' said Todd.

Paul pushed his hands into the pockets of his smart suit trousers, a patient look on his face, as he shot an amused smirk Sophie's way. 'OK, Mr Man About Town. Where do you suggest?'

'There's a great place opened in Williamsburg. Craft beers and gin. I bet English here loves her gin.'

Sophie was about to nod enthusiastically, she was definitely rather partial to a midweek cheeky gin and tonic in London. For a brief second she was almost felled by the unexpected wave of homesickness. A gin would have gone down a treat but before she could say anything, Paul shook his head.

'Williamsburg? Brooklyn? McLennan, man, you've got to be kidding. Why would I want to schlepp all the way over there? Hipster city. No thanks. I'm not interested in joining the beardy brigade. Manhattan is where it's at.'

Todd's mouth tightened. 'Your loss.'

'Sorry man, I forgot you like to slum it out that way. No offence, but it's not my scene.' Paul punched him on the arm. 'Nice try, but Sophie's English, she probably likes a bit of class when someone takes her out for a drink. Not so Man About Town after all.'

With a shrug Todd sat down at his desk and within seconds was engrossed with something on the screen.

Paul turned to Sophie, again the full beam of his attention focused on her. 'I'll swing by and pick you up at about six-forty-five'

'Six-forty-five?' repeated Sophie faintly. She was normally well on her way home by then. What was she going to do in the office for an extra forty-five minutes?

'See you later. See you, Todd. And keep me posted on those tickets.'

Todd gave him a casual wave, not looking up from his laptop.

'He likes you,' observed Todd a few minutes later, still focused on the screen in front of him.

Sophie swallowed. 'I'm sure it's just work.'

Todd looked up and raised an exaggerated eyebrow. 'A nice place across the street? Jeez. He hasn't got a clue. And if he took you to Brooklyn, you wouldn't have so far to travel home on your own. He could even see you home.'

'Like I said, it's just work.'

Todd snorted. 'If you think so, English. Paul doesn't come down here that often. He's scented new blood. Bit like a shark. You're fresh meat.'

'Charming,' said Sophie, surprised by the unexpected sting his words dealt to her feminine pride.

With a sudden start, he pulled an apologetic face. 'I didn't mean you're not, you know ...'

Sophie raised an imperious eyebrow, waiting for him to finish. She might not be gracing the front of a magazine anytime soon but she wasn't a complete heffer either.

'In fact you're very ...' Todd turned a delicate shade of pink.

She responded with a distinct snap in her voice, although why should she care what Todd McLennan thought of her? 'Thanks, nice to know.'

'Shit, sorry Sophie. Look, I'm around this weekend. Why don't I give you a tour of Brooklyn?'

'Don't worry. I'm sure you've got better things to do.'

At six-thirty Sophie left her desk, clutching her handbag and an H&M carrier bag and retired to the ladies. The office was virtually empty and Todd had disappeared mid-afternoon, although his jacket was still draped over his chair.

Driven by something, OK, that feminine pride again, she'd made a rare foray out at lunchtime and had been relieved to see the familiar store. Whipping off her plain cream jumper, she put on the newly purchased pretty lacy top and for some reason she took extra care with her make-up, making sure that it was perfect, using a little more than usual. She was going out, why not? With a final tug she pulled her hair out of its loose bun and let the blonde curls tumble down, fluffing them up with her fingers.

With one last look in the mirror, she gave herself a determined smile, mouthing 'Fresh meat.' Huh, she'd show Todd McLennan.

When she returned, Todd was leaning against his desk, tapping away at his phone.

'Hey English.' As he looked up, his smile dimmed and for a moment he looked disconcerted, which gave Sophie a brief smug moment of satisfaction. 'You look ... nice. Paul phoned down, he's running late. Some meeting running over. He'll be here around seven-fifteen.'

'Oh right, thanks.' Sophie swallowed, feeling less smug and a bit foolish. Paul wanted to pick her brains, that was all. She'd completely misread those flirty, eye-meet, full-on smiles. Was she really that desperate to prove that after James, someone might find her attractive again? Chewing at her lip, she sat down at her desk, wondering whether to switch her laptop back on and start work again but her heart wasn't really in it.

She began to tidy her desk, scanning through her in-tray. There were a few memos and meeting dates she needed to take note of and a couple of press releases and invitations to launch events to consider.

'Got any of that shortbread left, English?' Todd put his phone down and sat down at his desk, pulling his overflowing in-tray towards him. 'I need some strength to sort this lot out.'

With a smile, she reached into her desk and pulled out the tin. There was one solitary sugar-dusted triangle left. 'Hmm, I think the mice have been at it today.'

He grinned at her. 'A man's got to eat. Do you think you could make some more?'

'I'll see what I can do.' She pulled a wry face. 'Although I think it's going to take more than sugar to do your filing.'

Todd picked up the stack of paper and dropped it with a thud on his desk.

'Most of it can go in the bin. It's mainly press releases, but there are some invites to launches and things.' He lifted the top one. 'June 29th, launch of Paws for Thought. Introducing mindfulness classes for stressed-out pets.'

'What? You are joking?' Sophie frowned, trying to decide whether he was serious.

'Nope, you're not in Kansas any more. Welcome to the Big Apple. How about this one?' His eyes twinkled with mischief. 'You'll like this. Vajazzle with Dazzle invites you to the launch of this season's rhinestone cowboy designs.'

Sophie shuddered. 'Ugh, no.'

'Ah, this one's more up your street. Flavour sensations. Come along and taste over a hundred exotic fruits, rare herbs and interesting spices from around the world.' He pushed over the pineapple-shaped invitation card.

'That does look interesting. Thanks.'

'See, don't say I don't spoil you. In fact, here, take a look. See if there's anything else you fancy?' He halved his pile and pushed it across to her desk before adding, 'And let me know if there's anything you think might interest me.'

Sophie tipped her head on one side, unable to hide her smile. 'So basically, you want me to help you with your filing?'

He grinned unrepentantly. 'That's about the size of it, English.'

'Oh go on, then.' It was impossible to stay cross with Todd for any length of time. Besides, she had half an hour to kill.

At seven-fifteen, Sophie was giggling as Todd, hamming it up for all he was worth, read out another bizarre press release about a new range of men's support tights, when the phone rang on his desk, making them both jump. She'd completely forgotten the time as they'd worked through his pile, most of it going into the bin.

Todd handed the handset over to her. 'Paul.'

'Hi Paul.'

'I'm so sorry. My meeting has dragged on. I've got a few more bits to do but I could be with you just after seven-thirty. You know how it is.'

'Mm,' said Sophie, wishing she'd known how it was about an hour ago. 'Maybe we can catch up another time. It sounds as if you've got a lot on.'

'It's all go on the way to the top. I could do with staying for another hour, to be honest.'

'No problem,' said Sophie, stifling her irritation.

'You're a star. Thanks for being so understanding.' He paused and then said, his voice lowering, 'Why don't I do this properly? I'd like to take you out to dinner. I'd like to get to know you a bit better. And I should have done that first instead of pretending I wanted to talk work.'

She let out a gentle laugh, charmed by his admission and conscious of Todd opposite her listening in with a sceptical look on his face. 'Now that sounds like a better plan.'

'Let's sync our diaries, tomorrow. I'll call you. Night, Sophie.'

'Night, Paul.' She put down the phone, realising what she'd just agreed was tantamount to going on a date.

'Blown you out?' asked Todd, his mouth curling.

'No.' Sophie smiled, still touched by Paul's words and the little butterflies dancing in her stomach. She wasn't sure she was ready to date, not after James, but she couldn't deny that it was flattering to be asked. 'We agreed to rearrange.'

'You headed home then? I'll see you back and check in with Bels.'

'Mmm.' Sophie's mind was elsewhere. Picturing dinner with Paul. What would she wear? What would she say? It had been years since she'd been out with anyone other than James. Was she doing the right thing? But she had to start somewhere. Why not here in New York? There was no one to see her if she made a fool of herself. It would be temporary. It would be dipping her toe back in the water. And after someone like James, she didn't need to worry about her heart being damaged again. It was still so torn up, nothing could do any more harm. Not that she would let anyone come close for a very long time.

'Earth to English. You coming?' His voice had dropped and when she looked up she caught him staring at her, a strange intense expression on his face. Her heart did a funny little salmon leap in her chest. Flustered, she made herself busy, checking her bag for her subway ticket, looking in her purse and realising that she'd agreed to travel back to Brooklyn with him.

Ready at last, she stood up. He'd pulled on his jacket and was waiting for her. He flashed her his usual thousand-kilowatt smile and her pulse stuttered. Every now and then it hit her how damn good looking he was. Irritated with the stupid shallow observation and the ridiculous bubbling feeling in her stomach, she grabbed her bag.

'Let's go,' she said, deliberately business-like and brisk.

'Looks like she's still working,' observed Sophie as they came up to the front of the bakery. The shop was empty of customers but the lights in the kitchen were on and there was a shadowy figure behind the counter.

Their subway journey home had been a painless ride now that rush hour had died down and to Sophie's relief, they'd fallen into an easy discussion when she'd spotted he was reading Jack Kerouac's *On The Road*. Having seen the film recently – on her own, as usual, since James never wanted to go to the pictures (probably because he'd already been with his wife) – she was interested to find out what he thought of the bleak story.

Todd followed her as she pushed open the still-open door of the bakery.

'Hey, Sophie, how is it going?' asked Wes, his big rumbling voice very quiet as he wiped his hands on a tea towel before stepping out from behind the counter. 'Todd.'

'Good. Where's Bella?'

Wes's face crumpled in concern and he jerked his head towards the kitchen. 'She's taking a moment.'

'Is she OK?'

A slight hint of panic darted in his eyes and his mouth pulled that *I have no idea what to say that's not going to get me into trouble* shape. 'Kinda. I've been helping to hold the fort.'

It didn't occur to Sophie not to go straight in to see Bella. She seemed to have a gene which made her incapable of not offering to help.

She found Bella in the kitchen, her hair tied up in a blue gingham scarf, head on her forearms on the stainless-steel table.

'Don't tell me it's not hygienic. I don't care,' she intoned without raising her head.

'I wasn't planning to.'

Bella looked up, her eyes red-rimmed and baggy. 'Sophie. Sorry. Didn't know it was you.'

'I came to say hello. Are you OK? Is there anything I can do to help?'

'Stop me being so damn successful.' Bella shook her head. 'Crazy. For the last three months, I've been working for a break like this. Today ... the phone has not stopped. Mrs Baydon has some serious friends. The rainbow cakes for her nephew's coming-out party have been a major hit. Which is great but ... four cupcake commissions. Hell, I can't turn them down. I need to figure out when I'm going to find time to bake five hundred cakes, run the café and come up with the preliminary designs for a wedding cake by next Saturday. It's a seriously big break for me, top-notch society wedding. The cake has got to be a showstopper that everyone is going to talk about. And get my name out there. And I haven't got a single original, creative idea at the moment.' Bella sank her head back into her arms. 'I'm being a wimp. Ignore me. I'm tired and emotional. Damn hormones all over the place. Bastards.'

'So what you're basically saying is that you need a shit-hot assistant, who can bake like a dream when she's not at the day job. And someone who interned on a wedding magazine one summer and can brainstorm wedding-cake ideas until the cows come home.' Sophie hopped up onto the stainless-steel top next to her, swinging her legs as she looked at Bella, whose head shot up like a startled ostrich.

'Seriously?'

'Yes.' Sophie nodded, delighted she could help.

'You know I'm going to take shameless advantage of you and I really can't afford to pay you.'

'Bella,' Sophie put on her assertive voice, one that didn't come out that often. 'I *want* to help.'

'Well, I'm not going to say no.'

'Actually, there is a payback.' She'd realised last week that it was all very well suggesting parkin, but she was going to have to do some playing with the recipe to get it right, as they didn't sell exactly the same ingredients in America. 'Can I use your kitchen to do some recipe testing?'

'Sure. Course you can.'

'And I might want to pick your brains, about a few ideas.'

'Two heads are better than one. You might be able to help me come up with some ideas for this darn wedding cake.'

Sophie put out her hand.

Bella grasped it and shook it.

'It's a deal,' said Sophie. 'Right, when do you want me to get started?'

'Are you sure? I mean … this Saturday would be great. Wes, just about the sweetest, although dumbest, man on the planet

– don't get me started on him – offered to come in, but he has his own shop to run. Left his own place short-handed today to help me and he's still here now. But I couldn't say no, I had to make three batches of cookie dough for the breakfast crowd tomorrow and knock up a couple of cheese-cakes. Normally I'd have done them before but with the rainbow-cake commission, I got a bit behind.'

'No problem,' said Sophie, jumping off the counter. 'I'll be here bright and early on Saturday.'

'Saturday?' Todd's voice came from the doorway.

'Sophie's going to be my right-hand girl.'

'Is she now?' His casual stance, arms folded as he leaned against the doorway, didn't fool Sophie.

'OK, OK. Todd, yes I need some help. I bit off more than I can chew. Happy now?' Bella sounded defensive.

'Of course not, Bels. And I'm not going to say anything to the family. And if you need some help, why didn't you ask me?'

'I didn't ask Sophie, she offered.'

Todd's mouth pursed as he shot an accusing look at Sophie. 'She would. All work and no play is making English a very dull girl. She needs to get out more.'

'*She* is right here,' said Sophie stoutly. 'Besides, it's not work ...'

Bella snorted.

'Well, not the same. Not *work*, work. It'll be fun as well.'

Todd's eyebrows rose in amusement.

'Now you're making me feel guilty,' said Bella.

'I've got a deal for you. Sophie works for you on Saturday

111

and on Sunday I'll take her out and show her Brooklyn. It's about time English did some sightseeing.'

'Perfect,' said Bella. 'Then everyone's happy.'

'Er hello,' piped up Sophie. 'Do I have any say in this?'

Wes stood behind Todd and laughed, 'Not with these two, you don't. I'd go with the flow if I were you. It's much easier.'

Chapter 8

'That's nine dollars and ninety-five cents,' said Sophie, handing over two large espressos, a cinnamon bagel and a very generous slice of Maisie's strawberry cheesecake, which was the last one. They'd already sold out of the cinnamon-and-caramel cheesecake within an hour of opening this morning, but Maisie was on her way, as promised, with fresh supplies.

'Thanks. I love your accent. Where are you from? London?'

'Yes.'

'I love London. The royal family. Buckingham Palace. Harry Potter. Those red buses. Black cabs. It's all so cute. We were there last fall. Hey Mollie, this girl's from London.' Sophie smiled. In the last two hours, she'd had much the same conversation, about ten times.

Mollie looked up from where she was draping a jacket over the back of a chair and came over. 'We loved London. What are you doing over here?'

Sophie explained about her job swap to the friendly couple and spent another few minutes as they told her they lived around the corner, were renovating an apartment and had

113

been out for a bike ride. It wasn't just Mollie and Jim that stopped to chat. As the morning passed, Sophie found the mixed Saturday-morning crowd of happening and hip Brooklynites fascinating. This place was so different to London. The few times she'd worked in Katie's Kanesnegle, the café her friend owned, she'd enjoyed serving busy office workers and tourists, but here there was a surprising sense of community. After a week in Manhattan, Brooklyn was a welcome antidote to the city buzz and that sense of manic activity, where people on the street marched with purpose, seeming to need to be somewhere yesterday. On the subway, like on the tube, everyone avoided catching anyone's eyes.

There were young families; smart, slender and fit-looking parents who opted for super-skinny lattes and ordered Bella's special Stealthy Healthy cupcakes for their very well-behaved children who invariably came complete with mini iPad. There were also trendy young couples, some in Lycra leggings and fleece tops, clearly rewarding themselves after their morning run with Bella's daily Cappuccino and Cookie combo special. And dotted between them, poring over newspapers or laptops, devouring bagels and black coffee, were other couples, in their early and mid thirties, uniform in jeans, white sneakers and coloured T-shirts, with the sort of logos and branding that put them in the upper price bracket.

It was interesting to see the way in which their preferred seating choices immediately zoned the bakery into distinct areas. The sporty couples tended to sit in neat corners taking up the minimum space at the bistro tables at the front of the bakery, while the families spread themselves out around the tables, filling the space around them with coats, bags, buggies and toys. The weekend execs, as Sophie had labelled them, had colonised the sofas but politely shifted up to let others of their tribe share the area.

Judging by the number of people that greeted Bella by name whenever she popped out of the kitchen, a lot of the customers were regulars. There was a homely, friendly feel to the bakery as if everyone's visit was integral to their weekend, part of their weekly routine. No one seemed hurried or harried and they were happy to chat to each other as they waited in line.

Bella's Saturday girls, high-school students Beth and Gina, expertly weaved around the tables collecting cups and plates with the youthful grace of dancers, collecting up tips and depositing them in the glass jar behind the till. Both had been a great help in the first hour as Sophie found her feet.

Towards eleven the vibe changed as the families drifted away, the exercise bunnies left and the hungover brunch crew descended, craving sugar hits and large coffees.

Sophie took a break for lunch with Bella in the kitchen.

'How's it going?'

'Good. I had no idea there was such a community feel.'

'There is round here. A village vibe, if you like.'

Sophie laughed. 'That's the New York version of village, I think.'

Bella smiled back. 'Not an English ye olde village?'

'Definitely not, but there's something. Everyone seems so – I don't know – positive. Upbeat. Cheerful.'

'I think people respond to the environment. I deliberately tried to create that positive feel.'

Sophie looked up at the message above the counter, which changed daily. Today it read: *Every morning you wake up with two options, to continue to sleep with your dreams or to wake up and chase them. The choice is yours.*

Following her gaze, Bella beamed. 'Not just that, but take the girls, Gina and Beth. Took me weeks to find the right people to work here. I want can-do, happy people. If you weren't like you are, even though I was desperate for help, I wouldn't have asked you. And as a result I have a real core of regulars from the neighbourhood. During the week, it's the commuters who grab a coffee and my homemade breakfast bars en route to work. Then there are the oldies who come in after their morning hike. Lunchtimes are busy with local workers grabbing bagels. And early afternoon is bedlam. All the yummy mummies come in with their kids for my Stealthy Healthy cakes.'

'I was wondering about those. What's in them?'

'Fruit and vegetables. Courgette and lemon, carrot and orange, pumpkin and apple. The kids have no idea what's in them but it makes the mums feel a lot better about giving them a post-school treat.'

'What a brilliant idea. I might steal that for the magazine. Would be a great feature.'

'Feel free. I'll show you how to make them.'

In the last half hour, the numbers of customers had slowed to a trickle and the glass shelves were pleasingly almost bare. The door opened despite the *Closed* sign and Sophie was about to call, 'We're closing,' when she realised it was Wes.

'Hey Sophie. All done yet?'

'Just about.' She indicated the last table where three people were chatting over the dregs of their coffee.

All of the other tables had been wiped clean, their chairs pushed neatly underneath, most of the washing-up had been done and only now could Sophie appreciate that her feet were starting to complain.

'I came by to see if y'all needed any more help. And to bring some more cinnamon and nutmeg over. Bella said she was running low.'

He deposited two large paper bags on the counter top, a puff of spices pumping out of the top, perfuming the air.

'Mm, they smell gorgeous. Actually, I need to get some recipe ingredients for next week. Do you do ginger?'

'Do we do ginger? Girl, of course we do. You should come on by.'

'I will. I'm sorry I haven't already. And I never thanked you properly for the Rosemary. I was a bit spaced out that night.'

'No worries.'

'And I'd really like to buy some herb plants for the deck.'

'I can sort you out there, what sort of things would you like?'

'Basil.'

He laughed and corrected her pronunciation, 'You mean *baazel*. We've got basil. Lemon basil. Sweet basil. Thai basil. Cinnamon basil. Genovese basil.'

'Wow. That's a lot of b-b ...' nope, she couldn't bring herself to say it the American way, 'basil.'

Wes winked at her. 'You say tomato, I say tomato.'

117

'I'd love some Thai basil.'

'You cook?'

Sophie smiled. 'I haven't been cooking for myself recently, but I think I'm about to change that.'

'Hey, Wes.' Bella bustled out of the kitchen as the last customers wandered out with cheery waves. She shot across and bolted the door behind them. 'We're about all done, thanks to Sophie. She's been amazing.'

Sophie untied her gingham apron and wilted against the counter.

'How about I take you for a drink, to say thank you, Sophie. I *so* need a bucket of wine and then Chinese take-away, my treat. If you're up for it. You too Wes, if you fancy it?'

'That's very kind but I'm sure you two ladies have plenty to talk about. I'll be heading off. See you tomorrow.'

'You could come just for a drink,' said Bella.

Wes shrugged and ambled to the door with a wave. Sophie noticed a wistful expression in Bella's eyes as she watched him lope down the street.

'Right, drink?'

'Sounds perfect,' said Sophie. 'As long as I get to sit down. I'm used to standing cooking all day at work but I hadn't counted on doing that when I put these on this morning.' She looked down at her beloved Converse.

'I have to shower and change first. I'll knock for you in twenty.'

'Done,' said Sophie, figuring she could be ready in twenty minutes, liking the fact Bella was the sort of person who didn't waste any time dithering.

True to her word, Bella knocked exactly twenty minutes later, looking fresh and bright in skinny jeans and a red-and-white Breton-striped T-shirt. Sophie had been so hot and sticky, she'd opted for her favourite dress. A Joules T-shirt dress, with a floral pattern overlaying pale-blue intermittent stripes. She liked the Englishness of it. Made her feel like herself again.

'I can't tell you how grateful I am,' said Bella, linking her arm through Sophie's and steering her along the street which bustled with people. The evening was balmy and there was a holiday-like atmosphere. They arrived at a door with blacked-out windows on one side and Bella led the way into what felt as if it had once been a front room. Wooden benches and tables in rows were crammed in but most of them were empty.

'This place is a well-kept secret.'

'I can see that,' said Sophie as her words echoed in the empty space.

'Come on.' With a nod at the silent barman who gave her a barely-there greeting, Bella ordered a bottle of wine and, clutching two glasses, led the way up a small, dimly lit, narrow staircase.

The door at the head of the stairs opened out onto a broad rooftop and it was like stepping out of a long, dark tunnel. The rooftop buzzed with noise and chatter, and every table was full of bearded hipsters, young couples and groups of girls in strappy tops and big sunglasses.

'I wasn't expecting this,' said Sophie, looking around.

'Great vibe, isn't it?' said Bella proudly. 'We tend to keep quiet about it. It's like the neighbourhood bar.' She waved to a couple on a table on the other side of the terrace, as she set the glasses onto the last free table and poured two very generous portions.

'Cheers. And thank you.'

'No, thank *you*,' said Sophie. 'I enjoyed myself today.'

'You shouldn't have said that. Like I said, I will take advantage. Shout if my demands get too much.'

Together they took a long sip of wine.

The cold liquid hit the spot and for a minute Sophie felt things might just be alright.

'Are you still going with Todd tomorrow?' asked Bella, looking worried.

'Something wrong?'

'I'm just warning you not to get your hopes up too much. Saturdays are a big night out with the crowd he runs around with. They party hard. Trust-fund preppy types.'

'Thanks, I'm not sure he thought ahead that much, I think he was being kind,' she broke off, remembering the scene in the office, 'and a bit miffed that someone had dissed his beloved Brooklyn. It was a bit of one-upmanship.'

'That sounds more like Todd.' Bella's quick acceptance was followed by a considered breath and then she added, 'Although don't get me wrong. Todd is kind. He's my cousin. I love him. He's not had it easy ... but don't ... don't mistake it for anything else. He's lovely, or rather can be lovely, but whatever you do, don't make the mistake of falling in love with him. I've seen it too many times before. Girls are always falling for him, but he's never interested.'

'You don't need to worry on my account.' Sophie relaxed back into her chair. 'I've been burned. Not going back for quite some time.'

'Ah, I did wonder. You have that ... sort of bruised-around-the-soul look about you. Every now and then you drift off.'

'Damn, I thought I was doing a good job of hiding things.'

'Was it a hideous break-up?'

'Something like that.' Sophie looked away towards the pink glow where the sun was starting to sink, carefully examining the silhouetted roof lines.

'And you're not ready to talk about it?' observed Bella, candid as ever.

'Sorry.' Her eyes met Bella's with quiet apology. 'It's ...'

'Don't you worry, honey. I understand. Men, eh? Although with me, it's more a case of unrequited love rather than the man done me wrong.'

'Oh, that sounds ... sad.'

'Or darn frustrating. You know it's right but ... he's so pig-headed. Can't or won't see it. I really need to move on. Find someone else. But it's hard when you see them all the time and you keep wondering if maybe ...'

'Wes?'

Bella slammed her hand down on the wooden bench table. 'Aw, shoot, is it that obvious?'

Sophie bit back a smile. 'You kind of gave it away then, but I did wonder when you asked him earlier to join us.'

'And he turned me down in a flat minute.'

'Maybe he didn't want to intrude.'

Bella gave her a stern look. 'Really? I'm not buying that. If he was interested, I don't think he'd worry about being an unwanted third. But then sometimes he seems ... Why help in the bakery the minute I'm under pressure? He's the knight in shining armour whenever I need him. He doesn't have to do that. That's the bit I don't get. It's like he blows hot and cold ... Sometimes I think he might be interested and then I think I'm imagining it.'

'Is he seeing anyone else?'

'Not that I know of. But if he was I'd back right off. He's never mentioned anyone. And I'm pretty sure he's not gay.'

'That's a bonus,' said Sophie, laughing at Bella's suddenly gloomy expression.

'You're telling me. My high-school crush, unrequited throughout my teens, came out not long after we graduated. I was devastated.'

'Oooh, not good.'

'Tell me about it. But I don't think Wes is gay. He's mentioned girlfriends in the past. Not that that's necessarily an indicator.'

'You could always be direct, invite him out.'

Bella gave her a very sharp look. 'You think I haven't tried? Although, to be fair, I might have to be sort of circuitous about it. I haven't actually come out and invited him on a date. Is that what you would do?'

With wide-eyed horror Sophie shook her head. 'No way. I would never have the nerve, but you ... you've got that New York directness.'

'You think? I still couldn't do it. Despite my big mouth, I'm not that out there. How would I bear it if he turned me down?'

'But what if he said yes?' said Sophie, her little ray of sunshine finally reasserting itself. It had been dormant for so long, it was like trying on a new pair of wings for size.

'What if he said no?'

'Er, hello, what happened to all the positive vibes you channel in the bakery? If you asked him, then you'd know. What's the worst that can happen? What's the best that could happen? You can survive the worst, you can move on. It might be a bit wobbly for a while ... but think what if the best happened? Wes said yes. You went out on a date. Wouldn't that be wonderful? You'll never know if you don't ask. At least you'd know one way or the other.'

'Jeez, are you Pollyanna's love child or something?'

'Or something. I learned a long time ago. You can choose how you feel about things. You can choose to be sad. You can choose to ignore something ...' Sophie stopped short and then let out a tiny sigh, '... and I am very, very bad at following my own advice.'

'You've not been choosing wisely?'

'I've not been choosing at all,' said Sophie stoutly. 'But ... there's a guy at work.'

'Oh, do tell.'

'He's asked me out to dinner.'

'And?'

'I don't know. After ... I'm not sure.'

'Girl, you have to get back on the bike. And what have you got to lose?'

'Er, hello?'

Bella gave her an impish grin. 'I'm great at telling other people what to do.'

'OK,' said Sophie, suddenly sitting straighter, 'I'll go out with Paul, if you ask Wes out.'

Chapter 9

Sophie pulled a face at herself in the mirror and with her brush tugged at her hair, split it in two and plaited it into scruffy plaits. She didn't want to impress Todd. Where the hell had the incipient excitement dancing low in her belly come from? It could just sod off. It was like being fifteen again and you spot the best-looking boy in the school glancing your way across the corridor and your stomach gets in a bit of a spin before you realise that actually he's looking at Laura Westfield who's already got a 36C bust.

Pulling on her favourite pair of jeans, she rubbed her finger over the threadbare worn-out patch on her thigh with a laugh. They were now officially trendy, although it was only because they were so old and comfortable that she couldn't bear to part with them. OK, they also did good things to the shape of her arse, but that was an added bonus. The faded blue T-shirt vest came out because it was clean and then she topped it with a baggy white linen shirt.

She gave herself an approving look in the mirror. It didn't look as if she were trying to impress anyone, and then she added battered royal-blue Converse not because they matched the vest but because they were practical. She had no idea where Todd planned to take her, but he'd said it was a tour of Brooklyn, so she surmised there'd be quite a bit of walking involved.

At the last minute, she slapped on some of her favourite tinted moisturiser that gave her skin a golden glow, a touch of her standard understated Lancôme lipstick and a quick brush of mascara. There were some limits to her pride.

Packing her favourite Love Food tote bag with essentials like water, a camera, her phone, plasters, paracetamol and an umbrella, she felt like a proper tourist and for the first time since she'd arrived had that holiday feeling of excitement and enthusiasm.

When Todd rang the bell on the intercom, she patted her bag and skipped down the stairs, throwing open the door with a wide smile.

'Morning.'

'Oh Jeez, you're a morning person.' Todd lifted his sunglasses to reveal rather bleary eyes.

'Late one?'

'Just a bit. Party in Tribeca. New club opening. Didn't get to bed until after three. The things I do for my job.'

'Poor you. That's work?'

'Hell yeah, it's work.' He sounded fierce and very slightly defensive.

'Are you OK for today?' she asked, her spirits plummeting slightly. She'd been looking forward to this all morning and the thought of having to find something to do for the rest of the day suddenly made her feel hollow inside. 'We can always take a rain check. Perhaps go for a coffee.' She was rather proud of herself, using the phrase made her sound like a local, or at least she thought it did, and made light of her disappointment.

'No way, José. No lightweights here. I'm fine. Just keep the volume down and a bit less of the Heidi, wide-eyed bounce. Loving the plaits, by the way.'

'I'll do my best. And thank you. So where are we going?' She looked down the street. At ten o'clock in the morning it was busy with families and groups, everyone heading out for brunch.

'Bella's first for coffee to go, and then nine blocks north to Hoyt-Schermerhorn to pick up the subway. And then,' he paused, smiling to himself, 'actually, do you know what English, let's make it a surprise.' He steered her towards the bakery and pushed open the door, ushering her through first.

Sophie paused in the doorway and grinned. 'I love surprises.'

'Somehow I thought you might. Not normally my thing. I like to know.' His jaw tensed very slightly. 'That way no one ends up disappointed.'

'I won't be disappointed.' Sophie, still poised in the doorway, tipped up her face with a happy sigh. 'The sun is shining and it feels like I'm on holiday. And I have my own personal guide, which makes it even better. I don't even have to do any thinking. I can relax.'

'What, you think you're in safe hands?' asked Todd, a flirtatious dimple appearing to the right of his mouth.

'I didn't say that.' Sophie shot him a severe, quelling look. 'I don't think any woman should ever think of you as a safe pair of hands.' She walked into the bakery and joined the queue in front of the counter.

'Have you been listening to my cousin again? She's not a reliable witness. Bears grudges. I wouldn't listen to a word she says.'

'Not just her … remember, I spend half my days fending off calls from Amy, Lacey and Charlene.'

He grinned wolfishly. 'I can't help it if I'm irresistible.' His eyes danced with amusement and she knew he was sending himself up.

'Who knew girls in New York were so desperate?' said Sophie, grinning back at him.

'Are English girls more discerning?' asked Todd.

'Absolutely,' said Sophie, her lips twitching. 'We like a touch of brains with our brawn and good looks.'

'Ouch. What happened to Heidi?'

'Heidi's alive and well, she's just in touch with her inner minx some days,' retorted Sophie.

'For that you can buy the coffees.'

'Morning Sophie,' said Bella. 'Todd. What can I get you guys?'

'Morning Bella, ooh you look rough.'

Sophie nudged him in the ribs. 'And you wonder why she gives you a bad press.' She shook her head in sympathy at Bella, who smiled warmly back before simpering at Todd, 'Thanks, dear cous … wanna take your sunglasses off?'

'Not yet.'

Bella turned back to Sophie. 'And how come you look so bright-eyed and bushy tailed this morning?'

'You two were out on the town last night?' asked Todd, giving Sophie's face a quick study.

'I drank lots of water when I got in,' said Sophie, smugly. 'And took two paracetamol.'

'I should have. Or maybe we shouldn't have had that second bottle of Pinot. Was fun though.'

'It was. Thanks Bella. I had a great time.' It was the best night she'd had since she'd arrived in New York.

'What were you doing?'

'Just went to Harry's bar and then Chinese take-away at mine,' said Bella, handing over their coffees.

'And that constitutes a great night out? You two need to get out more.'

'We can't all be *Mr I'm papped coming out of the top clubs at 2 a.m.*,' said Bella, waving her hand at Sophie's proffered ten-dollar bill. 'On the house.'

'How come I never get any on the house?'

'One, because you put a corn snake in my bed,' said Bella, snapping on the lids to their coffees and pushing them towards them, 'and two, because Sophie helped out yesterday and is going to help out this week.'

Sophie picked up the coffees as Bella turned to take the next customer's order.

'See, that's the grudge I told you about,' muttered Todd, clutching his coffee as they stepped out onto the street again.

'I'm not surprised, you must have been a horrible child.' She levelled a reproving look at him.

His face split in a wide grin, 'I did that when I was twenty-five.'

As they emerged from Fulton Station in Manhattan, Sophie felt a touch ashamed that she'd not ventured further afield in the last few weeks.

'Wow, I feel like we're in a different place altogether,' she said, staring round at the crowded streets and wide road full of traffic.

'There's nowhere quite like Manhattan, it's got a very different vibe to Brooklyn. Come on, we're not staying.'

Sophie followed him as he took them down a side street with a determined stride, his hand periodically sliding under her elbow to guide her or bumping into her to let other pedestrians squeeze past on the crowded pavements.

Todd's phone buzzed, which it had been doing rather frequently.

'Do you want to get that?'

'No, it'll go to voicemail.'

They headed towards a very busy road and then Todd pointed. In the distance she could see water, the sunlight glinting off the surface, and ahead of them the towering pillars of Brooklyn Bridge.

'I'm going to take you across the East River, across the bridge. The world's oldest suspension bridge. And one of my favourite walks in the whole city. There's nothing quite like it. You get the best of both worlds, a view of Brooklyn and then back the other way towards the Manhattan skyline. And I might treat you to an ice cream at the other end.'

As they joined the throng of people headed onto the bridge he pointed out a few landmarks including City Hall just across the street from them. Their walk was punctuated with another two calls on Todd's mobile. Both times he pulled the phone out, checked the caller id and then slid it back into his pocket.

There was an infectious sense of gaiety on the path, as they strolled alongside walkers, tourists and the runners and cyclists separated by a designated lane. Under the midday sun with no shade, the breeze from the water was more than welcome. Beneath them, the cars made a rhythmic thunk, thunk noise as they crossed the sections of the road.

Todd came to stand behind her, pointing out the different skyscrapers, resting one hand on her shoulder, his animated face barely inches from hers. 'That's the World Trade Center, Four Seasons Hotel. That one with the green roof is the Woolworth's Building and once, can you believe it, the tallest building in New York.'

As usual, his face was alive and alight with enthusiasm, his casual touch natural and at ease. It brought back a sudden memory: James, stiff and impatient, on a rare outing to see an exhibition at the National Portrait Museum and he discreetly shaking her hand off his arm as he dug through his pockets to check his wallet was still there.

'Hey, English, there's a new restaurant opening on the Upper West side in a couple of weeks,' Todd piped up as they resumed walking. 'You can come and be my foodie wingman.'

'Oh, I can, can I? Because I've got nothing better to do with my time, than drop everything to go with you.' Sophie put her hands on her hips and shook her head, half teasing about his calm assumption she'd be happy to accompany him. He really was just too sure of himself.

'English, please, I could really use your help.'

Sophie immediately softened. 'Why me? I'm more than happy to help but,' she lifted her shoulders, 'from what I can gather, you've got a queue of volunteers only too happy to step in at any time.'

'That's part of the problem. I ask them to come with me, then they get the wrong idea.'

'Must be tough being so irresistible,' Sophie teased. 'Can't you take a mate?'

Todd was no doubt used to women trying to impress him all the time. She wasn't about to fall into that camp.

'I could, but it's useful to get a female perspective. You tend to get some funny looks if you start checking out the ladies' restrooms. Besides, this time I can talk about the club vibe, the people, and you can tell me if the chef is any good or too high on coke to know his saffron from his paprika.' He turned to her, those dazzling blue eyes like headlamps focused directly on her. For a dizzying second her pulse took off at a canter, mistaking his earnest look for something else completely. Luckily her head was in charge. 'Please, Sophie. I need your help.'

Damn, was it even possible to say no to him? 'You know, don't you?'

'Know what?' he asked, suddenly all innocence.

She narrowed her eyes and studied his face, watching as that dimple flashed and his eyes slid over her head in studied avoidance.

'That I'm incapable of saying no, if someone uses the magic word *help*.'

'I might have noticed. Pleeease, Sophie. I really, really need your help.'

'Put the puppy-dog eyes away. They won't work.'

'Sure?' His winsome blinking made her burst out laughing. 'Too much?' he asked.

'Way too much.'

They carried on walking, Sophie, like the other tourists, stopping to snap away. It was a blissful day and Todd was good company, telling her various interesting facts about the bridge.

His phone went again and he pulled it out of his pocket. With a wince he rubbed at his chin.

'Will you excuse me? I ought to take this.'

With so much to look at, Sophie told him it wasn't a problem.

'Hey Amy. I got your message. Yeah, I'm sorry, I've been tied up. Babe,' his voiced deepened, 'not that sort of tied up.'

Sophie, hearing the laughter on the other end of the phone, immediately remembered Amy, of the high-pitched giggles, leaving messages at work.

'Amy, you're a *very* bad girl,' he admonished, his face crinkling in a broad smile as he winked at Sophie.

She wanted to roll her eyes but his cheerful good-natured teasing of Amy was so open and friendly, it was difficult to disapprove, but it was very amusing when sudden horror crossed his face. 'Of course I haven't forgotten. Sure. The table's booked. I'll text you the address. You're in for a treat.'

'Nice save,' she teased when he said goodbye and began tapping at the screen on his phone.

'I don't like to disappoint the ladies,' he winked again, his eyebrows waggling lasciviously.

Sophie studied him, holding his gaze.

'What?'

'Nothing.' His lady-killer routine seemed a little bit too hammed up.

'Sorry, I need to make another call, d'you mind? And then I'll be all yours.'

He scrolled through his phone, tapping away.

'Aha, gotcha.' He held his phone up to his ear. 'Darla. Todd McLennan here. I've been trying to get in to do a proper review of the à *la carte* restaurant. Aw, no problem ... The food was great ... Yeah, I got the stain out. Poor guy, it *was* his first shift ... Hell, no. No one died and I have a hundred other shirts ... It was no sweat. I don't suppose there's any chance you could squeeze me in on Tuesday ... table for two? That's fantastic. Eight-fifteen. Darla, you're a star. I owe you one.'

He caught Sophie's eye and she gave him a cool look.

'Handy ... and presumably Amy need never know.'

Todd shrugged. 'I like to keep my dates happy.'

Sophie winced.

'What's the matter?'

'I'd hate to be referred to as a "date", it seems so impersonal. As if you're a pair of shoes being tried out for size. And the plural. Dates. Like they're dresses hanging in a wardrobe and you choose one to take out for an airing.'

Todd burst out laughing. 'I love that analogy, English. It's pretty accurate but dates are to find out if someone suits you.'

'Yes, but a stream of dates implies you're not taking it that seriously.'

'Or that you are taking it very seriously.'

She pursed sceptical lips, which failed to dilute the amusement on his face.

'They're dinner dates. Drinks. Dinner. Nights out.'

'I'd like to say I think the dating scene is quite different here, but the truth is, I wouldn't know.'

'So how did you meet two-year man?'

'Through work. I went to a launch party. New product.'

'Oh, I love those gigs. Last one I went to had daiquiris and Armani goody bags.'

'Mmm.' Sophie thought back to the Benson's Baking Powder event, more Darjeeling and Asda carrier bags.

'Do you know how far it is across?' asked Sophie suddenly, as a swathe of runners came jogging by in the separate lane.

'Just over a mile.'

'Do you think they run back again?' asked Sophie.

'Never thought about it.'

'I ought to start running again,' she mused out loud. 'I'm a bit nervous running on the streets around the apartment, I don't know the areas that well.' At home, you knew where to avoid. In Brooklyn, you could walk down a street and in an instant it would turn into a very different area. 'This would be quite a nice place to run, but it's a bit too far to get to.'

'I run in Prospect Park, it's about ten blocks from the bakery. I cycle up there first. You could come with me sometime if you like.'

'I don't think I want to go running with you.'

'Why not?' He actually looked quite put out, which made Sophie smile.

'Because you're probably super fit.' And would probably run at a pace she couldn't possibly keep up with and no doubt had half the female population of Brooklyn looking out for him over their cornflakes. 'And I don't have a bike. I can't remember the last time I went cycling.'

'No problem. My neighbour on the floor below me has a couple. We could cycle up and then go for a run.'

'Don't you think you ought to ask him first?'

His lips quirked. 'My neighbour's a she and I'm sure she won't say no.'

'Does anyone *ever* say no to you?' sighed Sophie, shaking her head with a rueful smile.

His face broadened with a wide beam. 'No,' he said simply. 'But I'll ask her tonight and let you know at work. Did you run with your boyfriend?'

'Ha! You're joking. I ran at the weekends, he wasn't around then.' She gave a hollow laugh, suddenly realising that it had been her way of chasing away the loneliness at the weekends when everyone else was coupled up.

They reached the end of the bridge and took a flight of stairs down to the waterfront, and Todd headed towards a white clapboard building with pale-sage green trim around the windows.

'Come on, this is the place for an ice cream and the view from the deck is great.'

'Sounds bliss. And just what I need. I hadn't realised it was going to be quite so warm.'

The ice creams were huge and Sophie wanted to try everything and dithered over Peaches and Cream, which she'd never had before and really felt she ought to try, and Butter Pecan, which sounded so delicious and she knew she'd love it.

'The lady will have Butter Pecan,' said Todd firmly, putting a casual arm around her shoulders. Sophie stiffened for a second but he seemed totally focused on the ice cream choices. 'You said today felt like a holiday. So you should have want you want.' He paused, appraising the ice creams in front of them and leaned forward and then shook his head, looking at the pretty young girl behind the counter in her red-and-white striped hat and matching apron. 'Sorry, can't do it. Peaches and Cream. Seriously, that is not a proper ice cream flavour. I was going to have it so that you could try it but no, I'll have the Double Chocolate Chunk.' The girl behind the counter smiled back at him, because who wouldn't when Todd was giving you his full attention?

Ice creams bought and paid for, they wandered out onto the wide wooden deck and crossed to the far rail right on the water. Sophie couldn't take her eyes from the view of the towering skyscrapers.

'This is one of my favourite views,' sighed Todd.

'City boy, then?'

'Hmm, no, because I love the beach too. My family has a place out in Long Island. The beach there is incredible, another one of my favourite places. What about you – city girl, beach or country?'

'Well, not so much the beach. Have you seen the weather

in Britain? I grew up in the country, which was ... OK, but going to the city, to London, was an escape. I think I'm a city girl. I love London, Barcelona, Paris, and I've been to Copenhagen. That was gorgeous.'

They swapped stories of the places they'd seen while admiring the high rises of downtown Manhattan opposite them.

'It almost doesn't look real. It's so perfect today. I feel like I'm in a film or a photograph.' She pointed across at the water, where the cerulean-blue sky, with the odd cloud, was reflected in the mirrored windows of the skyscrapers opposite. 'I ought to take some pictures. Prove to my friend Kate that I'm getting out and about.'

Todd seemed perfectly happy to walk alongside her as she took lots of pictures of the Manhattan skyline and the bridge above. Two stereotypically perfect all-American cheerleading-type girls, their blonde hair, immaculate teeth and long tanned limbs shown to their best advantage in Daisy Dukes and vest-top T-shirts, slowed and nudged each other as they walked towards Sophie and Todd. One of them gave Todd the sort of smile that hinted at a lot more than friendliness.

As they passed, Sophie took a look over her shoulder and saw that both of them had stopped and were unashamedly watching him.

'Really, some women have no shame,' said Sophie with a hint of laughter in her voice. 'I can't believe those two were blatantly ogling your bottom.'

Todd's mouth quirked at one side, something she recognised now as a precursor to his teasing. 'And you're not impressed?'

'What, by your bottom? No, not at all,' she lied, feeling a sudden flush. Since when had she started imagining men naked? Or specifically Todd. 'Is it particularly special?' she asked, keeping her voice light.

'That's what I like about you, English,' Todd punched her arm gently, 'you're good for my ego.'

'Glad I can be of service,' she said crisply, grateful that he wasn't a mind reader. At least if those two young women's reaction was anything to go by, it meant that her response to him was perfectly normal and nothing she should worry about.

Chapter 10

The maître d' fussed over her, shaking out her napkin and handing them each a menu as if it were the Holy Grail. Sophie took hers, conscious that there was a slight tremble in her hand. It had been a long time since she'd done this and the way her stomach was behaving, she wasn't sure she was going to be able to eat anything. *Relax, Sophie. Relax.* She nodded her thanks to the hovering man before looking over at Paul and giving him a smile.

'This is very nice.' It was the sort of restaurant that shimmered with quiet elegance and understated style and you knew the prices would be ferociously high. Classic formality was etched on every table with their crisp white cloths which were impeccably laid out with a collection of long-stemmed crystal glassware, starched napkins and silvery cutlery arranged with parallel precision. None of which was helping her to feel at ease.

'Yes, it's French. I figured being from Europe you'd be OK with French food.' Paul looked worried for a moment.

'As long as it's not escargot,' said Sophie, feeling that perhaps he was as anxious as she was. Talking snails was always a good ice-breaker. 'Really not my favourite thing.'

'The chef here is renowned,' Paul said, his face impassive as he picked up the menu. 'It's a very good restaurant.'

Under the table she pleated the edge of her napkin. OK, say perhaps Paul didn't know what escargot were, rather than missing her opening cue for more light-hearted conversation.

'Have you been here before?' she asked, gazing around at the other smartly dressed diners talking in hushed tones. For a minute she wondered how expensive the menu was.

'Yes, a few times. Mainly for business lunches. It's the first time,' he paused, his eyes meeting and holding hers with charming intent, 'I've brought a date here.'

Sophie shifted in her chair, crossing her legs, suddenly unsure how she felt about that. Ignoring the flicker of what-the-hell-am-I-doing unease, she said, 'I'm honoured,' adding a big smile to show she was teasing. She wasn't ready for this. James had taken her for dinner the first time they'd been out. To a restaurant not dissimilar to this.

'You look very nice, by the way.'

'Thank you.' Now she was glad, despite the very quick turnaround, that she'd dashed home after work to change into a dress and heels before travelling back to Manhattan to meet him. The quick pep talk from Bella had helped too, although as yet she hadn't held up her end of the bargain. 'So do you,' she said with a quick smile. The man definitely wore a suit well. 'Nice tie.'

He peeled the tie from his shirt and held it up, looking slightly bemused, as if he'd forgotten he owned it. 'Oh, thanks. I've had it a while.'

'It's not your special going-out-to-dinner tie, then?' asked Sophie, desperate to lighten things up.

For a minute Paul wavered, as if it might go either way – take himself seriously or give in to Sophie's teasing. Thankfully his face relaxed. 'Busted. I was too busy to go home and change before dinner. It's been another mad day in the office. I almost envy you down on your floor. It always seems so laid back down there. I guess you're all more creative.'

Relieved that they'd moved onto easier ground, Sophie stopped fiddling with her napkin.

'I think we're more like ducks, it looks like we're gliding along on the surface but underneath we're paddling like mad. We're always chasing a deadline. But when you're writing copy you tend to hunker down and keep quiet. That's probably why you think it's laid back. All the noise and commotion takes place in the test kitchens.'

Paul shuddered. 'I never go in there. That really does look like chaos!'

'It is,' said Sophie, 'but it's great fun.'

'You enjoy your work, then?'

'Yeah, I love food. Writing about food. Eating food. Sharing my knowledge about it. Educating people. Getting people to try new things.'

'Wow.' Paul seemed taken aback by her sudden burst of enthusiasm. 'I meant being a journalist. Writing copy. I mean, presumably you trained and you can write about anything?'

Sophie shook her head. 'Not really. I was lucky. I kind of fell into food writing. I don't really see myself as a journalist.

Food is my passion and what I know. I can't imagine writing about anything else.'

'But where do you see yourself in ten years' time? If you want to be an editor, you're going to have to branch out. I guess you could go into broadcasting.' His blue eyes softened. 'You're certainly pretty enough.'

Sophie blushed and picked at the tines of the fork on the table in front of her. 'Gosh, not something I'd thought of. At the moment, I'm taking things one day at a time.' She gave him a direct look. 'Last time I thought I'd got things all mapped out, they went drastically wrong.'

Paul frowned. 'But you need a plan, don't you? Especially when things have gone wrong. Otherwise how else are you going to pick yourself back up? You'll end up drifting. I mean, you must have a plan. You're here for what ... a couple of months? And then you'll go back to London. So you know what you're doing then, right?'

Sophie stared at him, a wry smile coming to her face. 'At the moment, I'm the girl without a plan. I'm here for six months and then I go back to London. And I have absolutely no idea what I'm going to do when I get back.' She put out a hand and patted his on the opposite side of the table. 'You've gone white.'

He laughed. 'Too right. I've got my career mapped out for the next seven years.'

'Wow. Seven. That's very precise.'

'I've built in some contingency,' he gave a nonchalant shrug, 'it could be five.'

'And will you still be in magazines by then? New York? I

mean, how do you know? I've got a friend who was aiming high in PR but gave it all up to run her own café in London. And she's much happier.'

'Never going to happen.' With a shake of his head, he picked up his menu. 'I'm going to be sales director of the company in the next two years, move to a major news outlet in the two years after that, and ultimately I'll be on the board of a major media conglomerate in the next ten years. I'm not planning on leaving New York anytime soon.'

'Gosh, I admire your determination,' she said, following suit and taking a look at the list of dishes. 'Now, Mr Hotshot, what do you recommend?'

'Depends what you like.' He looked worried for a moment. 'I should have checked your dietary preferences.'

Sophie let out a shout of laughter. 'I'm a food writer, remember. We like everything.'

'That's a relief. I should have asked before. One girl I took out was a vegetarian and every restaurant we went to, she was so picky. I mean, if there's no vegetarian dishes on the menu, why not have a plate of vegetables? Or a fish dish. I'm glad you're so easy ... I mean, you, er, like everything.'

She wanted to tease him again but he'd ducked his head and was studying the menu for all he was worth.

'Right.' She focused on a couple of entrées that sounded interesting: a crayfish-and-prawn timbale and a tarte flambé of Alsatian bacon and onion. Mind made up, she folded her menu.

'I think I'm going to have two starters.'

'Two starters?' Paul glanced over his shoulder as if he

expected the menu police to pounce on such maverick behaviour. 'Are you sure?'

'Yes, one instead of a main course. They both sound delicious and I can't decide between either of them. I always like to try new things whenever I get the chance.'

'Now, that sounds like a good plan,' said Paul, propping his elbows on the table and putting his chin in his hands. 'I like that idea. Expand your horizons. That sort of thing is always going to be useful in business. You never know who you're going to have to meet and impress. Sophie, you are full of surprises.'

When they'd ordered, the maître d' not so much blinking an eyelid at Sophie's request, and the wine waiter had opened an expensive bottle of wine, Paul lifted his glass in toast.

'To you, Sophie. A belated welcome to New York. Maybe I could show you around sometime? I'd like to spend some time with you. Get to know you.'

Sophie sucked in a careful breath and played with her glass for a minute, taking a long slow sip of wine. 'That ... that would be nice. To be honest, I've recently come out of a long relationship.' She gave a self-deprecating sigh. 'I did have a plan, actually. To steer clear of men for the next five hundred years.' She took another swallow of wine and looked down at the pristine white tablecloth.

She felt Paul's warm hand laid on top of hers.

'Now that would be a terrible shame. You deserve to have some fun. Enjoy the city while you're here. New York can be a pretty lonely place, especially at the weekends. I could show you round.'

It was the mention of the weekends. Sharing Sunday with Todd had been the best day since she'd arrived. It would be awful to go back to London and not have seen New York properly. And exploring it with a native was going to be so much more fun than doing it on her own. She couldn't imagine Todd would have too many more free weekends, what with his harem of girls on the go.

Sophie lifted a cheeky eyebrow. 'How do you feel about taking me to the Empire State Building?'

Paul looked nonplussed for a second. 'Is that a trick question? I'd love to. When would you like to go?'

'And I said to Ed, that we wouldn't let him have our bread again.' Edie finished her story and put her coffee cup down with a decisive flourish to demonstrate her assertiveness.

Sophie sipped at her coffee, enjoying the cosy atmosphere of the bakery kitchen as she and Bella took a well-deserved break. They'd been hard at it since seven o'clock, baking and decorating cupcakes for a birthday party and cutting up a Genoese sponge into intricate shapes for a sixtieth wedding anniversary cake. Thankfully Beth and Gina had everything under control in the bakery, managing the mid-morning rush.

It was now apparent that Ed and Edie's Saturday morning delivery round finished at the bakery in time for coffee and cake, and that invariably Maisie made an appearance at the same time.

'Go you,' said Bella. 'It's brave turning business down, but sometimes it's the right thing to do. I might have to turn down a wedding-cake commission.'

'Why?' asked Sophie, sitting up straighter and stifling a yawn, brought on by the warm kitchen combined with getting home late the previous evening. 'Who?' She knew that every commission counted while Bella was still trying to establish herself as a cake designer.

'Eleanor Doyle, the interior designer. She's impossible.'

'I thought all brides were impossible,' said Ed.

'Don't you go falling for the bridezilla cliché, young man,' chided Maisie, pretending to clip him around the ear.

'Remember, *Impossible* is *I'm possible*,' piped up Edie.

'Thanks for the reminder,' said Bella, her voice dry. 'But on this occasion, believe me, I'm struggling to say positive. Most brides are lovely. Excited. Enthusiastic. Sweet.' Bella shook her head in uncharacteristic despair. 'Eleanor's ... so cool. Unemotional. I can't get a handle on what she wants at all. And I need to because she could be a very influential client. Well connected.'

'Has she given you a brief?' asked Maisie, patting Bella on the knee. 'You're not going to turn this one down.'

'Only over the phone and it's so vague. *I want something that evokes me, the person, and the man I'm marrying,*' Bella mimicked in a clipped accent.

'You need to meet her,' said Sophie so decisively that everyone around the coffee table looked up at her, almost startled by her unexpected firmness.

'Why?' asked Bella, looking interested.

'She said "I want", "me" – it's all about her. She talks about the man she's marrying, not the man *I love*. Not even his name. I'd say the cake has to be about her, who she is, what she does. And it's got to be about status. You need to get to know a bit more about her. What makes her tick. What she likes. What makes her feel important.'

'Whoa! Go Sophie!' said Maisie. 'She's right.'

'You are,' said Bella, immediately picking up her mobile. 'If I fix up a meeting with her, will you come with me?'

Before Sophie even had a chance to nod in agreement, the call was in progress and an appointment was fixed up with Eleanor for the beginning of the following week.

'Well, that's sorted out my Tuesday night,' laughed Sophie.

'Darn, you haven't got another date, have you?'

'Another date?' Maisie's warm brown eyes glowed with sudden interest.

'Yes.' Bella threw a proud arm across Sophie's shoulders. 'She went out last night.'

'See, I told you,' Maisie beamed. 'And what's he like?'

'Are you going to see him again?' asked Edie. 'And did he take you somewhere nice?'

Sophie laughed and threw up her hands. 'It's like the Spanish Inquisition. He's called Paul. I met him at work. He's nice. We went for dinner.'

'And?' pressed Maisie.

'And?' Sophie frowned, looking round at the four faces, unsure what she was supposed to say.

'The spark. Was it there?'

'It's too early to say.'

Maisie shook her head, her mouth crumpling. 'The first time I laid eyes on Carl, I knew.'

Edie turned to Ed. 'Did you know?'

His eyes widened. 'I was terrified of you. If you recall, I'd taken the last sack of bread flour from the shelf and you were spitting.'

Edie's grin was smug. 'I knew. There was no way I was letting him get away. I followed him home.'

'Some people might say that was stalking.'

'Or that I was desperate for flour.'

He leaned into her and rubbed his nose up against hers. 'And my body.'

'That too.' She kissed him.

'Oh get a room, you two,' said Bella in mock disgust. 'So, Sophie, are you going to see Paul again?'

Sophie's throat felt tight. Envy flooded her at the easy affection between Ed and Edie. The date with Paul had been perfectly pleasant but for a minute she wondered if it had also been a little dull.

Chapter 11

Her shoulders ached slightly but she was determined to put the finishing touches to her fall afternoon tea feature for Trudi. After quite a few false starts over the last few weeks (who knew that you couldn't get black treacle in the US?) she'd finally produced a parkin that she was happy with.

The final recipe was a compromise on the traditional English one, but the universal verdict, bar one (Madison, of course), was that it tasted 'mighty fine'.

Just as she was describing how she'd substituted molasses, the phone rang. She looked up and as usual Todd nodded, indicating he'd like her to pick it up. She rolled her eyes.

'Sophie Bennings speaking.'

'Hey Sophie, its Amy, how are you today?'

'Hello Amy.' Todd shook his head and mouthed *not here*. 'I'm good, thank you. And you?'

'I'm just great, Sophie. I just love your accent ... it's just so ... English.' She giggled. 'Is Todd around?'

'I'm sorry, Amy. He's not at his desk. Can I take a message?' Sophie shot a glare at him.

'I just wanted to check up on him, I've not seen him since we went out for dinner a couple of weeks back.'

'He's fine,' said Sophie, glowering across the desk at Todd pretending not to listen in. 'Very busy.' She gave the magazine he was flipping through a pointed look.

'He works so hard. But he's such a gentleman.'

'That's Todd,' agreed Sophie, giving him a sickly smile across the desk. 'Just perfect.' She pulled a face at him that said he was anything but. He simply waved and went back to scanning his computer screen.

'I'll let him know you called.'

'Thanks, Sophie.'

She put the phone down. 'Poor deluded child. She thinks you're a proper gentleman.'

'Thanks, English.'

'Are you going to ring her back?'

'Of course I will.'

Sophie raised a sceptical eyebrow. 'Treat 'em mean, keep 'em keen?'

He shot her a reproachful look and clasped his hands to his heart. 'You wound me. It's not my fault I'm irresistible.' For a brief second he looked like a naughty pixie. 'I will call her,' he looked at his phone and pressed the calendar app, 'in two days' time.'

'What, you have them all on a schedule?' asked Sophie, horrified as she watched him tapping the details into his phone.

'I'm being organised.'

'So how many women are you seeing at the moment?'

151

demanded Sophie, pleased to see that he actually looked sheepish.

'Just Amy.' His eyes slid to a point above her head, just a bit too guileless, a bit too innocent and far too serious.

She quirked a disbelieving eyebrow. 'Yes, and I've seen a herd of wildebeest sweep past the window, accompanied by six unicorns and a dragon. What happened to Charlene?'

'Charlene ... well, she won't take no for an answer and keeps ringing. Honest, I went out for a drink with her. Once.'

'What about Lacey and Cherie?'

Todd sat up straighter. 'They called me.'

'And you gave them no encouragement?'

He had the grace to look discomfited for a second. 'I like women. Enjoy their company. I never make any promises or mislead anyone.' He gave her a sharp look, which made Sophie feel guilty. What right had she to judge him?

'And ...' he lifted his chin, his blue eyes boring into hers, semaphoring determined intent, 'I never sleep with more than one woman at a time.'

For a second she blanched, thinking he was alluding to James. But of course, he wasn't. He didn't know about James. No one knew about James. She hadn't told a soul, apart from Kate, who'd arrived in time to pick up the shattered pieces.

'I don't,' said Todd, a flash of anger on his face as he mistook her sudden withdrawal. He'd stiffened and leaned forward towards her.

'I-I never said you did,' said Sophie, startled by his vehemence.

'And I never would.' With a sudden movement, he pushed himself away from his desk, stood up and walked away.

She watched him with dismay, realising she'd touched a raw nerve. Guilt nagged at her. Had she become so embittered that she'd lost her judgement?

Sophie closed her eyes, reliving the awful scene with Anna again.

Feeling the familiar heaviness that settled whenever she thought about James, she ducked her head and went back to her laptop screen. She'd been doing really well this last week. Ever since dinner with Paul, in fact. Not that she'd seen him since, although they'd spoken on the phone a couple of times and exchanged a few texts. The man worked hard and played squash a lot.

Her fingers hovered over the keys as she tried to concentrate on her article again. Parkin. Teacakes. Fall. She clutched at the words, drawing them into her, focusing back on the words she'd already written. The feature wasn't bad and she was on the last leg.

The first two days of this week had been taken up with cooking the final recipes, decorating and preparing everything for the photo shoot yesterday. It had been a stressful couple of days, not helped when Madison dropped a tray of the cupcakes at the very last minute. Despite wanting to strangle the girl, Sophie set to, scraped clean the tops of her cakes and painstakingly redecorated them with swirls of orange frosting, topped with little black witches' hats which had been individually hand fashioned from fondant icing. Of course that would be the very day that she needed to get away smartly to meet with Bella and the bride, Eleanor Doyle.

'Do you know what Madison? I think this lot are better,' said Sophie cheerfully, sliding the plate of cakes into the vacant slot in the autumn display that the photographer had set up. 'I've had more practice. What do you think?'

Madison's face tightened and she made no comment.

Despite her cheer offensive, Sophie had not yet managed to win the younger girl over, but she suspected a lot of that had to do with the location of her desk and the fact that Todd had casually mentioned their walk over Brooklyn Bridge in front of her.

She tweaked her copy again. This first feature was important and she really wanted to make a good impression. She was still playing around with a sentence when Todd came to stand behind her chair.

'English, it's twelve-thirty. You need some lunch.'

'Right ...' She carried on typing.

'Lunch-time.'

'Yeah ...' Absorbed, Sophie moved a sentence. Did that sound better?

'Lunch, English.' He walked around, took the mouse out of her hands, saved her document and pulled out her chair.

'Haven't you got someone to go with?' She was cross with him for not giving her the chance to explain to him earlier. 'I'm kind of busy here. Couldn't you call up one of your harem?'

'Very funny.' He gave her a serious look. 'You haven't taken a break since nine-thirty this morning.'

'I'm on a roll.' She lifted her shoulders. They felt really stiff and she didn't like this uncomfortable feeling of being at odds with him, but she was still cross with him for jumping to the wrong conclusion. 'I can't stop now. I'm too busy for lunch.'

'I disagree,' said Todd firmly, clamping his hands on the tops of her shoulders, rubbing his thumbs into the muscles there. 'Tight as a ... a very tight thing. You need a proper break.'

'Hey, Sophie. Todd.' Paul's voice came from beyond Todd and for some reason Sophie tensed, feeling guilty.

'Paul! Hi.' Her voiced squeaked unbecomingly.

'Paul.' Todd kept his hands on her shoulders, his touch gentling but still moving over the tense muscles which had just got a whole heap tenser.

'Massage part of the Man About Town remit now?' asked Paul pointedly.

'Part of office wellbeing. This girl's got knots you wouldn't believe,' said Todd cheerfully, gliding his touch into the knots and making Sophie wince.

Paul's jaw firmed although he managed to smile at the same time. In yet another of his sharp-cut suits, with the sunshine slanting across his blond hair, he looked handsome and golden and the epitome of success already.

Sophie shook Todd off impatiently and turned to Paul, feeling a slight blush staining her cheeks. 'How are you doing? How's your week?'

'Busy. I've had a management meeting with Trudy on this floor, thought I'd swing by and say hi.'

'Well, you came at the right time,' she said in an over-bright voice, shooting a glare over her shoulder at Todd. 'I'm finishing this article and about to take a break. Have you got time for lunch or a coffee?'

'Oh babe, I'd love to, but I've got a stack of calls to make and a meeting to prepare for. I'd better not. I'll text you later. Next week's a bit quieter. Maybe we can grab a drink one night after work.'

'OK,' said Sophie, slightly surprised by being addressed as 'babe'. 'Let me know.'

After their dinner, Paul had taken her arm as they'd walked to the subway and pecked her on the cheek to say goodnight, but they certainly hadn't taken any steps that might suggest 'babe'.

'So,' said Todd as Paul disappeared. 'Lunch then. You've just finished your article and you're ready for a break. I tell you babe, those shoulders need a serious break.' He winked at her. 'Come on, English. I need to say I'm sorry properly. Come for lunch.'

Central Park in the sunshine. Sophie looked around her, marvelling at the greenery, looking up at the skyscrapers visible through the canopy of the trees. It was difficult to believe they were a ten-minute walk from the office.

'I feel bad, now, that I've never ventured out before,' she said, sighing, stretching her bare legs out in front of her and wiping crumbs from her mouth. Todd had insisted on buying them pastrami subs from one of the stands on the pavement outside the park. They were perched on a rock warmed by the sun and if it weren't for the not-so-distant sounds of the city traffic, horses' hooves and wailing sirens, you could almost imagine you were in the country. Almost. The country certainly didn't have this many joggers, skateboarders or push-chair- perambulating parents, it was surprising to see so many trendy hipster dads out with their children on their own.

'So you should. We're lucky to be so close to the park. And I wanted to talk to you about next week.'

'Next week?'

'Remember you said you'd come with me to a restaurant opening?'

'Yes, but I didn't realise you were serious. What's Amy doing? Isn't she free?' As soon as she said it, she wanted to take it back. 'Look, I'm sorry about earlier.'

'It's OK,' said Todd with a casual shrug. 'She knows we're not exclusive.'

'I never really know what that means,' she spread her hands in defeat.

'It means I date other people, but I'm honest about it and I don't sleep with more than one woman at a time.' Todd's tone was firm and almost fierce.

'I guess I should congratulate you on that. Quite an achieve-ment.' As soon as the bitter comment left her mouth, she wanted to take it back.

Todd raised an enquiring eyebrow as she blushed bright scarlet, picking at the grass with one hand.

'My ex ...' she couldn't bring herself to admit the shame of him being married, 'he was ... unfaithful.'

Todd turned his head slowly and his blue eyes softened as they met hers. 'Ah, and you found out.'

Sophie nodded, a lump in her throat as once again the

enormity of James's lies enveloped her like a black cloud and the familiar prickle of tears welled up in her eyes.

'That is shit.' He reached for her hand. 'I'm so sorry, English, but it wasn't your fault.'

Sophie clenched her jaw, determined not to cry as the familiar weight in her chest constricted her lungs. 'Maybe not my fault but ...' she rubbed a hand over her face, the familiar guilt crowding in. 'I think I closed my eyes. Didn't see what I didn't want to see.' She bit her lip, suddenly wanting to make a clean breast of things, get out the poison she'd been harbouring. Apart from Kate, she hadn't told a soul what had really happened with James.

She sat up. 'It's really not a pretty story.'

Todd frowned. 'Are you worried it'll change my view of you?'

'No,' she closed her eyes, turning to him. 'More that I'll hate myself when I tell you and I realise I should have known all along ...

'James, his name was James.' Her mouth crumpled. 'Probably about the only thing about himself that he told the truth about.'

Todd somehow snuck up next to her, his shoulder nudging hers as if to say, I'm right here with you.

'It turned out he forgot to mention that he had a wife and,' she swallowed, thinking of the gorgeous little girl in the café, 'a baby.'

'Baby?' Todd was quick. The shock in his voice confirmed that.

'Yeah, baby. Eleven months old.'

She watched as he did the calculation.

'Shit. That's got to hurt.' Shock flared in his eyes. 'Hang on. He lived with you? How does that work?'

'Well, basically ... because apparently I'm exceptionally stupid. Very gullible and downright dumb.'

'Aside from all that.'

'He told me his mother lived in Cornwall, that's two hundred miles from London. She wasn't well and he went home at weekends to look after her.'

'And?'

'In fact it turned out, she lived virtually around the corner from me. Luckily for him, his mother and wife disliked each other intensely, so he was able to keep up the story to his wife that he was staying with her during the week.'

'Ouch. So how did you find out? He slipped up?'

'No, even worse. His wife confronted me. She'd been following me at weekends for a few weeks. I always catch up with my friend Kate for a couple of hours on a Saturday while her boyfriend plays football. She was in the café. This woman. With her child, Emma.' Sophie winced, back in the coffee bar. Feeling again the spreading ink leak of disbelief. 'Poor woman, I felt awful ... for her. Her poor baby. It was worse for them.'

Todd's eyes widened in horror and he reached out to lay a hand on hers. 'That's shit. What an ... a-hole. Two years.'

'Yeah, how stupid am I?' Tears threatened. She thought she'd stopped crying over James. 'You're the first person apart from Kate I've told. I feel so ashamed.'

'But you didn't do anything wrong.' Todd rubbed her arm

and took her hand in his, threading his fingers through hers. 'He was the one that lied to you.'

'Ha! You think so. I'm not so sure. I think I should have known. I keep wondering whether subliminally I did know.' She'd been over it so many times in her head. 'He was a bloody good liar. It never occurred to me ... I loved him.' With a disdainful sniff, she berated herself. 'Thought he was a good guy because he took care of his mother.' She let out a bitter laugh. 'What a fool.

'But how could I have not known? Even on a subconscious level, I should have done.' She ducked her head, avoiding his gaze. 'I'm so ashamed.'

'You didn't do this. And you haven't told anyone?' He enfolded her in a hug and held her tight, stroking her hair as she tried hard not to let the tears out. With a sniff she pulled back. 'Don't feel sorry for me. What about poor Anna?'

'What did you do?'

She bit her lip and raised her eyes to his. 'After she'd dropped her bombshell, I was so shocked. I basically ran. Chickened out of confronting him.' Sophie blinked away more tears. 'I should have been braver. Told him what a bastard he was, but I couldn't face him. When you said that time in *Café Luluc*, that love turns to hate. It takes a while. I don't hate James, I-I ... shouldn't love him any more. But after two years it's hard. I went home, changed the locks, blocked him on my phone. Social media. And phoned my boss. She'd offered me the job swap a week before and I turned it down. She was delighted I'd changed my mind. I didn't tell her why.'

'I went to stay with my friends Connie and Kate, so that I

could avoid James in case he came to my flat. And then went back at the weekend to pack everything up when I knew it would be safe.'

'Did he go back to his wife? Did she want him back?'

'I've no idea. Like I said, I ran away. Came here. And started over. I didn't have any idea what I was going to do when I got here. I wanted to get as far away as possible.

'And I struck lucky when I met you and Bella. If it weren't for Bella I probably would have stayed holed up in the apartment watching reruns of *Friends*, *The Big Bang Theory* and *Before I Met Your Mother* and slowly going doolally.'

Todd looked thoughtful.

'Do you think I should have confronted him?'

'It might have given you, forgive the phrase, closure. Don't you wonder why he did it? To keep that level of subterfuge up for so long.' He shook his head. 'Part of me wants to take my hat off to …' He stopped as Sophie glared at him. 'I mean seriously, that's a lot of hard work. Why? Why would you do that? Constantly juggling the truth, remembering the lies you've told.'

Todd squeezed her hand gently. 'Do you know what you need to do? Make sure you enjoy yourself while you're here, instead of holing yourself up in your apartment. Live a little. Have a good time. You can do a lot better than Paul. There are plenty of guys in New York.' He winked. 'I could introduce you to a few. Good-looking babe like you.'

Sophie stood up and brushed the crumbs from her skirt. 'Don't call me a babe.'

'Sorry, babe.' He grinned.

'And there's nothing wrong with Paul.'

Todd pulled a face and Sophie pursed her lips.

'He's a decent enough guy, but seriously English – unless, of course, you want to play safe. He's rather wedded to his career. I suppose there are worse people you could have a fling with. But I think you could do a lot better.'

'I'm not planning to have a fling,' said Sophie tartly. That suggested something a lot more involved. A fling sounded far too emotionally turbulent, exciting, unpredictable and finite.

'Why not?' Todd spread his hands. 'Live a little.'

'Sadly ...' She looked at his handsome, smiling face. He had no idea. He'd probably never had a serious, stable relationship in his life. 'I'm not built for flings. I'm an all-or-nothing girl.'

Chapter 12

'Hey Bella, I've had an idea.' Sophie rushed into the kitchen, waving her notepad, having come straight from her subway journey. Calling in on Bella on her way home from work had become part of her daily routine. After a quick cup of coffee and a chat together, she'd nip upstairs, change and then come back down for an hour or two of baking cupcakes and cookies. Her icing skills had improved dramatically and under Bella's exacting eye she'd even been allowed to frost the last three batches of cakes.

Bella straightened and put down her frosting bag, rubbing her back. 'Hello, you. Coffee?'

'I'll do it. Decaff?' Sophie nipped over to the small Nespresso machine, still feeling rather pleased with herself.

'I think I've nailed Eleanor's cake.' It was no good, Sophie couldn't wait for coffee. She danced back to Bella's side. 'I realised Eleanor's wedding is as much a celebration of her success in her career as about getting married. Her job is her top priority. So I was thinking ... How about this?' She opened up the notebook to show a few sketches. 'Each layer features a different wallpaper pattern in contrasting colours.' She pointed. 'You need to get Eleanor to choose her favourite three wallpapers, which would make it really personal.'

Bella threw her arms around her. 'Yes! You clever thing. It's perfect.' Bella studied the page in the notebook, flipping through the pages. 'These are brilliant sketches. You're a genius.'

'No, you'll be the genius because I haven't a clue how you'll achieve it.' Although Sophie could bake, she was very much in awe of Bella's decorating skills.

'Neither do I ... yet. But I can teach you, if you're interested.'

'Yes please,' said Sophie with such alacrity that Bella burst out laughing.

'You don't know what you've let yourself in for yet.'

'I don't care,' said Sophie, busying herself making their coffee. 'If I can make something that looks anywhere near as good as your stuff, I'll be thrilled.'

Her eyes shone with enthusiasm. 'And I'd love to learn. I've been dying to know how you did the lace on the *My Fair Lady* cake. It looks amazing. And so do these.' She pointed to Bella's work in progress.

Bella picked up her frosting bag and started adding the finishing touches to yellow petals spilling over the sides of wider, flatter cupcakes than she normally made. 'You like?'

'I love, they are so cute,' said Sophie, diverted by the sunflower cupcakes.

'They're for a commission but I thought I might start selling them regularly.'

'You could do seasonal flowers each month,' suggested Sophie, bending over to examine the details of the sunflower seeds in the middle of the cakes.

Bella whirled around. 'What a brilliant idea! Sophie, I love you. We make a great team. Sure you don't want to give up the magazine gig and come work for me?' She broke off and gnawed at her lip with her teeth, 'Although you do most evenings. I shouldn't be encouraging you. I worry you're using helping me as an excuse to hide away, even though I love having your help.'

'But I love being here,' said Sophie, looking around Bella's kitchen, which felt like home these days. 'You don't need to worry. Honestly.' The whir and rattle of the blade in the Kitchen Aid, the comforting feeling of flour on her hands, the sound of caster sugar pitter-pattering into the bowl on the scales and the sweet vanilla smell of cupcakes were universal. She could have been anywhere but they all signified home from home.

'Although tonight, I can't stay long. I'm going out later for dinner.'

'Good for you.'

'I can stay an hour before I need to go and get ready.'

'So, where's Paul taking you?'

Sophie hesitated for a fraction of a second. 'I'm going out with Todd actually. A restaurant/club launch. He wants a foodie to help him critique it.'

Bella gave her a sharp look. Sophie held up her hands. 'Don't worry, I'm immune to the legendary Todd McLennan charm.'

'Good.' Bella sighed and leaned against the stainless-steel counter, crossing her feet at the ankles. 'He's my cousin, I love him to bits, but lovely as he is, he's also seriously messed up.

He wouldn't thank me for telling you but it's enough to say that his parents' marriage is the first word in dysfunctional. If you can knock up a couple of batches of batter while I ice this lot, that would be a massive help, but only if you're sure. If it's only Todd, you're not going to want to doll yourself up, are you?'

'No, I've got time,' said Sophie airily, as she started gathering ingredients with familiar ease.

Todd texted to say he'd arrived and was with Bella downstairs. Sophie pulled a face in the mirror. She'd hoped to avoid seeing Bella before she went out. Of course she'd dolled herself up. She was going out with Todd McLennan, international playboy, for God's sake. Feminine pride alone dictated that she was ultra-careful with her eye make-up. She also put on her favourite top, which happened to be a designer cast-off from Kate.

You could tell it was expensive from the cut – which accentuated her waist and dipped demurely at the neckline, revealing the slight swell of her breasts without being overt – and from the way the delicate folds of turquoise silk shimmered in the mirror. Sophie smiled at herself.

The outfit was completed with ripped skinny jeans and sparkly Kurt Geiger flat sandals, and she felt she'd got it right. Hip without being too glitzy and still comfortable in her own skin. She felt like herself.

With a nod, she tucked her clutch bag under her arm and went downstairs.

Todd had made himself at home, as he invariably did

wherever he was, sitting on the kitchen counter, swinging his legs and licking clean the cake-mix bowl, chatting away to Bella.

For a minute Sophie hung back before walking into the kitchen, suddenly self-conscious. Before she had a chance to retreat and go and put on a different top, Todd spotted her. For a brief second, his eyes widened and he held her gaze for a further heart-stalling moment before he quickly jumped off the counter.

'English. You're ready and on time. Have that girl cloned.'

Bella looked up. 'Whoa, girl!'

Immediately Sophie felt awkward, clutching a hand to the neckline of her top. 'Too much?'

'No, no you look gorgeous,' said Bella. 'Far too good for Todd.' She shot him a sarcastic look. 'Hopefully you can ditch him as soon as you get there and find someone better.'

Sophie got the distinct impression there was a definite warning in her words but she wasn't sure quite who they were directed at.

'Charming,' said Todd, taking her arm. 'Shall we go before my lovely shrewish cous reduces my ego to a pile of dust?'

Onyx was everything it sounded – a smart, super-sophisticated bar and restaurant – and Sophie was mighty glad she'd put on the blue top. There was a very good-looking, chiselled-cheeked doorman at the entrance, dressed in an immaculately cut charcoal-grey suit, checking names off a list with icy disdain. From the moment they were ushered inside, it was five-star treatment all the way.

'I'm not sure about the black champagne,' she whispered, holding up her glass flute. 'It's a clever idea but it doesn't look that appetising to me. Champagne is best left alone.' She took a sip and swirled it around her mouth before wrinkling her nose. She preferred her champagne unadulterated. 'If you're going to muck about with it, you'd be better off doing it with cava or prosecco, which doesn't have the same yeasty bite.'

'It certainly makes a statement,' said Todd. 'What do you think is in it?' He peered into his glass with comical distrust, which made Sophie laugh before she took a hesitant sip.

'Not squid ink, thank goodness. Probably just food colouring.'

'I'm so glad you're here with me.'

Her breath caught in her throat at the sudden serious tone in his voice and when she raised her eyes to meet his, they were for once rather solemn and steady. A flush heated her skin as they stared at each other, and quite unaccountably her knees suddenly felt weak. It was a relief when, with a swallow, he broke eye-contact and added, 'That's the sort of detail I need for my notes. And I'm going to need your expertise when we eat, as I suspect the food is going to be horribly over-complicated.'

He led the way into the semi-dark interior, towards the restaurant area on the mezzanine floor. 'Although it won't matter because we probably won't be able to see it.' Suddenly she was rather glad it was so dark and he'd missed her blush.

Todd snagged another glass of champagne for her at the top of the stairs as they entered the restaurant, where they were shown to a table in the corner overlooking the bar below. Before picking up the menu, he took a couple of pictures of the restaurant and the bar, already packed with lots of very beautiful people.

'What do you think of the décor?' he asked, tucking his phone away, glancing up at the ceiling, where tiny LED lights shone from polished black stalactites.

Sophie nodded, trying to pick a few diplomatic phrases. 'It's very ... smart.' And very black.

As she shifted in her seat, the unforgiving sharp metal edge of one of the legs caught her shin. 'Interesting cutlery.' She picked up the heavy bronze knife, with its agate handle. It was a bit too gothic for her but everyone else seemed to be raving about the place. 'Clever concept. Onyx like the stone, hence the black and metal accents.'

Todd's lips twitched as he studied her gravely for a minute. He leaned over and whispered loudly, 'It's terrible.'

Sophie giggled and picked up her champagne flute.

'Vampire nest meets goblin lair. I need one of those head-torch things. The interior designer must have had a taste bypass.'

'It's different.'

'Different doesn't make it nice. I suppose we'd better check out the menu, although if there are any lizard tongues, bat wings or hairs of newt, we are going straight to the Wendy's down the road for a burger.'

He picked up the menu. 'Hmm, not as bad as I feared but you're going to have to translate. What the hell is wild garlic and cockle velouté, when it's at home? Langoustine custard?

Smoked florets of cauliflower? I'm not sure I want to put any of this stuff anywhere near my mouth.'

Sophie read the menu with rising dismay. It was everything she disliked on a menu. Fancy for fancy's sake. The descriptions of the dishes contained all of her top pet hates, from the pea mousse and basil foam through to the unappetising-sounding sorrel sorbet and morel essence, but despite that she believed you should always try everything at least once.

'For goodness' sake! Seriously, Sophie, what is this? Verrine of a julienne of prosciutto, rosemary gelée, foraged mushroom emulsion, topped with a potato and parmesan galette?'

'Ssh, you'll upset the chef.' She could see a man in whites, wandering from table to table. 'A verrine is a clear glass. So it's all those things stacked inside it.' She took a long sip of champagne, grateful that the second flute had not been doctored with colouring.

Todd frowned, widening his eyes at her. 'Julienne is strips of something, so I take it that's strips of prosciutto. Rosemary gelée sounds disgusting. The galette I could live with, but seriously – foraged mushroom anything? You're not telling me that the kitchen team here were out this morning foraging for fungi anywhere near here?'

Sophie sniggered at the wrong moment and started giggling, almost choking on her drink.

'Hand-reared kobo beef on a bed of hand-selected slices of onions. What were they going to do, pick them up with their teeth? Who writes this tosh?'

She really had the giggles now and had to put down her drink. Todd was on a roll.

'Toothsome chicken combined with ... sharks are toothsome, chickens aren't.'

'Stop ... enough.' She had to work hard to school her face when the waiter came to take their order. Of course Todd was perfectly polite.

'I'll take the seared turbot with the wild garlic and cockle velouté, followed by the chicken. And a bottle of the Pouilly Fume.'

'And for you, ma'am?'

Deliberately not looking at Todd in case he set her off again, she opted for the shrimp and caviar with langoustine custard followed by the kobo beef, with pea foam, carrot emulsion and batter soufflé and red-wine jus. 'Although I have no idea what batter soufflé is, that one has me stumped.'

When the food arrived, both plates looked like Jackson Pollock works of art with smears of this and that across the china.

'I'm expecting you to take notes,' said Todd, poking nervously at the cockles on his plate.

Sophie dipped a spoon into the tiny pot of langoustine custard which was more like a jelly. A large prawn wobbled on top, shaking tiny eggs of caviar like confetti around it. 'Mmm, not bad. It's like a very rich shellfish consommé that's thickened up. Tasty but you couldn't eat too much of it. The shrimp's delicious. Here, try some.' She scooped up a portion of the custard and the tail end of the prawn and offered it to him.

'Do I have to?'

'It's good for your food education. You need to constantly challenge your palate.'

'I think I'm plenty well educated. I've dined in Paris a time or two and I promise you, my palate was well and truly challenged in the backstreets of Cambodia.'

'Oh, I've never been there.'

'What's the best meal you've ever eaten, then?' asked Todd, tilting his head, watching her after she'd described an amazing paella she'd had in Barcelona one summer and how she'd stalked the chef and spent the next day in his kitchen learning how to make it. The sudden switch to serious again and being the focus of his attention made her feel light-headed.

'That's impossible.' Sophie smiled dreamily at him as she leaned back in her chair, to give it some thought. In the last half hour they'd shared so many tales of their travels and food experiences. Todd was widely travelled and had plenty of stories to tell, as well as some fascinating insights into the places he'd been.

'Why?' His teasing smile did funny things to her pulse.

'A meal is the sum of many things, not simply the food. It's the atmosphere, who you're with, the memories you create. There's a special warmth about the perfect meal, a sum of all the right things coming together. This, for example, is superb food, but ...' she lifted her shoulders, not wanting to sound ungrateful, 'the ambience ... the atmosphere, it's not quite right ... well, not to me.'

'What about the company?' asked Todd, suddenly very still, as if the answer was important.

Nerves shimmered as Sophie looked back at him, unsure what to say. Was Todd flirting with her? She smoothed down the silk of her top, glad she'd made an effort to look nice this evening. *Who was she kidding?* Since the first day she'd met him her hormones had been clamouring to get to know him better. Little traitors. He was everything that James and Paul weren't. A complication in life she really didn't need, but when he looked at her like that ... she sighed.

'The company's not bad at all.' She smiled at him and his fingers brushed over her hand on the table in response, just as the waiter arrived with the second course.

'Is that it?' whispered Todd as the waiter left, having deposited the plates with a flourish. 'They're kidding, a snail has more meat on it than this.'

'Shh,' said Sophie, trying not to giggle at the mournful display on his face. Although the tiny cube of beef on her plate wasn't exactly generous.

Todd poked at the pea foam. 'Are you going to eat that? It looks like green spittlebug foam.'

'I'm guessing that's what we'd call cuckoo spit at home, white foam on plants made by insects.'

'That's the one. Why would you want to eat anything that looks like insect spittle?'

'Now you've completely put me off,' said Sophie, pointing her knife at him severely.

'And that orange stuff looks radioactive.'

'It's carrot emulsion.' Although it did glisten rather a lot.

'And what's the wrinkled thing?'

Sophie grinned at him and scooped up one of the two tiny cooked rounds of batter with a touch of the jus and half of the cube of beef and groaned. 'That, my friend, is what we call back home, roast beef, Yorkshire pud and gravy. And it's delicious.'

Todd, having polished off his own chicken dish in about five mouthfuls, then helped himself to the other Yorkshire pudding and the rest of the beef.

'Oi,' she tapped his hand. 'That was mine.'

'I need to try it for my food education.' Mischief danced all over his face. 'But you're right, that Yorkshire stuff is great. I've never had it before. Can you make it?'

'Make it? I'm a Yorkshire girl, of course I can.'

'Great, when I come to dinner? You can cook for me.'

'You're coming to dinner?'

Todd grinned at her. 'You can't tell a man all about the most divine paella you ever ate, say you've researched how to make it yourself and then not invite him to dinner.'

'I probably can,' she teased.

'You're a hard woman. I'll buy the wine.'

Sophie tipped her head to one side. She missed cooking. It wasn't always worth it for herself. She missed cooking for other people.

'Alright then, I'll cook you paella one night after work.'

'Excellent,' he rubbed his stomach in mock anticipation and then looked down at his empty plate. 'I hope the desserts are bigger. I'm still hungry.'

Sophie had to agree with him.

Dessert, delicious as it was, consisted of thumbnail portions of white-chocolate, coffee and dark-chocolate mousse dusted with edible gold leaf, which both of them polished off within seconds. Todd sighed heavily as he laid down the heavy teaspoon.

'Do you want coffee?' he asked, in that leading, I'm-hoping-you'll-say-no sort of way, as he dabbed at the last smear of mousse as if more might materialise like magic.

'I don't mind,' said Sophie easily.

'Good, let's get out of here.' He'd already risen to his feet and was holding out his hand. 'Come on.' He lowered his voice and looked around furtively. 'Don't suppose you fancy a burger? I'm still hungry,' he said again.

'Where do you put it all?'

'Come on, English. Don't tell me you couldn't put a quarter pounder away.'

'I could but I shouldn't. I still haven't been out running.'

'Why didn't you say? I'll take you out this weekend. When's a good time for you?'

'I'm not sure.'

'Well, let me know in the week, but in the meantime, my stomach is begging me to get out of here.'

She burst out laughing and hushed him. 'You'll upset the chef. I'll go to the loo and I'll meet you downstairs.'

'Todd! Darling.' A blonde of Amazonian proportions draped her endless limbs around him as Sophie emerged from the loo. 'It's been forever.'

'Liesl, how are you?' He kissed her on both cheeks, his smile broad and welcoming.

'All the better for seeing you. Where have you been? And isn't this place divine? Everyone's raving about it. Dino's done it again. I'm thinking about asking him to redecorate the penthouse for me. Apparently he's finished working for Paris. When are you coming out to the beach?' She reached a hand up towards Todd's face, smiling up at him. 'I've missed you.'

Sophie stood on her own, not sure whether to join them or not. From here she couldn't see Todd's face to read his reaction.

'How are Brett and Jan?' he asked.

'Mum and Dad are fine.' She pulled out a pale-blue leather diary from her snakeskin clutch. 'There's a party at the Swansons' this weekend, you should come. And Maggie and Bill are throwing a twenty-first for their youngest. It will be a killer.'

'Sounds great.' Todd put his hand over hers and pulled it away from his face in a smooth move, typical of his easy charm. 'I'll have to get back to you. I'm quite tied up at the moment.'

'I can't believe you missed the race season at Saratoga.' It was one of a litany of calendar dates that Todd appeared to have missed.

'You know what it's like. Weekends are so hectic. Busy, busy, busy. I never seem to have a spare minute.'

Sophie frowned. That didn't quite add up. Busy, busy was very vague, he didn't exactly spell out what he was busy doing. From what she'd seen, weekends weren't too busy to deliver cupcakes for his cousin, take an impromptu brunch or arrange a sight-seeing walk over Brooklyn Bridge.

Over the last few weeks she'd come to realise that much of his socialising was invariably work related. Last week's dinner date with Amy doubled as a restaurant review. He'd accompanied Charlene to a fashion show that he was covering for another magazine and Lacey, who he'd had several lunches with, worked for a company that was sponsoring the dating evenings that he was writing a series of features about.

'Oh my goodness, is that Chris Martin over there talking to Gwynie? They are so civilised. I must go say hi.' And with that Liesl uncoiled herself from Todd with several noisy kisses.

Sophie moved out of the shadows to join Todd.

'Hey English, ready for a burger?'

She nodded as he linked his arms through hers with his usual easy camaraderie, reminding her that Todd was friends with everyone. He liked women and they liked him.

Chapter 13

It had taken considerable juggling of their diaries and at eight o'clock in the morning there was a stiff chilly breeze at the top of the Empire State Building but it was so worth it, even if Paul had surreptitiously checked his watch for the second time in half an hour.

'Thanks for this,' Sophie beamed at him. 'It really does live up to all the hype.' Should she admit she'd watched *Sleepless in Seattle* five times and the scene located up here was one of her all-time favourites? The early morning sunshine turned the city into a dappled collage of light and shade, with diamond twinkles reflected from the sharp columns of glass and steel, and her gaze darted this way and that trying to take in the enormity of the view.

'My pleasure, and it was worth getting up early to see that smile. And now I'm really sorry I'd arranged to play squash later this morning.'

'I hope you don't lose, after all those stairs.'

Just getting to the top of the building was a marathon. Even at that time of day the queue was already lengthy and they'd opted to duck the final line by walking up the last few flights of the stairs to the top.

'Wow, everything looks so small,' said Sophie, peering down and looking at the streets far below and the tiny cars moving along. She laughed as the wind whipped at her hair, plastering the ends of her ponytail over her mouth. 'I bet everyone says that.'

'They do,' said Paul, with a quick smile pushing back unruly blond curls. The fierce breeze had played havoc with his usual neat style and it made him look much younger and, to Sophie's mind, a lot more attractive. Today was the first time she'd seen him out of his habitual suit. When she met him outside the subway station she almost hadn't recognised him in his jeans and a leather jacket.

'I'm sorry, I'm going to talk in tourist clichés because it's so amazing and you can see so far and it's all so fascinating. And I sound like a burbling idiot but it's ... I'm on top of the Empire State Building! I've always wanted to come here.'

'Don't worry. I love listening to your English accent, it sounds so classy. But then you are ... what is it in England? Upper class.'

Sophie stiffened. 'Why do you think that?'

Paul smiled, pushing his hands through his hair again. 'I've met a few English people, none of them speak as much like the Queen as you do.'

'Oh.' Sophie relaxed, she was being silly. There was no way that Paul would know about her family background. There were always people who were impressed by a title, which why she was at pains to keep it quiet. 'Gosh, is that a helicopter?' She pointed out towards the river, where it flew below, looking more like a toy.

'Yes, you can do helicopter tours of the city. That's the helipad right over there on the waterfront.' He stood behind her and one hand encircling her waist. She leaned back against him, suddenly relishing the feeling of being with someone else again. They stood like that for a few minutes, as Paul pointed out the distant shoreline. 'That's the Hudson River. And across on the other shore, New Jersey.'

They walked around each side of the tower, Sophie happily spotting famous landmarks like the Chrysler Building, Bryant Park, the new World Trade Center and musing over the surprising vastness of Central Park, which from this angle disappeared into the hazy horizon. From up here everything looked very angular and square, the towers like building blocks placed along the straight roads that stretched away out of sight, and the buildings dotted with thousands of tiny black-holed windows that reminded her of old-fashioned peg boards. An industrial landscape of sharp edges and straight lines. Exhilarating and exciting to be sure, but it certainly wasn't pretty.

The more she looked at the city, the smaller she felt. Insignificant and inconsequential. The view emphasised the sheer size of the place, the packed density of people living and working there, and for a moment Sophie felt horribly anonymous and lost. Thank goodness she'd landed in Brooklyn above the warmth and welcome of Bella's Bakery. If she'd been in the thick of the city, she wasn't sure she would have survived.

They spent another half an hour circling the observation deck before the wind finally got the better of them and Sophie's cheeks felt wind burned. Going down was a much quicker process, although the queues coming up had lengthened considerably.

When they exited the art deco hallways, Sophie noticed Paul checking his watch again.

'What time's your squash match?' she asked. This brief Saturday morning slot was the only free time he had this weekend.

'I've got another hour. For you I can squeeze in a coffee.'

'Are you sure?'

He took her hand. 'Yeah, I've built in plenty of time. There'll be somewhere around here.'

'So how often do you play squash? I've never played but it always looks very energetic and full of oomph. People play with great gusto.'

'Can you say that again in English?' asked Paul, a slight frown on his face.

Sophie smiled at the serious expression. She was learning that he didn't really do gentle teasing. Best not to mention that she thought squash looked quite an aggressive, angry sort of game. You didn't smash a ball around like that without a bit of testosterone-fuelled attitude. 'You know, they put lots of effort in. It looks very hard work.'

'It's a good work-out, that's for sure. I play a couple of times a week and I'm in a couple of different leagues.'

'Competitive then?'

'Not really. It's great networking. Most of the guys I play

with work in the media or business. What about you, what sort of sport do food writers do?'

'Apart from eating, you mean?' She laughed. 'We're very good at that.'

When Paul looked a touch nonplussed, she added, 'I don't really have a sport. I'm not very competitive at all, but I run.'

'Running's good. You should join a gym. There's a good one a block down from the office.'

'I'll bear it in mind. I'm ...' She was about to mention that Todd had threatened making her go for a run yesterday at work, and then thought better of it. It was the first time she'd seen him since Wednesday night when they'd ended up eating Wendy's burgers on a park bench.

'Here we go. This will do. Starbucks.'

Paul stopped outside the doorway and pushed it open for her. Sophie ignored the pang of disappointment. She could go to Starbucks anywhere in the world.

'I enjoyed the trip this morning. It's fun playing tourist in your own city. I haven't been up there in years. We should do it again sometime.'

'That would be nice.'

'Have you done Grand Central Station yet?'

Sophie shook her head. 'Not yet.'

'The Guggenheim? The Met? The High Line?'

Sophie shook her head at each mention.

'What *have* you been doing?' With a shake of his head, he wagged his finger. 'I admire your work ethic, but you're working way too hard.'

Sophie let out a delicate snort at his assumption. 'I've been ... busy.' The truth was, she realised with a sudden warm glow, that she felt settled in Brooklyn. The bakery and apartment were comfortable and familiar. Coming out into Manhattan felt like too much effort when she did it every day already.

'Where is it you live, again?'

'I share a place in the West Side, pricey but central. It must be a real schlepp for you getting to work.'

'It's not too bad and I like where I live. It's got a nice feel to it.'

Paul winced. 'Not my scene at all. If you're not going to be in the city, you want to move out proper to one of the nice suburbs with decent housing and a garden. That's what my folks did. They've got a place in Kensington. It's an hour out of the city.'

'How funny. I live in Kensington, London. I suspect it's very different.'

'There is a link. When Kensington, Great Neck was built the gates were copied from the ones at Kensington Park in London and the village was named after the gates.'

'Now that is spooky. I run in Kensington Gardens sometimes. I know the gates. I've got to see the ones here. Take a picture.'

'Yeah.' Paul looked awkward. 'I don't get out there too often.'

'No, no,' Sophie shook her head vehemently. 'I wasn't inviting myself to meet your parents.'

He toyed with the cardboard sleeve on his coffee cup. 'It's cool. I didn't think you were. It's fine. I guess I could take you sometime, if you wanted to see the gates. I'm going up ...' He winced. 'Fourth of July. You've probably got plans already.'

'To be honest, I hadn't thought about it. I guess I hadn't realised until last week at work what a big deal it is.' She took a long slurp of coffee, remembering Madison's endless bragging about her family's place in Southampton, which was, according to the smart young intern, the place to be during the summer.

'Oh,' his dismay was palpable.

'Honestly Paul, it's fine. I'm not going to crash a family party. I know it's a big deal over here but it's not to me.'

'No ... you'd be welcome. It's ... well. It's complicated.'

'Paul, it's fine.'

'Now I feel bad. What will you do?'

'Probably nothing, but it's not a problem.'

'You've got to do something.' He frowned. 'You can't spend the holiday on your own.' Rubbing at his forehead, he seemed, for Paul, quite agitated. 'I suppose I could invite you to my folks.' He sighed and drained his coffee and fiddled with the empty cup, circling it on the table.

Sophie smiled, he looked so excruciatingly uncomfortable. It was kind of sweet that he was worried about her being alone for the holiday. 'Don't worry. I understand. My mum and dad are the same whenever I take someone home. Dad's a terror, only a hair's breadth from asking what someone's intentions are.' A lump settled in her throat. Actually, she'd only taken James. Just the once. They'd both really liked him.

'Phew, I'm glad you get it.' His eyes swivelled her way again. 'I have to be careful. It's not just my parents. There's Pamela too.'

'Pamela?'

'Yeah,' he laughed, finally bringing his gaze back to her with a candid snap. 'The girl next door. She's ... well, one day we'll ... you know.'

Sophie felt as if she'd been thumped in the stomach.

'When you've achieved your seven-year plan,' prompted Sophie, her mouth as dry as the Sahara.

'Not necessarily. That's what I love about you Sophie, you are the perfect girl. You really get me. I mean, I really, really like you but the future's a bit grey. But in four months' time, who knows what will happen? Things might have changed. London's not that far away.'

'And if they don't, there's always good old Pamela.' It was unlike Sophie to take refuge in sarcasm, and she could see Paul trying to work out whether she was being serious or not.

'Like I said, who knows what the future will bring?'

'Who indeed?'

Chapter 14

'Morning English, ready for that bike ride and a run?' Todd stood in the doorway, his hair tousled, a cycling helmet dangling from one hand, wearing a Lycra running kit which showed lean muscular legs to great advantage.

'What?' She rubbed at her bleary eyes, she'd only just got up. 'What are you doing here?'

'I was passing and I knew you'd be in.'

'That's because I was sleeping.'

He looked accusingly at her. 'I did mention it on Friday.'

'And I said I was too busy.' It was the last thing she'd said to him in the office.

He grinned. 'Yes, but you didn't mean it. I could see in your eyes and your leg was jigging up and down saying,' he put on a fake falsetto voice, '"Yes please, take me out for a run."'

Sophie hid her smile, ducking her head. 'I'm busy.'

Todd put his hand on the doorframe and leaned against it. 'Busy doing what?'

'I said I'd help Bella.'

He turned and stomped down the stairs.

'You've left your rucksack,' she called as he reached the

186

bottom but he didn't turn around, instead simply giving a casual wave, he disappeared from view.

Shaking her head, she shot a quick regretful look out of the window. The blue sky was dotted with tiny fluffy white clouds and Todd was right, she'd spent most of the week inside, aside from yesterday's trip to the top of the Empire State Building, which she was still stewing about.

In weather like this, if she'd been at home, she'd have packed a small bag and already be on a circuit of Hyde Park. Although after yesterday she'd have happily done a round or two in a boxing ring.

Two minutes later he was back.

'I've cleared it with Bella, you've got two hours.'

'Pardon?' Sophie couldn't believe the cheek.

'Two hours. Perfect. We can run before it gets too hot.'

'But ...'

'Sophie,' he put a hand on her arm, 'it's a gorgeous day. Come on, you can go and be Bella's bitch later.'

'I'm not ...' she squeaked.

He grinned at her outraged response.

'Oh, alright then.'

Changing quickly, she returned to the lounge and gulped when she found Todd bending down to tighten the laces of one of his trainers, the Lycra throwing his rather delicious bottom into sharp relief.

Brimming with energy and bounce, he looked the epitome of health and fitness. For a second, she wasn't sure she wanted to be seen next to him, it was so long since she'd been out for a run.

'Mind if I leave this here?' He dropped his rucksack on the floor, taking a couple of bottles of water out. 'Here you go. You're going to need it. The bikes are outside. It's a gorgeous day and we need to make a move before it gets too hot.'

'How did you get two bikes here?' she asked, with a vision of him doing some herculean one-handed cycling.

'Dropped one off earlier and then went back to get mine,' he said with a triumphant tone, making Sophie realise there'd never been any hope of her getting out of this.

'I'm very out of practice,' she said. 'I probably won't be able to keep up with you.'

'No sweat ... actually, there probably will be. You set?'

'Yes,' she smoothed down her top. It amazed her that in her haphazard running-away packing she'd had the foresight to include trainers and her best running leggings.

The bike Todd had borrowed was a lot more expensive than any she'd been on before. She'd often borrowed ones in London, but this was a thoroughbred in comparison. It made cycling much easier and once she was used to it, she was able to enjoy the ride, especially as the view upfront was not to be sneezed at.

It was the sort of morning that made you feel glad to be alive. The streets buzzed with every race and nationality represented. Union Street was a vibrant eclectic mix, one minute down at heel with graffiti and run-down, abandoned buildings, and then the next, an amazing variety of shops offering everything from African drums to maternity wear and antiques. They crossed the canal which moved sluggishly beneath the blue-painted iron-work bridge that rattled ominously as cars passed. Away to their right the water stretched towards high-rise blocks in the distance.

Brownstone houses criss-crossed with fire escapes, made familiar by countless hours of Saturday-night TV, lined the street up here, with wide broad steps leading up to imposing doorways, while narrow gated flights of stairs led down to basements below street level.

At last the street opened into a big intersection, the park just beyond. They navigated the complicated crossings until Todd came to a stop outside an imposing building.

'The Brooklyn Public Library,' he gestured, hopping down from his saddle.

'Wow, that's impressive. Very Egyptian.'

'Yeah, not sure where that come from, but it's a local landmark.'

With its wide, high, flat walls and the twin columns decorated in golden hieroglyphics, it reminded her of an ancient tomb that had been unwittingly transported to modern-day America.

'You OK?'

'I'm keeping up,' said Sophie.

'Cool, we're headed that way.' He pointed across the road to the park entrance and they cycled along a wide, flat road cutting through the park, before he pulled up to dismount and lock the bikes.

'Remember,' she reminded him as they set off at a gentle pace, 'go easy with me.'

'Worried you won't be able to keep up?' he asked with a challenge twinkling in his eyes.

'Not at all,' she retorted, tossing her ponytail. 'I'm trying to lull you into a false sense of security.' At home, she usually went out for a least an hour and she was hoping her habitual weekend runs had embedded themselves into her muscle memory and that he wouldn't leave her too far behind.

Matching her stride to his, which thankfully seemed reasonably paced, they took it slowly and once her breathing had adjusted, she eased into the rhythm, listening to her feet pounding the path and feeling the muscles in her legs working and her arms pumping. As they picked up the pace, she'd forgotten how much she enjoyed the sensation of feeling her body working, being out in the sunshine and surrounded by greenery. After the first mile, her spirits had lifted and she could feel the smile on her face as she lifted it up to the sunshine. Why hadn't she done this before?

She was cross with herself for being so pathetic recently and now as she ran, smooth strides one after the other, the realisation settled in, she'd invested far too damn much of her life in James and his betrayal had left her bereft, which meant that he was winning. And now bloody Paul, keeping someone up his sleeve. The fact that he had someone waiting in the wings for the future felt inherently dishonest. As if he'd already made up his mind that Sophie was never going to matter in his life. She knew she was being contrary but it felt as if he'd closed the door before they'd even started.

They ran steadily for half an hour until the lake came into view and Todd slowed.

'Want to stop here for a breather?'

They sat down on the gravel beach next to the lake, where

swans on the far side glided across the surface and a couple of small children ran up and down trying to skim stones.

'This is lovely,' said Sophie, peering up at the skyline above the trees. 'Hard to believe we're not in the countryside.'

'It was designed deliberately so that the trees shield the view outside the park,' explained Todd. 'I like to come here at the weekends, recharge the batteries.' He stared out over the lake and almost looked wistful. 'There's something about seeing trees ... kinda restful.'

Sophie raised a sceptical eyebrow. It didn't sound like a Man About Town sort of thing to say, and then guilt pinched when he looked a little hurt.

'I'm serious. They're grounding. Seeing them in all the different seasons, it's reassuring. You know, that consistency. Buds in the spring, springing to life, blossoming in the summer, a last hurrah in the fall with colourful finery. The leaves don't just die, they go out in a blaze of glory,' he paused and shot a quick uncertain glance at her.

Charmed by his poetry and seeing this different side to him, she nodded in encouragement.

'Fall here is spectacular and even when they're bare in the winter, the branches look strong, reaching up, reaching forward. Symbolic as well. Roots, branches. Giving us oxygen.' He stopped suddenly, as if worried he'd said too much. 'Sorry, I came over all lyrical. You should take a trip up to New England in the fall, the colours up there are really—'

'*You have a message from dark side.*'

Sophie began to giggle, it was such an un-Todd-like ring tone.

'Sorry,' Todd looked endearingly sheepish as he unzipped a pocket to retrieve his phone. 'My kid brother put it on here. It's set to his text messages.'

He pulled out the phone, read the message and frowned. 'Sorry, I need to answer this.'

'No worries,' said Sophie as he began to tap away.

When he finally put his phone away, Todd said, 'Sorry about that. Martin ... he's having a tough time.'

'How old is he?'

'Thirteen.'

'Oh,' said Sophie, surprised. 'That's quite an age gap.'

'Yeah, my parents thought it would help their marriage.' Todd didn't elaborate but there was a bitter twist to his mouth that stopped her from asking any more, and with a quick change of subject he asked, 'Do you have any brothers and sisters?'

'No, only child. I always wanted a brother or a sister. Do you get on with your brother?'

'Yes.' Todd's face brightened. 'How could I not? He worships me. I'm the older brother who buys him the Xbox games. Plays *Minecraft* with him online. Sneaks him the odd beer and takes him to basketball games.'

'Ah, the perfect big brother then,' said Sophie, 'and modest with it.'

Todd's mouth twisted. 'Not really, I'm probably over-compensating because I don't see him enough and I feel guilty. My parents ... aren't easy. He's on his own a lot. He might as well be an only child. I ought to go for the holiday, that's what he was texting about.' His shoulders slumped slightly. 'I was hoping to avoid going but I can't leave him on his own. Well, my folks will be there, but there'll be lots of guests.'

Sophie thought of her parents with a pang. Her brief WhatsApp chats with her mother over the last few weeks had been masterpieces of subterfuge, not once had she let on how miserable she'd been or how little she'd done since she'd been here.

'What are your plans for the holiday?' he asked suddenly.

Sophie stiffened and shrugged. 'I haven't really thought about it.'

'What about Paul? Has he invited you to go home with him?'

Sophie gave him a mutinous glare.

'Sore point?'

'Paul has a girl next door waiting for him.' Sophie tried to sound bright and uncaring. 'Apparently I would upset the apple cart.'

'Ouch.' He gave her a sympathetic smile. 'He's an idiot. I told you, you could do better for a fling.'

'I-it's ... OK.' For some stupid reason there was a lump the size of an egg in her throat all of a sudden.

'You could come out to the beach with me.' He blurted it out and then looked a bit confused as if he hadn't meant to.

'Don't worry Todd, you don't have to do that. I'm a big girl. I'll be fine.'

'I'm serious. You should come. You'd love the beach.'

'What? To your family's place?' Had he meant it or was it a spur-of-the-moment thing he was now thinking better of?

'Yeah,' Todd nodded vigorously. 'There's loads of room. Mom always has a big Fourth of July party. There'll be fireworks. Great food and the champagne will be flowing.'

'Won't your mum mind?' Her mouth pursed. 'Or get the wrong idea?'

'No,' he gave a half-laugh. 'With that accent they'll love you. I can tell them you're landed gentry.'

Sophie winced, grateful he was so taken with the idea that he didn't notice.

'It'll be great. Besides, they won't even notice one extra.'

'Where is it?' She was tempted, especially after Paul's rejection.

'The Hamptons. Amagansett, near to the end of Long Island. The beach is beautiful there. It goes on for miles. Apart from my family, I love it. Bella and I used to have great summers there. Dad and Uncle Bryan would come out at the weekend from the city and the adults would party and mostly they'd forget we were around. We could pretty much do what we wanted,' he grinned, 'and we pretty much did.'

'What d'ya think?' asked Bella, stepping back, placing the last strawberry on top of a fruit topped-cheesecake as Sophie and Todd walked into the kitchen.

'Very patriotic,' said Sophie, admiring the rows of red interspersed with piped cream next to the wedge of blackberries, enjoying the summer scent of the berries. It brought back memories of Wimbledon and sunshine, pick-your-own in the field on the estate farm and a delicious strawberry-and-rhubarb crumble she'd once made.

'Fourth of July is coming up. I thought I'd start getting people in the mood and,' her eyes sharpened, 'make them start thinking about putting in their holiday orders. But this is missing something.'

'Spangle,' said Sophie.

'What?' Bella frowned, looking at the cake.

'Your flag is always called the star-spangled banner, so you need some spangle. You could put some of those little silver balls on the top of the piped cream.'

'You mean the silver-ball dragees?' said Bella.

'Yes, I absolutely love them,' said Sophie, remembering making cakes with her mother and the tiny decorations invariably escaping and scattering all over the kitchen floor.

'I've heard of blue balls, English and I tell you that's not a good thing,' teased Todd, 'but now silver?' His eyes widened with mischief.

'Don't be rude,' said Sophie, biting back her smile. 'You'll spoil them for me. Those silver dragees, if you will,' she deliberately copied his accent, 'are my favourite thing. They add something special to a cake. A little touch of star-shine, at least that's what my mum always used to say. And you can never have too much star-shine, can you?'

'Cute,' said Bella, before adding, 'how was the run? And do you guys want some coffee?'

'I could murder a cold drink,' said Todd, sauntering over to the large fridge and pulling out a couple of cans of Coke. 'Want one, Sophie?'

'Help yourself,' said Bella sarcastically.

'Thanks,' said Sophie.

'You are welcome, him not so. Unless he's prepared to do dishes.'

The kitchen, piled high with mixing bowls bearing traces of red, white and blue frosting, bore testament to a morning's hard work already and Sophie immediately felt guilty.

'Let me go shower and I'll come help. It's hot out there, you do not want to get too close to me.'

Bella bit her lip. 'You don't have to. Sorry, I'm feeling a bit stressed.' She slumped against the messy stainless-steel counter. 'I've taken an order for fifty cupcakes for a birthday party tomorrow but they don't want butter-icing frosting. They want something different and my head is full of July Fourth ideas. Although I could do with a few more of those too.'

'Don't worry, we'll come up with something,' said Sophie, patting her arm gently. 'Give me ten minutes.'

'I'll help. I can use Sophie's shower. Ever since we did the renovation, I've wanted to try it out. There are clean clothes in my backpack. I'll be your lean, mean washing-up machine.'

Before Sophie could protest, Bella gave a grateful sigh. 'Would you? I feel a bit out of control. All hands on deck would be gratefully received.'

'Do you want to go first?' asked Sophie, her voice bright and casual as she opened her front door. The thought of a naked Todd in her shower shouldn't have any effect but her stupid hormones had other ideas and were leaping about, getting all giddy and silly.

'No, I'll wait, if I could borrow a towel.'

'Of course.'

She went straight into the bedroom and as she pulled out the storage box from under the bed, she realised that he'd followed her in.

'I helped Bella decorate in here. Looks good.' He paused, clearly taking a good look around. She was glad her face was hidden from him. 'You didn't bring much stuff with you.'

Yanking out a towel, she shuffled back on her knees and bumped into him.

'Here you go,' she said, turning and kneeling up, passing the towel up to him, inadvertently brushing his crotch and then coming face-level with it.

'Oops. I didn't mean to ... erm ... yes. Sorry.'

Todd's mouth twitched, his eyes dancing with amusement.

Suddenly the room was far too small and very, very hot and he looked as cool and unconcerned as a dozen flipping cucumbers.

He tucked a hand under her arm and helped her to her feet.

'I'll j-just go ... go in the ... the shower.'

'Yes,' said Todd gravely, his tone belying the twinkle in his eye. 'Why don't you?'

Grabbing a towel, Sophie bolted.

She glared at herself in the mirror. Why couldn't she have laughed it off instead of getting all flustered and embarrassed? Todd must think she was a complete idiot, no scrub that, he already did.

With a muffled groan, she wound her ponytail into a knot, stuck another band around it and peeled off her clothes to step into the warm flow of the shower, feeling the heat soothing her tired muscles. She'd enjoyed the run but knew that she'd probably pay for it tomorrow or the day after. Feeling much better, she wrapped her towel around her and tried not to think that there was only one shower gel and that Todd would be using it in her shower. *His* body in *her* shower. *Naked body in her shower.* Her stomach did a lumpy sort of forward roll, as if it weren't completely sure what the heck was going on.

Sophie did not want to think about what Todd might look like without any clothes, although she thought with vicious satisfaction, his body was probably a hell of a lot more buff than James' slightly pudgy-around-the-middle one. Yeah, it would be buff. And she should not be thinking about it. Absolutely not. She hadn't ever thought about Paul that way, even though he rocked a suit. Tall, slender ... OK, his shoulders weren't as broad as Todd's and they sloped down a little and he was ... a tad bony, possibly. Despite her best efforts, her mind refused to be redirected. A flood of heat flushed across her skin. OK, Todd had a hot bod in that Lycra gear. It wasn't a leap to imagine it naked. Natural curiosity. Although natural curiosity did not make you feel flushed, with that irritable spot-that-needs-scratching feeling. She fanned her face, feeling the soft towel chafe at her peaked nipples. With a yank she tightened the towel, regretting that she'd not brought a change of clothes in with her. She'd better make sure she hung onto this sucker tightly. Taking a moment, she drew in a breath and opened the bathroom door, walking through the hallway to her bedroom, where Todd had made himself comfortable. Very comfortable indeed.

'Oh,' squeaked Sophie, coming to a very quick halt, all the moisture in her mouth evaporating instantly.

He was lying on the bed, propped up on her pillows, wearing nothing but the pale-blue towel wrapped low around his hips, busy with his phone.

Buff? Her imagination had failed her spectacularly. This was buffest of the buff. Proper ab definition, muscular pecs, and that oh-so-sexy crease above his hips. If that towel got any lower, everything the dark trail of hair from his navel pointed to, would be on display.

He looked up. 'All ... done?' his voice trailed away and something flashed in his eyes before he raised his eyebrows, the usual look of mischief returning to his face as he said, 'Nice legs.'

'Shame about the wonky boobs.' It came out as she was desperately trying to stop staring at his chest and look him in the eye. Although probably it was the best thing she could have said, because it sort of broke the ... no, not ice, the temperature in the room had sky-rocketed.

'Wonky boobs?' Todd laughed. 'Never heard that before. Do I get to see?'

'No you do not,' said Sophie, her voice quivering with slight indignation before it gave way to laughter. 'I've no idea why I told you that.'

'Neither have I, but now I'm really intrigued. What constitutes wonky boobs?' He tilted his head and stared at her chest, which she could hardly complain about as she'd pretty much invited him to.

Sophie blushed, waving her hand in front of her chest as

if to dislodge his attention. 'One of them is bigger than the other. As someone,' someone whose name she was not going to mention, 'once said, I have a boob and a half, rather than a pair.'

'Harsh, I'm sure they're perfectly lovely,' he smiled into her eyes. 'They look absolutely fine from here.'

'Thanks,' she said, now fervently wishing they could end this conversation and that he would just go on into the bathroom. She was rather proud of the fact that her voice sounded firm and in control, because seriously, any minute now she might dissolve into a pile of drool. For the love of God, would he please take his perfect body, get cleaned up and put some clothes on? 'Help yourself. To everything you need.'

'Will do.' He sauntered past her, as if this was all completely natural for him.

When he finally closed the bathroom door behind him, Sophie sank onto the bed, and dropped her head into her hands. Dear lord, how was she ever going to get the image of his perfect body out of her head? She was so screwed. Despite everything, she totally fancied the pants off the man. He was bad news. A relationship no-no and despite all her resolutions, she couldn't help thinking that if she were that sort of girl, after a no-strings fling with Todd, she could die a very happy woman.

Chapter 15

When they walked back into the kitchen at ten-thirty, Bella had lined up what looked like dozens and dozens of cupcakes ready for icing and Wes was standing drinking a glass of water.

'Thanks for coming back, I wouldn't have blamed you for doing a runner.' Bella wiped her hand across her forehead. 'I'm so tired, I can't think straight. Any ideas for another holiday theme, Soph? I'm relying on you. And I am so sick of red, white and blue frigging frosting.' She pointed to the batches of cakes behind Wes which were already decorated in patriotic swirls. 'I also need to cook up more cookies, decorate another cheesecake and come up with an idea for a showstopper of a Fourth of July cake to take home with me.'

'I did think of an idea for the cupcakes. How about white fondant icing with bunting triangles of red, white and blue, some spotty, some not? A bit Cath Kidston.' Sophie wasn't sure how big Cath Kidston was over here, but Bella nodded as if she knew what she was talking about. She tried to catch Bella's eye while Todd and Wes weren't looking.

'Brilliant. They'll look lovely. In fact, I could do those year round, change the colours to match the seasons. You're a genius, Sophie,' said Bella, her words running into each other as she did everything she could to avoid looking directly at Sophie.

'Once Todd's done the washing-up, we can get him to cut out the triangles.'

'I can do that too,' rumbled Wes's low voice.

'OK,' said Sophie. 'Bella, why don't you carry on making the cakes, while I colour the icing and roll it out, and then the boys can use the cutters to make the bunting flags.'

There was a flurry of activity around the kitchen as everyone took up their new positions.

Sophie sidled up to Bella. 'You haven't asked him yet, have you?'

Bella yanked open a drawer and pulled out a rolling pin and some metal cutters. 'Here, Todd. As soon as Sophie gets cracking, you'll have a job.' She gave Sophie a sharp nudge.

'Coward,' said Sophie with a teasing smile.

'I just need the right moment,' Bella muttered back.

'What are you two whispering about?' asked Todd. 'Coming up with more jobs for us poor hapless skivvies?'

'Yes, although it would help if you made a start on the washing-up,' said Sophie.

'You're quite bossy, when you get going,' observed Todd with a quick gentle nudge in the ribs, as he rolled up his sleeves.

'I have my moments. Now get to work, my man.'

'Aye aye.' He crossed over to the big industrial sink piled high and calmly began to run water.

For the next hour the four of them worked in quiet sync,

gentle chatter punctuating their flow, as Sophie and Bella guided operations. Sophie noticed that Bella avoided looking at or touching Wes, while he, when Bella wasn't looking, watched her with a naked hunger in his eyes that had Sophie puzzled. He clearly liked Bella and she liked him, so what was the problem and why was Bella so wary of asking him out?

When several dozen cupcakes had been baked and frosted, three batches of cookies had been baked and the second cheesecake had been decorated, Bella called for a coffee break.

'Thank you, God,' said Todd, heading straight to the machine, abandoning his post at the sink with glee.

'I need to head off, I'll take my coffee to go,' said Wes.

Bella watched him go, her mouth slightly pinched. 'Thanks for your help.'

'Anytime, Bella babes, anytime.' The wide, white-toothed, crescent smile he gave her didn't quite reach his amber eyes.

'So Sophie,' said Bella, dismissing Wes with brittle determination, 'I've seen this amazing cake on Pinterest.'

Wes took his coffee and as he walked out he raised his fingers in a casual salute.

'You did?' Sophie could spot a diversion tactic a mile away.

'Yes, look,' she showed Sophie a picture on her phone, 'you cut it and you can see the stars and stripes in every slice. I'm trying to work out how the heck you assemble it.'

Todd had made Sophie a coffee, and she nodded thanks to him as she poured milk into her mug. 'Alternate sponges of red and cream filling ... hmm, and then if you made a blue sponge but cut out most of the middle and filled it with a red sponge ... yes, that would work. Although I'm not sure how you'd get the stars running through. White chocolate chips in the blue sponge, perhaps?'

'You beauty!' shouted Bella. 'Genius, of course.' She slapped Sophie on the back, narrowly missing spilling her coffee.

Sophie lifted her cup as if to bat away the compliment. 'Team work. Actually, I stole that off *The Great British Bake Off*.'

'I don't care, it works for me and I love that show. Did I say how grateful I am for all your help?' She shot Todd a quick, warm look. 'Even yours.'

He toasted her with his coffee. 'Anytime, cous.'

'You did,' said Sophie, examining the contents of her coffee cup.

'No really, I'd have struggled with this many commissions. With you helping, I've been able to keep on top of those. Now that wedding season is coming up, it's getting busier.' She turned pleading eyes on Sophie. 'You are sticking around, aren't you?'

Todd rolled his eyes.

Sophie patted her hand with a reassuring smile. 'Don't worry. I'm here until the end of November.'

'Darn it, can't you stay a bit longer, I'll have Christmas cakes to do.'

'I'll be wanting to go home for a rest. You're a slave driver.'

'Sorry, am I too much? I am, aren't I?' Bella bit her lip, her face creasing in sudden worry.

'You're fine. I love helping you. I'm most at home in a

kitchen.' Sophie paused and then looked at her and Todd, his invitation to the beach still in her mind. 'You've been a life-saver. Both of you.' She swallowed slightly, ashamed of admitting it, but with Bella it was hard not to tell her everything. 'Without you ... and Todd, I'd have hidden away in the apartment. You've kind of dragged me out. I've always thought I was quite sociable and outgoing – and I am, once I'm out – but I've realised I spent quite a lot of time on my own ... waiting for things to happen, letting things happen to me, rather than going out and making them happen, like I used to do.' She realised there'd been a before-James life and a post-James life and now, in hindsight, the latter hadn't been quite as good as she'd hoped at the time. Even with Paul, she'd pretended that going out with him was stretching her wings again, but she'd been kidding herself. She'd known all along that she was playing safe and avoiding doing anything that would really challenge her.

If she'd acted that way when she'd failed her A levels she'd still be at home waiting on tables in the local pub. It was almost as if she'd been sleepwalking through life for the last two years.

'Does that mean you're going to come out to the beach?' asked Todd, as if he could read her mind.

'I—'

'You should go,' said Bella suddenly, nodding as if it solved a huge problem. 'Todd needs back-up and my family isn't going this year.'

'I heard,' said Todd, his face dimming.

'Sorry.' She patted him on the shoulder and turned back

to Sophie. 'We normally go to our beach house, which is down the road from Uncle Ross, but we're staying home this year. Todd and Martin usually end up spending more time at our place.' She risked a glance at Todd. 'My mom's a bit less ... formal.'

'That's the understatement of the century. Bella's mom would welcome a porcupine that wandered in off the highway.'

'You don't get porcupines on Long Island. National Geographic fact.'

'OK, a deer.'

'Mmm, not sure, Mom gets pretty mad that they eat all the roses in the yard.'

Sophie pressed her lips together hard to stop laughing at them but a tiny snigger slipped out.

'Honestly, you two are worse than brother and sister.'

Bella laughed. 'If you go out to Long Island, you'll have a ... great time. Todd's mom is a fabulous hostess. You'll be well looked after, that's for sure. And the house is wonderful, right on the beach. And you can spend every day there. And the weather will be great. And the fireworks are amazing. Yeah, you should go.'

Todd rolled his eyes at her. 'Keep going Bella, you're really selling it.'

'OK, Todd's mom is a little bit anal about everything being perfect.'

'You said it, not me,' he quipped, folding his arms and crossing his legs at his ankles. For once his smile seemed forced and his stance wary, as if he were ready to bolt at any second.

'But she's OK ... like I said ... a great hostess. And ... she'll probably love you. Just tell her you know Prince William and ... yeah, actually do that, she will love you.' Bella turned to Todd. 'And that will stop your dad thrusting the latest debutante your way.'

Todd glared at her. 'That's not why I invited Sophie,' he bit out. 'Don't make it sound like I'm using her.' Fury flashed in his face.

'Oooh,' said Bella in a high-pitched teasing tone that only a cousin or a sister could get away with. 'Touchy much.'

'Bella, leave it,' he growled, not meeting Sophie's eyes.

'OK. OK. Well, I, for one, am so looking forward to the holiday. I'm going to sleep three days straight and let Mom wait on me hand and foot.

'Yikes! The cookies.' She jumped up and rushed over to the oven, rescuing the chocolate-chunk cookies in the nick of time.

Todd had turned away and was looking into his coffee cup. Sophie wasn't sure what to say, still slightly surprised that Bella, who'd spent the last few weeks warning her off Todd, seemed so keen for her to go with him all of a sudden. Bella was clearly worried about him and thought that Sophie going with him would help in some way, which of course was what made her decide to go.

Todd had done so much for her, it sounded like he needed her support.

Chapter 16

Todd's text arrived as she zipped her bag up, struggling to pull the sides together. The leather holdall she'd borrowed from Bella bulged but after a thorough briefing from Bella on dress code – 'smart, definitely smart dresses for dinner, a cover-up is fine over your suit at breakfast, bikinis are OK at lunch if you're at a pool party and just about anything goes on the beach, although not topless' – and a quick Google on the Hamptons, Sophie was confident that she'd packed and shopped accordingly. The second bag, with its still-warm foil-wrapped contents, she was even more confident of. It had been worth getting up an extra hour early.

Following a post-work shopping spree at Nordstrom Rack and Banana Republic, she now had the perfect capsule wardrobe which included some floral shorts, two gorgeous summer dresses, high- and low-heeled sandals as well as a vest top and two new T-shirts for the beach. Like most of her purchases, the tiny bikini had been an impulse, vanity buy.

Just because Todd was out of bounds didn't mean she wasn't going to feel good in what she wore. She didn't want to let him down in front of his mother, who in her imagination was a patrician older lady, a dead ringer for Nancy Reagan or some elder states-lady.

It felt good to be getting away for a few days. Paul had popped down twice, inviting her for coffee during the week, and both times she'd blown him off citing pressure of work, which of course he was completely understanding about. She had no intention of explaining herself or letting him realise that she'd been a fool ... again.

Over the last few evenings, she'd been busy helping Bella with the July Fourth cakes and proud as she was of them, she'd reached the point where she never wanted to assemble red, vanilla and blue sponges again. The fiddly cake construction had been a roaring success and once the first one had gone on display, she and Bella could barely keep up with the orders. Yup, she definitely deserved a break and with the weather forecast predicting temperatures up in the thirties, it felt like she was going on holiday.

Todd's eyesore of a car rumbled at the kerbside as he hopped out and took her bag.

'That all you got?' he asked, peering beyond her as if a fleet of Louis Vuitton suitcases might come rolling out any second.

'That's it.'

'Fine by me.' He sniffed. 'Something smells good. Bella baking already?'

Sophie nodded, not elaborating, and stowed her second bag by her feet.

'Let's get out of here,' he said as she strapped herself in, 'the traffic is hellish once you get off the highway. There are only a couple of roads in. And the train is painful. Unless you're a Coldplay fan and you time it right and get the same train out as Chris Martin.'

'What?' asked Sophie, not convinced he wasn't pulling her leg but he looked pretty serious.

'Well, now Gwynie's remarried, he probably doesn't make the trip out so often, and probably by helicopter, but once quite a few years ago I caught the train and he was there, playing his guitar quietly in the corner of the carriage.'

'Wow, that is cool. Do you actually see many celebrities out there?'

Todd lifted his shoulders. 'There are plenty around, but the ones who don't want the fuss act normal, and there's a kind of code, you leave them alone. Even the paps play fair. Besides, there are plenty of wannabes who are looking for lots of attention and loving the limelight. Thankfully they tend to steer clear of the beach, and stick to the pool parties.'

'I thought that's where Mr Man About Town would want to be?' teased Sophie. 'I'm sure an armful of bikini-clad babes would be a good look on you.'

'Why don't I think that's a compliment, English?' He poked at her leg.

'Sorry, I don't have you down as a beach bum or a surfie. You have creases down your Ralph Lauren shorts and you wear deck shoes.'

'That's habit and charm, my laundry lady can't help herself,' he said, casually easing the car into the faster stream of traffic as they headed along Atlantic Avenue. 'I kick back when I get to the beach, I might even have a pair of denim cut-offs in there.' He indicated the horribly expensive-looking leather bag in the back seat.

'Oh lord, how will the beach bunnies cope?'

He grinned at her. 'I'm sure I don't know, although one look at your legs, English, and they'll be breaking out in hives of jealousy.'

Sophie snorted. 'I'm not sure about that.' Although it was nice to get a compliment.

'Although I'm dying to see these famous wonky boobs of yours.'

'I so wish I'd never told you that.' She shut her eyes, wincing, but he laughed and flicked on the radio. 'Fancy some music?'

For the next mile they squabbled light-heartedly about their respective music tastes. When Sophie said that her favourite bands were Wolf Alice and London Grammar as well as singers like Sam Smith and Rag N Bone Man, she knew that Todd would have a comment to make.

'I'd have had you down for up-beat Jess Glynn, Megan Trainor kind of stuff,' said Todd. 'You're the original sunshine girl.'

'Just goes to show, I have hidden depths,' she said smartly. 'Whereas you have Foo Fighters written all over you.'

'Really. No hidden depths here at all?' Todd pouted with toddler cuteness that made Sophie laugh.

'None.'

'Sure?' he asked, the pet lip trembling now.

'One hundred per cent certain.'

He sighed with mock pain. 'English, you wound me.'

'Good. Although this track is quite good, I don't mind a bit of Muse.'

They drove for little over an hour, before Todd said, 'Fancy a break? A walk on the beach before we try and find breakfast?'

Sophie stretched, already feeling a bit stiff. 'That would be great. And,' she gave him a slightly smug and very triumphant smile, 'I brought breakfast. A flask of coffee and ... home-made cinnamon rolls, baked this morning.'

'No way! English, I might just have to marry you.'

'The last man that said that to me turned out to be married already.' Sophie turned her head to look out of the window, grateful for Todd's timely reminder. James, Paul, Todd – they were all as bad as one another. Commitment-shy in different ways.

He turned off the highway and they followed signs to Jones Beach Island. She was following their route on her iPhone on the maps app and could see that it was a long narrow island with a beach running the whole length and a road running straight down the middle. She felt slightly disappointed, there was absolutely nothing to see, just black tarmac that seemed to stretch forward in a dead-straight line, with signs announcing less than romantically named Fields.

They parked in something called Field Six, the most enormous car park off the highway.

'It's early yet. By 10 a.m. this car park will be filling up. We're only twenty miles from New York, it gets pretty busy out here.'

She grabbed her bag. A stiff sea breeze tossed at her curls, pushing them into her face, bringing the slight taste of salt on the air. Dragging in a hefty lungful, she stood for a second, closing her eyes while she savoured the fresh bite of the wind and the warm sunbeams on her face.

Low-level utilitarian buildings fronted the beach. It wasn't pretty in any way.

Todd caught her scrunching her face in disappointment and tapped her playfully on the tip of the nose. 'I know, but it's the first ocean stop. I get my first fix here. When we get out along the beach away from here, you'll see. It stretches for miles.'

As they rounded the squat concrete buildings, the beach opened out, the sea quite some distance away. Todd took her bag and slung it over his shoulder as they ploughed through the sand down towards the sea.

The rolling walk, sinking and sliding across the beach, took a while and Sophie's muscles started to ache by the time they reached the damper and much easier-to-walk-on sand. It wasn't nine yet but there were already a couple of families that had set up camp for the day. Umbrellas up, rugs out and cool boxes no doubt laden with supplies. The white lifeguard tower was manned and a large American flag flew from the top, the stars and stripes flapping in the brisk wind.

Sea spray peppered the air as the waves rushed in and out, foaming white. Sunlight danced and glinted off the waves as far as the eye could see. A few threadbare clouds were strewn across the sky, teased apart like candyfloss, the sort that would be long gone by the time the sun reached its peak.

There was something about sea air, thought Sophie, taking in a deep breath. Immediately you felt soothed. Maybe it was the constant rhythm of the sea, the somnolent inevitability of wave after wave rolling in and sucking the last one away. Or maybe it was the crash of the breaking waves before the gentle lapping as the spent water ran up the sand. Or perhaps the plaintive cries of the gulls wheeling overhead.

They walked in silence, both carrying their shoes in their hands until they had the beach to themselves.

In complete accord they sat down on the drier sand, on Todd's windcheater (she would have called it a waterproof), side by side, their thighs touching. Sophie took the bag from Todd, offered him the flask and two cups while she unwrapped the cinnamon rolls and opened the paper around them like a plate and put it on the sand.

Todd handed her a steaming plastic cup of coffee and chinked his against hers. 'Cheers.'

She nodded towards the pastries. 'Breakfast.'

He took one with a crooked smile, munching and looking out to sea while perching the edge of his coffee cup on his bent knee.

It was a perfect moment. Quiet companionship. Good coffee. Food. No demands on their time. No need to be anywhere, no pressure to talk, to be anything but herself. There was something special about Todd's company, he seemed to have an innate ability to know when to tease, when to talk, when to be serious and when not to say anything at all. It probably came from the fact that he was comfortable in his own skin. He seemed to know who he was. Sophie had thought she'd got it all taped and now she questioned her own judgement, which had turned out to be incredibly bad.

'You're pulling faces, English,' observed Todd quietly, and she turned to find his face inches from hers, the blue eyes earnest and steady. 'You alright?'

'Yes. Just lost in thought for a second.'

'They looked like they weren't the best thoughts. Anything to do with Mr Married?'

Sophie held his gaze and frowned at him, still trying to figure him out. 'You're actually very perceptive, aren't you?' she asked.

His blue eyes skated away towards the sea.

'And nothing like the shallow socialite you pretend to be.' She watched his profile carefully as he carried on gazing out over the waves, noticing how his Adam's apple dipped slightly. 'For someone who's supposedly out with a different girl every night, at a new bar opening every other evening and partying hard every weekend,' she gentled her voice, making it sound less accusatory, 'you seem to be able to drop things very easily whenever Bella needs help, or to show me around Brooklyn.' He was, she realised with a warm glow in her chest, a very kind man and, judging by the way his lips suddenly compressed together, not very comfortable acknowledging it.

'Why is that?'

He took her hand and laced his fingers through hers and put them on his knee.

'Don't go thinking I'm a good guy. I'm not. Bella's family. And by extension, you are. You've been good to her and I'd do anything to help Bella. When we were kids, she was my best bud. I'm good at being the party animal, I enjoy the clubs, the bars, the restaurants and I get paid for writing about them. It's a great job but ... after a while, it's the same old, same old and it *is* a job. And you, well ... you never give me an inch.' He turned to face her. 'Without sounding ... you know ... girls tend to ... I'm not complaining – I got damn lucky with the genes, but that's all some people see. Hell, I can't believe I'm even saying this ... eye candy. Those girls don't know the real me. Nice as they are. You,' he smiled at her, a proper smile that met his eyes and turned her to mush, 'you treat me like a *real* person. I like you, English. When we went to Onyx that night, I realised ... we're friends.'

Friends. Sophie ignored the quick pang she felt and gave him a big smile as if that was the best news she'd heard all week. Then he went and spoiled things by leaning toward her and giving her a feather-brush of a kiss on the very corner of her mouth. As he pulled back the warmth in his eyes set off a slow burn, heat radiating from the inside out, but she kept the serene, smiling, we're-just-friends expression on her face, while inside her heart took up some serious gymnastic rhythms. 'I really enjoy being with you ... it kind of feels like I can be me. I never have to think about what I'm saying. It's easy being in your company.'

'Amy always sounded nice,' said Sophie, conscious of the tingling of her skin where his lips had left the whisper of a touch and the weight of his hand on her thigh, with his fingers wrapped around hers.

'Yeah, nice but ...' he pulled a face, 'how do I say this

without sounding like a complete ass? She's nice but insubstantial. Conversation stops at what do you do for a living, where do you come from? She would never tease me about my harem. Or ...' his eyes twinkled, 'threaten me with her washing.'

Todd took another bite of his cinnamon roll and waved it at her. 'These are amazing.'

'And you're changing the subject.'

He shot her his irrepressible grin, a hint of naughtiness playing around his mouth. 'I always pay my debts. Happy to get my hands on a lady's panties anytime.'

A flood of relief filled her as the mood lightened and she poked him in the ribs, retorting, 'And you're all talk. When was the last time you actually ...?' her voice trailed away as she realised that perhaps she'd strayed over the personal line.

'Been a while, English. Been a while.'

'Sorry, I shouldn't have ...' Sophie flushed scarlet. *What was she thinking?*

'No sweat.' With a lift of his shoulders, he turned his head away, looking out towards the sea before saying quietly, 'I'm not quite the horn dog that everyone in the office thinks.'

'They don't—'

'Yeah they do.' He turned his head quickly, his eyes suddenly serious, boring into her.

'Well, you do rather cultivate it,' she said, wincing at her bluntness, but she realised she felt irritated with him. 'Why do you?'

He shrugged. 'People believe what they want to, it doesn't take much to lead them. It's only because you actually took the time to talk to Amy and co., that you realised it isn't what it seems. The rest of the office believe I'm playing the field. Especially Madison. I tell you, she's put some work into those come-to-bed eyes. If I weren't a gentleman I'd have a free pass there. I tick all the right WASP boxes for her and her daddy.'

'White Anglo-Saxon Protestant?'

'That's the baby. Her daddy knows my daddy, so that makes me perfect boyfriend material.'

'Nothing to do with your hot bod and movie-star good looks, then?' Sophie tilted her head to one side with a quick teasing smile to make it quite clear that she was joking and had definitely not noticed said hot bod or perfectly put-together face.

'Why, thank you, ma'am, but no. She's on the lookout for a husband from the same socio-economic background.'

'Potentially a marriage made in hell,' said Sophie, thinking of her father and his first wife who'd definitely married him for his title, his stately pile and precious little else.

'You've met my parents,' quipped Todd, and for a second they shared a rueful look before lapsing into thoughtful silence. 'Sorry, I should have warned you. They're ... kind of hard work.'

A seagull swooped nearby, making them both start, and Todd protectively snatched up the rest of his pastry. 'Did you really make these? They're delicious.'

'Yes. I went to Copenhagen and learned from an expert.'

Telling him all about her trip to Denmark the previous year sparked an easy segue into an exchange of European countries they'd each visited. Swapping stories, they fell into their usual easy banter and Sophie was laughing so hard at his tale of finding himself in a brothel in Paris that Todd had to pull her to her feet when they decided to head back onto the highway.

Sophie's eyes widened, it was almost as if they'd passed an invisible barrier. Suddenly the houses were prettier and the countryside seemed to have been tamed into well-pruned precision.

She knew it was a wealthy area, but that knowledge didn't prepare her for the astonishing number of Porsches and Range Rovers, which made the many BMWs and Mercedes look commonplace. When she commented, after spotting her third Ferrari, Todd laughed.

'Welcome to the Hamptons.'

He suggested they took a detour from the highway and they drove through Southampton along Main Street where she stared through the window. It was as if the pages of a glossy magazine had come to life in super 3D, everything perfect and bright under a brilliant blue sky and a blazing sun. Even the people walking along the pavements, swinging handfuls of expensive-looking shopping bags, were beautifully tanned and impeccably dressed in a uniform of coloured shorts and smart white polo shirts and designer loafers.

As they drove out through a residential area, the houses were all immaculate, many with white wooden trim surrounding windows and doors, highlighting traditional grey-painted clapboard walls. Nearly every garden was manicured to within an inch of its life with lush, rolling, green lawns, abundant window baskets which co-ordinated perfectly with the paintwork, and sculpted shrubs lining the gravel drives behind the gated entrances.

'It's another world,' said Sophie, wide eyed, trying to take it all in and decide whether she loved it or whether it was a little bit too perfect in an unreal Disney sort of way. 'Very different from Brooklyn.'

'Wait until you see the beach.'

Finally, they came to Amagansett, equally pretty but a little less designer than its earlier neighbours, and at last they turned into a road called Further Lane and Todd pulled into a gap in the sleeping-beauty-proportioned hedge, where two huge oak gates punctuated the entrance like solemn sentries. He punched a code into the intercom on the driver's side and the gates rolled open with portentous slowness and silence. The wide drive wound through immaculately trimmed shrubs to arrive at a turning circle that was the size of an average garden in front of an imposing house.

Todd gave her an anxious look when she didn't say anything.

'Maybe I should have given you a heads up,' he said.

'Maybe you should. But it's OK, I know which cutlery to use and how to address the butler.'

Todd let out a relieved laugh and patted her on the knee. 'I knew I could count on you, English. You take it all in your stride.'

Todd parked next to a convertible Porsche which had its roof down. As he pulled up alongside it, Sophie immediately remembered the first time she'd seen his car.

'You're not really going to leave it here, are you?' asked Sophie, amusement sparkling in her eyes.

'Why not?'

'You know why not.' She gave his petulant scowl a reproving look. 'You're better than that.'

'Am I?'

'Yes. And you're not six years old. Park this heap with all the other cars. I'm presuming there's some enormous garage somewhere.'

'Ooh, I love it when you get all English and school-marmy.'

She simply gave him 'the look' over the top of her sunglasses and waited until, with a dejected huff, he turned on the ignition and drove the car around to the back of the house where there was a carport filled with flashy motors.

As they walked towards the house to a side entrance, Todd suddenly grabbed her wrist and wrapped his fingers through hers, pulling her to a stop. 'Promise you won't judge me after you've met this lot.' The low, urgent tone made her heart ache.

Although he wore sunglasses, she could tell by the set of his face that he looked unhappy and uncertain. There was a wary stillness about him as if he were afraid of her bolting.

Remembering his earlier easy kiss of friendship, she reached up and placed a gentle kiss on his cheek.

'I promise.'

His mouth relaxed and with a quick squeeze of her fingers, he dropped her hand. 'Right then, into the fray. Let the fun begin.'

Carrying their bags, they walked along a short corridor which opened out into a gracious, airy entrance hall taken up with a beautiful, dark, wide-planked staircase, tastefully covered in a narrow cream carpet held in place with gleaming brass stair-rods. The polished chestnut wood of the banister shone with the glossy hue of conkers, making Sophie smile. It was the sort of banister that cried out for small boys to slide down and come flying off the end.

'What?' asked Todd.

'Nothing,' said Sophie, all innocence. 'I was wondering if you ever slid down.' She nodded to the glowing woodwork.

'A time or two ... when no one was looking.'

They shared a conspiratorial smile as he stopped at the bottom of the stairs, putting his hand on the carved end of the banister.

Chapter 17

'Toddy, baby!' A tanned, lithe blonde wrapped in a stunning royal-blue sarong, exactly the right shade to accentuate her tan and the golden hue of her hair, appeared as Todd escorted Sophie into what he called the breakfast room.

The woman placed both hands on his shoulders and kissed each cheek with a loud 'mwah, mwah'.

She looked oddly familiar next to Todd. A relative? An aunt? Another cousin? He hadn't mentioned an older sister. There was no way this model-like creature could possibly be his mother.

'Darling, when did you get here?' There was genuine puzzlement on the woman's face. 'Did Brett pick you up from the airport?'

'We drove. Left very early. Arrived about half an hour ago.' Todd's stiff stance and uncharacteristic coolness made Sophie immediately wary.

'Drove.' The woman rolled her eyes as if it were the oddest thing she'd ever heard. 'At this time of year. You must have left at a godawful time.' She gave a delicate shudder. 'Well, don't let your father know, otherwise I will never hear the end of it,' she said, pursing her lips, which Sophie had been trying hard not to stare at for the last minute. There was something not quite right about them, but she couldn't quite identify what. It was almost as if they belonged to another person.

The woman gave herself a visible sort of shake as if suddenly spotting Sophie standing behind Todd.

'And who's this?' she asked, all arch and winsome.

Todd stepped aside and slid an arm along Sophie's shoulder, letting it rest there with reassuring weight as if he were laying claim to a staunch team-mate.

'Mom, this is my friend Sophie. Sophie, this is my mom, Celine.'

'Mom!' Sophie's mouth fell open in unchecked surprise and she stared. This stunning woman with the amazing figure, in her casual knotted sarong over bikini, with her Jackie O sunglasses perched on top of her white-blonde hair, was nothing like the Nancy Reagan matron she'd pictured. 'You look far too young. My goodness, I thought you were a cousin or something. You can't possibly be ...'

With a dazzling smile, Todd's mother turned to her. 'Well, *you* can be my new best friend. That's so adorable of you to say. And you're English. What a darling accent! Where are you from?'

'I live in London.'

'I adore London. We always stay at the Savoy when we're in town. Do you know it?'

Sophie nodded, bemused, wondering if *you know it* meant, have you stayed there, or have you heard of it?

'Old fashioned but so English. I love it. Todd's father always wants to stay at the Marriott, because he's an old friend of Bill's, Bill Marriott.' She paused for breath before adding, 'And you're a friend of Todd's?' With her raised eyebrow and the sultry lowering of her voice, she hinted at a thousand questions.

'We work together, Mom. And Sophie was going to be on her own for the holidays.' Todd shut her down, without answering the question.

'Oh.' Frigid disinterest echoed in her voice. 'You work at this magazine place too? You have a job.'

Sophie nodded. His mother pinched those strange lips together and busily brushed an invisible speck from her sarong and huffed. 'Well, it's not as if Todd even needs to work there. I think he does it to annoy his father. Which I suppose is as good an incentive as any.'

Todd didn't say anything but from the look on his face, it wasn't the first time such views had been expressed.

'I think it must be our generation,' said Sophie with an understanding smile at Celine, ignoring the slightly shrewish tone. 'My father says exactly the same.'

'He does?' Celine seemed mollified by Sophie's quick nod, while Todd flashed her a grateful smile. 'I guess it's a phase then. Hopefully he'll grow out of it.'

'Now, I want you to make yourselves at home. Todd, you can show Sophie around. If you have any special dietary requests, do let chef know. We're having dinner tonight in the dining room. Just the family party, the rest of the guests are flying in tomorrow. And then we'll have a houseful. The party on Saturday night is formal dress. Todd, you did bring your tuxedo?'

'Of course.'

A small Filipino woman approached them and waited patiently until Celine turned her attention to her. 'Ah, this is my housekeeper, Mahalia. If you need anything, Mahalia can help you.'

The woman's eyes lit up. 'Mr Todd, welcome.'

'Hey, Ma, how are you?' He gave the pint-size woman a big hug, picking her up off her feet, as her severe face relaxed into giggles.

'Todd! Really.' Despite her remonstration, Sophie was relieved to see that Celine's frown didn't quite meet her eyes. 'Honestly, he is naughty. With everyone else Mahalia is an absolute martinet. Quite why she dotes on him so much, I'll never know.'

Mahalia giggled and when Todd put her down, she pinched his cheeks. 'He so good looking, Cee. Now Chef want you to try the beef Carpaccio and you need make up your mind which crystal for tomorrow. The Lalique or the Baccarat?' The diminutive woman put her hands on her hips. 'I need decision today, lady.'

'I was thinking the Swarovski.'

'Eeeugh, no,' screeched Mahalia, swatting at the other woman with her hands. 'Too trashy. They no good.'

'She is so bossy,' said Celine. 'And I couldn't live without her. See you later.'

And the two of them walked away, Celine's blonde head bowing down next to the dark head.

Todd watched them go with a wistful smile. 'There they go, the Rottweiler and the Pekinese. You know they're best friends.'

'Really?'

'Yes, when no one else is around, Mom spends all her time in the kitchen with Mahalia, gossiping and drinking coffee and watching repeats of *Gilmore Girls* and *Riverdale*. Not that she'd ever admit it and if she heard me say that, she'd have my tongue cut out.'

'That's so sweet, although it sounds familiar.' Sophie thought of her parents and how they first met. The tale of her dad taking refuge in the kitchen, getting under the feet of his new housekeeper at Felston Hall after his ex-wife refused to move out, was one of Sophie's favourites.

'Hmm, *sweet* is not a word I associate with my mother.'

'She's very glamorous.' Sophie smoothed down her linen dress, worrying that maybe it was a bit too casual. Even dressed in a sarong, Celine looked a million dollars.

Todd tugged at the loose dress over her swimming costume. 'Don't worry. You always look gorgeous. Come on, I'll show you around.'

'Fancy a dip?' asked Todd.

'I'm not sure I dare,' answered Sophie, looking around the pool area, the last stop on the grand tour, which was grand. 'It's so ... quiet.' The word *perfect* had been her first choice.

Wooden decking surrounded the long rectangular pool which had been tiled in deep blue with a wave design picked out in a glittery twinkling mosaic. White rattan sun loungers, topped with navy-and-white cushions, all propped up at the same height, were arranged in pairs with a matching table and a co-ordinating parasol separating the two. Rolled navy towels had been placed exactly two thirds of the way up each bed and a little pot of bright-red geraniums sat on each table.

'It is lovely,' said Sophie, not wanting to sound ungrateful at the offer, but she didn't want to be the first to move one of those carefully placed rolled-up towels. To litter up one of the sunbeds. Put her sunglasses and sun cream on a table.

You couldn't deny the house was gorgeous and seriously sumptuous, the superlatives were endless ... but it didn't feel like a home. Everything had been placed. Nothing left. Nothing scattered. Even the family photos, all formal pictures, were grouped in silver frames on the grand piano in the sort of lines that felt as if they owed everything to military precision and nothing to family pride.

Suddenly she realised she was biting her lip and from the slightly amused expression on Todd's face, she knew every thought had been transparently displayed on her face.

'Come on, come and meet my brother.' He grabbed her hand and led her towards the back of the house and down a corridor she'd missed spotting earlier.

No wonder this room was tucked away, with its battered leather sofa, pile of video games and a huge wide-screen TV. It looked comfortable, slightly worn and much more like a family den. A boy of about thirteen sat on the edge of the sofa hunched over a controller, completely focused on the screen in front of him, on which airborne dragons ridden by longbow-wielding elves, which Sophie knew were called Lairfolk, battled with an alien species which bore a marked resemblance to flying otters.

'Hey little dude,' said Todd.

The boy's head whipped round and he jumped up, abandoning his controller. 'Todd!'

'Marty!' teased Todd, mirroring his brother's excited arm waving.

The boy skidded to a halt just short of Todd's outstretched arms as he noticed Sophie, and his own lanky arms dropped awkwardly to dangle at his sides.

'Hey,' he muttered. 'You're back.'

Todd ignored the sudden loss of enthusiasm and swept his brother into a hug, rubbing his knuckles into the top of the boy's head until Marty wriggled and started play-fighting back.

'How are you, little dude?'

'Taller than Mom,' said Marty with a pugnacious lift of his chin that belied his reedy build and thin shoulders.

'This is my friend Sophie. This here's my little brother.'

Marty scowled at him and gave Sophie a perfunctory nod but she spotted the give-away firming of his lips.

'Hi Marty. Good game.' She nodded towards the screen.

His shoulders lifted. 'Do you play?'

She smiled at his sudden eagerness. 'I have been known to,' she said with a self-deprecating twist to her mouth.

'Wanna play?'

'Not just now,' said Todd.

As Marty started to turn away, a flash of disappointment in his eyes, Sophie jumped in.

'I'd love to.' She moved around to the front of the sofa, ready to take a seat. 'But only if I can be a Swirenguard and have a Rating Nine Dragon Wraith.'

She giggled at Todd's startled look while Marty immediately perked up, rubbing his hands together, and handed her a second controller. 'Cool. You're on.'

He looked back at his older brother. 'Todd?' and even before he could answer, the boy was already scrabbling under the sofa and pulling out a third controller.

'What the heck?' He gave Marty a cocky grin. 'I've never even heard of this game ... but looking at the opposition, little dude and English, I feel a victory coming my way.'

Sophie winked at Marty. 'I think we need to show him a thing or two. This is war.'

'This is war,' echoed Marty and fist-bumped Sophie. Her heart turned over at his easy acceptance of her as over his head Todd mouthed, 'Thank you,' to Sophie with a warm smile.

Half an hour later, Todd was pleading for a break. 'Seriously, you guys are monsters. Ganging up on me like that.'

'What did you expect?' said Sophie with a superior tilt to her head, nudging Marty.

'Yeah, bro. Me and Sophie creamed you.'

'Sophie cheated,' said Todd, laughter dancing on his face.

'How did I cheat?' asked Sophie with mock indignation.

'You didn't say you'd played before.'

'You didn't ask.'

'Yeah Todd, you didn't ask,' chorused Marty.

Todd rolled his eyes. 'And how did you know those evil fairy things were down the mine-shaft before you got there?'

'Yeah, actually that was pretty cool.' Marty's admiration made her grin. 'And when you raided the serpent's nest to get more arrows. This version only came out two days ago.'

'I never had you down as a gamer.' Todd's puzzlement made her raise her eyebrows at both of them with an impish smirk.

'Well ...' she paused, unable to keep the glee from her face. 'I might have had a bit of inside knowledge.'

'You had a preview copy?' asked Marty, his eyes growing wide.

'Better than that. I've seen its inception. My neighbour is Conrad Welsh.'

Marty's mouth dropped open, his eyes even wider now, while Todd looked blank.

'Should I know who that is?' he asked.

'H-he ... h-he ...' Marty spluttered.

'He's, well actually, he's a she, is a games developer. And quite well known.' Marty nodded vigorously at that. 'She lives next door to me in London.'

Marty was now blinking furiously, holding his chest as if he were hyperventilating.

'She's a ... well, *friend* is stretching it. Conrad is a loner, she doesn't really do friends, or rather, she doesn't know what to do with them.' Sophie often thought of her as a stray kitten she'd adopted. Her neighbour rarely tore herself away from the computer screen to bother with things like visits to super-markets, so Sophie had taken to visiting with regular food parcels as if she were some elderly impoverished neighbour instead of a socially awkward twenty-three-year-old with more money than she knew what to do with.

'I get dragged in to help her test the games. She's a bit ... she doesn't like strangers in her flat and won't let the games leave her place before she's happy with them, so it was me or nothing.'

Marty had just about found his breath. 'That's seriously sick,' he said, his awestruck attitude lasting for another few minutes as he peppered Sophie with questions, much to Todd's silent amusement.

At last Marty ran out of steam on the games front. 'Can we go boarding?'

'Sure,' said Todd. 'I'm dying to get out on the beach.'

Chapter 18

As the three of them crested the top of the dunes, Sophie stopped and gazed down the endless length of the beach, the spit of yellow sand contrasting against the blue for as far as the eye could see.

Todd, with a body-board tucked under one arm and a bag loaded with beach towels, turned back to look at her with an I-told-you-so grin. 'Wonderful, isn't it?'

'Unbelievable.' The wind tossed her hair across her face as she stared out towards the vast expanse of the sea. It was sobering to think that there was nothing between here and Portugal. It was also a very handy distraction from Todd's tanned muscular legs covered in dark hair. Did the man ever look anything less than delicious? Even super-casual today in colourful patterned board shorts and a faded Timberland T-shirt, with the wind tugging the dark hair into tufts, he still looked like he was modelling surf gear.

With a whoop at the sight of the sea, Marty ran off down the dune, his feet churning up the surface of the beach, leaving a wake in the wind like the Roadrunner.

Underfoot, the pale fine sand felt like cool waves as she

sank up to her ankles, wincing at the occasional prickle of pine needles and twigs. It was hard work, especially when she also carried a cool box which might as well have been weighted with rocks. 'Come on.' Todd grabbed her hand and tugged her down the dunes and together they floundered down towards the water.

Marty had already run down to the sea, his indecipherable shout of joy carrying back to them, his lanky limbs flailing like a mad scarecrow as he dragged his body-board behind him.

They set up camp to a chorus of yells from Marty, chiding them for their slowness as he ploughed straight into the water.

'That is the Atlantic, isn't it?' asked Sophie dubiously.

Todd nodded.

'Isn't it cold?'

'Only when you first get in, but he's like a fish. Never seems to feel it.' He spread the towels out. 'Thanks for joining in with him – that was ... good. He gets a bit lonely out here all summer surrounded by adults. Mom and Dad's friends' kids are all our age.'

'It wasn't a problem. And who doesn't love a bit of hero-worship?' teased Sophie.

'Yeah, you've definitely made a hit.'

'Ah well, definitely a case of who you know in this instance.'

Todd looked up from smoothing down one of the towels over the sand. 'No, Sophie. You were kind, like you always are. I bet you'd have had a go at that game even if you'd had two left thumbs, when you saw how much spending some time with me mattered to him.'

Sophie shrugged his comments off. 'He clearly adores his big brother.'

Todd screwed up his face and looked out to where Marty was already diving into the waves. 'He's a good kid. I wish I could do more to ... I feel bad that he's stuck out here.'

Over the crash of the sea they could hear Marty yelling for Todd to come in.

He hesitated, one hand already pulling at the hem of his T-shirt.

'Go on.' She eyed his body-board. 'I think I'll leave that to the experts. Spend ...' she gulped and busied herself, pulling a book and sun cream out of her bag as, in one fluid move, Todd pulled his T-shirt off over his head, 's-some time with Marty. I'll be quite happy. Here. Watching people. People watching.' She pushed her sunglasses firmly up her nose. Gosh, it was hot. Her mouth had gone very dry. 'Yes. Go. I'm fine. Fine.' *Please go. Please take that exceptionally hot bod with you.*

With a quick wave, and was there a slight twist of amusement to his lips, *Oh please no*, Todd jogged away and Sophie sucked in a long breath. Honestly. *Get a grip, woman.* She was as bad as a teenager. Yes, he was very pretty, to look at. Look, not touch. Her flipping hormones needed reminding who was in charge here, but even as she was trying to remind herself that he was a friend, as he'd been at pains to make clear this morning at Jones Beach, her imagination had progressed from wondering what it might be like to touch that smooth skin around his waist, to what it would be like to be held against a very, *oh yes*, manly chest.

Cross with herself, she opened the cool box, picked out a bottle of water and took a long cool swallow. Enough. She was going to relax. Enjoy the sensation of being on holiday. It had been a long time since she had nothing to do but sit in the sunshine with a book and soak in the atmosphere. It was also highly entertaining watching Marty and Todd ploughing through the waves, teasing and laughing at each other, joining another group of young men who all looked very similar in their board shorts hanging off lean, lanky torsos.

The beach wasn't exactly crowded but there were plenty of interesting people to observe from behind her sunglasses. Down where the waves ran out of steam and licked at the sand, a woman who looked like Sarah Jessica Parker strolled past hand in hand with a handsome man ... Oh my goodness, it was Matthew Broderick.

After surreptitiously watching them until they were out of sight, she leaned back on her elbows enjoying the sun on her face, and Sophie realised that for the first time in a very long time, she actually felt content and happy with her lot. Carefree, as if a load had been lifted from her shoulders.

Shocked with the realisation, she sat up, digging her hands through the sand, letting the grains run through her fingers, like the memories sifting through her head as she tried to pick through where things had gone wrong.

When she'd come out to the US, she'd been running, with no thought beyond getting on the plane and escaping. Putting herself into limbo. Now she was here, it was liberating because there was no pressure. And with that weightless lack of responsibility here, it came to her that in London she'd been ground down by expectation. So busy waiting for the next step, she'd neglected the *now*. Ground down by waiting for James. Putting her life on hold in readiness for when he would ask her to marry him, when in fact she'd not been happy. She let out a half-laugh. She'd turned this trip down originally because of him. The usual pattern of not doing things because she was waiting for when he would commit to her. Sitting on the sidelines playing second fiddle to his mother. Playing video games with her neighbour, feeling superior because Conrad needed looking after, when the truth was, she had nothing better to do while she was waiting for James. A continual rubbing away of her self-esteem. Tension cramped her stomach as she remembered being reasonable and not stamping her feet because James always put his mother first. Now she knew why, her stomach knotted with the familiar fury. She'd been so bloody spineless and pathetic. She'd wasted so much time. Her own fault. She'd let herself do that. She couldn't blame James for that.

And worse still, she'd almost started to walk the same path with Paul. Playing second fiddle at the outset.

She picked up a handful of sand and let it seep away through her fingers. It was a painful analogy for her life at this moment. Letting it seep away.

A shadow came over her and she looked up to see Todd, droplets of water glistening on the hairs on his forearms, standing in front of her.

'You look fierce,' he said and with a start she realised she'd been grinding her teeth.

'And hot ...' he grinned, exuding his usual confident charm. 'Want to come and cool down in the sea?' He held out a hand.

All her anger drained away, replaced by amusement at his deliberate double meaning. What was she doing brooding when she should be enjoying the here and now? Life didn't get better than this. The Hamptons. Sunshine. Todd. With an answering grin, she threw out her hand to grasp his. 'Sounds like just the thing,' she said, letting him haul her to her feet. 'What happened to Marty?'

'He hooked up with some boys his own age whose parents have a beach house down the street.'

'That's good.'

'Yeah, they're here for a month. Hopefully it'll be company for him. I don't feel quite so bad about only being here for the weekend.'

As they neared the water, she took off, throwing a cheeky grin over her shoulder. 'Last one in buys champagne at Onyx.'

Laughing, Todd gave chase, splashing after her, deliberately kicking up the water, making her flinch and squeal at the cold spatters. Just keeping in front of him, she ploughed in, slowing as the wet sand caught at her feet, taking sharp indrawn breaths at the water's icy bite on her sun-warmed skin.

'Cold, cold, cold,' she rasped, thrashing through the waves, sucking in her stomach as if that might somehow delay the touch of the water. Todd caught her up, pulled at her hand again to try and slow her down.

'Not fair,' she yelled, her hair plastering across her face as she turned to him. He nodded over her shoulder, grinning from ear to ear. When she wheeled round she found a huge wave gathering momentum and heading straight towards them.

Bracing herself for the hit, she felt Todd grab her waist as the wave rolled into them. It was stronger than she'd expected, making her stagger to her knees. Frothing water crashing over her shoulders and chest, dousing her in a wall of instant cold, turning her nipples into tiny pain-filled pebbles, and she was glad of Todd's support as the undertow sucked at the sand under her forelegs.

'You OK?' he asked, laughter dancing in his eyes.

'Yes,' she beamed back at him, exhilarated by the rush. With a brief do-or-die moment of hesitation, she rose to her feet, threw herself forward into the water before the next wave came splashing furiously as the cold enveloped her whole body. She swam into the rising swell, hoping her muscles would warm her up.

'Cold. Cold. Cold. Cold,' she gasped as the breath stalled in her lungs, her ribcage almost frozen stiff by the chill.

Todd laughed, swimming alongside her, like an expert dolphin. 'Of course it's cold. It's the Atlantic.'

Thankfully, it didn't take long for her to warm up and together they swam, bobbing over the swell of the waves as they rose and gathered momentum to crash onto the beach. Sophie had forgotten how lovely it was to swim in the sea, but she was nowhere near as good a swimmer as Todd, who dived in and out of the waves. He also stayed close, for which she was grateful, even though there was a lifeguard on the beach. The sea here was much stronger than she was used to.

'Fancy lunch soon?' asked Todd as they lazily floated on their backs.

'Mm,' said Sophie, closing her eyes, tipping her head up to the sun. 'That would be nice.'

'Nice? Don't let Mahalia hear you say that.'

'Well, I'm expecting there to be plenty, after I lugged that box all the way here. It weighed a ton.'

'It would be a stain on her mortal soul for anyone to go hungry on her watch. You should hear her and Rick go at it. He's the cook, although Mom insists its *chef*.' In a falsetto he mimicked, '"You no put enough on those plates. What, you want people to starve?" She'll have packed enough for a voyage to Mars.'

'Now you've made me hungry,' complained Sophie as her stomach grumbled. 'Those cinnamon rolls were hours ago.'

'They were good. You can make them again.'

'I can, can I?' she teased, amused by his confident assumption that she would.

'After those Yorkshire pudding things you promised me, I want to try those again.'

'You'll have to wait until autumn, I'll do a roast. Invite Bella and maybe ...' She didn't get the chance to finish. Another wave had swelled up in front of them, this one bigger than any of the others. Transfixed for a second, Sophie watched it growing and growing as it headed their way. Like a fish, Todd dived under it while Sophie hoped to bob over it, but she'd mistimed it and just as it reached her it curled over itself, crashing down with white froth coiling around her, gathering pace, and before she knew it she was under the water, being spun around as if she were on a roller-coaster, until she was spat out, skidding onto the sand. She emerged choking and wheezing, thinking she must look like a drowned rat as she surreptitiously tried to shake out the sand which had accumulated in her bikini bottoms.

'Hey, you OK?' Todd bounded over, his face holding a touch of uncertain anxiety. 'That was a ...' His voice died away as she straightened.

'Huh, j-just got my breath back.' She swiped her wet hair from her face, trying to smile through the splutters. 'That certainly woke me up.'

She wasn't sure he was listening, he looked oddly strained. Then something flared in his eyes, launching a sudden flutter in her chest.

'Mmm, and me,' he breathed with a wobbly half-smile, nodding his head towards her chest. 'Erm, you might want to er ... might want to ... before you give half the guys on the beach a bonus today.'

She glanced down and blushed, hastily rearranging her bikini.

'Oh. Sorry.'

'No need to apologise to me.' His lips curved in a broad smile. 'For the record, there's nothing wonky-looking about those babies to me.'

The warmth in his voice made her nipples tingle and, to her horror, she could feel them tightening into hussy take-me-I'm-here points accentuated by the flimsy Lycra of her bikini top.

241

She looked away and focused on thrashing through the foaming waves back up the beach, fighting against the sand sucking under their feet.

From behind her another wave caught her and she fell over again, dragging Todd down with her.

He hauled her up again and as she got to her feet another wave crashed into him, sending him toppling into her, and she crashed backwards onto the sand. Todd went with her, landing on top of her, and immediately raising himself onto his arms to take some of his weight from squashing her.

For a moment she lay there as their eyes locked onto one another. A breath caught in her throat, her body going still with heightened awareness as they stared at each other. Her heart thudded, a wake of adrenaline coursing through her system.

As he began to lower his head, never taking his gaze from her, she could scarcely breathe.

The first tender graze of his mouth, so soft, so slow, so tentative, made her chest tighten. His lips were cold, but his breath felt warm. Her pulse kicked in objection when she felt him stop, an infinitesimal moment of hesitation. Without thinking, she slid her hands over his shoulders, even though she knew this was a big mistake, but it was a delicious mistake, made even more delicious when with a tiny moan, he deepened the kiss with slow sure movements, lazily teasing at her lips. Holding himself on his elbows, his mouth roved over hers but with an all-the-time-in-the-world leisureliness and determined, sedate thoroughness that left her reeling.

Despite the careful, unhurried attention, it was without

doubt the most passionate kiss Sophie had ever had. Even knowing it was wrong, she couldn't help herself. With a sigh she melted, giving herself up to pure sensation, her body totally limp.

Every nerve ending was alert to the feel of him, the hair-roughened skin of his thigh, the bone of hip to hip and the odd, cold/hot sensation of their water-cooled skins touching each other.

His heartfelt groan as she pressed her chest into his made her heart leap and she could feel his heart pounding too.

Above them a gull screamed, penetrating Sophie's conscious-ness. What the hell was she doing? This was Todd. They were friends. Stiffening, she started to pull away, her eyes darting down to his chest to avoid looking at him. 'I think that's Seagull for *Get a room*,' he said wryly, rolling to one side and scrambling to his feet before holding out a hand to pull her up.

Sophie's cheeks turned bright pink and she ducked her head as she took his hand and clambered upright.

'Well, that was ...' The husky timbre of his voice almost made her heart stop. She closed her eyes and swallowed hard, feeling her heart pounding crazily in her chest. *What had she done?* Todd was so far out of bounds, it was ridiculous. Too gorgeous for his own good and for her peace of mind. And thoroughly, thoroughly intoxicating. Oh God, she needed to be cool. This was probably all in a day's work for him.

'Very nice,' she said, stretching her mouth into a desperate grin. *Keep it light, Sophie. Keep it light.* 'Now I get what all those girls see in you.'

It would have been nice to believe that there was a brief shadow in his eyes before his usual broad smile lit up his face, but Sophie knew better.

'All part of the service, English. Come on, let's see what Mahalia's got lined up for us. I'm hungry.'

Together they walked back to their spot where Marty was sitting on a towel, his back to them, headphones on, attached to his phone, nodding away to an inaudible beat.

'Hey guys, I'm starving,' said Marty, looking up as soon as Todd's shadow fell over him.

Sophie was impressed he hadn't already made inroads into the cool box. Mahalia had done them proud and as Todd unpacked the picnic lunch, she tried to focus on laying out the different plastic boxes on the towels, but she couldn't help sneaking the odd peek at him. She found herself drawn to watching his mobile lips as he teased his brother, who was making short work of several rustic, well-filled sandwiches, wolfing them down as if he hadn't seen food in weeks. Every now and then Todd would shoot her a glance and several times she was mortified when she wasn't quick enough to look away.

As soon as they'd eaten and Marty had finally given up trying to wheedle his own bottle of beer out of Todd, he spotted his friends who'd also taken a lunch break and, with a spray of sand over the towels, he bounded off to join them.

As Sophie packed away Todd lay on his back, his arms behind his head, his eyes hidden behind the dark sunglasses. With that innate sense, she knew he was watching her. Despite the sun high in the sky, giving off a steady heat, she shivered, packing up quickly.

She needed to clear the air. Wriggling the lid to get it back into place, she sat back on her heels, pursing her mouth.

'English.' His low voice and the serious set to his mouth made the butterflies in her stomach take flight and race around like windblown lunatics. 'You're thinking so loud you're giving me a headache.'

'Sorry. We shouldn't have done that.'

'Done what?' his mouth quirked in one corner, but behind the sunglasses she couldn't see his face properly. It made her feel at a major disadvantage.

'You know,' she said severely.

'English, it's fine.'

'Hey guys, we're going to play volleyball. We need a couple more on the team. You'll play won't you?' Marty's yell came from a few yards away.

'Of course, we will,' said Sophie, jumping up immediately, kicking sand all over Todd. 'Although I'm not sure I'm dressed appropriately.'

Marty shrugged with a *whatever* sort of gesture. Todd narrowed his eyes as he looked at Sophie's cleavage and then dug around under the bags until he found his Timberland T-shirt.

'Here you go. Wear this. It'll stop you getting burned.'

Chapter 19

Sophie felt the glow on her skin as she stepped into the shower, her legs aching from the unexpected volleyball marathon. Thank goodness for Marty and his friends and their inexhaustible supply of energy. It had meant she didn't have time to think about that kiss, but now she couldn't get it out of her head or the image of Todd's golden body when he'd stripped off his T-shirt.

With an annoyed huff at herself, she yanked the big white super-fluffy towel from the rail and wrapped herself up in it. She wasn't fifteen, for heaven's sake. She glared at herself in the mirror as, with tentative fingers, she traced her lips. No, definitely not fifteen, that had been one adult kiss.

And she was a grown-up. Beyond this sort of silly ... infatuation. This was just a crush. Wayward hormones distracted by extreme good looks.

She lay on the bed and picked up one of three complimentary magazines from the table. Dinner wasn't until six-thirty. There were a few hours to kill. After flipping through the pages, she threw the magazine down in disgust. Bloody hell, why couldn't she get her mind off Todd?

With a sigh, she snatched up her phone.

'Hey Sophie.' Kate's face appeared on her phone. 'What's up?'

'Nothing. I thought I'd ring you from ... the Hamptons.'

'No! How come?'

'I got an invite for Fourth of July. Look.' Getting off the bed, she flipped the phone around and gave Kate a walk-through of the bedroom and the huge bathroom. 'And look at this.' She stepped out onto the wide wooden balcony over-looking the pool. Damn, there was Todd ploughing up and down, cutting through the water with a fearsome front crawl.

'Whoa. You lucky thing. And who's the hot bod in the pool?'

'Todd,' said Sophie, hoping her voice wouldn't give her current turmoil away.

'That's Todd! *The* Todd. And you're staying with him in the Hamptons? You kept that quiet. What happened to Paul?'

'Nothing happened to Paul, except that he has a girl next door in waiting and so it wasn't convenient for me to spend the holiday with him. Todd invited me to his parents' place because they have a big, huge party here.'

'Back up a spot. Paul has a girl in waiting?'

'Yeah, turns out that there's an understanding between them.' She did the quote marks with one hand.

'And how do you feel about that?'

'When he told me, at first it didn't matter because I'll be back in London in six months, but now I've had time to think about it, I feel a bit shit, to be honest. It's like James all over again.'

'Ouch.'

Sophie shrugged.

'And what about the lovely Todd? He invited you to his parents'.'

Sophie looked away, back towards the pool.

'He's ... he's a friend.'

Kate smirked.

'What?' asked Sophie.

The smirk turned into a full-blown grin. 'You like him.'

'How old are you?' said Sophie, which was ironic given she'd been asking herself that question a little while before.

'Distraction-technique alert. I'm onto you.'

Sophie pursed her lips but Kate's eyes bored into hers. Damn, half the time Facetime froze and blurred but today the signal was absolutely perfect.

'He kissed me today.' The words tumbled out.

'Who? Todd?'

'Yes.'

'Well, you don't exactly look chuffed about it. Is he a crap kisser? Halitosis? Slobbery?'

Sophie giggled. 'I bloody wish.'

'Run that by me again. You want a slobberer?'

'No,' she paused, feeling a slight flush run up her body at the memory of that heart-stopping, time-freezing, momentous kiss. 'He's bloody sublime. A champion, hormone-exploding kisser. That's the problem. He wasn't supposed to kiss me. I don't want him to be a good kisser.'

'Why not? He sounds rather yum to me.'

'And that's another problem. He's too yum.'

'No one is too yum.'

Sophie looked glum. Todd was too everything. He had danger written all over him. A danger to her equilibrium in complete contrast to James and Paul, who'd both seemed safe. And look how they'd turned out.

'When you met Ben ... did you know?' The pair of them seemed to fit so well now, although it hadn't been plain sailing.

A warm light lit Kate's eyes and her mouth curved, her whole face instantly serene. 'The very first time I met him, I knew that he might be. The first time he kissed me, I knew for sure.'

Sophie closed her eyes for a second. Oh shit.

'What was it like kissing him?' Kate's question made her start and she opened her eyes wide.

'Like falling off a cliff.' There, she'd said, good as admitted it.

'Oh,' breathed Kate, with a smile.

'No, not oh!' Sophie shook her head, feeling slightly sick inside.

'Oh, yes.'

'Kate, he doesn't do relationships,' her voice was suddenly desperate. 'He has a whole harem on speed dial.'

'Are you looking for a relationship?' she demanded, her face looming large on the screen.

'No.'

'Well then.' Kate leaned back again, much to Sophie's relief. It felt a bit like being under a microscope, as if she might see too much.

'Well then what?'

'Soph, I can't believe you're being so obtuse. You're only there for another four months. What have you got to lose? Go for it. Have some fun. Dive off the cliff. Embrace the ride. Live a little.'

'Kate ... one more cliché and I'll drop you over the balcony.' Sophie waved the phone about in threat.

'Diversion again. Being serious and cliché free, James hurt you and getting over that is going to take some time. Perhaps having a rip-roaring fling will do you some good, especially if you know it's not going to come to anything. Why not? And if Todd's as gorgeous as he sounds—'

'Oh he is, believe me,' said Sophie, watching the sleek form slicing through the water down below.

'Then ... enjoy.'

Todd did a racing turn and streaked back down the length of the pool. She could see the muscles in his back and shoulders working, driving him through the water, and her mouth dried as she remembered the moment he stripped off his T-shirt. There was no denying she found him attractive and that kiss had been something else.

'Sophie?'

'Mmm.'

'You still there?'

'I'm still here.' She sighed and bit her lip. 'You know what? I'm seriously considering your advice.'

'You know it makes sense.'

'Don't be smug now, missy. I said considering.'

'Who, me?'

'And how's Ben?'

'He's fine,' drawled a voice and Ben's face appeared next to Kate's. 'And appalled at you two objectifying this poor man.'

An imperious rap at the door startled Sophie.

'Oh, there's someone knocking. I'd better go.' With a hasty goodbye, she put down the phone and opened the door to find Mahalia with a bundle of towels.

'Brought fresh supplies. You want your beach swimming things laundered?' Even as she spoke Mahalia had darted out onto the balcony where Sophie's wet bikini was draped over a chair.

As she snatched it up, Mahalia glanced towards the pool and Todd's relentless pace. 'That boy. He's got some demons chasing him.' She shook her head, her dark eyes clouded as she gave Sophie a steady assessment. 'Something's bothering him. He's a troubled soul. Needs some kindness in his life. A loving heart.'

Turning away from that direct gaze, Sophie closed her eyes, barely hearing the diminutive housekeeper leave.

With a quick flourish, watching the silk fabric flutter with movement, Sophie pulled out her new dress from the wardrobe, holding it up in front of her, suddenly wanting to look more than her best. Teamed with a little cardigan and the new low-heeled sandals, it looked feminine rather than sexy. She put her hair up, leaving a few tendrils down, and gave her lips one last slick of pale lipstick and texted him to say she was ready. He'd said he'd knock for her before dinner.

A brief rap at the door seconds later announced his arrival, and her pulse lifted in uncontrolled anticipation. There was a definite disconnect between her brain and her body at the moment. From the neck downwards, everything seemed to have gone haywire. She swallowed, took in a calming breath and opened it. To her surprise, Todd was dressed in a scruffy T-shirt and shorts that looked as if they'd been worn to service a dozen cars.

'Oh,' she looked down, smoothing the fabric of her dress.

'You're fine,' said Todd with a grimace. 'I ... You look lovely. I ...' His face contorted. Sophie was intrigued by the conflict she could see there. 'My parents dress for dinner.'

'Aha.'

His eyes slid away in an un-Todd-like manner. Normally he was open, gregarious and easy to read. She frowned and was about to ask him if he was OK but he straightened up and crooked his arm with as much debonair charm as if he were dressed in a dinner suit. 'Shall we go?' Todd the playboy was back, eyes twinkling, smile broad. 'Would you like a drink on the terrace? The view out over the sea is rather nice and there'll be a bottle of fizz chilling.'

'Why not?' Sophie took his arm, squashing the brief feeling of misgiving. 'Just promise me it's not been messed with.'

'Don't say a word about black champagne.' He shuddered with great show. 'My mother would love that idea. She loves a theme. I can imagine it. Batcave by McLennan. It doesn't bear thinking about it. Only Mahalia keeps her in check and keeps her taste this side of understated tacky.'

Sophie laughed at his mock theatrics as they descended, because with a staircase like that you couldn't really do anything but descend down to the ground floor. At the bottom,

Todd steered her down the hallway and they were about to turn left past a door that was ajar when he stopped dead. A sort of halt-in-the-shoes standard comedy freeze, except he didn't look as if this was funny. From inside voices hissing with venom spoke in low, vicious tones.

'You don't have to flaunt your floozies in front of me. Have some respect.'

'Respect ... that's rich. You earn respect. And she's my secretary, so make sure you're damn polite to her.'

A bland mask slipped down over Todd's face, like an eraser rubbing away the sunshine and light Sophie was so used to seeing. She was disconcerted by the lack of expression on his face. It was as if someone had snuffed him out.

'Secretary, my ass.' Fury simmered in the words. 'Like the last three secretaries you've had.'

'Jesus, Celine, you're a paranoid neurotic. And if we're talking numbers, I've lost count of your tennis coaches.'

'They are *tennis coaches*,' came the hot denial.

'Like my secretaries are *secretaries*, for crying out loud, woman.'

This was followed by a derisory snort in response.

'Doesn't seem to have done much for your game. Hope you've entered us for the mixed doubles at the Allenbrooks'.'

And then Todd's mother replied with icy disdain, 'Of course, I always do. Although if I'm so bad at it, why would you want to play with me?'

'Because you're my wife.' The angry, raspy voice must belong to Todd's father. 'And that's what we do. Can you imagine if the McLennans didn't show up?' The voice lowered with a hint of incipient menace. 'I expect you to behave in a fitting manner. The Allenbrooks are big sponsors at the golf club, not to mention Jeff Allenbrook is now the CEO at the bank. And Jeanie Allenbrook seems to like you.' This was added with decidedly unkind incredulity.

'Why, thanks. I'm so glad I'm useful for something,' Celine spat. 'You have no idea, have you? No concept of how much work goes into running this house? The apartment in Manhattan? The ski-lodge in Aspen? You think everything magically appears on the table? The menus choose themselves? The designers throw up the decorations without a brief?' The pitch of her voice rose with each sentence with the power of a soprano. 'You think it's easy entertaining your important guests, business contacts? You seem to think I sit here twiddling my thumbs.'

'You're being emotional again, Celine.'

'Emotional,' screeched Todd's mother. 'You think *this* is emotional?'

Todd closed his eyes and winced, freezing in anticipation. There was an almighty crash. '*That's* emotional.'

'Pull yourself together, woman.'

Todd suddenly looked up and, following his gaze, Sophie could see Marty plugged into his phone, heading down the stairs. Todd grasped the handle and marched in.

'Marty will be here any moment. At least try and be civil in front of him,' he snarled in a voice that Sophie had never heard him use before.

Celine hastily schooled her face while an older-looking version of Todd sighed impatiently.

'We'll have drinks in the salon while Mahalia cleans up in here.' He looked pointedly at the floor where a thousand shards of crystal were strewn. There was a definite indentation in the wall above. 'And I'll thank you, Todd, not to take that tone with us.'

'Marty darling, take those ridiculous earphones off your head.' Celine's voice was suddenly sugar sweet.

'Yes son, you look like hoodlum.' Todd's father glanced at him, a quick enough once up and down, as if to check he met with approval. 'And tuck your shirt in. You're not a child any more. Unlike your brother, who seems to have forgotten that we dress for dinner.'

Marty tucked in his shirt, his face an exact copy of Todd's, completely devoid of expression.

Sophie realised that she'd edged closer to Todd. Neither his mother nor father had acknowledged her, for which she was fervently grateful. It felt as if she'd been pitched headfirst into a play as an understudy without a script. It also struck her that she'd never seen Todd dressed less than impeccably.

'Dad, this is my friend Sophie. She's renting Bella's apartment over the business for a couple of months. She's over from England. Sophie, my dad, Ross.'

'England. London?' With an utterly charming smile, as if the last ten minutes had never happened, he stepped forward and took her hand to shake it. 'Does that mean you like gin? We have an excellent selection, don't we Celine? I believe the rhubarb is particularly good.' The sudden turnabout in tone and atmosphere, as Todd's mum's face transformed with an obliging smile, threw her.

'I ... er, yes,' said Sophie, completely confused.

'Excellent.' With smooth, pleased confidence, he ushered her and Celine towards the salon. 'Come and have a drink before dinner.'

The sofas in the salon were built for style rather than comfort and Sophie had to hold herself upright, clutching her gin as the conversation unfolded. Luckily years of training kicked right in and she was able to summon up her very best social manners to tide her through the odd undercurrents.

'Todd, would you pop down and tell Chef we'll be ready for dinner in twenty minutes?'

'I thought you'd already—'

'Todd, do as you mother tells you.' Despite the snapped order, Todd rose slowly and ambled out of the room. At the door he shot Sophie a quick anxious look and she responded with a reassuring smile.

'Celine tells me you work ...' Ross paused as if that was bad enough before adding, '... you're a colleague of Todd's at the magazine place.' He and his wife sat side by side, suddenly unified in a powerhouse pose that reminded her of formal historical family portraits. She didn't think it was an unconscious pose.

'I am.'

'And what is it you do?' asked Celine.

'I'm a food writer.' Sophie smiled, exuding serenity.

'How fascinating.' Celine leaned forward, her eyes gleaming with sudden avaricious interest. 'So you know all about trends in food? The next big thing.'

'I guess,' said Sophie. 'I meet a lot of people in the food world, so you pick up on that sort of thing.'

'Excellent, because I am so over quinoa and goji berries.'

'Please tell me red meat is back in,' said Ross, amusement lighting his face and instantly reminding her of Todd. 'Not that I'm complaining, Celine runs a great home.' He preened a little and looked fondly at his wife. 'Everyone knows she throws the best parties. People love coming here for dinner.'

'Now, Ross darling. I'm sure you're exaggerating.' She laid her hand on his, the light catching the array of diamonds on her wedding finger.

Sophie schooled her face, hoping the amazement didn't show. Ten minutes ago, it sounded as if they'd been ready to kill each other.

'Ah Todd.'

'Chef says he's serving now.'

Celine rolled her eyes and sighed in a winsome, what-can-you-do sort of way. 'Oh, that man. We only put up with him because he cooks like an angel, but he does have a dreadful tendency to forget who he's working for. But,' she brushed a weary hand across her forehead and Sophie had to pinch her lips together, 'that's the price you pay for greatness.'

'And I'm paying a hefty price,' added Ross. 'He's the best-paid chef on the island.' The latter was added with bombastic pride.

They moved through to the dining room to sit at a formally laid table. Despite there only being five of them, there was a full set of crystal glasses, an ornate place setting of what looked like gold-plated cutlery and damask napkins wrapped in a golden laurel-leaf-shaped napkin ring.

The first course, a delicately flavoured saffron broth with mussels, was brought in by Mahalia with great ceremony and Sophie had to admit the chef was some kind of genius.

'What can you taste, Sophie?' asked Celine, watching her as she took a considered mouthful.

'Fennel? Cream.'

'Yes!' She clapped her hands in delight. 'You do know what you're talking about.'

'I'm pleased to see you parked that eyesore of a car out of sight this time.' Ross's voice cut through and there was a definite pause in the chink of cutlery on china, a palpable heaviness in the air.

Todd gave his father a level look and carried on eating.

'It shows some maturity at last. Can I assume that you might be coming to your senses and considering gainful employment?'

Todd's mouth flattened. 'I have gainful employment. I receive a salary each month.'

'Chicken feed. You need to get some corporate experience. I've been talking to Wayne Fullerton—'

'Dad, I'm not going to work in a merchant bank. Not now. Not ever.'

'Do you realise that what you do reflects on me? You look like a lightweight. Partying is not a man's job.'

'Ross,' interjected Celine. 'He's networking with some of the best-connected people in Manhattan. Just last month Joyce

Weinerberg said she and her husband saw Todd at the Guggenheim fundraiser.'

'Great, when's he going to use those connections?' Ross glared at Todd. 'And what sort of example is it setting Marty? The boy's flunking his grades. Sees his big brother bumming around in the city. Where's the incentive for him to do well? No wonder his mid-term papers were all C's.'

Marty's head drooped.

'Yes, you.'

'Dad, I don't think now's the time for this conversation,' Todd said firmly.

'No, you're right,' said Ross. 'Let's talk about Wayne Fullerton's boys. The elder one's just got into Harvard. The younger one scored the highest in his SATs in the whole state. Joyce Weinerberg's grandson landed an internship at Goldman Sachs and her granddaughter is playing the cello with the New York Symphony Orchestra.'

'That girl is so talented,' chipped in Celine. 'And didn't the grandson get a scholarship to Princeton?'

'I believe he did.'

Sophie caught Todd's eye. Why wasn't he telling them about the awards he'd won? There were several lining the shelf behind his desk. He was a talented writer and several of his more in-depth feature pieces had been picked up by the *New York Times*.

Ross and Celine continued to reel off various friends' offspring's super-achievements, throughout which Marty seemed to shrink into his seat.

'Wow, this looks amazing,' gushed Sophie when the main

course arrived. 'I haven't had beef tournedos for years. It's such a classic dish. Did you know it was created in honour of the Italian composer Rossini?'

'I did not know that,' said Celine. 'You hear that, Ross? This girl knows her food.'

'I've eaten some amazing food in New York.'

'Yes, we have some of the best restaurants. There's a new one opened. Ross has been promising to take me, haven't you darling?'

'And I will as soon as I can get a table.'

Celine's pout was a picture.

'Darling, I promised you. I'll make it happen.'

'By the time we get there, it will be old news.'

'Where is it?' asked Todd. 'I might be able to help.'

'I doubt it,' said Ross, tucking into the steak with gusto. 'Onyx is booked solid for months.'

'Oh! Todd took me there two weeks ago. Oh my goodness, the kobo beef is to die for.' Sophie beamed across the table at him. 'And what was that fabulous dish you had?'

Todd's mouth quirked. 'You mean the shrimp with langoustine custard and caviar. And don't forget the foraged mushroom emulsion.'

'Or the black champagne,' added Sophie with a naughty twinkle in her eye.

'Black champagne!'

Todd coughed, holding his napkin over his face.

'That sounds divine. What a fabulous idea. Black and gold.' Celine clapped her hands. 'Sophie, where do I buy black champagne? Ross, do you think you could get some flown in for the party tomorrow?'

'Sure, darling. Now that will make a statement. I bet Jeff and Jeanie Allenbrook won't be serving black champagne at the tennis tournament.'

The rest of the meal was consumed by the subject and Celine's musing on what else she could come up with to complete the theme. At last Mahalia came in to take orders for coffee and Marty announced he had an assignment for school to finish and scuttled away.

'Fancy a stroll on the beach?' asked Todd as Sophie drained her coffee cup. The start of a headache pinched at her temples.

Todd's offer of an escape to the beach came not a moment too soon.

'That would be lovely,' she said, jumping to her feet. *Oh heavens, was it that obvious she was so desperate to get away?* 'Thank you for a wonderful meal. That syllabub was amazing. I was trying to identify the flavour. Was it yuzu? I'd love to talk to your chef sometime.' Her words ran together in haste, even as she was backing out of the room.

Once out of the dining room, Todd took her hand and they ran out of the house, and they kept running until they reached the path down to the beach.

'Jeez, I'm sorry.' Todd's shoulders were hunched up to his ears when they finally came to a halt and sat down side by side amongst the scrubby grass at the top of the sand dunes. 'I shouldn't have subjected you to that. Each time I leave, I think it can't be as bad as I remember. And each time I come back, it's worse.'

'It's ... not ...' No, she couldn't lie. 'Yeah, it is that bad.' She shuffled closer to him to take the sting out of her uncharacteristically blunt words, so that they were hip to hip. She couldn't lie to him but it went against the grain to make him feel any worse.

She slipped her arm through his and squeezed, her heart ached for him. 'Do they have any idea what they're doing to Marty?'

'You got that?' Todd turned to face her, worrying at the hairline of his temples with one hand. 'Actually, he is superbright. A bit of a computer genius, but they have no idea. He deliberately doesn't make any effort at school. Does no work. He stays out of trouble, so keeps below the radar but he doesn't do more than the bare minimum. He puts all the effort into working out how little he needs to do to not get booted out but enough to stay beyond notice. His way, I guess, of flipping the bird to the parents. You don't see me, so I'm not going to do anything to try and please you.' Todd suddenly sighed, shuffling close to her. 'It's not funny and I am seriously worried he's going to get into big trouble one day. Skip the minor stuff and go straight for the big time. He got into Dad's computer, reset all the passwords and managed to get into his bank account and tripled his monthly allowance. They had no idea until I made Marty tell them what he'd done. Dad assumed Mom made the change, she assumed Dad did, so he got away with it for months. As you probably saw, their communication is ... confusing. I thought if they knew what he could do, they might be concerned and keep an eye on him. Stop him doing something really dumb like hacking into the Pentagon. But they don't get it.'

'From what I've seen of your Dad, I can't imagine that went down well.' Underneath Ross McLennan's charming bonhomie, there was an inflexibility and a ruthless need to be top dog.

'Dad reamed him. A full hour's lecture on what a disappointment Marty was, but it was a ten-second wonder. Naughty Marty. Don't do it again. Took his Xbox away and locked it in a cupboard for a month.' Todd sighed and then added, with a reluctant laugh, 'Little sod, bought another and a brand-new TV with Dad's credit card and holed up in one of the suites on the top floor that's hardly ever used. He had it all set up. They never even noticed. I didn't bother telling them that time.'

Sophie laughed and slapped her hand over her mouth. 'Oops. I shouldn't laugh, but I like that Marty still managed to come out on top, but it's pretty tragic that your parents had no idea he was doing that.'

'Too busy with their own lives.'

'Yes,' said Sophie, 'I ... er ...'

'Don't worry, nothing you say about them is going to offend me.'

'They seem quite ... erm, self-absorbed.'

'That's putting it mildly.'

'And I couldn't figure it. Do they love or hate each other?'

'Your guess is as good as mine. I don't think they know.' Todd sounded weary. With one arm looped through his, Sophie pulled him closer and laid her hand over his where it lay on his thigh. 'One minute they're at each other's throats, the next they're making big extravagant gestures. Dad will present Mom with a new car or a pair of diamond earrings, but everyone will know he's bought it for her as a *surprise*.' He laced his fingers through hers almost absently. 'They seem to revel in the drama of it all. As a kid it's horrible to be around. The constant bickering and sniping at each other. And then over-the-top declarations of affection. You walk on eggshells the whole time. That's why I worry about Marty. He's got no one, but at least I had Bella. And her folks.'

No wonder he was so cynical about relationships. That early conversation over brunch suddenly made a lot more sense.

'I'm sorry, that must be tough. My parents were solid. Gave me a really good sense of who I am. They genuinely love and respect each other.'

'Which is why you're such a nice person. More than nice. You're kind, thoughtful.'

'Yuk, I sound like someone's granny.'

Todd turned and looked at her and lifted the hand linked with hers, kissing her knuckles one by one before raising his other hand to touch her cheek, hesitating for a second. 'Sophie, you're definitely not like anyone's granny.'

His hand slid down her face to cup it. 'You're not ... not like anyone I've ever met.' At the husky tone, her stomach dropped away. In an unconscious nervous gesture, she clamped her lips together and his gaze followed the movement.

'I want to kiss you again ... and I know I shouldn't.'

Sophie bit back a smile, charmed by his gentle diffidence. Lines furrowed his forehead and he looked adorably irritated and annoyed. It was gratifying and rather cute.

'What if I wanted you to?' Her fingernails pricked her

palms as she scrunched up her hands under her thighs out of sight, her knuckles cold against the damp sand.

'Sophie ... you're ... you're ...' Equal touches of hope and denial flitted across his face, telling her all she needed to know.

Mahalia's words came back to her. After that hideous dinner, she knew exactly what the other woman meant. He really did need some kindness in his life. He would be an easy man to love, even if he didn't think so. And she shouldn't love him, but she could give him the care and kindness he deserved.

On the edge of precipice time. Jump and take flight or move back to safety. She could let him talk her out of this or she could let her mouth do the talking. Suddenly she didn't care about the future, the next few months, the next few weeks. She wanted Todd to kiss her. To give in to that heady free-fall sensation of crazy lust, longing and desire, and to give him what he needed, someone who would look after him and show him that they cared.

Laying a hand over his, she moved in and moulded her mouth to his, her lips moving against his in a soft feather-light kiss. For a few seconds he responded and then pulled back.

'You.' He frowned and lifted a hand, extending his index finger towards her lips. He paused for a second before delicately tracing their outline. 'I'm .... I don't do relationships, commitment ... and you seem like a commitment kind of girl.' He sighed and skimmed her lips again. 'You deserve better ... but I ...' His finger paused, the touch setting light to tiny electrical tingles running down her chest. 'I'm not sure I can ... leave you alone.'

'Maybe you don't have to,' suggested Sophie softly, not moving. She had a feeling that if she made one false move, like a skittish kitten, he'd back off.

'I can't give you what you want.'

For a second anger flared. 'How do you know what I want?'

'Sophie, you're a forever kind of girl.'

'And what if I decide to live a little? Have some fun. Have a fling. Everyone seems to think that's what I need.' She turned her head away, looking out at the sea, staring hard at the silver streams of moonlight dancing on the waves rippling into shore.

'I'm fed up with playing safe. I tried that for two years. And do you know what? It was dull.' Sex had always been a rather serious business with James. Perfunctory and, if she were honest, fairly passionless. Suddenly she wanted to know what it might be like to have some fun. 'I want to *live*. To dive off the edge of that bloody cliff. And I'm telling you now Todd, if you don't want to kiss me, I'll find someone else who will.'

With a quick movement she twisted and pushed him down on the sand and lay on top of him.

His eyes displayed brief panic and then a slow smile emerged as she lowered her head very slowly to kiss him, signalling her intent all the way.

Just before their lips touched, a bare millimetre apart, she stopped.

'Last chance,' she breathed.

His hands slid into her hair and he pulled her head down to close the barely-there gap.

When they finally drew apart to draw breath, there was a wry smile on Todd's face. His chest rose and fell as if he'd been running. Sophie laid a hand on it, feeling a touch possessive and proud.

'Hell, where did you learn to kiss like that, English? I swear you've damn near seared the soles of my feet off.'

Her shoulders lifted in a tiny feminine shrug and she smiled at him.

He shuddered and shook his head. 'What am I going to do with you?'

Sophie sighed. 'Nothing. I know you're not a commitment kind of guy. But I'm not sure I believe in commitment any more. After …' She was not going to spoil the moment by saying his name. 'I've realised this last few weeks that I spent all that time waiting for him to be around. Not living properly. Not doing stuff. I'm not going to do that any more. I'm going to live for now. Enjoy myself and let myself enjoy myself instead of putting everything on hold until the right things happen. I'm only here until November, the last thing I'm looking for is commitment. The last time I tried that I made a terrible mistake.'

'You didn't make a mistake Sophie, he did. And he lost you, which was his biggest mistake. I'm no prize when it comes to relationships but I treat people well. I don't understand why anyone would do that. What did he get out of it … unless it was copious amounts of sex and I can think of far easier ways of getting that.'

'It definitely wasn't for that,' snapped Sophie indignantly. 'He was always too tired. And now I bloody know why.' Her lip curled in disgust. James had always said sex wasn't important, the cuddles were – and, stupid sap, she'd thought that was rather sweet. She sat up straighter, suddenly furious. 'All that bloody time, thinking I fancied a ...' no, she couldn't say it, 'and he was too tired. Of course he was, because he was bloody sleeping with his wife. Impregnating her. And I,' her mouth crumpled, 'I thought I wasn't that ... you know ...'

Todd lifted an eyebrow.

'I thought I was ... not very ...'

Still Todd waited, he wasn't going to help her out here.

'Not very sexually attractive,' she blurted out. 'I bet all your Amys, Charlenes and Cheries are all super-model thin, with silk-curtain hair and shoulders like clothes horses.'

'Sophie. Sophie. Sophie.' He let out a long-pent-up sigh and shook his head. 'Dumb bastard clearly never saw you in a bikini, babe,' he paused and lifted a finger, tracing the neckline of her dress, 'or rather, hanging out of it. And if he's the one that said you were lopsided, he should be shot.' He leaned in and kissed her gently and firmly on the lips. 'And he certainly never saw that delicious pert ass of yours in Lycra running shorts.' His hand shaped her face as he held her gaze, his eyes dancing with wicked amusement. 'And those legs, I've had a few fantasies about those legs wrapped around ...' His fingers skimmed her collar bone. 'Oh yes, those legs.'

Sophie stared at him, the words a balm to that constant sense of guilt she'd always felt about sex with James. It had always been tinged with disappointment, that guilt-ridden, slightly ashamed feeling that she was wrong to feel there should be more. Sex with James had always been hurried, in bed, in the dark and never mentioned. Now she realised it was probably a manifestation of his own guilt.

She gave Todd a wobbly smile.

'English, you have no idea.' He kissed the corner of her mouth, his fingers following to outline her lower lip. 'Although it might have something to do with that oh-so-cute English accent. You sound all buttoned up and straight, but with, as revealed on the beach today, the body of a goddess. And these ...' His hands drifted down, soft through the silk of her dress, his mouth curving in the gentlest of smiles, 'wonky boobs, they're really quite lovely.'

'Oh,' breathed Sophie, feeling light-headed and disconnected from the world as if a puff of wind could lift her and carry her away.

'You are lovely and ...' He pulled his hand away from her face and laced his fingers through hers. 'Sophie, this ... this could be a mistake.'

'No.' She sat up straighter with a sudden spurt of panic. Whatever this was with Todd, it made her feel more alive than she had done in years. So what if it wasn't destined to last? She had no idea what the future held, why the hell not live for the moment? Excitement fizzed at the prospect. She wanted to hold onto it, grab it with both hands and bloody well enjoy the feeling.

'Todd,' her voice rang out, clear and determined. Her mind made up. 'I've made the mistakes already. I did the serious thing for two years. Where did that get me? I want to have some fun. And I mean *fun*.' She gave him a look that should leave him in no doubt. 'I don't want serious. And I certainly don't want commitment.' With a lift of her head, she gave him a direct look, filled with challenge. 'If you're not interested, tell me now.'

'Oh boy. You know, you're even sexier when you get all haughty and posh on me.'

As he leaned forward, a wicked smile curving his lips, his eyes full of intent, Sophie felt a huge sense of relief and the sensation that a door had been kicked wide open.

When he planted his lips on hers, she went boneless, conscious only of the teasing determination of his touch. He pushed his hands up through her hair, a gentle but possessive hold, as he angled his head to deepen the kiss. She wound her arms around his neck and pulled him towards her, wanting more, even though she couldn't have articulated what more was to save her life. It was almost as if she couldn't get close enough. Almost as if he felt her desperation. Something had changed and his mouth began to explore hers with a heated thoroughness that made her heart bang so hard, it almost hurt to breathe.

One hand slid down her neck, brushing the edge of her breast in a barely-there tantalising touch before sliding around her hip to cup her bottom, pulling her tight against him. The seductive, tentative drift of his fingers teasing her skin through her dress made Sophie ache for more. With sudden boldness that surprised herself, she caressed his lower lip with her tongue, insistent and demanding, until he opened his mouth and sucked her tongue in.

In seconds the kiss went X-rated as Sophie refused to let up control. She deepened the kiss, feeling feminine and womanly as she pressed her breasts against him and rolled her hips against the erection pressing at his trousers. When Todd let out a heartfelt groan as she ground up against him, her pulse leapt in exhilarated delight.

'Jesus, Sophie,' he muttered in her ear as they pulled back, their breathing heavy. 'You're killing me.'

'Good,' she said and pulled his mouth back to hers. She'd been the good girl for too many years. This man knew how to kiss and she was going to enjoy every last damn moment.

It was Todd who finally put the brakes on things, wrenching his mouth away and putting some distance between them. In the moonlight, she could see the pulse jumping in his throat and the rise and fall of his chest.

'Sophie, unless you want our first time to be down and dirty in the sand, we have to stop.'

At that moment, common sense had all but gone up in a puff of smoke and down and dirty sounded rather appealing to a girl who'd never been down and dirty in her life.

With a challenging tilt to her head, she gazed back at him. 'Seriously, Sophie.'

'I'm game,' she said.

He groaned. 'You're making this really hard.'

'Well, I certainly hope so,' she said with a winsome smile.

He took her hand. 'Let's walk.'

'You're no fun. Here am I, thinking for the last few weeks that you're an international playboy with a string of women, and you want to *walk*.'

'Yes, Sophie. I want to walk.' He sounded almost cross. 'And as we both know, it's been a while, so unless you want me to go off like an express train, give me a little time here.'

She smiled to herself and gave his hand a squeeze, rather pleased with herself.

He pulled at her hand, leading her down to the shore. As they neared the waterline, right on cue the moon shot out from behind a cloud, lighting up the sea with silvery iridescence. The shush of the sea rolling in and out was almost hypnotic, adding to the atmosphere of calm otherworldliness.

'Gosh, it's beautiful out here. You can almost forget that cities exist.' There were only a few lights from the houses hidden beyond the dunes. 'It seems impossible that New York is just along the same coast, full of people and buildings.'

Todd nodded but didn't say anything as he stared out at the horizon where the silver-rimmed clouds scudded around the moon.

'I need to …' He stopped and Sophie, looking at his profile silhouetted against the pale sand lit up by the moonlight, saw him swallow as if in pain, his Adam's apple bobbing. 'I need to tell you … this, between us, it … it's … I don't want to … I don't want you to get the wrong idea. I like you. A lot but … it won't ever be … anything permanent. I'm being honest. I've been with girls who thought that they could change me. The love of a good woman and all that. I'm not being a dick. I sound like one,' he squeezed her hand, 'but I'm trying to be completely honest with you. If you want to duck out now, that would be fine … but you have to know, I'm *not* going to fall in love with you.'

Sophie felt a tiny pinch of regret, not for herself but for him. Being so adamant he was never going to fall in love. Being so against the idea. At the moment, she was out of love with the idea of being in love, she didn't want to get hurt like that again, but one day she'd feel ready again. There was hope, whereas Todd seemed to have effectively closed himself off from any hope at all.

'And I don't want to fall in love with you. Done that, got the T-shirt. But I do want to enjoy myself. You're not my type at all.'

'Yes I am.'

Sophie narrowed her eyes, trying to figure out whether he was being serious or not.

'No, you're not.'

'Yeah, I am, English. I saw you giving me the eye the first time we met.' He nudged her with his arm.

'I wasn't giving you the eye, I was trying to stop you eating my cupcake, if you recall.'

'No, you were flirting with me at the get-go.'

'I wasn't.'

'You were.'

'Todd McLennan, you have such a big head. If you think the blue eyes, charming smile and big Hollywood teeth are all it takes to make women fall at your feet, you need a reality check.'

He laughed out loud. 'And that right there is exactly why I like you.'

'I made the mistake of falling in love with someone who didn't deserve it, I'm not going to do that again in a hurry,' said Sophie and then, worried she sounded bitter, she quickly added, 'and yes on a good day, from a very long distance, if I squint a bit, there's nearly a resemblance to a young Rob Lowe, so I might fancy you a teeny tiny little bit, but don't let it go to your head. I'm more of an Ed Sheeran kind of girl.'

Todd burst out laughing. 'Well, that's put me in my place.'

Sophie winked at him, ignoring the mocking voice at the very back of her head asking just how long did she think she could keep him in his place. And what if she had enough love for both of them?

Chapter 20

'Morning, Marty.' Sophie sat down at the breakfast table, having snagged some yoghurt and fruit from the side table behind them. It was already a glorious day and she'd slept well, although it had taken her a long time to get to sleep. Too busy reliving Todd's kisses, her mind going backwards and forwards over every word they'd exchanged. This morning she'd woken full of hope and crazy joy that zinged about in her stomach like a demented moth.

'Hey,' he mumbled through a mouthful of bacon. His plate was piled high with bacon and waffles swimming in maple syrup.

'Looks good,' she teased.

He looked furtively around and shrugged.

'Mom would go ape. She's like, your body is what you put in it. But,' he slumped in his seat, 'she won't be up for ages and Dad is already on the golf course.'

'I won't tell,' she said. 'Although I might be boring about fruit later.' She winked.

Marty gave her a considering look. 'Me and Todd are going to the lighthouse this morning. We always go.' There was a certain defiance in his tone as if he were daring her to contradict him.

'That sounds fun. When I go home, me and my dad always go down to the stables. Not that we have any horses or anything. Just something we always do. Kind of like, me-and-Dad time.'

Marty nodded. 'We're going to the beach afterwards. Maybe you can come then?'

'That sounds like a plan.'

'What does?' Todd sauntered in the room and Sophie's breath caught. A flood of sensation hit her. Fresh from the shower, he looked absolutely edible.

'You two making plans without me? Dude, you're not running off with my pal, are you?'

'No,' said Marty, grinning. 'Although she's better off with me.'

'So still up for the lighthouse this morning?' Todd scooped up a couple of slices of bacon and some waffles from the side, glanced at his brother and added some grilled tomatoes and two bananas. 'Here you go, junior.' He tossed the second banana next to Marty's place setting. 'Build up your strength.'

Marty rolled his eyes.

'Fancy coming with us, Sophie?' Todd sat down next to her, his ankle nudging hers. She glanced at the younger brother, whose shoulders were now level with his ears.

'Do you know what? I think I might stay put, if you don't mind. It's such a gorgeous day and being totally selfish, it would be lovely to laze by the pool with a book. Us Brits aren't used to this weather, I want to soak up the rays. Make the most of it.'

Marty shot her a look, part relief and part guilt. Todd noticed the exchange and raised an eyebrow but didn't say anything.

'You can come if you like, Sophie,' he suddenly blurted out.

With a gentle smile, she shook her head. 'I wouldn't want to come between brothers. Todd would never forgive me if I decided I like you better.'

'OK, beach this afternoon?'

'Sounds like a plan.'

After a lazy morning by the pool, where Mahalia had brought lunch to her, which seemed deliciously decadent, especially when followed by a sneaky snooze, Sophie decided to investigate the library, as she'd finished the book she'd brought with her. There was a good selection and when she'd grabbed a paperback, she decided to head back to her room to sit on the balcony for a while. Crossing through the salon, she entered a second lounge area which she remembered from her tour with Todd. Today it had been transformed and she paused to take in the beautifully arranged table set up for afternoon tea.

Red, white and blue bunting hung around the edge of the white damask-covered table, upon which champagne flutes and pretty china cups had been arranged along with little dessert forks and fine bone china tea-plates, interspersed with floral napkins. She almost did a double take when she saw the cakes on glass cake stands and, intrigued, she crossed the room to examine them.

'Surprise,' yelled a voice from behind her.

'Bella!' She turned and before she could say anything else she was enveloped in a huge hug. 'What are you doing here?'

Bella beamed, her eyes twinkling with mischief. 'Personal delivery. Aunty C saw my cakes on mom's Facebook page and just had to have some.' Bella wiped her brow with exaggerated feeling. Sophie grinned at her, delighted to have her here.

'Honestly, I thought I was done with the darned things. But what Aunty C wants, Aunty C gets.' Her freckled face danced with glee. 'Uncle Ross sent the Lear to get me and five cakes. Heck, I'm not complaining, it'll be great advertising.'

'The Lear?'

'Jet, darling. Welcome to the Hamptons.'

Wow, it really was another world.

'I'm rather enjoying them, so far. Oh Bella, it's so good to see you.'

'You too. How are you finding it all?'

'Fine,' said Sophie, with a sudden qualm. Eeek, what was Bella going to say about her and Todd?

'I hope you don't mind but the house is pretty full, so I offered to bunk in with you.'

'No problem. Er, Bella, there's—'

'Ah there you are, Bella. I completely forgot to ask. Can you tell me if there are any additives in the frosting? The colouring is all natural. And did you make a gluten-free version too?' Celine breezed in wearing a white linen sheath dress that showed off her tan and a youthful figure that looked far too young to have Todd as a son. As she teased her blonde hair, the single piece of jewellery – a diamond tennis bracelet – on her slim wrist sparkled and glinted in the sunlight streaming through the window.

'Yes,' said Bella with the type of patience that suggested she'd been asked the question a few times before. Sophie shot her a sceptical look, which Bella met with blithe innocence.

'Marvellous. They do look wonderful. I'll see you later. Tea at four.' She tutted. 'I really should have said tea at three. It has a better ring to it.' She sighed heavily and drifted off, straightening champagne glasses and fiddling with the plates.

'Let's get out of here,' Bella whispered.

Only when they'd reached the foot of the stairs did Sophie round on her. 'Natural blue food colouring?'

Bella shrugged, looking like a naughty pixie, her red curls bouncing as she then shook her head in disgust. 'Like any of her friends are going to touch it, because of the carbs anyway. She wanted red, white and blue cake. She got red, white and blue cake.'

Both Marty and Todd were pleased to see their cousin and the three of them exchanged family news as they walked down to the beach. Carrying his body-board and towel, Todd teased his cousin as he walked alongside Sophie, their arms brushing frequently enough for her to know that he wanted to make her aware he was there. Oh, she knew he was there, alright. Each touch brought the brush of his soft hair against hers, igniting a giddy warmth and lightening her step. Something about being with Todd made her feel happy, despite the slight apprehension she felt at the thought of telling Bella.

Luckily, although that probably wasn't quite the word, the

cat was well and truly let out of the bag when they stopped at an appropriate spot and Todd dropped a quick kiss on Sophie's lips before he and Marty charged off into the surf, already clutching their boards to their stomachs.

'Oh lordy, it's like *Baywatch*,' said Sophie, watching them go and feeling her face turning pink, busying herself getting out her towel and laying it on the sand, hiding her face as she peeled off her T-shirt.

'So-phie.'

With an inward sigh, Sophie turned to face the music, wriggling out of her shorts.

'Seriously? *Todd?* After everything I said?' Bella had planted both feet in the sand with her hands on her hips, and she looked as if she wouldn't be budging until she'd had answers.

'I'm a big girl, Bella.' Sophie flicked the corner of her towel and sat down, rummaged in her bag for her book. 'I know what I'm doing.'

'Really?' Bella dropped to her hands and knees on the towel, so they were eye-level. 'Please don't be like all the other girls and think he'll change. He won't. You must have seen Aunty C and Uncle Ross in action.'

'Bella.' Sophie lifted her head and raised her sunglasses, 'I'm not like those other girls. I know what I'm doing.'

'Hmmmph.' Bella's face twisted in disgust as she reared back on her heels. 'I know you're not like the other girls. That's what worries me even more.' She fixed Sophie with an assessing look. 'They're usually the smart, sophisticated, cool types who only want Todd for his □ oh darn it, I'm going to have to say it □ looks. Who wouldn't love those baby blues and that manly jawline? Not to mention the slight bonus of status and pedigree. You do realise that his dad is on the Forbes richest list? Among a certain social circle, Todd is a serious catch.'

'Bella.' Sophie's tone was firm and kind. She really didn't want Bella raising all her own doubts. 'I know Todd isn't a keeper. He might be a catch for those girls, but he's a fish I'm going to throw back into the sea.' She gave Bella a sad smile. 'After my last boyfriend, I'm not in the market for anything serious. I want to have some fun.' Her jaw clenched as Bella looked sceptical. 'I really loved my last boyfriend. I thought we were going to get married, everything. Then I found out he was cheating. It was such a shock, I packed up and left. I've not seen him since.'

'Wow. How does that feel?'

With a shrug, Sophie looked out to sea, just about making out Todd and Marty's dark heads bobbing in the frothing waves.

'Do you still love him?' With her usual directness, Bella gave her a look that left Sophie with nowhere to go.

'I shouldn't after everything he's done, but ...' With a beseeching look she turned to Bella. 'I know you think I'll fall for Todd, but I won't. It's going to take me a very long time to get over James properly. Todd is his polar opposite. And not someone I'd ever normally go out with.'

'Your rebound?'

'That's a good way of putting it. I want to have some fun. Enjoy myself while I'm here.'

'OK,' Bella screwed up her face and gave a wry frown. 'And

now I'm in the weird position of saying, don't hurt my cousin, even though I know he's a player, but he's ... like my brother.'

Sophie reached over and patted her on the hand. 'Don't worry, I'll look after him.'

'Make sure you do,' said Bella with more than a touch of menace in her voice, before she lay back, propping herself on her elbows and tilting her face up to the sun saying, 'Heavens to Betsy, this is just darn blissful.'

Chapter 21

Thank goodness for Nordstrom Rack. Sophie's little black number, Calvin Klein no less, was exactly right. It also helped that during the last hour she'd giggled until her sides hurt as she and Bella got ready. Definitely one of the upsides to sharing a room. Now walking into the crowded salon, full of peacock-bright ladies in showy dresses, lit up with enough diamonds to put the crown jewels to shame, she felt perfectly relaxed. Formal dos didn't faze her, there'd been enough of them at home.

Although he was talking to an elderly couple, Todd spotted her immediately and shot her a smile of such focused warmth it made her knees wobble. It didn't help that in black tie, he looked even more ridiculously film-starry handsome.

'Put your tongue away,' muttered Bella in her ear. 'Oh darn. I've just realised. Are you two doing the dirty yet?'

'Bella!' Sophie punched her arm.

'Didn't think so.' Bella grinned unrepentantly. 'And I've cramped your style. Sorry.'

'I meant that's a horrible phrase. And I don't think I could ... at his parents' house. Not the first time.'

'Oh, Sophie you're so sweet. That's the whole point of these house parties. Beds available at any part of the day. No one knowing where anyone is.'

Sophie giggled. 'Sounds like a house party in a regency novel. Clearly things haven't changed that much.'

'Thank goodness they have. You and I would probably have been scullery maids if we traced our family trees back. My grandad made his money through technology and built up a huge telecoms company. And Dad and Uncle Ross built it up even more.'

And what did she say to that? What would Bella's reaction be if she told her that on her father's side she could trace her family tree back to 1660 to the first Earl of Hanbury?

'Bella darling!' Celine interrupted, bringing another lady with her. 'Sandy, this is my clever, clever niece.'

'Oh, I adored your little cakes. Now, I have a party coming up ...'

Sophie drifted outside onto the terrace overlooking the gardens, enjoying the background hum of chatter and laughter. The balmy evening air carried the faint clean scent of pine, rather welcome after the overwhelming fug of rich perfumes.

'I'm starting to wish I was back in New York,' said Todd as he slipped his arms around her middle and came to stand behind her, resting his cheek against hers.

'And why's that?' asked Sophie, turning around with a flirtatious smile.

He kissed her firmly on the mouth.

'Because then I could get you all to myself.'

'And why would you want to do that?' Her voice came out slightly breathless and a touch husky, which she hadn't meant to do, at least she didn't think she had.

Todd's eyes darkened and his direct smile that held more than a hint of smoulder made her swallow hard. Oh dear heaven, the man simply oozed sex appeal and she was drunk on it.

With a feather-light touch, he stroked one hand down her arm, his thumbs skimming the outside of her breast. She didn't normally play sexy siren, but when his smile ratcheted up the smoulder to damn near combustible, she smiled back, letting the desire swim in her eyes. Which was pretty tricky given that she was about to go cross-eyed with lust.

'Do you really need me to answer that?' he asked with smooth self-assurance, looking down at her as she stood bare inches apart from him.

Sophie's *femme fatale* upped and left. Todd was so much more experienced at this kind of stuff. Biting her lip, she lifted her shoulders in a half shrug, ducking her gaze.

'Hey,' he tilted her chin with a hand and gave her a gentle kiss on her lips. 'We've got plenty of time.'

'Sorry,' she muttered, feeling stupidly gauche and suddenly near to tears.

'Don't worry,' he gave her a quick kiss on her forehead. 'Sorry, I realise it's probably still quite soon. Come on, let's mingle.'

That's not what she'd meant at all, but Todd was already leading her back through the French windows and into the crush. There had to be nearly two hundred people there. Of course, everyone wanted to talk to Todd. Why wouldn't you? He was easily the most handsome guy in the room.

'Can you see Marty anywhere?'

Sophie glanced around the room.

'I'm worried he's up to something.'

'Like what?'

'With him, it could be anything, but he seemed a little bit too pleased with himself when we came off the beach. And when I went into the study he was on his laptop and shut it pretty quickly as if he had something to hide.'

'Do you want—'

'Sophie! Sophie Bennings-Beauchamp. It *is* you. Gosh, whatever in the world are you doing here?'

'Margery!'

'My dear gel. Don't you look just delicious and isn't this a lovely party? Don't you just love the uninhibited trashiness of new money? Dear lord above, black champagne, in gold goblets. What fun! And who's this handsome young man?'

Sophie couldn't help smiling back. Margery Forbes-Bryson was one of her parents' oldest friends and famed for her social *faux pas*. Luckily she had such a warm, eager manner, she was quickly forgiven for her tactless observations which usually came from garrulous enthusiasm rather than unkindness.

'Margery,' Sophie kissed her on either cheek before stepping back to introduce Todd. 'This is one of our hosts. Todd McLennan. This is his parents' party.'

'Whoops,' she patted Todd's arm. 'Lovely to meet you and pay no mind to me. Known for planting my size nines in just about everything. Now Sophie, I had no idea you were over here. I'm staying with my dear friend Cissie Newham, she moved here over forty years ago. She's Johnny's daughter. Was Cissie Blenkinsop, wouldn't you marry just to get rid of that name? Caused a great scandal at Diana and Charles' wedding. There she is.' Margery started to wave at a woman across the other side of the room, her big voice bellowing, 'Cissie! Cissie! Come here. Come meet Sophie, Lady Bennings-Beauchamp. You remember Freddie, the Earl of Hanbury? This is his daughter.'

Sophie wanted to sink through the floor as half the faces in the room seemed to turn and stare. Bella's open-mouthed surprise registered, as did Celine's delighted, approving smile. Luckily the approaching Cissie and her rather magnificent bulk shielded Sophie from the curious gazes. She didn't dare look at Todd, although she felt his hand slip into hers and give it a squeeze.

'Oh my word. Freddie. Haven't seen him in yonks. Is he still an old reprobate?' Cissie let out a larger-than-life cackle. 'Although I probably shouldn't be asking his daughter that? Dear lord, Margery. Do you remember when you, Freddie and Charlie went for a dip in the lake at Buck House?'

Thankfully the two of them launched into a trip down memory lane and all she had to do was nod and smile as, out of the corner of her eye, she spotted Bella advancing.

'Well, someone's made Celine's day,' muttered Bella in her ear. 'She's telling everyone that you know Prince William. You don't, do you?'

Sophie ducked her head.

'Oh, shit. You do!'

Sophie moved away from the two ladies, now deep in conversation, to face Bella with Todd flanking her.

'Bella ...'

'*Lady* Sophie. Forgot to mention that one, didn't you?' Although there was a teasing note in her words, her voice cracked slightly and Sophie could tell she was hurt. Before she could say anything, Bella turned to her cousin, 'Did you know, Todd?'

'Yeah, I did.' Sophie did a double take but her attention was held by Bella's furious blinking and the tell-tale glisten in her eyes.

'Bella,' Sophie reached out and touched her on the forearm. 'I wasn't keeping it from you.'

'I thought we were friends.'

'We are ... I never tell anyone. Honest. The only reason my friend Kate knows is because she saw my passport. People I work with in London have no idea. It's not that important to me, but other people ... well, it affects their perception of me. Look at Celine's reaction.'

'So is your dad a ... you know ... a real-life lord?'

Sophie smiled at Bella's sudden diffidence.

'Yup, the fourteenth Earl of Hanbury. And I'm still exactly the same person I was yesterday morning, before you knew.' She sneaked a look at Todd's profile. To her relief he turned his head and gave her a quick wink and a warm smile.

'Wow,' said Bella. 'Fourteenth whoa! You really are an aristocrat. Not a scullery maid in sight. And do you have a place like Downton Abbey?'

Sophie laughed. 'No, nothing like! That's Highclere Castle which is huge and a proper stately home. Felton Hall is ... well, it's not that big.'

'No wonder you weren't thrown by my parents' house,' said Todd.

'You're kidding. Felton Hall is old but it's nowhere near as grand and luxurious as your parents' place. No swimming pools or private access to the beach.' Sophie laughed. 'Can I put this in context? My dad is the Earl and his first wife was Lady something or other before she married Dad. When they divorced he married my mum, who is very ordinary. She was his housekeeper before they got together.'

'So you're only half posh, then,' said Bella. 'Phew.'

'Does that make it alright?' asked Sophie with a grin.

'Yes, half posh I can cope with, but whatever you do, don't tell Wes. He'll never speak to you again.'

'Why, is he some kind of Trotskyite?' Sophie frowned. The big, gentle guy seemed too shy and thoughtful to indulge in forceful politics.

'No,' bitterness roughened Bella's voice, 'but he doesn't believe people from very different backgrounds are compatible. That's why I'm too chicken to ask him out.'

'You still haven't done it, then?'

'No, because I know what will happen. Last year I invited him out here and that's when it all went balls up.'

'Ah, and was he was a bit uncomfortable when he saw the house? I guess that's natural, if you're out of your comfort zone.'

'You're kidding, the concept of a house in the Hamptons

freaked him out. He refused to set foot out of Brooklyn with me. Dunderhead male.'

'Harsh, Bels,' interjected Todd.

'No, he's an idiot. Said we were too different. But I know he still likes me. Too freaking proud. His loss.' Bella's bravado didn't quite ring true. Suddenly she changed the subject. 'So how come Todd knows?'

'Yes,' Sophie frowned. 'How do you know and why didn't you say anything?'

'You never mentioned it, so I didn't.'

Sophie's eyes narrowed. 'When? And how ...?'

'Work. Your visa paperwork. Trudy mentioned it in a meeting. Ages ago.'

Sophie groaned, putting both hands over her face. 'Does everyone know?'

'I've never heard anyone else mention it and there were only four of us in the meeting. Trudy, Paul, me and a woman from HR.'

'Paul knew.' Sophie grimaced and rocked back on her heels. Now some of his comments made sense. No wonder he'd been so unexpectedly keen. Him and his seven-year plan. He probably thought her name could open a few doors.

'Sorry,' mouthed Todd. She gave him a sad smile. He might not do commitment or long term, but at least he was honest about it. She knew exactly where she stood with him. She didn't need to trust him because she wouldn't be making an emotional investment. From now on, she was keeping things light and fun.

Chapter 22

Thanksgiving had been put to bed at the magazine and come Monday morning Sophie was plunged into Christmas, even though the temperatures outside had touched the high forties.

Going to work was suddenly a challenge. July had hit big time. Walking along the streets was a hot sticky business, whereas going into the subway was like plunging into an icy fridge. This, combined with the more bearable temperature in the offices, meant that deciding what to wear was fraught with difficulties.

By Friday, quite frankly, Sophie was crabby. And ... she knew exactly why. Since Sunday there'd been absolutely no sign of Todd. It was as if he'd vanished. She hadn't received a single text from him. He'd been absent from his desk all week, which was doubly irritating because Sophie was still fielding calls from Amy, Cherie and Charlene.

They'd travelled back from the Hamptons on Sunday morning to beat the traffic. When Todd pulled up outside Bella's, he'd handed Bella her bag outside Sophie's door. Her grumpy stare in response had had Sophie hiding her smile. 'The treatment only goes up one floor, does it?'

'Be grateful it went this far. Last year I dropped you outside and as I seem to recall, you were more than happy to get a lift home.'

Bella hefted her bag over her shoulder. 'Behave, kids. I don't know who to warn off first.' With a comical grimace she'd looked from one to the other, wagging a finger. 'If you can't be good, be careful.'

'Bels, get lost.'

'Going, going, gone.' Like one of the seven dwarves with a heavy load she trooped off up the stairs.

When they'd stepped over the threshold to her apartment, Sophie had held her breath, fanciful that she might startle the air. The apartment had that still, stopped-in-time feel, as if not even so much as a dust mote had moved while she'd been gone.

Sitting here now at her desk, she allowed herself a little smile at the memory of Todd dropping her holdall, letting it land with a graceless thud.

'Come here, you.'

He'd pulled her into his arms, saying, 'So much for the nice leisurely journey home I'd planned without my cousin cramping my style. Lunch in West Hempstead and I wanted to take you to this great little coffee shop.' He dipped his head and grazed her lips with his. 'And I'd factored in a lot of kissing.'

'A lot of kissing?'

He nodded solemnly. 'An awful lot of kissing.'

'Ah, so you're behind now.' Sophie linked her arms around his neck.

'Very behind. Any suggestions?'

'I'm fresh out of ideas, probably,' she peeked through her lashes at him, her eyes brimming with mischief, 'because I haven't been kissed enough.'

Todd had done his very best to remedy the situation and Sophie had done her very best to help. Wriggling in her chair and staring out of the window beyond Todd's desk, she remembered how things had started to get a little heated.

'This could go one of two ways. I can carry on kissing you, neglect all my domestic chores, which will mean I go to work commando tomorrow—'

'Eek, please tell me you don't really do that,' Sophie blushed as she looked at Todd's low-slung jeans and the gap where his T-shirt rode up.

'Wouldn't you like to find out?' His naughty smile almost turned her inside out. 'But I need to do some catching up. Dinner?' He stopped. 'Er ... how about Saturday?'

'Saturday?' *Damn, that sounded like dismay.* 'Yes, yes,' she collected herself quickly. 'That would be ... lovely,' she said. *Saturday was forever away.* Nearly a whole week. Clearly that was the way things were done when you were having a fling thing.

Todd gave her a quick frown. 'Something wrong?'

'No. No. Right, I need to get on too.'

It was only when she closed her door and leant against it that she sagged slightly with a tiny plaintive smile. Saturday was fine. Disappointment wasn't part of this deal. And she was a fool to expect any more. It wasn't as if Todd hadn't made the parameters perfectly clear.

And he'd stuck to them, thought Sophie later that morning when she finally said in exasperation to Charlene, on her third call of the day, 'I think he must have dropped his cellphone down the loo.'

'You will tell him I called,' she said insistently as if Sophie was his PA or something.

'I've left three Post-it notes on his desk,' said Sophie, 'but I haven't seen him since last week.'

'Has he been in to work?'

'I've no idea,' replied Sophie, 'and quite frankly I don't care. I'm sorry, I've got work to do. I'm sure when he resurfaces, he'll call you.' She slammed the phone down perhaps a little more forcibly than poor Charlene warranted. Where the hell was Todd? She had plenty to do without answering his phone every five blessed minutes.

With a start she realised it was ten past eleven and she was due to join a meeting to finalise the plans for the Christmas recipe pages. With a heavy sigh, she grabbed her notebook and shot a glare at Todd's empty seat. She was already pig-sick, quite literally, of Christmas. By then she'd be back home. All this would be in the past. And she didn't want to think about it.

With a huff, she left her desk. She normally loved everything festive and now she was irritated by the indecision of the editorial team charged with the dessert end of the article, who had yet to decide whether they should focus on Christmas cake or Christmas pudding for the December issue.

She sat down in the board room with an audible thump in her chair, feeling guilty when Paul shot her a warm smile from the other side of the table.

'Everything OK?' asked Trudy.

'Fine,' said Sophie, clenching her hands into fists under her thighs. They'd discussed this once already and she really didn't feel they needed to go over it again.

Five minutes into the discussion, when it had virtually been agreed that a feature on a classic Christmas-cake recipe would be the centrepiece of the December magazine, Madison piped up.

'Don't you think that's all a bit old fashioned?' she asked with her usual superior sneer. 'We should do modern twists on Christmas cakes. People don't want stodgy dried fruit. They want chocolate cake. Sponges. Only old people want that sort of stuff.' She looked around the table, flicking her shiny hair over her designer-clad shoulders, reminding Sophie of the weekend and the other guests at Celine's party.

Immediately she thought of the Artic Monkeys and the refrain, *I bet you look good in the Hamptons* burst into her head, bringing with it a quick zing of rebellion. With a brief pause, the sort that isn't quite enough to stop you saying something you know you shouldn't, she clenched her hands tighter, and then suddenly found herself saying, 'Actually, you're wrong. People want nostalgia at Christmas. Tradition. They want to reproduce what their families had. They want a cake to be special, not something they can have the rest of the year. They want to take time and trouble over it, they want it to be made with love. I think readers want to soak their fruit in brandy, I think they want to make their cake over a few weeks. The perfect Christmas cake is almost an antidote to technology and the fast pace we live in. Making it takes time and care.'

'Well said, Sophie.' Trudy put her pen down. 'Actually I think that's a theme we can focus on for the whole issue. Abandon the cell-phones, reconnect with the family. It's exactly what people are looking for at the moment.'

When Sophie walked out of the room, heading back to her desk down the corridor, her back positively itched. It wasn't difficult to imagine Madison hurling a dozen knives her way, but she was pleased she'd said her piece even though it was now down to her to come up with a very traditional recipe that involved steeping fruit for several days and designing a show-stopping topper. Thank goodness for Bella and her icing skills. Sophie would be picking her brains again this weekend.

The sight of Todd on the far side of the office, lounging back on two legs of his chair, brought her to a sudden halt. He looked completely relaxed and at home. With a swallow she bent to touch her foot, as if there was something in her shoe that had stopped her. She bet his pulse didn't do stupid things when he saw her. In fact, he was probably on the phone with Amy or Charlene right now, fixing up to see them later in the week. *Act normal. Pleased to see him.* She straightened and carried on, weaving through the desks, pasting a big fat casual smile on her face, one that she didn't really feel.

Todd smiled when he saw her, and he waved, with the phone tucked under his chin. Being friendly, just like he had in all the weeks previously.

'Hey,' he mouthed as she sat down opposite him. Somehow she found herself doing one of those cute little waves in greeting as she drew in her chair and flipped up her laptop.

'Sure ... That would be great ... Seven ...Yeah ... See you there.'

Checking her emails, she studiously kept her head down. She'd got this.

When he put the phone down, she didn't look up but kept tapping away.

'Hey English, how you doing?'

'Good thanks,' she managed the full-on, twinkly, isn't-this-fun smile back at him. *Not aggrieved, not disappointed. No promises made.* The last thing she wanted Todd to realise was that actually, she was a little bit disappointed that he'd not been in touch since Sunday. Not so much as a text or a call. Which was fine, really. Because after all, they'd agreed this wasn't ... permanent. She had no right to feel that way. They'd made it perfectly clear between them. This was a thing, a fling thing. Except ... when they were in the Hamptons away from the everyday routine, she hadn't really appreciated the difficulty of sitting opposite him at work, or equally, the difficulty of him not sitting opposite her at work.

It wasn't Todd's fault. He'd been quite clear. She hadn't done casual before. She'd get used to it.

Treating him like a colleague, she gave him a brief nod and got back to her email inbox which stared blankly back at her. Not a sausage in there that needed dealing with.

'You OK, English?' Above the top of his desk, Sophie could see one of Todd's legs bouncing up and down with nervous energy. *Oh lord, could he sense her annoyance with him?*

'Me? Yeah, fine. Busy. Christmas.' She needed to do better than this. At the moment she was acting as if she expected something from him. *Remember the rules, Sophie.* 'Can you believe it? You could probably fry eggs on the bonnets of cars out there, and I'm writing about making Christmas cakes.'

'You still on for tomorrow night?' Todd's forehead was marred by the faintest of frowns.

'Tomorrow night?'

'Dinner.'

'Oh,' Sophie frowned in puzzlement as if she'd forgotten all about it. He paused for a moment, his eyes searching hers. 'Yes.'

Now he was the one that looked puzzled.

They worked in silence, strained silence. Sophie didn't dare look up at him. She'd blown it. Completely blown it. Feeling slightly sick, she tensed in her seat.

'Hungry?' Todd jumped to his feet. Before she could answer, he was beside her, putting a hand underneath her elbow, gently guiding her to her feet. 'I bet you've been eating at your desk all week, haven't you? I told you it's bad for you. Come on, I'll take you to a fantastic Mexican street-food stall around the corner and we can eat in the park.'

With a casual shrug, she agreed. *Here it was, she was going to get the brush-off. He knew.* With reluctant steps she followed him through the desks towards the lift.

They stood in front of the doors and she kept herself ramrod straight so there was no accidental touching. Not that he seemed aware, as soon as they got into the lift he leaned right across her to press the button for the ground floor, brushing his hand across her stomach.

She stiffened, but then as the doors began to close he

twirled her around, muttering, 'Been too long, English.' He was just lowering his head, her heart exploding in a series of mini explosions of relief, when the doors stuttered open again and Sophie looked over Todd's shoulder to see Madison's very startled face, her mouth dropping into an 'O' of surprise. Then Madison, being Madison, regained her super-cool equilibrium and strode into the lift.

'Todd. Nice to see you,' she said, completely ignoring Sophie. 'I hear you were in the Hamptons at the weekend. I've discovered we have mutual friends.'

'We do?' asked Todd, turning around with the sort of formal politeness that Sophie now knew was his way of signalling complete disinterest.

Sophie stared down at the floor, as the lift did that into-hyperspace speed-drop downwards.

'Yes, my friend Stacy Van der Straten was at your party.'

'Well, technically it was my parents' party.' Sophie ventured a look at his face and saw his friendly smile, which clearly reassured Madison, judging by the simpering grin on her face. But Sophie thought smugly that the smile didn't hold the usual kilowatt twinkle that did funny things to *her* stomach.

'Stacy said it was fabulous. Shame I had to stay in the city for my father's sixtieth. Family do at The Metropolitan Club. I'm sure I'd have had a lot more fun at your place.'

'Like I said, it's my parents' place. They're in charge of the frivolities.'

'Maybe next year,' purred Madison, shooting a look of triumph at Sophie as if to say, *because I'll still be here and you won't.*

With that jolting vibration that signified they'd landed, the lift stopped and as soon as the doors opened Todd marched out of the door, like a man on a mission.

'Nice seeing you, Madison. Come on Sophie, we'll be late.'

She had to lengthen her stride to keep up with him as they left the building, walking out into hot soupy air filled with fumes and the sound of sirens and horns tooting. He slowed as the heat hit and took her hand, linking his fingers through hers.

'She is one royal pain in the ass. Do you know how long it is since I last kissed you?'

A burst of sunshine lit up inside her.

It looked as if most of the office workers in downtown Manhattan had had the same idea and almost every patch of shade in the immediate vicinity was taken up, but with unerring confidence Todd led her to an area of grass next to a shimmering expanse of water.

'Come here you,' he pulled her into his arms and gave her a thorough kiss that left them both looking a little bemused. He pushed away a stray tendril of hair that had escaped her ponytail, looking into her eyes with a quick puzzled frown, before saying very quietly, 'I missed you.'

She gave him a quick squeeze in response, not wanting to say anything, as if it might scare him away. He looked as surprised at the revelation as she was.

'Are you going to feed me or not?' she asked, popping a quick kiss on the corner of his mouth.

With a quick roll of his eyes he shook the brown paper bag in his hand. 'It's always about the food with you.'

They sat down side by side on the grass and he quickly unpacked an interesting array of little plastic trays. He'd insisted on selecting the tapas-style dishes for her at the food stall, so that 'lunch would be a surprise'.

'Here you go, English, try that.' Todd scooped up a tiny tortilla piled with broad beans, chili, coriander and slivers of lime and offered it to her, sneaking in a quick kiss which made her insides flutter, before she put it into her mouth.

Tasting the fragrant combination, Sophie closed her eyes in bliss. 'Mmm, that is heaven and a nice change from turkey. I've been busy putting the Christmas edition together. Seems crazy, doesn't it, when the weather is like this.'

'It does.' His fingers skated over her lower lip teasingly. She stared at his chin while her pulse short-circuited for a second. 'Where,' his hand slipped under her chin and he nudged it up very slightly so that she was forced to meet his eyes, 'do you fancy going to dinner tomorrow – no turkey drumsticks?' The warmth in his gaze was quickly replaced with flirty mischief.

'You're kidding. There is such a thing? They'd be huge.'

'Oh yes, they're a thing. So tomorrow? There's a great Meze place or an Italian which does seriously good pizza.' He leaned back on the grass next to her, propping himself up on his elbows, lifting his face up to the sun, a slight wariness in his stillness.

'Do you know what, I haven't had pizza for ages. That would be perfect.'

'Phew,' she saw him relax, 'because it's seriously stressful taking a foodie out for dinner. I've been checking recommendations for the last two days.'

'You have?' Suddenly all the hesitation and uncertainty she'd been feeling since Monday vanished as quickly as an extinguished match.

'Yes, it's too hard. Unless it's a work thing, a launch or an opening, in future you have to decide where we go. Do you know how many restaurants there are in Brooklyn?'

'Ever heard of Trip Advisor?' laughed Sophie.

'Yes,' said Todd, sitting up and wrapping an arm around her, 'and then you get sucked into reading all the reviews. You think you've got it nailed and then someone says it was the worst meal of their life. So you cross that one off the list. And how do you know how discerning these people are?'

'You're not trying to impress me, are you?'

'Of course, I am,' said Todd, the twinkle back in his eye. 'I have my international playboy reputation to think of.

'What time shall I pick you up tomorrow? I won't see you later, I'm leaving the office this afternoon and heading up to Queens for a press launch. Some new men's grooming product. I shall come back smelling of "Courage", "All Man" or "Noble". The press releases are highly amusing.'

Sophie pulled a face. '*Grooming product* always sounds slightly wrong. As if you're a poodle or something.'

Todd's face fell comically, 'Wet-dog smell? You really do my ego the power of good.'

When Sophie went back to work her spirits had been lifted – so high, in fact, that she thought she might be able to float up to her office without the aid of the lift. Todd had clearly been thinking about her and their date. Sitting at her desk, she spent half an hour gazing out of the window, reliving the lunch-time conversation and the way Todd's shirt had ridden up, leaving a tantalising glimpse of bare tanned stomach. And how his eyes had twinkled even damn more when he'd caught her looking. Even now she felt a little flustered and scratchy. Was it wrong to be so looking forward to tomorrow night? She must remember to put fresh sheets on the bed. *Whoa! Sophie, where did that thought come from?* She'd turned into a complete slapper. But she was due some fun and these next few months were going to be that.

She almost ignored the phone ringing on the desk, until she realised it was hers and not Todd's.

'Sophie, we've got a bit of a problem. Pigs in blankets.' Trudy's voice sounded furious.

'Sorry?'

'Tell me what a pig in blanket looks like?'

'Bacon wrapped around a chipolata sausage.'

'Do you know what a pig in blanket looks like here?'

Sophie paused and did a quick search on Google. 'Oh shoot ...' The pastry-wrapped sausages looked more like sausage rolls and definitely very different.

'You haven't seen the shots from the Christmas shoot yesterday, have you?'

'No,' said Sophie. She'd prepared the turkey and the vegetables for the stylist and had okayed the props and the set. The photographer was experienced enough to take it from there and Madison had insisted she was happy to stay and supervise.

'I think you might want to come to my office to take a look and explain to me how I'm going to find a spare thousand dollars for another day's photography shoot.'

Chapter 23

'I honestly thought I was going to get the sack. Trudy was mad as hell,' said Sophie, cupping her hands around a cup of coffee and inhaling the familiar scent. She'd sought out Bella in the kitchen, attracted by the welcome smell of baking. 'I was worried sick until I got home half an hour ago.' It had been the longest afternoon of her life as she'd sat with an incandescent Trudy and the photographer while they'd looked at every possible permutation of cropping or Photoshopping the picture to remove the offending items.

'It was only when I got home that I got a text from Trudy, apologising. Lauren, one of the food techs, had been to see her. She'd been there when I handed over my recipe to Madison, who'd commented on how different they were to US pigs in blankets. She'd also been there when the stylist had queried them and Madison had insisted that I'd said that's what I wanted. So instead of nice bacon-wrapped sausages, there were these bulky pastry-wrapped things that looked completely out of place.'

'The cow. The absolute cow.' Bella paced around the kitchen waving an icing bag. 'What a bitch. I can't believe Madison deliberately set you up.'

'It didn't do her much good because Trudy told her straight that she knew she'd done it on purpose. When Madison tried to protest, Trudy said you query everything Sophie says in the editorial meetings, what changed? Apparently that shut her up.'

'What have you done to upset her?'

'I don't think being invited to the Hamptons with Todd was my best move.'

'And that's your fault?'

'Maybe not, but after today the knives will be out. She caught Todd kissing me in the lift.'

'Dirty trollop. How is he? I haven't seen him since he dropped us off.'

'Today was the first time I'd seen him since Sunday. We're going out tomorrow. Want me to send your love?'

'No, its fine. Right, I'm going to shut up shop. I'm actually going out tonight.' Bella brightened. 'Wine and food not cooked by me.'

'With Wes?'

'No chance.' Bella's mouth turned downwards. 'I asked him if he fancied coming out for a drink, but he turned me down again.'

The first hit of ice-cold white wine down her throat was so welcome, it was tempting to knock back the whole glass and pour another straight away. The day's heat seemed to have collected and pooled in the apartment, and the day's stress had left her restless and unable to settle. Already she felt a new trickle of sweat starting to collect at the back of her neck where her damp ponytail hung. It was Friday night, for goodness' sake. She should be out. There was nothing on television she fancied, the book she'd filched at the weekend from Celine's library wasn't holding her interest and the families enjoying the early evening in the neighbouring gardens had put her off sitting solo on the deck.

She lifted the edge of her vest and flapped it, trying to cool herself down, even putting her cold wineglass on her belly. The unexpected knock at the door startled her. With a jerk of her arm, she jolted the glass, tipping a cold steam of wine across her skin, trickling down over her cotton shorts as if she'd wet herself. 'Damn.' It was probably Bella checking up on her on her way out.

Opening the door, she came face to face with a navy-blue linen shirt and had to adjust her eye-line upwards. 'Todd!'

'Hi.'

Everything inside her suddenly turned to mush. His hair was damp around the edges but he had that just-showered delicious man-smell, a combination of cedar, sandalwood and something indefinable.

'What are you ...?' her voice petered out.

He stepped forward, ducking his head as if suddenly shy. 'I was ... er, passing. Wondered if you ... er ... fancied a drink or something.' His voice grew a bit stronger. 'It's a lovely evening.'

'Oh,' she looked down at herself, 'I'm not dressed. And I've just spilled my wine. I haven't ...'

'I can see that,' he said gravely, before a tell-tale quirk to his lips gave him away. 'I'm not sure whether I want you to get dressed or not. It's a very fetching ...' He nodded his head towards her skimpy vest. She didn't need to look down to know that both nipples were making a spectacle of themselves. It seemed ridiculously coy to try and cover herself.

She turned her back on him, saying over her shoulder, 'Would you like to come in? I've just opened a bottle of wine and I've got some beer in the fridge.'

'Beer would be great, it's hot ...' he paused, 'out there.'

Without looking at him, she crossed quickly to the kitchen area and yanked open the fridge, grateful for the cool flow of air that hit her. The temperature in the apartment had just hit a thousand degrees Fahrenheit, or was that just her? Any minute now she was about to spontaneously combust, and by the looks of things, she wasn't the only one. Flipping off the top, she put the beer bottle to her face before turning to find that he'd followed her across the room.

'Here,' she thrust the bottle at him. Calmly he took it from her and put it down on the bench, before sliding his hands around her waist under her vest top and slowly pulling her to him.

'Sorry, I should have called, but I've been thinking about you all day,' his thumbs stroked her skin in small circles, 'and tomorrow night seemed ...'

Whatever it seemed, she never found out because his words ended as his lips homed in on hers with magnetic accuracy. Like a sunflower she tipped up her head in happy anticipation and the minute his mouth touched hers, her stomach went into free fall, her heart flickering like a lantern in a storm.

No denying it – the breathless excitement of kissing Todd

McLennan was utterly addictive. Whether it was playboy technique or maybe they fitted, she couldn't say, but it felt like fireworks and sunbeams every time. Little fizzing explosions and gorgeous warmth.

Just as all the joints in her limbs appeared to have dissolved and she was in danger of melting into him, they backed into the bench and were brought up short by a sudden clink and rattle. With a handy save Todd reached out and managed to catch the bottle, spewing foaming beer from the neck, before it plunged over the side.

For a minute he stood there with the beer foaming over his wrist.

'Between us we seem to be wasting alcohol at a vast rate of knots,' he said, taking a quick sip to stop the flow.

For a second she considered licking the drips of beer running down his forearm and caught his eye. She blushed as he raised one eyebrow with an I-know-exactly-what-you're-thinking lift.

'Shall we go out on the deck?' she asked hurriedly and, before he could answer, she picked up her wineglass and was out of the door.

Of course, he looked amused when he followed her. None of this was new to him, whereas she was feeling a little bit out of her depth. James had been a strictly lights-off, in-bed-and-after-dark man, whereas she had a feeling Todd was more of a Martini man, anywhere and anyplace.

'I thought maybe you'd heard about the disaster in the office today.'

'No? What happened?'

Sophie nibbled at her lip, a dull ache settling in her stomach as she looked at him. Yup, he was absolutely, bloody gorgeous, especially now he was slightly dishevelled. The linen shirt was crumpled around the hem where she'd pushed it up to touch his skin. Run her hands over his lean hips. Her mouth dried, she wanted to get her hands on him again. She felt herself turn pink again at the thought of running her fingers down his abs, over his chest. Those days on the beach had revealed exactly what was on offer.

'Do you know what, I don't want to talk about it now. I'd rather do something else.' She stood up and took the beer bottle out of his hand, putting it down on the table. Something glittered in his eyes as he looked up at her. Remaining seated, he held her gaze. Her breath stalled in her chest. The next move was hers. Grateful that he'd left her in control, she held out her hand. 'Coming?'

His swallow, the widening of his eyes and the almost dumb-struck nod made her smile with a rush of womanly pride.

He put his hand in hers and allowed himself to be gently tugged to his feet.

Rising excitement filled her with every step, along with a sudden confidence that she was doing the right thing. He might be out of reach for the long term, but she was going to grab everything she could right now. Things could change in a heartbeat and she didn't want to miss a minute of life any more.

Unfortunately her confidence upped and left the minute her feet hit the centre of her bedroom floor and she turned to face Todd, but she needn't have worried. As if he knew exactly how she felt, he cupped her face in his hands and kissed her gently on her mouth.

'I think I should be a gentleman about this, ask if you're sure ...' he took a sharp indrawn breath, 'but it might kill me ...'

She laid a finger on his lips, warmth blossoming at his words, 'Shh,' she whispered.

For a moment, heady with anticipation, they held each other's eyes in solemn promise. Sophie's heart pumped so hard she could feel it vibrating through her body.

Then his fingertips were sliding up under her vest top, inching rib by rib, upwards, taking the flimsy fabric with them. He eased the scrap of jersey over her head and she let out a tiny breath as he gazed down at her breasts. With infinite slowness he traced the back of his hand down her throat, down to the vee, his fingers widening to brush each breast before continuing down.

Biting back a tiny gasp, she stood there as he removed her panties. Before she could take stock he picked her up and laid her on the bed. And before she could feel a hint of self-consciousness, he began to unbutton his shirt.

Of course this was playboy perfection, wasn't it, and as the snake of a thought slithered, it was quickly repelled by the sight of his fingers shaking as they fumbled with the buttons.

'Oh fuck it,' he said and whipped the shirt off over his head, almost falling over as he tried to get his shorts off, while digging in one of the pockets. 'I've never wanted to get naked as much as I do right now.'

And right there, the mood lifted and it wasn't quite so scary or important that she got this right. Sophie giggled.

'Are you laughing at me?' he growled, tossing a couple of condoms on her bedside table and lunging onto the bed and taking her into his arms.

'No.' Her attempt at a straight face fell far short and she giggled again at his mock outrage when he began to tickle her. At some point the silly wrestling tipped over into teasing caresses before sliding into full-blown seduction.

Making love with Todd was an utter revelation. At first he was generous, careful and attentive as he eased her onto her back, his hands dancing over her skin, setting light to her nerve endings. Then he moved into playfulness; talkative, teasing and frustrating as he gently tormented her, homing in on every erogenous zone she had and quite a few more she never realised were there. As her temperature rose, her desire rocketing and a burning need fired up, he laughed down at her as she played back, her hands exploring, running over the contours of his chest, sliding across his waist and dipping below. Twisting and turning, they tangled in the sheets, slightly sweaty in the evening heat. At some point the mood slid into sexy, as if a switch had been pressed. Suddenly they were breathless, need pumped as fast as their pulses and the tempo of kisses and caresses had ramped up to passionate.

Suddenly they stilled, his hand on her breast, teasing the nipple, she whimpering with breathy moans, her hand cupping his balls as he groaned, moving his hips in a driving tempo.

When he tried to tear into the condom, she couldn't help smiling at his ineptitude.

'Do you know what you're doing?' she teased as she stroked him.

'With you, mmm, doing that ... I-I'm not sure I even know what my own name is.'

'Doing what?' she purred, circling her thumb over the very tip.

He tried to wriggle away out of her reach and she dipped her hand down, caressing his inner thigh.

'Jeez, Sophie.'

He ripped open the packet with his teeth. 'I'd offer to let you do this but I'm not sure I'd survive.'

With quick efficiency, he rolled on the condom, his hand sliding between her legs.

'Someone's ready,' he said, his finger sliding over the sweet spot, almost sending her cross-eyed with lust.

All she could do was pant, his touch had pushed her into desperation.

She lifted her hips, almost unable to help herself, her body's needs had taken over. 'Like that, do you?' He removed his hand.

'Please,' her strangled desperate plea surprised her but she could hardly think straight.

'Please what, Sophie?' She closed her eyes and whimpered.

His fingers teased again, dipping in before retreating, quick, fast movements that had her lifting her hips, grinding but with each lift, he retreated.

'You have to stay very still, I think, Sophie.'

It was almost impossible. He tormented her, if she so much as moved an inch, he retreated again. Soon she was breathless, a fine sheen coating her skin.

'Please,' she panted again.

His smile now was strained, as he bent his head to suck one nipple hard and fast into his mouth.

She cried out, an incoherent moan.

He continued sucking, his rhythm at one with the two fingers sliding relentlessly in and out.

Her pants were erratic, she tried to escape from the persistent touch and thrust. All the time Todd watched her but his breathing was strained.

'Todd, now, pleasepleasepleaseplease.'

In one fluid move he moved over her and slid inside her, stretching and filling while inflaming the already sensitive nerves. And then he pulled back before sliding slowly, slowly … she could hardly bear it. Greedily she grabbed his hips.

'More?' he asked, his voice taut.

'Yesssss, please.' She lifted her hips and he met them before picking up the pace. With every thrust she lifted to meet him, and it still felt as if it wasn't enough, would never be enough. And then suddenly, like breaking through the clouds to the sun above, they burst through the rhythm, hitting the perfect pace as they rode together. With one helpless cry she dissolved, the waves of feeling overtaking as she fell headlong into the climax and he stiffened, calling her name in a long, loud, heartfelt groan. For a while they lay together, sweat slicked in the humid atmosphere, the sound of Friday night coming in through the open window. Sophie wondered whether she might ever move again and then decided that she probably didn't want to. This was about as close to heaven as she could imagine and had just blown every other sexual experience she'd ever had out of the water.

They must have dozed together for a while because when she opened her eyes, it was half past seven.

'Wowsers,' Todd shifted, moving his weight from her but leaving his thigh over hers and one hand spanning her waist, 'I think you've killed me, woman. What the hell was that?'

A kaleidoscope of butterflies fluttered low in her belly at his heartfelt words. 'I've killed you? I think it's the other way round. You with your international playboy skills.'

He propped his head on his hand and with the other skimmed her ribcage, coming to rest on her hip.

'I promise you, I've never had sex like that before. That's intergalactic playgirl standard. I feel as if my whole body's been discombobulated.'

Sophie dropped her head, allowing herself a very small but very smug little smile.

'Pleased with yourself?' asked Todd, his hand grazing back along her side to lift her chin, peering into her face 'Rendering a man's brains incapable.' He punctuated each word with a quick kiss on her mouth.

'I think I am,' she gave him a lazy smile, her gaze drifting down his body.

'You want to watch that,' he said, his voice lowering. 'A man might get ideas.'

'What sort of ideas?' Sophie's voice was suitably husky.

'I'm sure I can think of a few.' His arm slid underneath her waist and he pulled her body to his side, nuzzling her neck.

She looped her arms around his neck, rubbing her chest against his. With a groan he kissed her again. 'You want round two now?'

'Why not?' she smiled up into his face.

'You sure you're up to it?' he asked, a cocky smile playing around his lips.

Blushing, she nodded.

'Bring it on.'

Finally untangling themselves from the sheets, Todd insisted on her joining him in the shower, where round three ensued with much giggling, soap suds and general silliness. The night was still young and the air had cooled considerably, so they decided to go out for a bite to eat.

Chapter 24

'Would you like chocolate or cinnamon sprinkles with that?' Sophie took a moment to roll her shoulders before picking up one of the shakers. This morning her body felt well-used and weary.

'I'll have both, my darling.' The woman chuckled, a rich, dark, rolling sound that matched her ebony skin and friendly, open smile. She was tall and, as Sophie's mum would have said, big boned. 'And don't you have a fine accent there. Where are you from?'

The woman was so deliciously cheery, that despite being asked that very question at least fifteen times this morning, Sophie cheerfully responded, even though she was starting to flag a bit. Since eight o'clock she'd been in the coffee shop, having helped Bella for an hour before in the kitchen cooking up several batches of cookies and cakes. Sleep was overrated. Who needed it when they had this delicious sense of excitement and happiness to hug to themselves? Still buzzing, she could feel herself blushing at last night's memories. Sleep had not been high on the agenda.

After dinner Todd had walked her back to the apartment,

both having agreed over dinner that as she was working in the bakery in the morning, they would see each other for dinner the following evening. But the minute he kissed her outside her front door, all their good intentions went up in smoke. Soft kisses turned into sizzling in less than sixty seconds. By the time they came up for air they were back in Sophie's bed.

'So you're not Bella, then?' There was a distinct naughty sparkle in the woman's eyes, almost as if she could read Sophie's thoughts. She reeked of someone clearly up to no good.

'No,' said Sophie, enchanted by her mischievous air.

'I'm Dessie.' She looked back over her shoulder, like an inept spy, checking no one was in earshot. Although the café was busy, now that they'd passed the ten o'clock threshold, the morning rush of commuters had slowed. This was the pre-eleven coffee slot, comprising mainly solitary newspaper readers, laptop users and daydreamers, and the *après*-gym buddy set. All of them were absorbed in their own worlds.

'I think you're safe,' teased Sophie.

Dessie leaned over the counter. 'I'm Wes's mum.' She gave one of those this-is-between-us nods.

'Oh, how lovely to meet you. He was in here this morning.' Sophie paused. Wes came in every morning, without fail. Usually the first customer of the day, waiting patiently outside the door like a faithful hound. Every morning Bella made him wait until she'd switched on every light, put the sugar and vases on each table and the espresso machine was ready to go. It was Bella's subtle way of punishing him. Poor man.

He couldn't stay away, but he didn't seem to be able to move forward.

This morning, he'd been grateful when Sophie stopped him to ask if he had any lemon grass, red chillies, Thai basil, fresh ginger or coriander, which she still kept forgetting to call cilantro. He was impressed when she said she wanted to make an authentic Thai Green Curry, confirmed he had all of those things and offered to ring a friend to get hold of some pea aubergines that he could get delivered that afternoon.

'I've come to find out what's making my boy so miserable,' Dessie's ridiculously loud stage whisper echoed around the café and a dozen heads turned. Sophie might have giggled except Bella, who'd been clearing tables, stood right behind the older woman, her face looking decidedly grim. 'And I know, I know. I'm interfering but something's not right and that boy is so darned stubborn.'

'You're not wrong there,' snapped Bella, putting her tray down and resting her hands on her hips. 'I'm Bella.'

Sophie watched as the two of them sized each other up. They were almost polar opposites, Bella with her red-gold hair and pale skin and Dessie with her Amazonian stature and dark skin.

'Well, aren't you a dab of a thing.' Dessie's broad smile robbed the words of any offence.

'Yeah,' Bella said, her mouth turning down with a mournful twist. 'Which means we look one hell of an odd couple.'

'Surely he pays no mind to that.'

'It's a factor.'

Dessie frowned. 'I brought my boy up better than that.'

'Perhaps you should ask him what the problem is, then.'

'Well, if it were that simple, my darling, I wouldn't have trailed my tail all the way down here when I'm supposed to be doing a bake-sale for the stray-cat society. Honestly, those cat babies are better fed than half the kids in the neighbourhood, but the darn school keeps picking it as their charity of the year.'

'You could always buy some. Give me half an hour and I could knock you some up with cats' ears and whiskers on. I've got a couple of dozen cupcakes waiting to be iced.'

Dessie tipped her head on one side. 'Deal. Why don't I come chat to you while you're doing it?'

Bella raised an eyebrow. 'How many are you going to buy?'

'I like you, girl. Let's start with a dozen. Now,' she tucked her arm cosily into Bella's, 'I'm thinking we can get this sorted out in two ticks of a tailor's dash.' Over her shoulder Bella raised her eyebrows at Sophie as the older woman marched alongside her to the back of the bakery.

Sophie watched them go. Poor Wes, she wasn't sure he stood a chance with those two on his case.

Ten minutes later he stood in front of her with a basketful of herbs, looking everywhere but at Sophie.

'Where is she?'

'Bella?' asked Sophie, trying to play innocent. 'Are they for me?'

'My mother.'

'Your mother?'

'Yes, lady with a bright-red dress and a very a big nose.'

'Oh, that lady.' Sophie buried her face in the fragrant herbs. 'Don't you love the smell of Thai basil?'

Wes folded his arms but even at over six foot, with shoulders as wide as an ocean liner, he didn't look the least bit intimidating. Not any more. Sophie couldn't believe she'd been quite scared of him that first night when he'd loomed out of the dark. How could a man who tended his herbs with so much love and tender care possibly be a threat?

'Hey Wes, Sophie.' Her heart sprang into action like a sprightly springbok bouncing around with joy at the sight of Todd.

'Hi,' she squeaked, her voice suddenly going haywire.

'The day was dragging.' He pushed his hand through his hair, looking evasive. 'Nice herbs, Wes.'

'They're for Sophie, she wants to impress the guy she's cooking for tonight.' Wes nudged Todd. 'She's pulling out all the stops. Authentic ingredients. And here you go, pea aubergines.' He winked at Todd. 'Ultra-special ingredient.'

Sophie wanted to sink through the floor at Wes's unwitting teasing.

'Does she, now?' Todd grinned. 'Pea aubergines. Are they some kind of aphrodisiac, Sophie? What are you planning?'

'Thai Green Curry and no, they're not,' she said repressively. 'And if you don't behave you won't be getting any.'

Wes's mouth dropped open as he looked from Todd to Sophie and then back again. 'Right. I think I'll be going. Here you go.' He gave Todd another glance, fighting back a grin. 'Enjoy the curry. And tell Bella I was here. I'll deal with her later.' The latter was said with a touch of an ominous threat.

'Am I missing something?' asked Todd.

'I'll explain later,' said Sophie as Wes departed, handing over the basket of herbs.

'So do you fancy being my plus-one to review this place? Rooftop bar. Swanky hotel. It's the perfect evening. We can go for one drink, before you drag me back to your place to have your wicked way with me.'

'Your chances of being fed, aphrodisiacs or anything else, are rapidly declining.'

'English, you're not playing hard to get, are you? Do I have to beg?'

She laughed. 'I need to help Bella close up. And I'll need a quick shower. I can be ready by five. You can go dump the herbs in my fridge if you want to be useful.'

'OK. And then I could go warm the shower up for you.'

She felt her cheeks turn bright pink. 'I think my poor shower could do with a break this evening.'

'You're no fun.' Todd pouted before smiling. 'Tell you what, I'll dump this and nip back to my place for some supplies.'

'What sort of supplies?'

'More shower gel, you're running low.'

She threw the cloth at his departing back.

Todd drove to the Westlight, which was a stunning, sophisticated roof-top bar north of Williamsburg. Sophie felt she was starting to get the hang of Brooklyn, which she'd now realised was much bigger than Manhattan.

'You ain't seen nothing yet,' said Todd in response to her

observation as they drove back to her apartment. 'In fact, I know where we can go tomorrow.'

'Where?' A little thrill flashed through her that he was already planning tomorrow. After last weekend, when he'd not arranged to meet up until Saturday, she'd sort of assumed that he wanted to keep things very casual.

'It's a surprise.'

'It's always a surprise with you,' muttered Sophie.

'Don't you like surprises?' asked Todd.

'I love them, when they're instant surprises but not when I'm told there's going to be a surprise, because then I have to wait and I'm impatient.'

'OK. Would you like to go out tomorrow?'

'That would be lovely. Where?'

'I haven't decided yet,' he said, suddenly very prim, straightening up at the wheel and deliberately not looking at her. She burst out laughing.

And laughter seemed to be the theme of the night. He sat at the breakfast bar in the kitchen drinking beer as she cooked the curry, sniffing appreciatively as the subtle fragrances of lemon grass, ginger and Thai basil filled the air. What's more, he was interested, asking lots of questions like: why was she using shallots instead of onions, why did she bash the lemon grass before she chopped it? And as she answered – explaining that shallots had a more intense flavour than onions, so you used less and therefore made the paste less watery, and bashing lemon grass softened it and helped to release its natural aromatic oils – he listened carefully, his whole attention on her. He definitely knew how to make a girl feel good about herself.

After they'd eaten, he volunteered to wash up and she sat on the stool at the breakfast bar toying with the stem of her wineglass, watching him rolling up his sleeves, trying not to look at his hands and remember their skilful touch the previous night.

'You've used an awful lot of utensils.' Todd frowned, looking around at the kitchen. Sophie, who prided herself on being a tidy cook, was very slightly put out.

'You're not reneging on the internationally recognised convention that the cook skips the washing-up?'

'No, but I think in the interests of parity and Anglo-American relations, that we should make it more interesting.' There was something devious about the gleam in his eyes.

'How do you make washing-up more interesting?' Sophie leaned against the breakfast bar, one hand cupping her chin as she picked up her wineglass.

'Well, for example, this rice pan is going to need a bit of work. I'm going to need an incentive.' She couldn't miss the hint of challenge in his voice.

'And the best Thai curry you've ever eaten outside South-East Asia wasn't incentive enough?'

Todd shrugged. 'I've eaten it now.'

She looked pointedly at his empty plate by the sink. 'You certainly did.' He'd had three helpings.

'You have to take an item of clothing off.'

Sophie choked on her wine. 'I beg your pardon?'

'You're so sexy when you go all prim on me, English.'

She stared at him, her lips twitching.

'It's a big pan. Needs a lot of scrubbing.' He cocked his head.

She slipped off one shoe and held it up.

'That's one piece of flatware. Come on, this is a heavy-duty pan.'

Sophie took a long slow sip of wine, her mind racing.

'OK, but you have to keep washing up, until it's all done.'

'Naturally.'

Without a second thought she peeled off her dress and tossed it on the breakfast bar, hiding a smug smile when his eyes widened and he gulped. Oh, yes, he definitely gulped.

'Pan.' She nodded at the sink.

He dealt with the rice pan without another word and his voice was husky when he put it on the drainer and said, 'Next.'

She took another sip of wine, her eyes on his, and without flinching pulled down her underwear and laid her lace shorts on the bar next to the dress. He suddenly looked a little strained. Not that he could see her, tucked behind the breakfast bar.

'Carry on,' she said, deliberately demure.

'Right.' He reached for his beer bottle and took a quick swig, almost choking. 'Yes. Right.'

'Something wrong?' She crossed her legs on the stool, moving very slowly.

'No.' His low-pitched denial was a far cry from his usual confident tone as he hesitantly picked up the chopping board.

Without hesitation she slipped one strap down on her bra,

pausing to catch his eye, watching him as he watched her. She lowered the second before unhurriedly moving her hands behind her back to undo the strap. 'Don't stop on my account,' she said.

Without breaking his gaze, he dumped the board in the sudsy water. She unclipped her bra and let it fall. He dropped the board with a crash into the water.

'Gently,' she reprimanded him. He grabbed a tea-towel and rounded the breakfast bar, sweeping her into a hungry kiss.

The breakfast bar proved a handy support.

She woke the following morning with the sun streaming through the window. For a moment she lay there enjoying the feeling of the weight of Todd's arm across her hip and the warmth of another body spooned up to her. When his fingers began to stroke her skin she turned over to find him sleep-mussed with a dopey smile on his face.

'Morning, English.'

'Morning. What time is it?' She was too comfortable to reach for her phone.

'Who cares? We've got all day.'

'We have?' She hadn't thought that far ahead.

'You don't have any plans, do you?' Todd's hopeful face made her heart sing.

'Nothing particularly interesting.'

'You do now. Time to get your lazy but rather delectable ass out of bed.' He slapped her bottom gently. 'You're a terrible influence. Dragging me into bed.'

'Me!'

But Todd was already throwing back the sheets and tugging her hand. 'Into the shower with you. I have plans ... for you.'

'In the shower?' She cocked her head, a shiver of anticipation rolling through her.

'Jeez, woman.' He pulled her upright up against his naked body. 'You have a filthy mind. I'm going to be a shadow of my former self if you keep making these insatiable demands on my poor body.'

Sophie rolled her hips. If he was going to suggest she was a wanton harlot, she was more than happy to play along.

'Hell, woman, you're killing me. Get into that shower, before I drag you back to bed. We have a day planned.'

'We do?'

'Yes.'

From the top of the Wonder Wheel, the crowds below looked like busy ants. Coney Island reminded Sophie of a proper seaside resort with its snack bars, amusement arcades and the packed beach. The wind tossed her hair as the car they were in swung slightly as it rose to the very top of the wheel. Thank goodness she had a good head for heights, unlike her friend poor Kate. She craned her neck, keen to make the most of the view, and took out her phone to take a picture of it. With a quick smile she WhatsApp'd it to Kate, with a quick teasing caption, *you'd love it here*. It felt good to be normal again and not *pretend* that she was having a good time. Holding up her phone, she nudged Todd to take a quick selfie.

Since they'd arrived earlier, he had taken her hand as they'd ambled along, taking in the sights and smells. The hot dog seemed to be king here, the smell of fried onions permeated the air as people wandered along clutching napkin-wrapped bundles dripping with the bright-yellow mustard sauce. It made a welcome change to be one of two among the happy crowds of people who were all enjoying their weekend.

After the Wonder Wheel, they went on the dodgems before standing in front of the terrifying Thunderbolt ride.

'What do you think?' asked Todd, looking up at the death-defying vertical climb, the loop the loop and the waves of orange steel track.

'I'm game if you are,' she replied, remembering the last roller coaster she'd been on in Denmark. 'I survived The Demon in Tivoli Gardens last year.' She took another picture for Kate and sent it over.

'You're a brave woman, English,' said Todd, watching the cart inching up the ramp towards the top of the sheer drop.

'It's not brave if you're not scared,' said Sophie, noting the slight strain in his face. 'Brave is when you're scared, and you still do something, when you face your fear. That's real bravery. My friend Kate went on the Demon last year, even though she's terrified of heights and had never been on a roller coaster before. And that is not one to lose your ride virginity on, but she didn't want to spoil things for another member of our party. So she went for it. That's brave.'

He lifted his chin. 'I always thought being brave was recognising your limitations. Acknowledging you don't have to do something to try and prove you're brave. Saying I'm scared of roller coasters and living by it. Being honest to live by your beliefs and not try.'

'I hadn't thought about it like that.' She tipped her head up, looking back at the height. 'But sometimes the benefit is worth the risk.'

'Hmm, I'm not sure. Do you want to go on?' His deceptively casual tone didn't fool her.

'Not particularly, I'd rather have a hot dog.'

Relief loosened his shoulders which had been almost up to his chin. There was a story there. 'Hot dogs coming right up.'

'You've got mustard,' he nodded at her chin and then scooped it up with a quick dab of his finger, lifting it to her lips.

He'd insisted, for her 'food education', on taking her to Nathan's for the best dogs on the island and now they were sitting on the sand just off the boardwalk.

'Mmm, thanks.'

'My pleasure.' The warm smile he sent over the huge hot dog he was eating had definite undertones of no good thoughts. 'You look like you're really enjoying it.'

'It's delicious,' she said warily, immediately conscious of the incipient *double entendres*, 'and at home I'd probably never eat a hot dog.'

'Ah, that's because you've never had your mouth around ... an American dog before.'

'Don't start all that malarkey!' said Sophie, nudging him, immediately blushing as she remembered what they'd been up to in the shower that morning and inadvertently looking at his crotch. It appeared she'd left all her inhibitions at Heathrow when she boarded the plane.

'Malarkey?' said Todd, imitating her accent. 'Is that what it's called?'

'Shh,' said Sophie, blushing some more. The dratted man didn't miss a trick.

'Shower malarkey.' He nodded gravely, his intent gaze suddenly sharpening as she tried to take another bite of her hot dog.

'Stop it,' she ducked her head. 'I'll never be able to eat this if you don't stop watching me like that.'

'Yeah, but you look so cute when you blush.'

'Behave.' She gave him a repressive glare and was about to take another bite when he said, in a deliberate husky, suggestive tone, 'I love your mouth.'

She wriggled in the sand, now starting to feel warm in all the right places. What was it about Todd that he could do this to her at any moment?

That naughty knowing look in his eye suggested he knew exactly what he was doing and then he waggled his eyebrows in a ridiculously over-the-top expression.

With an impish smile his way, she lifted the dog, playing along, blowing on the meat for a second, trying to look seductive and come hither, and then as she opened her mouth, she took a firm, snappy bite.

Todd's head shot up. 'Ouch!'

And she burst into giggles.

The silliness continued until she'd finished the hot dog and he scooped up the wrappers and jogged off to the nearest bin. She watched him cross the beach, with a light heart and a big smile on her face.

When they'd finished eating, they sat on the beach, side by side, Todd's arm slung around her, watching the people around them, enjoying the touch of the brilliant sunshine. Sophie rested her chin on her knees, happy to watch the children on the shoreline dancing in and out of the sea, shrieking as the waves sped up the beach, splashing them with the cold Atlantic waters. She tipped her face up to the sun, glad she'd put sunscreen on.

'Mind if I have a snooze?' asked Todd, leaning back. 'I'm exhausted.'

'Exhausted?' asked Sophie.

'Yeah, you've worn me out, English. You're a demanding woman. I'm not sure I can keep up.'

'Todd,' she said.

'Yeah?'

'Go to sleep,' she said over her shoulder.

'Yes, ma'am.'

He stretched out beside her, one arm tucked around her bottom as if he wanted to anchor himself to her. She checked her mobile phone, enjoying the feeling of having him close, knowing he wanted to *keep* her close. Kate had texted back.

Blimey, girl. You didn't say he was that bloody gorgeous. A smile touched Sophie's mouth and she glanced back at Todd. In six months' time this would be just a lovely memory.

For the first time in months, Sophie opened up the Facebook app on her phone. She'd not posted anything since she'd left London.

Posting a picture of the Thunderbolt on her page, she wrote: *Enjoying life in New York. A day out on Coney Island. Blackpool it isn't.*

Like opening a bottle and letting the genie out, she began scrolling through her Facebook feed. A sudden wave of home-sickness rolled over her, taking her breath away as she began thinking about friends and family back home. She'd cut herself off so sharply, she hadn't thought about what they were all up to. There were lots of messages from people including Angela and Ella in the office. And there, a whole stream from James sent through Messenger.

At the flat. Can't get in. When will you be home? Jx

Where are you? Jx

Sophie, we need to talk. I love you. It sounds a terrible cliché, but I can explain everything. Jx

Darling, I'm worried about you. Please get in touch. Just let me know you are OK. Jx

Please don't cut me out of your life. There's been a terrible mistake. We need to talk. Jx

A slew of other messages in a similar vein followed and then there was a break of a couple of months. And then last week there'd been a new message.

Sophie. I love you. I want you back in my life. I'm an empty shell without you. I'm so lost without you.

With a curl of her lip, she stabbed at the screen, her heart aching at her stupidity. She'd invested so much in him. So much love. So much hope. Her future. Six months ago she'd never have dreamed she'd be here. If you'd asked her then, her hope would have been to be engaged. For James to have finally popped the question. She'd been so convinced that he was about to propose. How had she got it so wrong?

She looked down at Todd, realising that he was watching her through half-closed lids.

'You OK?' he asked, lazily tracing circles on her thigh. 'You look a bit sad.'

'Fine,' she said, keeping her voice bright, trying not to let the memories dampen the day.

'Ready for a cold beer? Or would you like to go on another ride? Would you like to go on the dodgems?'

And there, she realised, was the difference. The magic word 'you'. He might not take anything too seriously. He might be all about having fun, living for the moment and enjoying everything that life threw at him. But he *cared* about her. He did things for her. Even last night when he'd seduced her into bed, he constantly checked that she was happy, that she was comfortable.

Even with his harem he was solicitous. Making sure he took them to places they'd like. Looking out for other people. He might not realise it, but he was an absolute gentleman. Thoughtful and considerate. But not a man who was for keeps.

'Dodgems,' she said, jumping up. 'I love the dodgems.'

Chapter 25

'How do you fancy a trip on the Staten Island ferry?' asked Todd, draining his coffee cup and already starting to rise to his feet. 'If we go now, we can beat the tourist crowds.'

'Ooh, yes. I've always wanted to do that since I saw *Working Girl*.' She looked at her watch. It was still early. 'I have promised Bella I'd help her later. I've neglected her a bit this week.'

They were finishing breakfast on the deck, having had a lazy start to a glorious Saturday morning. The sun was climbing into a pure-blue sky and the grey clouds of the week had finally been washed away.

In the last few weeks since their trip to Coney Island, they'd spent each weekend exploring Brooklyn but this weekend they'd decided, if the weather was nice, to head to Manhattan. They'd been to the Barclay Center to see a basketball game, where Sophie had spent more time watching the antics of the crowd than the game, which was totally unintelligible. They'd been to a rooftop cinema, they'd eaten pizza, Lebanese and Brazilian food and they'd been on the boating lake at Prospect Park, making the most of the warm balmy days.

This last week the weather had turned, with low grey clouds

skimming the tops of downtown's skyscrapers, the view from the windows blurred with drizzle. Not that either of them had noticed. It meant that their lunch breaks were spent in a cosy Italian deli that Todd had introduced her to. Of course, it was a great opportunity for her to pick Mario's brains: Mario the fifth-generation Italian owner, who much to Todd's amusement had taken a shine to Sophie and would pull up a chair at their table to talk food and recipes with her. It was rapidly becoming another one of her favourite places. She was really starting to feel as settled in Manhattan as she was in Brooklyn.

Sophie was secretly amazed and surprised by the way they'd fallen into such an easy regular routine. Each night on the days when Todd was in the office, they'd travel home together, stopping to pick up groceries at the store by their subway station. By unspoken agreement they hadn't gone public about their relationship at work, although Sophie wondered whether Madison had said anything. If she had, no one made any comment. A couple of times they'd been to Todd's apartment, which was only two blocks away. Looking at the stark white walls and minimal flat-packed furniture, Sophie could see why he preferred spending time at her place.

Most nights she'd cook for him, while he sat at the break-fast bar watching her, stealing kisses and complaining about being an unwilling slave when she made him chop vegetables. Without fail he'd wash and tidy up afterwards, constantly suggesting she took her clothes off again. He only stopped when one night she'd nipped off after dinner to add a dozen extra layers of underwear under her clothes. She laughed so hard her sides hurt, when in exasperation he started taking clean teaspoons out of the kitchen drawer to wash when he failed to get her naked.

He'd spent every night at hers, not that she was complaining. Her favourite part of the day was waking up next to him.

Todd came behind and nuzzled her neck, his hands sliding down to her waist. 'Are you sure you want to go on the ferry this morning?' His lips slid to capture her mouth in a kiss. 'We could stay here,' he muttered.

With a sigh she looked up at him, her eyes dancing. 'And if you start that, we'll never get out.'

'I'm not complaining,' he replied, his hands moving up along her ribs. 'Are you?'

She sucked in a breath as his fingers skirted her breasts.

'I mean if you have any complaints, I'd be more than happy to have a replay ... maybe I need to practise ...' His hand closed over her breast, finger and thumb capturing her nipple.

With a fractured breath she leaned back into him, starting to feel heated. They'd only left the bedroom half an hour ago, but already she wanted him again. Sex was a constant adventure, hot and hard some days, soft and tender on others, but always a revelation. It was as if she couldn't get enough of him.

The shrill tones of Todd's phone interrupted, and he frowned as he looked down at the phone on the table. With reluctance he peeled his hands from her ribcage. 'It's Marty. Sorry, I'd better take this.'

'Hey, little dude. What's up? ... What?' Todd turned away and walked back into the apartment, his shoulders hunching as he went.

Sophie picked up her orange juice, leaning back in her chair and watching the children playing in the back yard two doors away. With a brief pang she thought of James's daughter. Was he still with his wife and Emma? And if his wife hadn't confronted her, how long would James have kept up his double life? Sophie still had the occasional daydream of their future, of children. She screwed up her face. Children. Todd would have beautiful children. She knocked back her orange juice with a quick jerk of her hand. If he ever had any. Sadness washed over her. Not for herself but for him. He deserved to be loved, to be happy. This last week they'd spent every available moment together and he'd been lovely. He might not realise it but he was good in a relationship. Perhaps one day he might change his mind. Realise that love was worth taking the risk and that not all relationships were as toxic as his parents'. She wasn't stupid enough to think she was the one to do that.

'Marty's in trouble again. I'm going to have to take a rain check on the ferry trip. I have to go to the Upper East Side. Dad's making all sorts of threats. Marty's in a terrible state.'

She jumped, so lost in thought, she'd not heard his approach.

'What's he done?'

'You look bright eyed and bushy tailed.' Bella's teasing drawl greeted Sophie as she went into the bakery kitchen. 'You've got that thoroughly ravished look about you.'

She pulled on an apron and gave Bella a sunny smile.

'My cousin is keeping you … busy.' This time there was an

underlying touch of cynicism in her words. 'I'm surprised the novelty hasn't worn off yet.'

'We're having fun, Bella.' Sophie tried not to sound defensive, but she was getting a little fed up with Bella's regular warnings. 'I got the memo. Todd doesn't do commitment. He won't fall in love with me. I get all that. I'm not going to fall in love with him.'

'Sorry, hon.' Bella came over and put her arms around her, with a quick squeeze. 'That was mean. I'm not trying to be a bitch. I worry about you. This might be the most attentive I've seen him ... but I know what he's like. I love him to bits, but he's not a stayer. Hell knows, he could do with someone like you on his side but he's ... well, you've seen his folks in action. As far as he's concerned, love is a blackmail tool.'

'Hardly surprising. Have they always been like that?' She and Todd rarely talked about his family.

'Always. It's like treading on eggshells around them. One minute they're ready to kill each other and heading to the lawyers for a divorce and then they're all over each other again. They've calmed down in recent years.' Bella sighed. 'I remember one time. It was Christmas, darn it. Ross made one of his disparaging comments, she lost it and pushed the whole damn tree over. Ornaments smashed everywhere. She flounced off and refused to come back downstairs. Can you imagine Christmas dinner that day?'

Sophie winced, picturing a young Todd.

'So where is lover boy today?' asked Bella. 'I have to say, he seems remarkably attentive. Has he been home this week? I might have to double your rent, it's like he's moved in.'

'He's gone to see his folks. Marty is in trouble again. Apparently he hacked into a few Facebook accounts of guests at the party. Added horns and a tail to the pictures of Ross's business partner's wife, which has not gone down well.'

Bella started to snigger and started to sing, '*Beware the devil woman ...*'

Sophie shook her head. 'She wasn't the only one. Quite a few of the guests that weekend were visited by the Photoshop fairy.'

'You're kidding ... oh, Marty.' Bella put a hand over her mouth to hide her smile. 'He's a ...'

'He's in a lot of trouble ... again. Todd's gone to run interference.'

'That's hilarious,' said Bella. 'Wish I'd seen them. Some of those folks are pompous idiots.'

'Unfortunately, Celine and Ross don't feel the same way. They're furious. Marty called Todd this morning, crying hysterically down the phone.'

'Poor kid. And smart. He chose their Achilles heel to make his point. They're obsessed with putting on the right image. It's pretty harmless in the scheme of things.'

'Yes,' Sophie sighed. 'But Todd worries about him getting into bigger trouble.'

'They should pay the poor little sod a bit more attention.'

'That's what Todd says.'

'Hmm, he's not wrong. But I'm grateful he's hot footing it to the rescue. It means I can use and abuse your help.'

Icing and decorating the wedding cake for the interior designer was Bella's priority for the day and for the rest of the morning the pair of them were absorbed in transferring the patterns of the three wallpapers the bride had selected for each of the different tiers of the cake. Sophie had been tasked with tracing the pattern onto the rolled-out sheet of icing. The painstaking work took all her concentration, as she used a pin to prick through the wallpaper design laid on top of the icing.

When they broke for coffee, they took their drinks into the café. Bella's Saturday staff were busy but they bagged a table at the back.

'And what's the latest with Wes?' asked Sophie. Bella had enough comments to make about her and Todd, so she had no compunction when it came to probing for the latest. 'Has his mother been in again?'

'No, which is a shame because she's an absolute doll.'

'Really? Formidable was my impression.'

'Yeah but in a good way. She thought I'd been leading her baby on.'

Sophie spluttered on her coffee at the thought of the strapping Wes being described as a baby.

'She dotes on him ... except when he's being an idiot.'

'And what did he say about her coming to see you?'

Bella's eyes sparkled with sudden glee. 'I haven't seen him for the last week or so. Deliberately. I had the girls on the counter on early-warning system. Every time he's been in, I've sneaked out the back. Dessie suggested that I've been making it too easy for him. Absence makes the heart grow fonder and all that.'

'Interesting strategy,' said Sophie, immediately thinking about James. Absence had given her a much clearer head.

'Always brings them to their knees,' said Bella with strident confidence. 'Or at least that's what Dessie says. And she should know. She's a marriage counsellor, at least that's what she told me. I could have sworn Wes said a while back his mother was a teacher. Maybe I got that wrong.'

Bella's iPhone suddenly beeped.

'Oh ... sh—'

'Looks like you can ask him yourself,' said Sophie, amused by the panic-stricken expression on her friend's face.

'No. Oh. I don't want ...' Bella's confidence had vanished and she'd paled. 'What do I say to him? He's going to be furious I talked to his mother.'

'Bellllaaa.'

She sank into her seat. Sophie rose. 'I'll leave you to it.'

Back in the kitchen, Sophie carried on working on the cake and wondering how Todd was getting on. He'd promised to text her later but her phone remained resolutely silent. When she reached a point where she could do no more without Bella, she realised that an hour had elapsed. When she went back into the café, there was no sign of her.

'She went out with Wes,' explained one of the girls serving coffee. 'Said she'd be back later.'

In the end, Sophie heard from Bella long before Todd, a brief text apologising for running out on her. At an unexpected loose end, Sophie had taken her laundry for a service wash, scooping up Todd's clothes that had amassed during the week, which he'd tossed into her basket. There hadn't been any awkwardness about those domestic details. Since the first week he'd stayed over when he'd brought his toothbrush and shaving kit over, they'd taken up residence in the bathroom with seamless ease, even though every night he asked if it was OK if he stayed over.

As she wandered through the bustling neighbourhood, she marvelled at how at home she felt now compared to when she'd first arrived. A couple of faces were even familiar.

She decided to head for Union Street to an interesting supermarket she'd passed a couple of times on her morning run with Todd, enjoying the Saturday-afternoon buzz of people going about their business. After loading up her groceries, wishing that Todd was with her to help carry them home, she headed back towards the apartment. Tonight, she'd cook him one of the pasta recipes that Mario had given her. It was still too hot to be cooking Yorkshire puddings, despite his daily request every time she asked him what he fancied eating.

When she arrived home, unloading the shopping, she checked her phone again. Still no word from Todd. She sent him a quick text.

For the rest of the afternoon she sat out on the deck with a book, her phone beside her. When she heard the knock at the door, it was a relief and she raced to the door, but it wasn't Todd.

'Hi, can I come in?' asked Bella.

'Sure, how's Wes? You ran out on me.' Bella followed her into the apartment.

'He wanted to talk.'

'Absence made the heart grow fonder?' Sophie opened the fridge.

'After being thoroughly pissed, yes,' said Bella with a triumphant smirk.

'And? Do you want a cold drink?'

'Progress. We're going on a proper date on Friday. I'd love a glass of water.'

Bella stayed a while, thanking her for helping with the cake. 'If you can spare any time tomorrow, that would be cool. I need to deliver it next week but if I know it's finished this week, it'll take off the pressure.'

'And Cinders can go out on Friday,' teased Sophie.

'Well, there is that.' Bella winked. 'Although, I'm starting to get nervous already. What the heck am I going to wear?'

'Clothes?'

'Very funny. You heard from Todd? How's Marty?'

'No word yet.'

There was no word for the rest of the day. Eventually, having watched wall-to-wall rubbish on the television all evening, constantly checking her phone, Sophie went to bed.

Chapter 26

'Great job, Sophie.' Trudy nodded down the table as they wrapped up the meeting for the January edition. How had that happened? Suddenly her time here was racing by. It was September this week.

As soon as she left the meeting room, she spotted Todd at his desk, lounging back in his chair, his feet on the desktop, talking into the phone. Her stomach clenched at the sight of him as a sudden punch of longing hit her. *Ridiculous*. How could she miss him after two nights? She hadn't heard a word from him since Saturday morning and almost hadn't expected to see him at work this morning. Things must have been bad at his parents', but she was dying to know if Marty was alright.

'That would be great, Amy. What time? Eight? Why don't we do six-thirty Amy, then we could do dinner afterwards.' Cradling the phone under his chin, he looked up and gave her a casual wave. 'Now Amy, don't go putting ideas in my head.' He laughed, not looking at Sophie.

With a flicker of anger she approached her desk, suddenly aware that her hands had tightened into fists. It wasn't jealousy, she told herself. Flirting was like breathing to him. She narrowed her eyes, no she wasn't jealous but she was mildly pissed off that he hadn't let her know what had happened with Marty and his parents. Perhaps he was too upset to talk about it. She studied his face. Yes, there were tiny lines around his eyes. He looked tired. Strained.

'Cheers Amy. See you later.' He put the phone down. 'Hey English, how are you?'

She raised an eyebrow, not taken in for a minute by the studied casualness. 'I'm fine, how are you?'

'I'm good.'

'Good. Great ... And Amy. Good to see you haven't forgotten her name.'

Todd's mouth straightened in a mutinous line. Did she sound like a jealous girlfriend? He hadn't made any promises but over the last few weeks, the calls had dried up. Determined to be pleasant, she asked, 'And Marty?'

He frowned and slid his shoes from the desk, pulling his laptop towards him.

'Todd?' Sophie wasn't about to let go.

'Just leave it, Sophie.'

'Leave it?' Now she was puzzled.

'I've got a lot of work to get done today. I need to get my head down.'

She took a step back, feeling as if he'd punched her. 'Right.'

Clearly the weekend had been far worse than he wanted to let on. Knowing how close he was to Marty, she turned on her laptop and engrossed herself in work as best she could.

At lunchtime she looked up. Todd had been working hard, typing away. He caught her eye.

'I'm going for some lunch. Fancy coming?'

With an offhand shrug he shook his head. 'Bit too much to do. You carry on.'

'No Todd, today?' asked Mario as she toyed with a solitary cup of espresso. She'd given up drinking tea since she'd been in New York. Too often it either had a slight taint of coffee or was made with hot water instead of boiling, while the coffee was always good. With coffee shops on every street, it seemed as though the city was powered on caffeine.

'He's busy,' she said, ignoring the dart of hurt at his sudden seeming indifference.

'You should take him back a slice of my lasagne or some of my wife's cannoli.'

Todd did love his food, maybe that would cheer him up. She put her cup down in the tiny saucer with a clatter, as a spurt of shame hit her. She of all people knew the effect his parents had on him, witnessed it first hand, and here she was, focusing on her hurt feelings when he needed some support. 'I'll take some cannoli.'

Mario bustled off, pleased with his suggestion, and she checked her phone to catch up with her Facebook and WhatsApp messages. She'd been posting much more regularly of late, putting up pictures of the places she'd visited and making contributions to FoodLovers, one of the groups she belonged to. Her recent post on the Lebanese restaurant along with a recipe she'd blagged from the owner, a lovely plump balding Egyptian who was delighted in her interest, had garnered a record number of likes and shares. As she was scrolling through the many comments, she sat upright. Damn, she'd forgotten James's company had an account following food bloggers and groups.

Good to see you on here Sophie. James x

Frantically she checked her post. OK, it was obvious she was in New York, but one restaurant was hardly a giveaway. Quickly, she tried to remember what else she'd posted recently as she scrolled through her updates. Pictures of the July Fourth cakes she'd iced in a Bella's Bakery branded box. Pictures of wedding cakes she'd researched when she was trying to help Bella design the cake. Most of it was fairly innocuous stuff and then she paused, her finger over the screen as she came across one conversation with another food writer, who asked where she was. In black and white, she'd said she was in New York on a job swap for six months. Would James have searched for any other mentions? And did it matter if he knew where she was? By the time she got back, hopefully he'd have forgotten about her. The desperate attempts to contact her on messenger had died away two months ago. He wouldn't come knocking when she came back, and if he did, she'd be ready to face him.

Todd was leaning against Madison's desk, juggling with a couple of branded stress balls as the young intern laughed up at him. Sophie walked past them and neither gave her a second look. *Too busy? He didn't look that busy to her.*

Hurt or not, that didn't give him the right to be rude to her. Ignoring the sudden sour taste in her mouth, she walked calmly over to her desk and dropped the brown paper bag on it as she stowed her handbag beside her chair. The smell of cannoli teased the air. With pursed lips, she dumped the bag in the bin that stood between her and Todd's desks. OK, she got that he was upset. Got that with bells on, but he didn't need to take it out on her.

Thank goodness she had a photo shoot to supervise in the test kitchen. She didn't think she could stomach watching him flirt with Madison for the rest of the afternoon. The photo shoot took up the rest of the day.

'Just a bit more melted chocolate,' said Sophie to the food stylist. Getting the right shine on the gravy was an exercise in frustration, involving careful alchemy and the addition of the right amount of chocolate to make the liquid look unctuous, smooth and glossy without taking on a darker hue.

'Are you sure? If you add too much, it won't look the right colour.'

'Well, it will have to be dark gravy,' snapped Sophie. They were running out of time before the chocolate/gravy mix started to thicken. It would lose the desired shiny appearance. 'Hurry up, otherwise we'll have to start again.' There was a shocked silence and Sophie's face burned with embarrassment. 'Oh my goodness, I'm sorry. I'm a bit stressed.' She looked into the surprised faces surrounding her. 'I do apologise.'

'Hey Soph, it's fine,' said the stylist. 'I've heard far worse. Jeez, you should hear Brandi. Every other word would have been an F-word.'

'But I ... gosh, I am sorry.' One of the other girls patted her on the arm.

'I think we deserve a glass of something after this. It's two for one on champagne at Flute. Why don't we go?'

Sophie nodded. Why the hell not? She'd spent too much time with Todd, she ought to branch out, spend some time with her co-workers.

For the rest of the afternoon, she was careful to keep herself in check even though inside she was cross that she'd let herself down. This was a timely reminder. She'd become too used to Todd being around. Perhaps a bit of space was needed. It was difficult to believe that she was two thirds of the way through her stay.

She had to remember that above everything, he'd been a good friend to her and that when whatever was between them had run its course, she was grown-up enough to focus on all the positives. If it weren't for him, she'd never have gone to the Hamptons, or the basketball. Never cycled in Prospect Park, gone running around the lake. Never had wild, uninhibited sex in the kitchen, the shower or on the deck at midnight.

Damn, she was definitely going out with the girls.

One glass of champagne turned into three or four and a round of tapas. Sophie had forgotten how good it was to go out with a bunch of girls. Since her Danish trip, she'd become good friends with Kate and they regularly met up with two other people she'd met in Copenhagen – Avril, a TV presenter, and Eva, who was Kate's business partner. She missed their prosecco-fuelled fests where Avril regaled them with tales of celebrities she'd interviewed on breakfast television. With a cosy warm glow, she boarded the subway and travelled most of the way home with one of the other girls, who was planning a trip to London and spent the whole journey picking Sophie's slightly addled brains about the best places to eat in the city and whether she should visit Scotland to try proper haggis.

It was nearly eight o'clock when she put her key in the front door. From outside she'd seen that Bella's lights were on. Maybe she'd see if Bella fancied a drink. After enjoying such good company that evening, she wasn't sure she fancied spending the rest of it alone.

Mounting the stairs, she heard a rustle and looked up in surprise. Todd rose to his feet, every inch of him looking weary and lost.

'Todd! What are you doing here? What's happened?' Wasn't he supposed to be with Amy?

'I'm sorry.' His voice vibrated with regret.

She stared. Crumpled shirt, ruffled hair and red-rimmed eyes. There was such a defeated droop to his wide-shouldered frame, Sophie wanted to wrap him in a big hug but she hung back, unsure. Spite didn't come by nature to her, nor kicking a man when he was down, but today's indifference had destroyed the easy comfort between them. It had hurt.

'How long have you been here?' She kept her voice expressionless and distant.

'What time is it now?'

'Ten to eight.'

'Since six.' The pleasant wooziness of the champagne and the cosy evening vanished instantaneously.

'Six!' She pushed past him to open the front door. The late

sunshine filtered through the windows, casting a golden shadowy glow over the room. 'You'd better come in.'

Dumping her handbag on the sofa, she tried to steel herself against his pull before turning to face him. The filtered sepia light had deepened the circles under his eyes and much as she wanted to hold him and rub away those strained lines around his mouth, she held back.

He stood alone, surrounded by dust motes dancing in the shaft of sunlight sliding in, looking lost and uncertain. Just looking at him almost caused her physical pain but everything melted when he stepped up to her and held out his arms. 'Hold me, Sophie. I need you.'

How could she turn him away? Those haunted eyes tugged at her. When she slid her hands around his waist, stepping into the circle of his arms, he immediately drew her forward, burying his head in her neck, holding on with a touch of desperation. She kissed his cheek and hugged him, holding him tight. Despite everything, it felt like coming home.

'They've ...' his voice broke and she felt him shudder in her arms with a quickly caught sob. 'Marty ... they've sent him away.'

'Oh, Todd.' Her heart melted at his distress. She held him for a while longer, feeling him trying to pull himself together. When he'd calmed in her arms, she led him to the sofa, pushing him down like a rag doll before sitting beside him and taking his hand. They sat together, his head bowed, until he straightened and kissed her cheek.

'Thanks, English,' he whispered.

She squeezed his hand. 'Can you tell me what happened?'

With a nod, he took a deep breath. 'When I went round Dad and Mom were having a full-blown row, threatening to divorce each other in front of Marty. Blaming each other for his behaviour.' Todd winced. 'Saying what a disappointment to the family he was.' He dropped his head in his hands. 'It was awful. Dad said he was going to send Marty to military academy, saying it would teach him some discipline. There'd be no computers. No contact. They'd make a man out of him. Teach him the right values. I spent all day there and things finally calmed down. Poor kid was absolutely exhausted. Flaked out in his room. I stayed until he'd gone to sleep.' Todd closed his eyes. 'Then I confronted Dad. Lost it. Told him and Mom that their crappy marriage was responsible. As you can imagine, that didn't go down well. Shit, it was fucking awful. I spent the night and all day Sunday. But when I left, I thought I'd persuaded Dad that military academy wasn't the answer, that perhaps a shrink might help. Some counselling. They seemed to buy that.' His mouth twisted bitterly. 'Of course, they did. Having a shrink is part of the New York lifestyle. But I thought at least someone like that would identify the real problem and my folks might listen to a professional. The last thing Mom said was that she'd get some recommendations in the morning for a psychologist for Marty.'

He turned to her. 'I'm sorry. I'm so angry with my Dad. Worried about Marty. He's going to hate it. I let him down. I should have said something earlier to my parents. Made them realise.'

'I don't think you could have stopped this.'

'No, maybe not ... but I should have texted you, phoned, but I felt so wrung out, I couldn't think straight.'

She rubbed her thumb along his knuckles and he gave her a grateful semblance of a smile.

'It's OK.'

'And today at work ...' he kissed her on the forehead, 'I was a shit. It ... running scared, I guess.' His eyes met her hers and she saw the fleeting panic in them. A hint of terror that hit her hard, fracturing the little shell she'd tried to erect around her heart.

It cracked wide open and with it came clanging alarm bells ringing out, vibrating through every last pore, and the weighty thump of realisation.

She loved him. Stupidly, she'd fallen in love with him.

She saw his throat working as he swallowed. She laid a finger on his lips, not wanting him to say any more.

'And then ... I phoned Mom. After w-work. She told me. Dad took Marty this morning. She w-wouldn't ... wouldn't tell me where. Just that they'd decided. He'd gone. I let him down. I didn't know ... what to do. Where ...' He raised his head, his eyes stricken with fear and confusion.

The instinct to comfort him overwhelmed her, crowding every other thought out as she took him into her arms, moulding her lips over his, pouring her love into the kiss. He clung to her, his hands clutching her back, pulling her into him as if trying to absorb her into his body. Between them need began to build, a desperate pull of gentle desire seated in comfort and longing.

Still kissing him, she pulled him to his feet. With unusual docility he let her take charge as she took him into her bedroom. When she pushed him to sit on the bed, he sat stiffly as she knelt to take off his shoes. As she went to peel off his socks, he slipped a jerky hand down to stroke her cheek, the barely-there touch so gentle, as if he might break if he moved too much. She parted his thighs and moved between them, rising to unbutton his shirt. He made no move to help, his eyes holding hers the whole time. When she slipped the linen fabric away from his shoulders she heard him sigh her name as her fingers grazed his warm skin. In front of him she undressed quickly before pushing him back to lie on the bed, unzipping his shorts. He lifted his hips as she removed them and then she climbed on the bed to lie next to him. His arms closed around her, pulling her until they were skin to skin, not an inch between them, his grip so tight as if he was scared she might leave. His lips grazed her forehead, skimming the hairline, his breaths light and shallow.

'Sophie,' he whispered.

'It's OK.' She traced a kiss up his neck, with a fleeting brush over his lips. 'It's OK.'

With a heavy sigh, he breathed out, the tension leaving his body, his hold on her not quite so desperate. Almost involuntarily she stroked his back as they lay together, her head tucked between his neck and shoulder, nothing but the sound of their breathing punctuating the close air of the bedroom.

At some point he shifted, kissing her neck and moving down to scatter tiny kisses along her collar bone, whispering her name. The sight of his dark head bent over her body brought a wave of unbearable tenderness and a warm ache between her thighs. Shifting slightly, she pulled him on top of her, lifting her hips in silent invitation, opening her legs.

He raised his head and looked down at her. The brief wordless exchange as he stared into her eyes made her heart hitch, the intense sensation of love blossoming and blooming in her chest almost too much to bear. With a muffled groan he dipped his head and kissed her hard on the lips, his tongue plunging into her mouth. He moved between them and slid slowly inside her.

Unlike their previous times, the air was charged with emotion, as if the gravity of the moment had infused the room. Each thrust and slide was slow and languid. The sensation of skin and heat built, slow and sure and with each push and pull her heart flooded with emotion. Holding her gaze, his eyes darkened. A heartfelt moan escaped as the feelings began to build, an overwhelming wave bearing down on her. She sucked in an almost panicked breath, a quick dart of fear that this was too much. Too much to take, to bear and then it hit. A punch of pleasure sending shockwaves bursting through her body, subsiding into ripple after ripple of feeling so intense it was almost painful. With a shudder and a guttural groan, Todd slid home one last time, his arms trembling before he collapsed on top of her, the weight of his body a welcome testament to the knowledge that filled her.

'I love you,' the words escaped on a whisper of sheer explosive joy. She could no more have kept them in than stopped breathing.

Todd's hold on her tightened and he rolled over, taking her with him. His ragged breath grazed her cheek, but he didn't say a word. It didn't matter. Sophie had no regrets. She loved him, heart and soul and in that moment. Placing a gentle kiss on his neck, she settled in his arms, bathed in a sense of utter contentment. Strangely confident, she smiled to herself, proud that she could say the words. She'd spoken the truth. If Todd couldn't deal with it, that was his problem.

As if exhausted by the weight of emotion, they both slept.

The smell of coffee woke her along with the dip of the mattress. When she opened her eyes, Todd smiled down at her, a cup in his hand, perched on the edge of the bed, twisting towards her.

'Morning.' The husky timbre in his voice held a touch of shyness.

'Hey, you,' she said, her words soft with sleep. This morning he looked so much better, his eyes less troubled and the dark shadows under them less pronounced. The familiar pull of desire tugged as she took in the sight of his bare chest, one of her towels wrapped around his lean hips. Feeling feminine and that prick of satisfied pride, that this gorgeous man was all hers, whether he knew it or not, she pulled herself up to sit against her pillow, covering her nudity with the sheet, taking the coffee from him.

'Thank you.'

'No, thank you.' He leaned forward and brushed her hair from her face. 'I'm sorry—'

'Shush. What time is it?'

'Seven.'

Sophie took a sip of coffee. 'I need to get ready for work. Are you coming into the office today?'

'Yeah, not sure I'll get much done. Yesterday was a write-off, but I need to do something.'

'I don't know, it looked as if you honed your juggling skills nicely.' Sophie's attempt at a teasing smile didn't quite hit the mark.

He winced. 'Sorry, I was—'

It was on the tip of her tongue to say, *Don't worry, I forgive you,* but that wasn't right and he needed to know. If she was brave enough to tell him she loved him, she was brave enough to tell him how he'd made her feel. 'Yes, you were. I know you were upset, but it hurt. No matter what happens, we're friends. You don't treat friends like that.' She tilted her chin up with an uncompromising stare.

Lifting her hand, he brought it to his mouth and kissed the knuckle on her thumb. 'You're right. And you didn't deserve it. You're ... too ...' Sadness tinged his smile as he looked at her.

'It's OK.' The words sounded so inadequate. 'I wish there was something I could do to help.'

'You already did.' Her pulse leapt at the expression in his eyes. 'You were there when I needed you, last night. Thank you.' He linked his fingers through hers where her hand lay on her lap and squeezed them. 'But, it doesn't mean ... I needed a friend ...'

Sophie held her breath, she knew what was coming. Watching his profile as he studied the opposite wall as if there was something completely fascinating about the point where it met the ceiling, she knew he was struggling with what she said to him last night. Could almost see him fighting with it.

'You said ...' his jaw clenched. 'You ...'

Reaching out, she touched his arm. 'I said I loved you.' Her voice was remarkably clear and steady, even though her heart pounded.

'That. Yes.'

For some reason she kept perfectly still, almost as if he were a deer she might frighten away.

He turned to her, bleakness etched in the lines around his eyes. 'You shouldn't. I don't deserve it.'

'Todd,' her voice gentled, the sense of pity for his confusion stronger than anything else. 'It's my choice.' Except there hadn't been any choice. Not for her anyway.

She saw him swallow again. 'I watch my parents, over and over declaring how much they love each other. The next minute they're tearing each other to shreds, picking at each other's vulnerabilities. It's like a battleground, where what they share when they're in love seems to give them the most ammunition and insight to hit the weakest, most hurtful spot. They can't even behave in front of other people. It's so damn public. I hate it. I couldn't bear to live like that. And I went and did it to you yesterday. I hurt you.'

'Not intentionally. You were hurting. There's a difference. Lots of people have happy relationships, but love does open you up to being hurt. But it's worth the risk because of all the wonderful bits that come with loving someone and being loved.'

'It's not a risk I want to take. I've spent most of my life observing the war zone that's my parents' marriage. It's like asking a war correspondent to ditch his pen and take up arms.'

'Interesting analogy.' She could think of far better ones.

'Sophie, you'll be going home soon and yeah, I'm going to miss you. I know that much. Who else is going to keep me in check? But, don't be in love with me. Please. I'm not worth it.'

She held her breath, wanting to tell him he was wrong, but the stubborn set of his jaw and the sadness haunting his half-smile made her pause. Twenty-odd years of conditioning weren't going to be overcome that easily. All she could do was share her love with him, but she wasn't going to deny its existence.

'Todd,' her voice was firm, 'I knew all that when we started this. Loving you is my choice. Well,' she let the smile slip through, deliberately teasing, 'I can't help it.' She stroked his bicep. 'You're fairly irresistible.'

One side of his mouth quirked.

'And quite sexy. Not bad looking either.' She lowered her voice to a whisper, 'And quite hot in the sack.'

With a sudden change in his mood, he removed the coffee cup from her hand and lunged at her, pinning her to the bed. 'What's with the *quite* hot?'

'Reasonably hot?'

He stroked a hand down her body, skimming her nipples, down across her stomach, brushing her skin and down between her thighs and back up again, making her moan with sudden desire.

'Smokin' hot?' he rasped in her ear before sliding his mouth over hers with possessive thoroughness, his tongue delving in, sending spikes of excitement dancing through her nerve endings.

'Smoking,' she gasped and then wriggled away. 'And some of us have to get to work.' She threw back the corner of the covers. 'I need to get in the shower and get ready.'

'Need a back scrub?' And just like that, they were back to normal. She wasn't going to stop loving him. Todd was just going to have to live with it.

Chapter 27

The phone on Todd's desk rang and Sophie reached over to pick it up realising, as she did, that none of the harem had phoned in the last two weeks. No word from Amy or Charlene.

'Hello.'

There was silence before a young, panicky voice asked, 'Can I speak to Todd McLennan? I think ... he works there.'

'Marty?'

'Yes,' the voice squeaked.

'It's Sophie. He's not here at the moment, but I know he'll want to speak to you.'

'When is he back? I've only got a minute but I really need to speak to him.'

'He's at a press launch, he's not going to be back until after lunch. Have you got his mobile number?'

'No, I ... I've ... erm ... borrowed someone's cell phone.' The diffidence suggested that the term *borrowed* might be relative.

'Have you got a pen? I'll give it to you.'

'Er, hang on.' There were sounds of drawers being opened and shut. 'Got one.'

Sophie reeled off the number from her own phone. 'Are you OK? Can he call you back on this number?'

'Not exactly. I'm in one of the offices. It took me ages to find Todd's work number. I'll probably get court martialled if I get caught in here,' Marty muttered, clearly not wanting to be overheard.

'Where are you? Are you OK?'

'I am OK,' Marty sounded surprised. 'It's not too bad. I was homesick the first week, but some of the other guys are cool. We get to do PT every day. It's kind of strict but I don't mind that. You know where you are with everything. Yeah, I don't mind it as much as I thought I would. But I don't have my laptop or phone. Dad took them, told me they weren't allowed, but they are. I wanted Todd ... to get them for me.'

Sophie almost laughed at his teenage self-absorption. Poor Todd had been worried sick about his brother over the last two weeks and Marty's greatest concern was not being online. Although it was probably a good thing. Todd would be relieved to hear that Marty was OK and not desperately unhappy.

'If you don't speak to him, I'll tell him you called. Give me your address?'

She wrote it down quickly before he hung up. Hopefully he'd have time to call Todd before he got caught. What a relief, she couldn't wait to speak to Todd, but she'd leave it a few minutes before she called him, to let Marty get through.

As it happened, she was called into a meeting with Trudy before she could speak to Todd and when she tried to phone him, his cell went straight to voicemail. She left a message, hoping that he'd pick it up soon, as she wouldn't be seeing him until later. They were double dating – Todd's terminology – meeting up with Wes and Bella, who were on date number four and taking things slowly.

'Sophie, I wanted to catch up with you.' Trudy sat behind her desk. 'How are you enjoying your time with us?'

'It's great,' said Sophie with enthusiasm. 'I'm loving working on my new feature.' She'd been so inspired by Mario and the stories he'd shared about his family setting up the restaurant and their original Tuscan roots that she'd suggested a regular feature for the magazine, each month focusing on a different ethnic culture, exploring the dishes and the restaurants in the city. 'I knew New York was diverse, but there's so much material. I've found this amazing Ethiopian place in Harlem that I'm thinking about featuring for the March issue. And then there's a really interesting Portuguese place, with *nata* to die for.'

'Fantastic. The feature you've done on the Italian family for the February issue looks wonderful. You've got a real flair for bringing food to life. One of the best food writers we've had working here. I'm going to come right out with it. Would you consider staying?'

Sophie's mouth literally dropped open.

'We can extend your working visa. I'd really like to keep you. Reader feedback on your English afternoon tea feature has been through the roof. The chief editorial director loved it and so did the advertising director. You're a seriously talented writer. It's a godsend having someone who knows food the way you do. *Please* say you'll consider it.'

'I … I don't know what to say. It never occurred to me that I might stay.'

'Say you'll think about it,' urged Trudy, echoing Angela's words all those months ago.

She thought about it all the way back to Brooklyn on the subway. Thought about it until her head spun. Todd. Bella. London. Her friends back home. Todd. What would he say? Since that night when she'd told him she loved him, there'd been tiny, almost infinitesimal changes. Somehow, he seemed softer. More tender. His touches more frequent and more intimate. The way he touched her face when he kissed her. The way he took her to bed with careful consideration. Some days she wondered if maybe he did love her just a little. They never talked about the future or referred to anything beyond the end of October which was when she was due to leave. Could she stay? How would he react to her staying?

When she arrived at the bar, he was already there, and as soon as he saw her he hailed a waiter to order a white wine. 'Hey English,' he brushed her mouth with a teasing kiss, while sliding his hand under her hair to stroke the back of her neck. 'How was your day?'

'Interesting,' she replied. 'Did you get my message?'

'No, I forgot to charge my cell this morning. I got distracted, if you will recall.' His direct stare made her blush.

'That wasn't my fault. I was cleaning my teeth.' Her legs turned to jelly at the memory of his naked body sliding up against hers early that morning. His hands cupping her breasts and his hungry expression staring back at her in the mirror.

'There's cleaning your teeth and cleaning your teeth, English,' he growled.

'How do I clean my teeth?' she asked, amused.

'Sexily,' said Todd.

She rolled her eyes and then remembered. 'Marty called.'

'Marty!' He immediately tensed, his fingers gripping his beer bottle so hard the tendons stood out white against his tanned skin.

She laid a hand over his wrist. 'He's OK.'

Quickly, she relayed the conversation, watching the tension leach out of his fingers.

'Thank goodness for that. I guess the discipline might do him good.' Draining his beer, he let out a half-laugh. 'Typical that what drives him to get in touch is wanting his computer. Maybe we could catch a flight down to Charleston this weekend. Go see the boy.' Eagerly, he pulled out his phone and then his face fell, as he remembered it was dead. 'I can sort out a laptop and a phone for him. Let's hope the Pentagon firewalls are Marty-proof.' With a thoughtful sigh, he shook his head. 'Maybe I should warn them.'

'I think you should go on your own,' said Sophie with a gentle smile. 'You probably want some time together. He needs to know that you're there for him.'

'Yes, but he likes you.'

'He needs stability in his life,' Sophie reminded him.

For a moment Todd looked blankly at her. 'You're pretty stable.'

'Exactly.' She wanted to shake him for being so damn obtuse.

'So why can't you come? Marty would love to see you. We

could get a nice hotel, fix up a whole weekend. Take him out for a burger, we'd have a nice meal.'

'Todd, if I come with you, what sort of signal is that going to send to Marty? What happens when next time you see him and he asks where I am?'

Todd picked at the label on his beer bottle, reminding her of Marty, mutinous and wary.

The awkward silence stretched out between them and as Sophie reached out to take his hand, he jumped up waving. 'Hey Bella, Wes.'

Sophie turned to see the other couple weaving their way through the busy tables, Bella in front, her hand clasped in Wes's.

This was the second time they'd been out as a foursome. Sophie had got to know Wes a little more and his quiet dry humour was a good foil for Bella's boisterous directness. Although completely different, they suited. Bella seemed a lot less frenetic in his company.

'I delivered the wedding cake to the interior-design bride today,' she said proudly.

'*You* delivered?' Wes's deep tone grumbled. 'I coulda sworn I put a big white cake box in the front seat of my van, with you flapping around like mama hen, convinced I was going to back end someone. She made me put the belt round it with two pillows.'

'I meant delivered as in completed,' said Bella, 'and there was no way I'd have trusted the darned thing with anyone else, so consider yourself honoured.'

'Yes, ma'am,' said Wes, saluting her.

'And does she love it?' asked Sophie, eager to hear, as Bella had given her free rein over the final design. It had taken them a whole day to put the finishing touches to the three-tiered cake, but once it was assembled, both Sophie and Bella had hugged each other with excitement. Each layer featured a different co-ordinating wallpaper in shades of purple, lilac, silver and white, the patterns picked out with three different icing techniques. It was quite simply a triumph.

'When I called her on her cell, she cried. She loves it. I really regret not being there to see her face when she saw it.'

Todd attempted to exchange a wry look with Wes.

'Hey man, don't include me.' Wes held up his hands in surrender. 'I saw the bride's face, when she opened the box. Damn near brought a tear to my eye.'

'It's a cake,' said Todd, genuine bewilderment on his face.

'It's a symbol,' Bella sighed. 'You don't have a romantic bone in your body, do you?' She curled her lip at her cousin.

'I can be romantic,' said Todd, folding his arms. 'Just not stupid. It's all part of the illusion. The cake. The dress. But when it comes to the vows, they mean Jack shit a few months down the line. The whole wedding probably makes things worse. Spending all that money, focusing on the crappy details, how much you're going to impress the audience, because that's what it is, one big show. And that's been my parents' marriage from the start, except theirs has been the biggest and the best. You can bet your bottom dollar that Mom's dress would have been the most expensive, the flowers the most extravagant and no doubt their cake would have been thirty darn tiers high. Tell me how that's a symbol of anything, but *look at us, look at us.*'

Bella raised sceptical eyebrows and put her hands on her hips. 'I declare, you have no soul, Todd McLennan. Not one shred of humanity. The cake is the centrepiece of the wedding. The design can symbolise so much. Sophie is amazing at picking up what the bride really wants. She has romance in her soul.'

Under the table Sophie kicked Bella, sure that he didn't want to know about it.

'Cutting the cake is the first joint act a couple do together once they're married. It's a symbol of their unity. Of doing things as a team. Their future together. And that future includes their family as they share the cake among their guests. Feeding their loved ones. Embracing the wider family. There's so much loveliness about it. It's not just cake,' snapped Bella.

'What she said,' added Wes.

Todd looked to Sophie as if for support. 'It's part of the trappings of the day.'

'I'm with them. Sorry, I think a wedding cake is a lovely tradition.'

'At least they taste good,' conceded Todd rather grumpily, looking at Sophie from under his lashes.

'Outnumbered, Mr Grinch,' she said, kissing him cheerfully on the cheek. 'And what's this about being romantic? I missed that.' Her eyes twinkled at him. He might not do romance, but he certainly knew how to make her body sing.

'I don't do hearts and flowers or the diamonds and pearls. That's easy stuff. Anybody can do that. Had a row? How bad was it? Worth one or two carats? Broken a date because you've been offered a day's golf at Pebble Beach, that's OK, an outsize bouquet of twelve dozen roses will fix that.'

'Anybody' being his dad, Sophie guessed, thinking of Celine's tennis bracelet and diamond earrings.

'You can be romantic without spending money,' said Bella, with a dreamy wistful smile that really wasn't her at all. 'Someone leaving lavender under your pillow because you couldn't sleep, well ... that's romantic.'

Wes ducked his head. Todd shot him an irritated look as if he'd let the side down somehow.

'Suddenly you're an expert, are you Bella?' Todd's voice held a low angry hum. 'You've wilted about for the last year, waiting for Wes to take notice. Moaning and not doing anything about it. Now, suddenly you know it all.'

'Todd!' Sophie nudged him, startled by his vehemence. He had the grace to send her an apologetic look although it didn't extend to his cousin.

Wes picked up two menus from the centre of the table and handed one over to Todd. 'Man, I think we could use a little food. You two are mighty testy.' He winked at Sophie. 'Not kissing cousins then.'

'Lord, no,' scowled Bella and then her face brightened. 'Although Todd was always very keen to make my Barbies kiss. What was it you used to say, "smoochy, smoochy" and rub their faces together.'

'I was seven.' Todd groaned and then he grinned. 'And when you were seven, you spent a whole summer running around in your panties and Wonder Woman sparkly red boots, refusing to get dressed.'

Bella giggled. 'I'd forgotten about that. I chased you with my special lasso.'

Sophie heaved an internal sigh of relief, sharing a small smile with Wes, as the two of them expounded on their youthful tormenting of each other.

Bella caught her in the restroom as Sophie was washing her hands.

'You OK?' she asked.

'Yes, why?' asked Sophie, sensing Bella had something on her mind.

'I ... you know ... Todd's attitude. I was worried about you. You're the traditional type. I know you are from what you've said about wanting to marry James. You get the whole wedding cake, romance, happy-ever-after schtick.

'Must be hard, that's all. I guess now I'm finally with Wes, I want everyone else to be madly in love. I want you to have that ... you know ... that you're-the-centre-of-someone's-universe feeling. You were so sad when you first arrived here. I wish I'd warned you off Todd more.'

'Bella, you warned me plenty of times.' Sophie sighed, she just hadn't paid any attention. Falling fathoms deep in love with Todd had never been her intention, but he had been nothing but honest with her. From day one he'd been clear he wasn't available for the long term. Better to know at the outset than to find out that someone wasn't available after all, when it was way too late.

Bella wasn't the type to compromise. She'd never understand, so Sophie added, 'Look, Todd isn't really my type. I'm enjoying myself while I'm here. My kind of man is serious, steady and reliable. Someone who's ready to settle down. Have children. Once I get back to the UK, that's the sort of man I'll be looking for.'

Her words sounded convincing but inside a voice was shouting, *No! That was old Sophie.* The Sophie who went out with men like James. She wasn't that Sophie any more. She wanted someone who made her laugh, someone spontaneous, someone with whom she could be uninhibited and passionate. *Someone like Todd.*

Chapter 28

When she saw the name come up on her phone, she snatched it up, taking the frying pan of browning chicken from the hob.

'Kate! How's it going? Let me just turn the ring off.'

'Ooh, what you cooking?'

'Thai curry,' she said with a crooked grin. It was Todd's favourite and a quick and easy mid-week dinner when they'd been distracted by other things.

'Yum. I ... I wasn't sure whether to tell you but I saw James this week. He came into the café.'

'James? What did he want?' Sophie's voice held a touch of healthy disdain.

Kate smiled happily across the miles at her. 'Nothing, apparently. Just wanted to know how you were.'

'I hope you told him I was absolutely brilliant.'

'Something like that.' Kate's eyes brimmed with mischief before her face sobered. 'You don't know how glad that makes me!'

'What?'

'You, you almost sound blasé. As if, who? James? I was worried about telling you.'

Which just went to show how far Sophie had come. Hearing his name was like a reference to another life.

'You don't need to be. I've definitely moved on.' Sophie's mouth curved in a wicked smile of satisfaction.

Kate burst out laughing. 'You look like the cat that's got the whole damn dairy, missy. Having fun, are we?'

Sophie blushed at the memory.

'I thought that was a very skimpy outfit for cooking.'

She cast a quick look down at the vest top and knickers she'd pulled on while Todd nipped out to the liquor store to get a bottle of wine.

'It was hot when we got back from work.'

'I bet it was,' teased Kate. 'You look good, Soph. Happy. Ravished.' She winked. 'He's good for you.'

'Yeah, and I think I'm good for him. Although he doesn't realise it.' Sophie grinned at the screen, grateful for the miles between them. If Kate were here she'd spot the bravado in her words. Time was running out and she had no idea what she was going to do.

'Kate, they've asked me if I'd like to extend my stay.'

'In New York?'

'Yeah.' Sophie bit her lip.

'Wow, that's fantastic. Oh my goodness, I am so coming out to see you.' Kate pulled up. 'You are going to stay, aren't you?'

'I don't know.' She pulled an agonised face, glancing over her shoulder to make sure Todd hadn't come back yet. 'Part of me would love to, but I'm not sure what Todd's reaction would be.'

'I'd have thought he'd be pleased.' Mama-hen indignation rang in her voice.

'I don't know. This was always supposed to be temporary. Remember, a fling. I'm worried if I tell him, he'll run for the hills.'

'Sophie, that's crazy. The two of you practically live together. I mean, how many months is it? Two and a half? You seem pretty inseparable. Everyone says dumb things like that when they get together, basic self-protection, in case the other person doesn't feel the same. But things have obviously changed now. And he'd be stupid to let you go. He doesn't strike me as a stupid man.'

Sophie swallowed, wishing she had Kate's confidence. 'He does seem ... well, he never says anything but he acts like he cares.' It was in all the little things he did.

'Well there you go, typical man. Actions speak louder than words.'

'And talk of the devil, I can hear him coming back.'

'And I ought to head for bed, its nearly one here. I'm waiting for Ben to get home.'

Todd bowled into the room, blowing extravagant kisses at her as if he'd been away for a day rather than ten minutes, before miming drinking a glass of wine.

'Say hi to Kate, she's just going.' Sophie turned the phone around.

'Hey Kate. What's the weather like?' Todd loved to tease them about their obsession with the weather.

'Raining cats and dogs.'

'You get some wild stuff over there in the UK.'

He put the wine down and Sophie watched as he chinked glasses in the cupboard, sorting through to find her favourite. Despite teasing her about being fussy with her penchant for a bone-china cup that wasn't too small or too big, and her preference for fine wineglasses, he always made a point of using them for her. The gesture of familiarity and intimacy made her smile. It was the little things he did that gave her hope.

'I'd better go Kate, I need to feed my man. Take care. Night.'

As Sophie put the phone down, Todd put his arms around her waist and nuzzled at her neck. 'What time's dinner?'

'Another twenty minutes.'

'Sure you don't—'

With a peal of laughter, she pushed at his hands. 'I'm hungry even if you're not.'

'I'm always hungry for your ...' pausing, he raised his eyebrow wickedly, 'Thai curry. I'm going to miss your cooking when I go to Charleston.'

She rolled her eyes. 'You'll only be away two nights.'

'Yeah but Marty will make me eat burgers the whole time. I'll come back malnourished.'

She shook her head, laughing at his mournful expression. 'I'm sure you'll survive. What time's your flight on Saturday?'

'Seven. I need to leave just before five to get to JFK.' His hands dropped, moving to cup her bottom, dropping his voice with husky suggestion, 'I guess we'll have to have an early night tomorrow.'

'You're in luck.' She looped her arms around his neck, toying with the hair that ran into the nape. 'It just so happens, I've got that tasting thing near Prospect Park tomorrow afternoon. As it's near here, I wasn't planning on going back to the office.'

'Excellent, we can have a really early night.'

With the tang of exotic fruits still fresh in her mouth, Sophie turned onto Smith Street, her head full of ideas on how she might incorporate the flavours of yuzu, dragon fruit, lucuma and guava into a dessert feature. One thing was for sure, she was never trying durian again. With a shudder, thinking of the vile smell, she headed for Bella's. As she was finishing work early, she'd promised Bella she'd call in to help decorate some cookies for a children's birthday party on the Saturday.

When she walked through the door, Bella rushed up to her. 'You're early.' She glanced back over her shoulder.

'I left when they brought out the durian, also known as vomit fruit because it makes you want to. Eek, that stuff is seriously—'

'Sophie,' Bella's eyes were wide and she was jerking her head towards the back of the café. 'There's someone here to see you.'

'Who?'

Bella's face lit up with an excited smile. 'Go see.'

As Sophie stepped past, Bella gave her a little push as if to hurry her along. 'Good luck.'

Rounding the corner, Sophie stopped dead. Sick dread anchoring her to the spot.

'Sophie! Oh my. Sophie! Look at you. You look incredible. I've missed you so much.'

White noise buzzed in her ears and her body felt as if it

belonged to someone else. There wasn't a scrap of moisture in her mouth and her tongue was suddenly made of lead.

Unable to speak, she found her hands taken and she was being pulled to one of the bucket chairs around a round table. In the middle of the table was a small turquoise blue box. Dead centre.

She looked from the box to James, still too stunned to speak.

'Say something Sophie,' he beamed at her. 'I've surprised you, haven't I? It's good to see you.' He threw his arms around her and kissed her full on the mouth, completely oblivious to her instant recoil.

'James.' Her voice sounded dry and stiff. 'What are you doing here?'

'What do you think I'm doing?' He shook his head, smiling with patient indulgence. 'Something I should have done a long time ago.'

He grabbed the box, flipped open the lid and went down on one knee. 'Sophie Bennings-Beauchamp, will you do me the honour of becoming my wife?'

Completely taken aback, Sophie stared down at him, quite unable to believe what she was seeing.

'James?' She blinked, trying to take in the familiar face that suddenly wasn't familiar at all. The grey, pleading eyes that now looked like small, flat pebbles. The too-pink mouth that made her want to shudder in revulsion.

'Say yes, Sophie. I know you love me. It sounds a terrible cliché, but I can explain everything.'

To say she'd never been so stunned in her life would have

been an understatement. It felt as an Exocet missile had blown up inside her, leaving her disorientated and shell-shocked.

He jumped up, still holding the ring in one hand, and guided her into one of the chairs, pulling his up next to her. He took her hand and she flinched, taking it back and holding it up against her collar bone.

'I've shocked you. Sorry, but I came as soon as I found out where you were.'

Gradually she felt herself settle.

'Sophie, I know you were upset, when you found out about Anna. But it wasn't what it looked like.'

She frowned, sarcasm taking hold as she pulled together her scattered wits. 'You weren't married? Emma wasn't your child?'

He huffed impatiently. 'Hear me out. Believe me, I've always loved you. From the moment I met you. That was the problem. I loved you so much that I couldn't bear to lose you. It made me weak when I should have been strong.'

What was he wittering about? Why was he even here? It was a definite mind-out-of-body experience. She was watching and listening to a scene that she had no part in. It was tempting to check over her shoulder because it felt as if he were talking to another person. A different version of her. One that had loved him before she knew what love really was.

'When we met, Anna and I were separating. It was instant. I fell in love with you. Me and Anna were already over. Just living in the same house while we sorted money out. I was going to leave her but somehow she got pregnant.'

'Somehow?' It wasn't funny, it really wasn't, but it made her laugh.

'You know what I mean.' James's earnest gaze slipped. 'It wasn't planned. I felt sorry for her one night, let my guard down.'

Sophie laughed again as a comical vision of James, defending his honour in a darkened room with a shield and sword, popped into her head. 'That's a new euphemism for sex.'

With great dignity, James ignored her, ploughing on quite manfully with his speech, oblivious to her total detachment. 'I kept putting it off. And then when Emma was born, it was hard. I was so torn. Anna would never have let me see my daughter. I loved you so much, I was worried if I told you about Emma you'd leave me.'

It was like listening to a complete stranger. None of it mattered. Everything she'd felt for him had been expunged. She liked that word; completely expunged. Utterly expunged. Loving Todd had lightened her heart and helped her move on. She didn't care about James at all. The lies still stung, but more because she'd believed them. And there were so many. Weaving in and out of each other in growing complexity and deviousness. Piled one on top of another until it was a mountain, too high to get over or penetrate.

'Your mother didn't live in Cornwall.' Had never lived in Cornwall. How many times had he complained about the journey, sounding so sincere? Just like he sounded now. How many dinners had he cancelled because of emergency trips to the hospital? Dozens of ambulance call-outs he'd glibly described.

James shook his head. 'Sophie, that's not important. I need to tell you, I left Anna. We're getting divorced. I'm free to marry you. I was so furious with her for confronting you like that. How dare she?'

Seriously? He'd taken insensitivity to a new level! 'Perhaps because she was your wife.' She blinked back her incredulity. *Was he for real?*

'In name only. It's you I love, Sophie. You've got to believe me.'

Something inside her snapped. 'I don't,' she said, her voice crisp and cold. She refused to waste one iota of emotion on this man.

'What?'

'I don't have to believe you.'

'Well ... it's ... it's a figure of speech.'

'I'll never believe anything you say again. I stupidly thought I loved you—'

'Don't say it, please don't say it. Just give me another chance. You don't have to say yes now. Think about it. We can spend some time together. You loved me. We were good together.'

'No.' The bald repudiation stopped him in his tracks. 'We weren't.'

There was a genuine look of shock on his face as he peered at her.

'Don't be silly, of course we were. Don't you remember?'

'We weren't,' she repeated, surprised by her own *sang-froid*. She couldn't even get angry with him, which she was quite pleased about. Anger would give credence to what he was saying. Being able to be calm and unemotional confirmed what she knew: it was over and there was no going back.

'Of course, we were. We never rowed. Never fell out. We loved doing the same things. Food, wine. We're completely compatible.'

For some reason, Sophie's head crowded with more recent images. Todd washing up. The whisper of cotton over her ears as she pulled her dress over her head when he challenged her. The kick to her pulse at the sight of Todd's hopeful and surprised gaze. The beach and the first time she kissed him. The feel of cold sand on her back. Him stealing her beef at Onyx. Running together in Prospect Park and coming back to the apartment, peeling off his sweaty kit.

'Have you ever had sex in the shower? Up against the cold tiles? Soaped someone's nipples until they almost came?'

'Sophie!' He glanced around, his eyes wide with horror. 'What the hell are you talking about?'

'No, I thought not.' Sophie shivered, delicious memories warming her.

'What is wrong with you? Sayings things like that.'

'I thought you said we were compatible.'

'We are, when you're being sensible.'

'I don't want to be sensible any more.' She levelled a look at him, suddenly feeling a tiny bit sorry for his confusion. How could he possibly comprehend? She'd moved on and he hadn't. Gently, because she knew he saw her as she'd been months ago, she said, 'I'm not that Sophie. We weren't right together, we just thought we were. I'm a different person now.'

James' mouth opened and then closed as he tried to digest this. 'You've met someone else.' He shook his head sadly, 'Please don't tell me I've missed the boat.'

'No, James.' She'd had enough. 'The boat sank, weighed down by your lies.'

She stood up.

'Where are you going?'

'Home.'

'But what about me?'

Sophie shrugged, even though it went against her natural instinct. She hadn't invited him here. He wasn't her responsibility.

'Sophie, I've got nowhere to stay.'

'There are plenty of hotels in Brooklyn.'

'I can't afford a hotel.'

It was on the tip of her tongue to suggest that it was his problem, but she couldn't quite do it.

'Wait here a minute.' She was surprised when he nodded meekly.

Bella was wiping the counter of the coffee bar with methodical studiousness, as if she'd been doing the same thing for the last twenty minutes.

'Sophie! How are things?'

'Complicated.'

'That's James then.' Curiosity bristled from her like crackles of electricity. 'Your ex. Did he propose? I saw the Tiffany box. He must be serious.'

'He's deadly serious. Doesn't want to leave. I feel a bit bad that he's come all this way for nothing.'

'Nothing! But ... he said he really loves you. That he'd been an idiot and should have proposed before.'

382

'He says a lot of things.'

'But actions speak louder than words. Can't you give him a chance?'

Sophie let out a mirthless laugh at the words echoing Kate's from the other night. Now she regretted not telling Bella the full story before.

'He's married.'

'Yeah, he told me but he's getting divorced. He wouldn't come all this way if he weren't. I think you at least ought to talk.'

'We've talked. He needs somewhere to stay. Would you mind if I let him stay in the apartment for a night?'

'No, not at all.' Bella looked pleased. 'It's your apartment. You can have whoever you want to stay.'

'I'll text Todd. We can stay at his place.'

'Todd? But ...' Bella suddenly looked furtive. 'Why? I thought you'd want to spend some time with James.'

'Todd's leaving tomorrow morning, I'd rather be with him tonight.'

'But ... I mean ... Todd. Well ...'

A frisson of fear raced down Sophie's spine. 'Bella?'

'He ... well ... he came by. I told him ...'

'Told him what?' When Bella didn't say anything, Sophie grabbed Bella's shirt. 'What did you tell him?'

Bella wrenched herself away. 'I told him James was here. That he was proposing. That ... he should leave you and James alone. Give you a chance to sort things out. Let James say his piece.'

'And what did Todd say?' Cold fear settled in her stomach.

Bella bit her lip. 'He said I was right. It was probably for the best.'

Sophie ran all the way to Todd's apartment. He'd not picked up his phone to any of her calls. Despite knowing it was hopeless, she'd left a voicemail message. When she'd probed more with Bella she wanted to knock both of their heads together. In fact, as she panted her way up the stairs to the front door of his brownstone building, she couldn't decide which one of them she wanted to inflict bodily harm on the most.

Bella had only gone and repeated the conversation they'd had in the bar. The dumb one, where Sophie had told her what she wanted to hear. It turned out as soon as the American girl had laid eyes on James, her brain had zeroed in on Sophie's words. Safe. Steady. Reliable. Which she just had to go and repeat to Todd. And the stupid idiot, more stupid than stupid, had believed his cousin.

With three bells to choose from, her mind went blank and she couldn't remember which one was Todd's. She picked the one in the middle and left her finger on the buzzer as she hopped from one leg to the other, trying to catch her breath.

The door opened and a blonde woman peered through the crack, guarding the entrance. 'Gee honey, can you take your finger off the buzzer. The static you're producin' is giving me a headache.'

'Sorry. It's Todd McLennan. I got the wrong apartment.'

'No, you got the right one. I was on my way out, but I could hear it in the hallway.' She sighed, but didn't move. 'If

I had me a dollar for every chickadee that comes knockin' for that boy. Seriously, he's as good lookin' as shit, but he's no stayer.'

'I know exactly what's he like, believe me, but I need to talk to him.'

'Sure you're not wasting your time, honey? By rights I shouldn't let you in but,' she lifted her shoulders in an offhand shrug, 'what the hell? Heard him come in not so long back.'

Furious that Todd had ignored the buzzer, Sophie raced up the stairs to the first floor and hammered on the door, knowing that she was acting like a crazy woman. She'd never been crazy in her life. 'Todd McLennan, I know you're in there, so you'd better open this damn door.'

She carried on knocking until the door was wrenched open.

'OK, OK. I get the message.' He wore that slightly aloof, amused look she'd seen when they'd first met.

'Good.' Sophie marched past him into the apartment.

'Can I ask what's got your panties in a bunch?' drawled Todd.

Sophie narrowed her eyes, refusing to be drawn by the deliberately provocative attitude. Instead she put one hand on her hip and adopted the same calm tone. 'And can I ask why you didn't stick around at Bella's? I thought we were having dinner tonight.'

She was pleased to see him stiffen. 'You were otherwise engaged.'

'No, I wasn't.'

'Looked like it to me.'

'Well appearances can be deceptive.'

385

Todd ran his hand through his hair. 'Look … I get it. James came by with a ring. He's the commitment guy. I'm not.'

There was no way Sophie was going to let him off the hook with that asinine statement by challenging it, he could damn well explain himself. Instead of responding she looked at him impassively, or at least that was the expression she aimed for.

'Come on Sophie. James. He's left his wife for you. He's offering the whole deal.' Todd rubbed at the back of his neck. 'A man doesn't fly halfway across the world with a Tiffany ring box unless he's pretty confident of his welcome.'

He was definitely starting to flounder but Sophie refused to rescue him.

'What do you want from me?' He'd started to pace now. 'I can't compete with that.' Quick jerky steps punctuated his words, followed up with telling strained glares sent her way. 'I told you I don't … this is … you're going back to England soon.' He stopped in front of her, his eyes almost pleading. 'You'd be better off going back with James. You want marriage. The whole shebang.' She wasn't sure who he was working so hard to convince. Her or him. 'He can offer you what you want. Much more than me. I'm … I …'

'Are you done?' she asked, with a gentle smile. He was such an idiot. He was a million times the man James would ever be. Radiating the warmth that came when you were totally, utterly and absolutely certain of your own mind, she stepped forward. Todd was the only man for her, even though he didn't quite realise it yet. With the knowledge came confidence. She could show him how wrong he was.

'You're such an idiot,' she smiled and leaned forward to kiss him on the lips. For a moment his lips softened under hers and he kissed her back. 'I love you, not James.'

Todd stiffened and he gripped her forearms, pushing her away slightly. 'You're making a mistake. I'm not ...'

'Not what, Todd?' Sophie's voice hardened.

'Not right for you. This was only ever ...'

'Todd, how can you know what's right for me?' With sudden realisation, it dawned on her. She'd never fought for anything she wanted before. As a result she'd sleep-walked into and stayed in a bad relationship with James.

'I know what's right for me.' She gave him a fierce stare, letting her feelings show. 'It's you. I love *you* and I'm not going to apologise for that. You can fight it all you like but it's not going to change.' She took a breath, it needed to be said. 'And I think you could love me.'

His jaw clamped tightly and she could see the denial in his rigid posture. He was such a baby.

'Sophie. I'm not doing this. I told you. I think we should call it quits. You'll be better off—'

'You're a coward.' Sophie's sudden vehemence made him jump. 'Yes. You're not brave enough to try.'

Todd flushed at the accusation, his lips pinching together. 'We had this conversation once before. Being brave is acknowledging your limitations.' With his fists clenched by his sides, his vulnerability showed in the white around his knuckles. His stance hovering between fight or flight.

'No, that's being honest,' she gentled her tone. He looked as if he might run away at any second. 'Being brave is acknowledging those limitations and taking the risk anyway. You think you'll be no good in a committed relationship because you don't think you're worthy of one. You've seen your parents' relationship and the way they've neglected you and Marty for their selfish version of love and you want no part of that. I understand that. But that's only one version of a relationship. In their own strange way they probably do love each other. They're still together. But you're not giving yourself a chance to be happy. Saying you don't do commitment, you're ducking the issue. You're not prepared to take the risk. That's not being brave.'

Todd sighed, lifted his chin. Her heart sank at the bleakness in his eyes.

'Thanks for the amateur psychology half hour, but I think you're being naïve. Happy Sophie. Wants everyone else to be happy. You're a romantic. You think love will cure everything. Life's not like that.'

Stung, she flinched. 'And how would you know? You've never even tried. At least I have. OK, I made a mistake with James. It hurt at the time, but I learned something from it. I see now that I wouldn't have been happy with him, but at least I know what will make me happy. I know what I do want.' She stopped and swallowed. Despite his rigid stance, she reached up and touched his face. 'You might not be able to see it, but I want us. You've made me see things in a different way. I'm happy because you've made me happy.' It made her smile thinking about it. Grasping his wrists for balance, she stood on tiptoe and kissed the corner of his unmoving mouth. 'Perhaps love is as simple as making the person you're with happy.'

Only someone watching him closely would have seen the subtle movements, the tendons in his neck tensing, the still of his chest as he held onto a breath and the furious pulse under her fingers where she held his wrist; the battle as he weighed up her words.

Her eyes held his, unwavering and determined.

When he blinked, she knew. Even before he spoke, her heart began to drag, sinking slowly like a ship-wreck feathering down to the sea bed.

'You're wrong.' He looked right at her, his words brutally calm. Each one slicing in with the sharp pain of a knife blade. 'I was perfectly happy before you came along. And I'll still be happy when you've gone.'

If he'd shouted, sounded sad or laughed at her, she might have found the strength to argue back but ironically, the flat unemotional delivery mirrored hers to James exactly.

With a regal nod, she said, 'Give my love to Marty this weekend.'

Turning her back on him, keeping her head held high, she walked out of the apartment without a backward look, down the stairs, out of the door, down the front steps, one foot in front of the other, forcing her eyes wide open, only letting herself blink when she absolutely had to.

Chapter 29

Sophie faltered on the bottom step, bitterly regretting saying James could stay. With a decisive about turn, drawn by the scent of chocolate, she followed her nose to Bella's kitchen. Standing in the shadow of the doorway, she peered into the golden glow of the kitchen, where Bella was perched on the arm of the sofa next to Maisie holding court, her plump hands waving madly as Edie creased back into the pink armchair, clutching her stomach as if it hurt, her face lit up with laughter. Ed slouched up against the dresser, a whimsical smile on his face as he watched his girlfriend.

Like a delicious hug, the comforting smell of the chocolate muffins cooling on the side, the gentle hum of the fan oven and the sound of the others laughing and chatting, loosened the iron grip of tension gnawing at Sophie's shoulders and the fury that had carried her back to Smith Street dissipated a little.

Unnoticed, she slipped forward, her hand touching the familiar glossy red of the Kitchen Aid and a finger leaving a smear in the cocoa dust on the side.

'I told him there was no way I could do that many cakes

for less than forty dollars. Honestly. People want ...' Bella trailed to a halt. 'Sophie.'

Sophie gave her a grim smile.

'Hey, honey. Great timing. You must have smelt the honey-comb,' called Maisie, bouncing in her seat. 'You are just in time to try my new hokey-pokey cheesecake.'

'Oh my giddy aunts, it's amazing,' sighed Edie, raising a spoon and licking it, her eyes closed in bliss.

'Grab a spoon, girl, quick,' said Ed. 'Before she eats the lot. Your tastebuds are in for one helluva treat.'

Sophie pursed her mouth. They were all trying far too hard. Bella ducked her head at the accusing look she shot her.

'Let the girl come sit down,' said Maisie, shifting to make room on the sofa, patting the seat next to her and immediately slicing a portion of the cheesecake and serving it up.

With all eyes on her, all Sophie could do was automatically dig in and taste, even though she could have sworn her appetite had vanished. The second the sweet sugary confection wrapped itself around her tongue, she closed her eyes, blinking back the tears that threatened. Next to her she felt Maisie's warm body, Bella's hand on her knee and heard Edie's over-enthusiastic chatter to Ed. Maisie joined in and the three of them began talking a lot of nonsense about whether it should be called honeycomb or hokey-pokey.

Bless all of them, working hard to act normally, giving her the space and time to do what she needed to do. A burst of love for Bella and her generosity bloomed in Sophie's heart. Without any reservation, she'd shared her friends, her kitchen, her life and in turn these good people had opened their arms, offering easy acceptance through the common bond of food and a love of food. With a teary smile, she blinked at them and put her hand on top of Bella's.

'Thanks Bel.'

'You, OK?'

Sophie gave her a tremulous smile. 'Not really but ... I will be.'

'Yes, you will,' said Maisie, suddenly chipping in.

'Just don't be nice to me,' threatened Sophie, trying to keep the mood light. If she gave into the anger coursing through her veins, she might explode and she didn't want to upset them. 'Otherwise I might start blubbing all over you. I'm guessing Bella told you, my ex turned up.'

'I did. I'm so sorry. If I'd known I would never have let him wait for you. He seemed so sincere,' Bella wailed. 'Turning up with the ring and all. Shit, I can't believe it. Married and you never knew. In all that time. Two years. You had no idea. Seriously?'

Sophie raised her hands. 'What can I say? I'm an idiot.'

'No, you're not, honey,' Maisie shook her head vehemently, her dark curls bouncing in agreement. 'You're too darned nice.'

'Sheesh!' said Edie with a scowl. 'You let him stay in your place. I'd would have shown him the door ... after I'd rearranged his boys for him.'

'Ouch,' said Ed. 'That's my girl. Bloodthirsty warrior. I keep the knives away from her most of the time.'

'I'm kind of regretting that now.'

'What, regretting not doing him bodily harm or letting him stay?' asked Maisie, looking amused.

'Both, actually,' said Sophie with a quick rueful grin. 'I was so shocked to see him. There are a million and one things I wished I'd said to him now.'

'Don't worry, I told him he had to be out by eight in the morning,' said Bella. 'You can sleep on my couch, it's a pull-out. I'm guessing Todd wasn't home.'

'Thanks Bel, that would be great,' she said, deliberately avoiding talking about Todd. She wasn't sure she'd be able to hold it together. At the moment she was furious with him, but that was only going to last for so long. The heat of the battle would fade. Tomorrow would be another matter, when she was left to bear the weight of the loss.

'Well, I've got the very thing for you. Ed and Edie are here to give me and Maisie a masterclass in bread-making. We're making sourdough. You can join in.'

'Oh yes,' said Edie. 'Violence is always the answer. Pummelling dough is the perfect punchbag.'

'You can see why I avoid getting on the wrong side of her,' said Ed, the fond look on his face at complete odds with his words.

'Imagine it's your ex.' Edie jumped up. 'And we brought supplies.' With a clink and a rattle, she lifted a brown bag up from beside her armchair. 'My friend Jack.'

It turned out bread-making, drinking and laughter were not a bad way to spend an evening.

Drunken bread-making was to be highly recommended, decided Sophie the following morning, although she was all for divorcing any further association with Jack. When she opened her eyes, the tiny crack of the light streaming through Bella's lounge window hurt.

'Oh lordy, lordy,' croaked Bella, tiptoeing into the room with two steaming mugs. 'Please tell me you feel as bad as I do. And please tell me I didn't imagine texting the girls and asking them to open up the bakery today.'

'You texted the girls. You texted Wes.' Sophie reached for the coffee. 'You're off the hook.'

'It was worth it, we made damn fine bread, though.'

'My arms ache.' With a flex of her bicep, she winced. 'Who knew it would be such great therapy?'

'Knead that man right out of your life.'

'I wish,' said Sophie. 'I am such an idiot.'

'No, you're not. You keep saying that. He's not worth it,' said Bella stoutly. 'His wife can have him back.'

Sophie gave her a woebegone smile and from absolutely nowhere tears welled up in her eyes.

Bella frowned. 'We're not talking about James, are we?'

Sophie shook her head, fighting back a sob. Last night she'd succeeded in putting on a brave face but this morning it hit her, just as she knew it would. When Bella hugged her, all her defences crumbled and she broke down and cried. Slow, quiet, heartbroken tears of regret and frustration, while Bella held her and rubbed her back.

When her tears finally subsided, she felt wrung out and exhausted. Burying her head in her hands, feeling her puffy cheeks beneath her fingers, she whispered again, 'I am such an idiot.'

'Aw, hon.' Bella put her arm across her shoulder and pulled her close again.

'This is where you say, I told you so.'

'No, this is where I say my cousin's the idiot.'

'At least he's an honest idiot.'

'Still an idiot.'

'I'm not disagreeing with you there.'

'What happened?' Bella took her hand.

'He's running scared. When I saw him last night he tried the *you'll be better off with James* tack. And he should have known better.'

Bella squirmed. 'I promise I'd never have let James over the threshold if I'd had any idea. What a jerk. I wouldn't have said anything to Todd, if I'd known, either. I feel so bad. I'm so sorry.'

'Don't be silly. It's not your fault and it wouldn't have made any difference,' replied Sophie, bleakness threatening to overcome her. 'It was the perfect excuse for Todd to bail.' She sighed and gave Bella a rueful half-smile. 'I did tell him he was a coward.'

'Ouch, how did he take that? Not that he doesn't deserve it.'

'How you'd expect? He's stubborn but, like you said, he's consistent. He said he wasn't interested in anything permanent. And he meant it. To be fair to him, I agreed. There was always a shelf-life. It's not like this is a surprise.' Listen to her, she sounded positively stoic when inside her heart felt like a mangled wreck.

'Except,' Bella heaved a big sigh, 'I sort of thought, that maybe ... that maybe you were the one that was going to change him. The two of you looked good together. And you were good for him.' Her voice rose in frustration. 'Really good for him.' She hugged Sophie again. 'At least you've only got another month here.'

Sophie nodded, noncommittal before suddenly deciding to tell Bella about Trudy's offer. It had been playing on her mind ever since her boss had spoken to her. 'If I wanted to stay, would you let me lease the apartment, even if it pisses your cousin off?'

Bella sat up, her head bobbing up, alert like a small bird and a little smile hovering around her mouth. 'All the more reason to lease the apartment to you. In fact I'd negotiate a discount if it really makes him pissed.' Bella looked at her. 'Are you thinking of staying? That would be awesome.'

'You're only saying that because of the free labour,' teased Sophie, her mood lifting at Bella's unconditional enthusiasm.

'Well naturally. But how come?'

'I've been offered a permanent job at the magazine and I can extend my work visa for up to three years.'

'And you want to stay? What about Todd?' Her expression held a touch of mischief. 'That's going to be interesting. He bailed on you because he thought you wouldn't be around much longer. Made it easier for him. This changes things.'

Sophie screwed up her face, mutinous and defiant, although inside she felt anything but. 'It's not going to change anything with him. His mind is made up. He says he can't be in a committed relationship. And he genuinely believes that.' It was going to hurt seeing him every day, she had no idea how she was going to cope, but she wasn't running away for a second time.

'I'm staying.' Sophie looked out of the window, surprised by the tug of love she suddenly felt for the city. 'I love Brooklyn. I love living here. The bakery's become like home. When Trudy suggested it, I was surprised but the more I think about it, the more I want to stay, even though Todd has called time.' It wasn't that she had anything particular to go back to London for. She liked the person she'd become. Wanted to explore being that person. If she went back to London now, she might fall back into the old patterns. The same old routines.

'In that case I've got a proposition to put to you.'

Sophie managed to laugh, although it sounded forced. 'Businesswoman Bella, straight on it.'

'Hell yes.' Bella held out her fist and Sophie bumped it.

'Go on then, what's your latest fiendish plan?'

'I really want to expand the wedding-cake business, but ... well, you nailed it with the wallpaper cake. You're better with people than I am. Translating what they really want. You listen whereas I tend to think I know what they want. I can do the technical stuff, but ... and I really hate admitting it,' she scowled at Sophie with a twinkle in her eye, 'but your ideas are a hell of a lot better than mine.'

'Rubbish, look at the *My Fair Lady* cake.'

'Nothing particularly clever there. I used the picture as inspiration and then lots of technique and pretty window dressing, but the creativity was down to the dress designer. I just pinched various elements.'

'I don't agree but I would love to be your right-hand woman.'

'Excellent. We make a great team. And,' Bella paused,

looking at her watch, an impish grin tugging at the corners of her mouth, 'what are you doing on Wednesday after work?'

'Well.' Sophie's tired sigh made her feel irritated with herself. 'As of Friday, it looks like most nights are free.'

'Good, well not good because of the reason. I mean, I'm really sorry and ...'

Sophie held up her hand. 'Bella, stop. I know what you mean. What's happening on Wednesday?'

'Eleanor has been recommending me, us, left right and centre. I've had three enquiries by email this morning alone and on Wednesday we're meeting Alessandra di Fagolini.'

Sophie nodded, suddenly diverted by the text alert on her phone. 'I can do that.' She snatched up the phone, hope turning to sharp disappointment when it wasn't Todd's name on the screen.

Chapter 30

Butterflies hammered at her stomach, desperate for escape, as she stepped out of the lift on Monday morning. She was going to be cool and calm with him. Skirting the first desk, crossing the office, she looked over to the window. They were both reasonable people. They'd been friends first. It would be fine ... eventually. Oh shit. He was there. Sitting at his desk. Looking ... tired. Looking like the Todd he'd always been. Pain pinched at her heart, almost stopping her in her tracks. Damn, it wasn't supposed to feel this bad.

She'd been kept super-occupied over the weekend. Maisie had had an alleged babysitting emergency on Saturday night. Double trouble didn't begin to describe the twins and looking after them was the gold standard in distraction. Wes had asked for help potting up a delivery of herb seedlings and Edie had insisted Sophie should visit them at their workshop to see how bagels were made. Despite all that, it had been impossible to keep thoughts of Todd at bay but seeing him in the flesh, it was so much worse. Her stomach turned a dozen flips with each step she took.

Forcing herself to keep walking, she approached their desks, and he looked up.

'Sophie,' his smile was strained and it struck her that for once he looked uncertain.

'Todd.' See, she ignored the frantic pulse threading her veins, she could do this. Act normal. Even smile, although it felt plastic and didn't go anywhere near reaching her eyes. 'How's Marty? Did you see him?'

Relief flooded Todd's face. 'He was good. Really good,' he nodded his head with sudden enthusiasm, his eyes meeting hers in a genuine smile. 'He's happy. He likes it there. Wants to stay.' He laughed. 'He likes the discipline. Knowing where he is, what he's got to do. Who'd have thought?'

'Well that's ... good.' Lame, Sophie, lame but it was hard to think straight with that sudden direct smile. This was why she loved the idiot so much. Because he loved his brother. And suddenly from nowhere, she was absolutely furious with him. Rage buzzed like angry bees in her head. 'You could have let me know, I was worried about him too, you know.'

'I brought you coffee.'

The complete change in tack took the wind out of her sails momentarily, as Sophie looked down at the insulated cup on her desk, managing to mutter a tight, 'Thank you.'

'I ... I missed you this weekend.'

She froze. Anger fizzing even more furiously. The breath caught in her throat at his hesitant smile and a heavy weight settled on her chest.

'I ... do you want to go out to dinner tonight?'

'Dinner?' Her voice sounded rusty and distant, even though

she felt as if at any second the top of her head was going to explode with a flood of lava-like fury.

'Yes,' his voice had confidence now, as if he'd got over the first hurdle and the rest was plain sailing. There it was, that easy Todd charm. The man for whom everything came effortlessly. No one ever said no to him. 'There's a new Brazilian steak house opened on Fulton Street.'

'And then what?' Her oh-so-quiet deadly voice made his eyes cloud with the sudden attention of a man with a hand grenade in his palm, unsure whether the pin had been pulled or not.

'Er ... what do you mean?'

Her dark smile held the self-satisfaction of a praying mantis about to pick off her victim. She might love him but ...

'After dinner? Back to mine? A fantastic shag? Pick up where we left off?'

Todd flinched at the acidic bite of her staccato questions and his mouth moved as if he wanted to say something but knew better.

'You don't get to say you missed me,' Sophie said, deadly calm. 'You made a choice.'

'What if I made a mistake?' Todd sounded sincere.

'It's not enough. I've realised, I'm an all-or-nothing girl.'

Todd took a step back. 'What do you mean?'

'I want a proper relationship. One that has the potential to go somewhere. I want permanency. Promises. Exclusivity forever.'

Panic flared in his eyes. 'You know I can't do that.'

'I think you can.'

Todd shook his head. 'I can't.'

Sophie picked up the coffee cup. 'Thanks for the coffee. You know where I am,' she said over her shoulder as she sauntered off towards the test kitchens, where she spent the rest of the day.

'Sophie?' Bella's worried face greeted her as she rushed into the hotel foyer.

'Sorry I'm late. I got tied up and then there was a problem on the subway. Is she here yet?'

'No, thank goodness. I definitely couldn't handle this one on my own.'

'Of course you could.' Poor Bella's hands were shaking. 'It's another wedding cake.'

'Not this one. I thought Eleanor was big but this is massive. It's Alessandra Di Fagolini.' The cartoon saucer-wide eyes told Sophie she was missing something here.

'OK, I don't know who she is.'

'You've never seen *America's Next Supermodel*, have you? She's the top judge even though she's only twenty-six. She and her boyfriend are like royalty over here. She's interviewing us, with a view to deciding whether to even give us a shot at the design.'

It sounded a gig fraught with problems but this was Bella's business. 'And you really want the job?'

'You're kidding me, this would be a serious publicity boost. They've already sold the pictures to some magazine for a six-figure sum. I'm probably not a big enough name for them. I'm surprised I made it on the list. They—' she stopped with a sudden squeak.

A tall glamorous coffee-skinned woman prowled towards them, endless legs revealed by the split in a skirt that stopped inches from her crotch. Cat-like eyes made up with gold and green eye-shadow glittered at them in lazy assessment but she didn't say a word.

'Hi Alessandra. I'm Bella and this is my associate, S—'

'Lady Sophie Bennings-Beauchamp,' interrupted Sophie, holding out a hand, conscious of Bella's startled gasp.

'You're English,' Alessandra's drawl added an extra syllable to her words although her indifferent gaze sharpened a little. 'You know Harry and Meghan? William and Kate?'

Sophie gave a discreet shrug as if, of course she did, but she couldn't possibly say.

'Cool.' With a nod, Alessandra sank into one of the velvet tub chairs and crossed her legs with the sort of slow deliberation which left you in no doubt that she was aware that every masculine gaze had swivelled in her direction.

Like a pair of obedient lapdogs, Bella and Sophie sat down opposite her. There was a hush in the room as if everyone was straining to listen in.

'Lovely to meet you, Alessandra.' Bella's voice sounded horribly loud and she looked around. 'Perhaps you can tell us what you're looking for.'

'A cake.' She lifted one shoulder. 'A fabuloso, zinger of a cake.' With that she leaned back, the sleepy smile was back in place. It was a wonder she didn't just curl up and go to sleep, she was so relaxed.

'Right.' Bella tapped her notepad with her pencil. 'Any ideas on what sort of cake? Traditional fruit? Chocolate?'

'Uh.' Alessandra wilted as if even considering that information was too much, her eyes had wandered over to the reception desk where there were a number of people trying to manage the complicated feat of straining to get a look at her while pretending not to. 'Really? Aren't you the go-to guys? You tell me. Toddy said you were the best.' She sighed and stretched her mouth, turning it down in a disconsolate pout as if this was all too much effort.

'Toddy?' Bella's lips mashed together in a curious half-grimace that looked as if she was biting back a snort.

'Yeah, Toddy McLennan. You do know him, right? I mean, everyone knows Toddy.'

'Of course we know Todd,' interjected Sophie smoothly, sensing Alessandra's growing irritation. She was like a toddler, her attention span was of the short variety.

'How do you know him?' she asked with a sudden petulant frown.

Except when it came to Todd, apparently.

'He's ...' A sudden memory of him laughing across at her as he did the washing-up, insisting he deserved a reward, almost floored her. The words stalled in her throat and for a second she couldn't breathe, the pain felt so real.

'He's my cousin,' said Bella, interrupting, sending Sophie a quick concerned glance.

'Cool.' Alessandra flopped back in her chair. 'Does this place have any water? I'm exhausted already.'

'Do you want me to get you some?'

Alessandra lifted a slim wrist and squinted at her watch. 'Is this gonna take much longer?'

Seeing the tightness around Bella's mouth, Sophie laid a quick hand on her arm.

'No, I think I know what you're looking for. You want a showstopper. The best cake in town. Something everyone will be talking about weeks later.'

'You got it.' She flicked her hair over her shoulder in the first show of animation since she'd arrived.

'Have you decided on your dress yet?'

Alessandra uncrossed her legs and crossed them again, enthusiasm suddenly appearing on her face. 'Oh yes,' she purred with feline sultriness.

'How do you do it?' asked Bella as she put a glass of prosecco with a thump in front of Sophie, who'd already started a preliminary sketch for Alessandra. Sophie snorted, amused by the combination of irritation and admiration in her voice.

'It's a talent,' Sophie teased as Bella juggled her full glass and laptop while trying to sit down on the sofa opposite. 'You're going to spill that.' She rescued the glass and put it on the table as Bella flipped open the laptop.

'Hmph,' grunted Bella, tapping with one finger at the keyboard balanced precariously on her lap, while grabbing her glass again. 'What a diva, although the idea of modelling the cake on her dress is nothing short of brilliant. You're a genius.'

'Not really, it didn't take much to work out she wasn't the least bit interested in the cake *per se*. It's another tick on the list. An accessory. The minute she lit up about the dress, I knew. That's the main event for her, all she's interested in. She never even mentioned her fiancé.'

'You sound positively cynical. I thought you were the romantic. Men aren't that interested anyway.'

'They might not be, but the cake should be a reflection of the bride and groom's partnership. It should mean something. A unique reflection of your love. I know. I know.' She stopped to lean over the coffee table and poke Bella in the ribs, when the other girl pulled a *bleurgh* face. 'You think I'm being cheesy. But weren't you the one who said to me, *There's just something about a cake. It says love. It's like a tiny handheld hug?*'

Bell held her hands up in surrender, the laptop listing dangerously to one side. 'Yes, you're right. Do you think she's even factored a bridegroom into the whole thing? She didn't talk about him once.'

'Which is why the dress was the thing to focus on. Obvious, really.'

'Still think you're brilliant.'

'You're the one that will be doing all the fancy icing.' Sophie shuddered. 'Belgian lace sounds horrendously fiddly to me.'

'Yeah, but it will look stunning. You're a star. Especially for the name drop. She was dead impressed, Lady Sophie. I think that's what made her listen to start with.'

Sophie shrugged it off. 'You need to thank your cousin for the recommendation.' Her mouth twisted and the familiar sick feeling taunted her stomach.

Bella leaned over and patted her hand. 'He owes me. You don't. And I know you avoid using your title, so I really appreciate it.'

Sophie blinked hard. 'Don't. It's me that should be thanking you.'

'For what?'

'Looking after me this weekend and this week.'

'I need you. Just looking at my inbox is making my head hurt. There are quite a few enquiries, although some of them are, frankly, nuts.'

'Really?'

'Listen to this one: *I'm looking for a cake the weekend after next.*'

'Two weeks' time?'

'Yup, because I really am Wonder Woman.'

'You did have the sparkly boots,' Sophie pointed out with a mischievous grin.

Bella threw the prosecco cork at her.

'OK, how about this one: *We require a four-tier chocolate-sponge wedding cake to feed two hundred and fifty guests. Our budget is a hundred dollars.*'

'Teaspoon-sized portions?' suggested Sophie with another grin, getting up and moving to sit next to her to peer over her shoulder at the emails. 'That one's not so bad.'

'A cake that is dog friendly?'

'I didn't read that far down. How about that one? *My daughter's theme is rose-pink and cream and she'd like a traditional sponge cake with flowers.*'

'Ah, a sensible woman. I like her. She's a yes.'

'And what about that one?' Sophie pointed to an email entitled *Star Wars themed cake.*

'*Dear Sir or Madam, we're interested in having a Star Wars themed cake at our wedding. Would you be able to create a Death Star cake? The bride will be d-dressing …*' Bella stifled a giggle, '*as Princess Leia and the g-gr-oom as …*' she lost it, snorting prosecco out of her nose all over the screen, '*Chewbacca.*'

It took a while for the two of them to regain their equilibrium.

'Oh sweet Mary, this one takes the cake.' Bella flapped her hand. '*This cake has to be special* … that's good, because I regularly make non-special cakes.'

'Don't be mean.' Sophie leaned over to read the rest of the email.

'*On our wedding day* … Aw, it's a he,' Bella paused, 'OK, we'll forgive him. I want to give my bride the sun, the moon and the stars,' she slowed her words, '*show her that she makes my world a brighter place to be in and my life infinitely better for her being in it.*'

Bella sat back and both of them were momentarily silenced.

'Wow, that's rather lovely,' said Sophie.

'Lovely,' echoed Bella faintly. 'But as much use as a chocolate teapot if you're designing a wedding cake.'

'It's a challenge, for sure. And very romantic.'

'And flaky. This one sounds more promising: *Eleanor's cake was wonderful and as I'm a hat designer, I'd really love a hat-themed cake. When would be convenient to meet up for us to discuss ideas?*'

Sophie sat up, wriggling to gain purchase on the soft cushions of the sofa. 'Now that's a gift. I remember seeing a gorgeous cake made of a stack of vintage hat boxes in pastels.'

'Ooh yes, hat boxes. Perfect. Let me Google.'

Before long they had finished the bottle of prosecco and Sophie's notebook was full of scribbled notes, website addresses and rough sketches.

'What would I do without you?' asked Bella as they began to tidy up.

'You'd be fine.' Sophie rubbed at her eyes. Helping Bella was about the only thing that had got her through this week. 'What would I do without you? I ... I really appreciate you ...' her voice shook. 'Especially when he's your cousin. Don't feel you can't see him, because of me.'

'I don't want to see the useless oaf. In fact, maybe I should give him a piece of my mind, which is probably why he's avoiding me too. He hasn't called in for coffee all week.'

'Don't be mad at him. It's me that broke the rules. Promise me you'll call him, make sure you see him. He needs people around him who love him.'

'Sophie, you are far too nice.'

'Not really.'

'Yes, you are. He's been so much happier since you've been around. I wish he could see that he needs you. You're so good for him.'

'I think so too, but he's not listening. All I can do is be myself. I love him. He needs people even if he doesn't think he does.'

'Again, you are too nice. He doesn't deserve it.'

'Oh, I'm not being nice to him.' Sophie gave an evil grin, or as evil as was possible for her. 'He thinks he can charm me back into being friends. Don't you worry, I'm not going to make it easy for him.'

Chapter 31

'I hear you and Todd broke up.' Sophie turned to face the voice from the corner of the lift.

'Paul.'

'You OK?'

'Fine, thanks.'

'You still mad at me?'

'Not really. Just fed up with the male race in general.'

'Ouch. I realise I was a bit insensitive, mentioning Pamela. Just trying to be honest why I couldn't invite you for the holiday. I should have explained. She dates too. It's not—'

'Paul, it's fine.'

'You headed out for lunch?'

She nodded. She wasn't really that hungry but sitting opposite Todd, who was on the phone to his new flavour of the week, Leticia, was more than she could bear. It might have been easier if she thought he was OK. The worst thing was that he didn't look happy. To anyone else he might, but she knew him. His laugh was a little bit forced, the lines around his mouth were a little more pronounced and the purple shadows under his eyes seemed to darken on a daily basis.

Not that she was much better, continuing to channel Pollyanna's love child for all she was worth.

She gritted her teeth. It would get better. She had no false hope that he would change his mind, but one day they'd get back to that friendship. He needed a good friend. And one day she'd forgive his idiocy to be that friend again. It was going to take her a little time. Of course, he had no idea that she'd decided to stay and he certainly didn't have the right to know.

'Gee, there's a lot going on inside that head of yours,' commented Paul, making her realise she'd been pulling all sorts of faces.

With a forced laugh, she denied it. 'Nothing special.'

The words echoed in her head. Since she'd read the groom's rather heart-warming email last week, she'd been wrestling with ideas, much to Bella's disgust, who thought the brief was too cheesy and insubstantial to consider taking any further.

'Can I tempt you with lunch?' Paul's words interrupted her train of thought, chasing away the glimmer of an idea that had floated into the periphery of her mind. 'My treat. An apology for being a dickhead?'

Charmed by his unexpected bluntness, Sophie found herself agreeing.

They piled out onto the sidewalk with a tide of other office workers escaping their desks for a quick burst of sunshine. The weather over the weekend had been miserable, heralding the coming fall, although Sophie still wanted to say *autumn* all the time. She'd just about managed to come to terms with *sidewalk*, *cilantro* and *sweater*.

'Where do you fancy?'

'Would you mind Italian? Mario's. Do you know it?'

'Never been there, but didn't Trudy mention it in an editorial meeting?'

'Yes, I've been writing a feature on him and the history of the family and the restaurant. I wanted to check a couple of facts with him before I put the piece to bed.'

'Sure. Who doesn't love Italian food?'

Sophie was dithering over whether to have the lasagne or the chicken parmigiana, her appetite reignited by the usual delicious smells coming from Mario's kitchen, where she could see his wife of thirty years hard at work.

'Have the lasagne,' said Paul, snapping his menu shut. 'I'm having the pizza.'

'I don't know. I quite fancy the chicken.' Which was silly because she knew everything on the menu would be amazing. She'd spent enough time in here both eating and interviewing the whole family over the last few weeks.

'Well, have the chicken then.'

'I can't decide.' She wrinkled her nose and sighed, which made Paul look up from his phone with barely concealed exasperation. Clearly, he had no idea what his role here was.

'You've had the parmigiana a ton of times before. Have the lasagne,' came Todd's patient voice over her shoulder. She whipped around, startled.

'The lasagne, Sophie. Last time you ate half of mine,' he gave her a broad grin before adding, 'or Paul could have the lasagne, then you could share his and have the chicken.'

'I'm sure Sophie's quite capable of making her own choice,' drawled Paul, a possessive challenge hovering in his voice and body language. 'And I'm quite happy with mine.'

'I wouldn't count on that, English here is absolutely hopeless at deciding,' countered Todd cheerfully, as if he were completely oblivious to the atmosphere. 'She's a greedy wee piglet,' he said authoritatively, pulling out the chair next to Sophie and sitting down at the table with his usual casual confidence. 'I tell you what, I'll have the parmigiana and then you can have some.' He looked over at Mario and nodded. 'We're ready to order. Right, Sophie's having lasagne, I'm having parmigiana and Paul's having the pizza. And a jug of tap water.'

Sophie could have cheerfully strangled him, but he seemed completely at ease and she was damned if she was going to let her feelings show. Paul narrowed his eyes and studied Todd, who was now engrossed in a conversation with Mario about Italian football.

Sophie winced and mouthed 'Sorry' at Paul who lifted his shoulders in a terse shrug.

'You heard that the editor on *Supercars* has left,' said Todd as Mario left, having taken their order. He leaned back, stretching his arms, resting one on the back of Sophie's chair, his thumb grazing her back. Shooting him a sharp glare, she leant forward, putting her elbows on the table, although she might not have bothered, for all the notice the two of them were paying her, as Paul launched into an enthusiastic response about staff vacancies and moves in the building. Her mouth twitched in reluctant amusement, Todd had done it deliberately. What was he playing at?

Whatever it was, she refused to rise, instead she smiled serenely through every mouthful of her lasagne. Although she refused a single bite of his chicken, he still helped himself to the odd forkful of her dish as if nothing had changed.

Who was she kidding that they'd be friends? She might just kill him before they got to that stage.

She stomped into the kitchen and threw her bag onto the coffee table.

'Bad day?' asked Bella, looking up from the cake she was carefully icing.

Sophie was determined not to bad-mouth her cousin. Since lunch today, Todd had been under her nose at her every turn. Appearing in the test kitchen, raiding her desk drawer in search of cookies and barging in on a meeting with Trudy.

'Just ignore me for a while. I'll crack on and make a batch of muffins. What flavour are you doing this week?'

'Cinnamon and Orange,' mumbled Bella, tilting her head to one side, examining her work.

As Sophie whizzed about the kitchen collecting and lining up the ingredients, weighing everything out in her usual methodical fashion, she felt the irritation of the day start to fade. Cooking always had the power to soothe. Bella left her to it, completely absorbed in her task, the fiddly icing demanding almost mathematical precision.

Once the cakes were in the oven, she turned to watch Bella, humming along to the radio.

Sophie began to smile.

'What?' asked Bella, looking puzzled.

'That song.' Sophie began to sing along, '*I want to see the sunshine after the rain …*'

Bella joined in, '*I want to see bluebirds flying …*'

When it finished, Bella gave her a hug. 'You OK?'

'I will be. I've had the sunshine. I've seen the bluebirds. It might be raining right now, but I'll be OK.'

Bella rubbed her back and put down the icing bag. 'What do you think?'

'Oh my goodness, that is so pretty.' The cake was covered in the palest blue icing and Bella was halfway through over-laying it with a delicate lattice of white piped icing.

'It's also painstaking. I've reached a point where I can take a break. Fancy a glass of something?'

Curled up in her usual spot on one of the pink armchairs, Sophie lifted her glass and toasted Bella. 'To your beautiful cake. It's going to look amazing when you've finished.'

'I'm quite pleased with it, the bride wanted simple and elegant, incorporating her bridesmaid's colours.'

'I think you nailed it.'

'It was an easy one.'

Sophie took a sip of her cool white wine and tapped her fingernail on the glass, watching the condensation run down the side. 'I've been thinking about that brief. The really romantic one.'

'What, Mr Special? Why did I know that?'

'Because it came from the heart.'

'No, because I know you. You're a big softie. Go on, tell me you've come up with another one of your brilliant ideas.'

'I've got the germ of one.' Sophie faltered, looking across

at the beautiful half-finished cake, uncertainly. 'It's kind of my dream cake but ... I'm prepared to sacrifice it for someone who sounds as if he and his bride deserve it.'

'Are you sure? And what is your dream cake? Mine changes on a weekly basis, when I see all the amazing designs around.'

'Remember I told you I love the silver balls? I'd have a cake covered in those. Just that. I think it would look amazing.'

Bella wrinkled her nose. 'Cute.'

'It would,' insisted Sophie, conscious of the other girl's scepticism. 'Now you've got me worried. Look, I started to make some initial sketches.' Delving into her bag, she pulled out her notebook and gave her earlier sketches a cursory glance before she handed it over to Bella.

'Hmm,' said Bella, tilting the book this way and that.

'It's hard to make it come alive on paper.'

'Mmm,' agreed Bella.

'It will work.'

'Yes, but how are you going to convince the happy couple?'

'How would you feel if I mocked one up? A smaller version.'

'That would work. Could you do it this weekend? I'll email the guy and see if he can come here to see it. And I can take photos for my gallery. You're going to need a hell of a lot of those silver balls. I'd better get onto the wholesaler. This job will certainly keep you quiet over the weekend!'

'That's the idea,' said Sophie grimly. 'You don't mind if I work in the kitchen?'

By three o'clock on Sunday, Sophie's hands had almost cramped into a permanent lobster claw.

'I wish I'd never started this,' she moaned, her hands gripping a pair of tweezers, when Bella popped in with Wes.

'Jeez Louise, it's like a fairy hailstorm visited,' said Wes, surveying the floor.

'They're slippery little devils,' said Sophie with feeling.

'You should have just chucked the balls over the cake,' observed Bella.

'Then it wouldn't look right, or special,' snapped Sophie, immediately feeling guilty – but seriously, this was so romantic, it had to be perfect. 'Some would overlap, some wouldn't stick, it would have bald patches.'

'Sorry,' said Bella. 'Why don't you take a break? Have you eaten?'

Sophie shook her head, looking a little frantically at the clock. 'You did say six, didn't you?'

'Yes, but I can always ring and put them back.' The groom was due to bring his bride to see the cake today.

'No, I thought you said it was the only night both of them could do.'

'Yes, but you've got another three hours. You've been at this since nine. You need a break.'

'I daren't, the icing is starting to harden off. And I've only got the last third of the top tier to do.'

Making the cake had been the easy part. She'd made three mini-sized ones, each an inch bigger in radius than the next, yesterday morning. It still stood thirty centimetres tall. Yesterday afternoon Bella had helped her to assemble them one on top of the other, strengthening each cake with dowelling and a hidden platform, so that the weight of the top two cakes wouldn't sink into the base. The icing had been more problematic as it had to be exactly the right consistency, firm enough to ensure that the silver dragee balls stayed put and didn't slide down or sink, and soft enough that it didn't harden off while she was still working on the decorations.

Each silver ball had to be applied with a pair of tweezers, as the silver dust came off the balls if they were touched. Sophie suspected she looked as if she might be related to the fairy godmother, she was so covered in silver dust.

'At least have a coffee and a muffin,' said Bella firmly. 'And let me carry on.'

Sophie hesitated. Was she being too possessive? With each silver ball, she'd thought of a special memory. The early cakes she'd made with her mum. The day her dad took the stabilisers off her bike. Her first published article. Her first kiss. Her first kiss with Todd. The first time they'd gone to bed. The day on the beach at Coney Island. The day on Jones Beach. So many reasons to be happy. So many treasured memories that she'd always hold dear. Todd might be out of reach but he'd shown her how to live. He'd given her a new way of looking at life. He'd given her Brooklyn.

'Hello ... Sophie, come back to me.' Bella snatched the tweezers out of her hand. 'You can trust me! For goodness' sake, girl, take a seat and a caffeine hit. Wes, make her.'

'Don't involve me,' he rumbled, holding up his hands in mock surrender.

'I promise I won't mess it up. You need a break.'

Sophie took a seat and watched like an over-protective mother as Bella took over.

'Darn it! These things are like ... oh darn it, I've dropped another one. Whose bright idea was this?'

Sophie flexed her cramped hand and laughed at Bella's comical dismay. 'Wait until you've been at it for a few hours.'

'I'd have run out of patience about thirty seconds in.'

In fact Bella's patience ran out after about ten minutes, which being perfectly honest, Sophie was rather pleased about.

Sophie placed the final few balls into place and stepped back. It looked stunning. Simple but so effective.

'It's amazing,' said Bella, 'I take it all back, I'd never have believed how beautiful it is. This is definitely special.'

'I think so. I hope she likes it. You'd better keep any sharp implements out of reach, just in case.'

'How could she not love it?'

'She'd better, I've put my heart and soul into this one. It really is *my* cake.' Tears welled up in her eyes at the thought of each of the thousands of silver balls that she'd evenly placed exactly a fraction of a space from each other.

'Right. We have one last job to do,' announced Bella.

Sophie looked confused.

'This is a work of art, you can't leave it in here. We'll take it through to the bakery. I've had Wes do some work.'

'We need to move it,' he said. 'Let's hope we don't drop it.'

'Don't even say that,' Sophie shuddered. It didn't bear thinking about.

They carefully lifted the cake onto the trolley that Bella kept for this very purpose and pushed it through into the other room.

'Oh wow.' Wes had done an amazing job, stringing several lots of fairy lights around the walls of the far corner. All the furniture had been moved away with the exception of one circular table which Bella had covered with a pure-white damask tablecloth. 'It looks fab in here. It's going to set the cake off beautifully.'

Sophie let Bella lift it onto the little table and Wes switched out the main lights.

Like a gorgeous silver star, the cake twinkled in the fairy lights. Sophie clasped her hands together and let out a tiny gasp. 'It's perfect.' Her heart flipped over at the beautiful sight and she blinked back tears.

'Well, whoever the couple are, I bloody hope they love each other to bits,' she said fiercely.

Wes and Bella came and flanked her.

Bella squeezed her arm. 'It is beautiful and so romantic. And listen to that, bang on time. I'll get the door.'

They'd agreed that Sophie would present the cake and Bella would talk money and dates. Even if the couple didn't like it, Bella had arranged for some professional shots to be taken on Monday that she'd use on her website.

Wes melted away into the kitchen as Sophie lingered, giving the cake one last look. She could hear Bella unlocking the café door and talking in a low voice.

Then a shadow moved through the café towards her.

She waited, twisting her hands, suddenly anxious. What if they didn't like the cake? The shadow came closer and stepped into the circle of light, the tiny bulbs suddenly illuminating his face.

'Todd!'

'Sophie,' he said quietly.

Where was Bella? She looked at her watch.

'We're about to have a meeting with ...' her voice trailed away. With a slow smile, his eyes never leaving hers, he stepped forward and took her hand.

'That is one hell of a cake.'

'It is,' said Sophie, proud of every last inch of it.

'And exactly what I asked for.'

'Oh,' her mouth dropped open, she scarcely dared breathe as she looked at the cake and then back at him. Hope bubbled, singing in her veins. Her eyes widened, as she stared at him.

He lifted her hand to his mouth. 'I want to give you,' he gently kissed each knuckle with each word, 'the sun, the moon and the stars,' he said, holding her hand, his eyes never leaving her face. 'You make my world a brighter place and my life is infinitely better when you're at my side.'

His softly spoken words warmed her from the inside out and she couldn't bring herself to say anything, in case her brain had short-circuited and she wasn't understanding properly.

She frowned, scared she might have it wrong.

With gentle fingers he soothed the line away.

'English, I love you. I don't deserve you but I know you love me,' he gave her a lopsided smile, 'and I'm taking it.'

It was such a magical moment, she didn't want to spoil it. Instead she squeezed his fingers, her eyes locked on his, letting all the love in her heart pour out.

'And our spectacular wedding cake is absolutely perfect.'

His voice was so soft, her heart stalled and she stared up at him, wide eyed, scarcely daring to believe in case she'd misheard.

'Ours?' she asked in a breathless whisper.

He nodded. 'It's beautiful. Starlight and love. A million stars to wish upon.'

Her lips curved. 'Romantic.'

'I can do more.'

'For how long?' she asked softly, clutching his hand, praying she hadn't got this wrong.

'How about forever?'

'Forever's a long time.'

'All or nothing. I want it all.'

'You want to get married?' Sophie's whisper was incredulous.

He nodded and then a playful twinkle danced in his eyes. 'There is a proviso ... it has to be to you.'

'Why?' asked Sophie, still not quite able to believe that this gorgeous man wanted her.

He looked startled and then he looked at the cake. 'Because you're the moon and the stars in my life and I can't live without you any longer.'

'Are you sure?'

'Never been surer of anything in my life.'

'But ...' she frowned.

'I love you.' He gave her a giddy smile. 'Proper love.' He touched her arm as if to reassure himself that she hadn't run away. 'The sort of love that you read about in books, hear about in songs. The sort of love that's selfless. The sort of love that you've given me. That you offered me unconditionally even when I didn't think I could give it back. You took a risk saying it. You were right, I was a coward. I spent all weekend thinking about what you'd said. Even discussed it with Marty. He thinks you're cool, by the way.'

'Pleased to hear it.' She smiled up at him.

'All week I kept trying to think of reasons why I *didn't want* to be with you. And I could only think of reasons why I *wanted* to be with you. The harder I tried to think of reasons, the more I wanted to see you.'

'And what about your harem?'

'Given them up.'

'What about ...?'

'What about kissing me, Sophie, and agreeing to spend the rest of your life with me?'

With a teary smile, she gazed up at him. 'Sounds like a plan.'

Acknowledgements

I find writing the first draft of any book a painful process akin to pulling out your own teeth with a pair of pliers and this book was no exception. Heart-felt thanks go to my wonderful editor Charlotte Ledger and my darling agent, Broo Doherty, without whose support, encouragement and pep talks, this book probably wouldn't have made it into the big wide world. Equal gratitude goes to lovely copyeditor, Caroline Kirkpatrick, for her encouraging comments in the margin. Caroline, you've no idea what a confidence boost they were!

And now (and I can hear the 'told you so' comments) after all the self-indulgent angst I put them through, I think Todd McLennan might just have become my favourite character to date.

I was inspired to set Sophie's story in Brooklyn after a family holiday to New York a couple of years ago. We stayed in an Airbnb just off Smith Street and found the area to have a wonderful, buzzy vibe which I really wanted to use as a setting. From there we headed out to stay with my dear friend Professor Roberta Elins and her husband, Steven, in Amagansett and I just had to include a side trip to the Hamptons.

A massive thank you to Roberta who corrected my American slang and despite that generosity, I'm afraid I've blatantly stolen some of her and Steven's stories about the locality (well wouldn't you if Gywneth Paltrow and Sarah Jessica Parker were near neighbours) and the celebrities that can be spotted in the area. Guys, a massive thank you for your wonderful hospitality and for letting us stay in such a gorgeous spot. There's definitely something to be said to having a house on the beach!

A huge thank you is owed to Sherry Hostler, the most amazing and talented cake designer, who kindly shared some of her inside baking tips with me and also very generously let me steal her fabulous silver ball Eat Me wedding cake design. I urge you to Google it, simply stunning!

Thanks also go to Nick, my domestic god, who steers the household ship while I'm holed up in the writing cave, plying me with gin and making the occasional heroic effort on the ironing. I couldn't do without his or my children Ellie and Matt's unconditional support.

Last but not least my writing buddies Donna, Anita and Liz as well as the wonderful HarperImpulse gang; Jane Linfoot, Caroline Roberts, Zara Stoneley, Debbie Johnson, Bella Osborne and Georgia Hill who are all so fabulously supportive ... and write great books too.

Keep reading for an exclusive look at book three, Nina's story...

The Little Paris Patisserie

Chapter 1

Stamping her sore and tired feet on the gravelled surface trying to get some warmth into them, Nina looked at her phone for the ninety-fifth time in ten minutes, almost dropping it. Where the heck was Nick? Fifteen minutes late already and her fingers were about to snap off, adding to her general sense of misery. Standing here at the back entrance to the kitchens in the staff carpark there was little protection from the biting wind whistling around the sandstone manor house and certainly none from the bleak thoughts in her head.

'Hey Nina, are you sure you don't want to come to the club?' asked Marcela, one of the other waitresses, in her heavily accented voice, winding her car window down as she backed with some speed out of one of the spaces. 'Say goodbye to Sukie with some dancing and fun?'

'No,' she shook her head, 'it's alright thanks. My brother's on his way.' At least he had better be. Nina wished she was in the little steamed up car with Marcela and the other two staff members, and almost laughed at the rather annoying irony. Mum had insisted Nick pick her up so that she'd know Nina was safe and here she was standing on her own in a car park in the pitch black about to be completely on her own.

'OK then. See you in eight weeks' time.'

'Ha!' Piped up a gloomy East European voice from the back seat, Tomas the sommelier, a perennial pessimist. 'You think the builders finish on schedule.'

A good-natured chorus shouted him down.

'See you soon, Nina.' They all waved and shouted their goodbyes, Marcela winding the window back up as the ancient Polo roared away as if she couldn't wait to escape the end of her shift and put up her feet. Which was exactly what Nina was hoping to do, if her brother ever got here.

At last she spotted the headlights speeding down the drive towards her. This had to be Nick. Nearly everyone else had gone. With a speedy gravel-crunching turn, the car pulled to a halt in front of Nina.

She yanked the door open.

'Hi Sis. You been waiting long? Soz, sheep emergency.'

'Yes,' snapped Nina scrambling in grateful for the heat of the car. 'It's bloody freezing out there. I'll be so glad when my car's fixed.'

'Tell me about it. It took me all the way here to thaw out. Friggin sheep. There was a ewe stuck in the wire fencing up on the moor road. I had to stop and help the stupid creature.'

Was it really churlish to think that the sheep had a nice woolly coat while she was in a skirt and tights on a cold February evening?

'So how was it? The last night,' asked Nick, leaning down and turning the radio off, which had been blaring football commentary at full blast. 'And did your mate get a good send off?'

'Fine. Bit sad as we all won't see each other for a while. And Sukie will be in New York.'

'New York. That's a bit of change.'

'She's a brilliant chef. Going places.'

'Clearly. To New York. And what's everyone else doing?'

'The regular staff are being redeployed and having lots of training.'

'Seems a bit unfair. Why not you?'

'Because I'm just on a casual contract, I guess.'

'Well I'm sure we can find you a few extra hours at the farm shop as well as in the café. And Dan can give you a bit of work at the brewery. Gail might pay you for some babysitting and George can ask in the petrol station, they're always needing extra staff. Although that's late hours, so possibly not.'

Nina closed her eyes. She was absolutely certain that everyone in the family would pitch in to find something for poor Nina to do while the Bodenbroke Manor Restaurant was closed for refurbishment, whether she liked it or not. It wasn't that she was ungrateful, they all meant well, but she was a grown up, she was quite capable of finding work without the vast tentacles of her family network spreading their reach on her behalf. She loved her family to bits, she really did but...

'What's with the huffing and puffing?' asked Nick, turning his head to look her way.

'Nothing,' said Nina, closing her eyes. 'Holy moly I'm tired.

My feet feel like they've been stomped on by a dozen elephants.'

'Wuss,' teased Nick.

'I've been on the go since nine o'clock this morning,' said Nina. 'And the restaurant was rammed. I didn't even get lunch.'

'That's not on. You should say something.'

'It's not that easy. Everyone's busy. There wasn't time for a proper break.'

'Don't tell me you haven't eaten anything today?'

Nina shrugged, she'd rushed out without breakfast, much to her mother's consternation. 'A little.' Her stomach rumbled rather inconveniently at the very moment as if to dispute her answer. Clearly it didn't think that a bread roll and a slice of cheese constituted enough.

Nick frowned heavily. 'Even so. Do you want me to say something to the manager, when they re-open?'

'No, it's fine. We'll be having dinner when we get home.'

'Well it isn't—'

'You don't work there, you don't understand.' Nina's voice rose in heat. Typical Nick, assuming that he knew best.

'I don't need to understand. There are labour laws. You're entitled to breaks. It's—'

Whatever he was about to say was interrupted by the timely horn fanfare ringtone of his phone booming out through the radio on his handsfree set up.

'Nick Hadley,' he said pressing the accept call button on the dash board.

Nina slumped back in her chair, relieved at the interruption, it gave her the perfect opportunity to close her eyes, tune out and pretend to doze for the rest of the way home.

'Hey Shep, how're the socks?' Her brother was often referred to as Shep, short for shepherd.

Nina tensed, every sinew locking into place at the sound of familiar mocking voice.

'All good. How are you Knifeman? Still supporting that shite excuse for a rugby team?' And apparently Knifeman was the not-so clever nickname for a chef.

'No words mate. They were a bloody shout against France. And I paid good money for tickets.'

'What you went to Stade de France? You jammy git.'

'Not so jammy when the buggers lost.'

'Fancy coming over for the Calcutta Cup? You don't want to be too long in France you might pick up some bad habits.'

'Slight problem there.'

'What?' asked Nick.

'I'm laid up. That's why I'm ringing you.'

Nina pressed her lips together in what some might call a snarky smile. Sebastian clearly had no idea she was there and she didn't want him to either. Listening to this ridiculous conversation, no one would ever know they were grown men rather than a pair of adolescents, which would be the obvious inference. She definitely did not want to remember Sebastian as a teenager or how she'd made a complete dick of herself over him. Unfortunately having a teenage crush on your brother's best friend is possibly the worst thing you could do because ten years on, even now, someone in the family would occasionally bring it up.

'What's happened?'

'I've only gone and broken my leg.'

'Shit man, when?'

'Yesterday. Taken out by one of those bloody cabin bag pull along fuckers. Twisted as I fell.'

'Ouch. You Ok?'

'No,' Sebastian growled. 'Everything's gone tits up. Turns out one of the new places I bought in Paris has a metaphorical sitting tenant. It's a beautiful little patisserie but the previous owner ran cookery courses and forgot to tell me that there's a six-week course coming up that's all booked and paid for.'

'Can't you cancel?' asked Nick flicking the indicator and turning the car off the main road towards the village.

'Unfortunately, I committed to it. I thought I might as well because I can get my French contractors to start work on the other place first and they'll take a couple of months, so I might as well keep this going. Which would have been fine if I hadn't broken my sodding leg.'

In the darkness, Nina pressed her lips together. She wouldn't normally wish misfortune on anyone but somehow Sebastian just irked her. It wasn't his success she begrudged, lord knows he'd worked hard enough to become a top chef with a small chain of his own restaurants. Too hard if you asked her. No, it was his superior, dismissive attitude. Over the last ten years whenever she'd seen him, she'd always managed to appear at a disadvantage. And the last time had been truly mortifying.

'Can't you get someone else to do it?'

'I'm not sure I'm going to find anyone at such short notice. The course starts next week. Besides, all I need is a spare pair of legs for the next six weeks. Until I get this cast off.'

'Nina could help. She's just been laid off at the restaurant she works at.'

Nina shot up in her seat, narrowing her eyes at her impossibly stupid brother. Had he had a brain fart or something? Seeing the movement in the car, Nick turned and she saw the flash of his teeth in the dark as he gave her a great big grin.

'With respect Nick, your sister is the last person in the world I'd want helping me.'

Nick's grin faded. There was a lengthening silence in the car.

Then Sebastian muttered, 'Oh shit, she's there isn't she.'

With an icy smile, Nina drew herself up. 'Oh shit indeed. But don't worry, with respect Sebastian, I'd rather help castrate the lambs on the farm using my own teeth.'

With that she leaned forward and disconnected the call.

A Q&A with Julie Caplin

What was your inspiration for the series?

I used to work in public relations specialising in food and drink PR, so I organised a lot of press trips to European cities as well as liaising with food writers, who were always lovely to work with. For *The Little Café in Copenhagen*, I drew on my experiences of organising press trips abroad. They always sounded glamorous and exciting to my friends but in reality they were hard work and occasionally a bit fraught. Trying to round up grown adults on a press trip can be interesting and on one memorable trip I really did lose a journalist before we'd even left Heathrow! On another trip I took food writer Sophie Grigson to Milan, she was the most delightful company and had a real and enthusiastic passion for food. Her catch phrase when she was encouraging us to try new foods was that it was 'good for our food education' and I borrowed this line for Sophie who appears in both *The Little Café in Copenhagen* and *The Little Brooklyn Bakery*. When it came to writing *The Little Paris Patisserie* I wanted to learn more about cooking patisserie and found that Sophie Grigson was running a course in Oxford. Not having met her for a further twenty years, I signed up for the course and discovered that she was just as passionate and enthusiastic in her teaching about food as she was back then.

Have you always wanted to be a writer?

Since the age of eleven, when I announced that I was going to write a book, I've always wanted to be a writer. As I grew up and started working in PR that idea got put to the back of my mind. It resurfaced when I was put on gardening leave between jobs and decided that I would sit down and write that book. It was only a few years later, after I'd written several books, that an old school friend, now in Australia, contacted me and reminded me that as a child I'd always said I'd write a book one day.

Are any of the characters based on you or people you know? If so, which ones?

Very occasionally I might base a character on someone I know. For example Nan in *From Paris With Love This Christmas* (one of the book I've written under my real name, Jules Wake) was partly based on my paternal grandmother, who was what one might call a feisty character. However most of my characters pop fully formed into my head. To me they are like real people and while I'm writing a book, I often have conversations with them in my head.

It's amazing that you have the opportunity to travel so much and use your own experiences in your books, but how do you find time to write? And where do you write when you do?

I'm very lucky that I can write anywhere. Even when I'm travelling my laptop comes with me and I usually write first thing in the morning before taking the rest of the day off. I plan my research trips well in advance of writing a book, so that often I write the book once I'm home. I'm very disciplined when I'm working on a deadline and have a daily word count target which has to be met no matter where I am. Luckily my husband is self-employed, so no matter where in the world we are, you'll find us both tapping away at our laptops!

What has been your favourite place to visit?

Gosh, that's a tricky one. It's often the people I'm with that make a trip. When I went to Copenhagen, I took a couple of friends, now known as travel elves, with me. They were such good company that they really made the trip something special. Likewise when I went to Brooklyn and the Hamptons, it was a family holiday and we stayed in Armgansett with a very special friend, so that trip also holds a very dear place in my heart. When I went to Paris recently I took my husband and we had a wonderful time visiting various patisseries in the city, so that also has special memories.

Have you got any funny travel stories you can share with us?

I'm not sure that this is funny, but I'm rather accident prone and on my last trip to Paris I didn't *mind the gap* between the Metro and the platform. I came home with a rather nasty gash on my leg and now have a less than fetching scar as a permanent reminder of the trip. One story that I have used in *The Little Paris Patisserie* comes from the time I was in New Zealand and working in a rather busy wine bar. I took an order from a gentleman at the bar and had to ask his name. Unfortunately, with the noise in the crowded bar and his very strong Kiwi accent, I couldn't quite hear his name so had to ask three times. This proved to be rather hilarious to my colleagues as this man was actually very famous in New Zealand. It was akin to asking someone like David Walliams what his name was!

Do you have any advice for readers who want to follow in your footsteps and visit these gorgeous places?

I would heartily urge anyone to visit Copenhagen, it is a very small, compact city so it's easy to navigate on foot and you don't need to worry about public transport. Everyone speaks fantastic English and is so friendly and welcoming.

Wherever I'm going, I always buy a local guide book for the city and pick a few places before I go to visit when I'm there but I also make sure I leave some time to take up any tips from other tourists. I'm a bit of a chatterbox, so where ever I go I end up talking to people and it's a great ice breaker to ask other people for their tips and suggestions.

What would you like your readers to take away from your stories?

One of my favourite phrases is 'Walk a mile in another man's shoes'. It's important to remember that there are always two sides to a story and that other people think in different ways. I often explore this in my books. We need to learn our own strengths and weakness as well as recognise that other people have theirs, which won't be the same as ours. Sometimes we need to listen to what's not said in order to really understand each other.

Who are your favourites authors and have they influenced your writing in any way?

I'm a huge romance fan and always want a happy ending. I adore Jill Mansell's stories, particularly her happy-go-lucky characters and easy, sparky dialogue. I'd love to say that has influenced me, but it's still a work in progress! I'm also a big fan of Katie Fforde and I love her settings and the kind-hearted characters in her books. More recently I've become a big fan of Sue Moorcroft and I particularly like the way that her stories have plots that twist and turn to constantly keep the reader on their toes. All of them have influenced me in different ways, so that I focus on character, dialogue and plot and hopefully I produce stories that really engage you, the readers.

Julie Caplin

If you could run away to a paradise island, what or who would you take with you and why?

Well, obviously, Captain Wentworth from *Persuasion* is purely fictional, but in his absence, I'd take my very own hero, my husband. He's brilliant at looking after me (especially when I fall over, a frequent event!), makes me laugh and is super organised when we're traveling. And I always have to have a book with me. My trusty Kindle goes everywhere ... although on my last trip it died, which was an absolute disaster! I was half way through a really good book and had to finish it by using the Kindle app on my phone.